HUNT
ON THE FENS

A gripping crime thriller with a huge twist

JOY ELLIS

Detective Nikki Galena Book 3

JOFFE
BOOKS

Revised edition 2024
Joffe Books, London
www.joffebooks.com

First published in Great Britain in 2016

This paperback edition was first published
in Great Britain in 2024

Cover art by Nick Castle

ISBN: 978-1-83526-604-5

CHAPTER ONE

DS Joseph Easter's eyes snapped open. Instantly he was wide awake and experiencing a rush of automatic reactions left over from his years as a special ops soldier.

His ears strained for sounds that shouldn't be there. He sniffed the air for unexpected smells and his eyes systematically checked the moonlit bedroom. When he was certain that he was still alone, he noted the time on his backlit radio alarm and forced himself to relax. It would appear that old habits died hard.

Joseph sat up and pushed the duvet off. Okay, so it wasn't an enemy insurgent, but something had woken him, and a feeling of unease was clinging to his skin like a film of oil.

Without putting the light on, Joseph padded across the wooden floor to the window, and keeping back a little, carefully surveyed the area around his home.

Knot Cottage sat close the edge of the estuary of the River Wayland, in a remote part of the Cloud Fen Marsh. He had been told that way back, it had been an eel-catcher's cottage, and from the odd paraphernalia of traps and baskets that he had found in a decrepit stone shed, he thought this was probably true. One day he would trace the old place's history, but right now crime was on the up in the Fenland Constabulary's area and spare time was hard to come by.

He looked across the small, tidy garden and along the river bank, but nothing other than the deep flowing water moved. Joseph's narrowed eyes followed the lane across the marsh to where Cloud Cottage Farm could be seen clearly under the quick-silver light of the moon. It was some quarter of a mile up the lane and was the only other property for miles. He stared at the outline of the old farmhouse, and saw a thread of pale, wispy smoke drifting up into the night sky.

Immediately he stiffened. Earlier that evening he had called in to see Nikki Galena at Cloud Cottage Farm, and the fireplace in the sitting room had been cleaned out. No new fire had been laid. It was late spring and as she was not reliant on the open fire for hot water, there would be no more logs brought in until autumn.

Joseph scrambled across to an old oak dressing chest on the other side of the room, pulled open a drawer and grabbed a pair of binoculars. They were good quality, expensive, and gave him bright, clear night vision. He hurried back to the window, trained them on Nikki's home and adjusted the sights.

'Shit!' A flickering glow rose, faded, then rose again, this time a little brighter than before, and it was in the outbuilding nearest to the house itself.

Swearing again, Joseph threw himself across the bed and grabbed his phone. The first call was an emergency call to the fire service, and the second, directly to Nikki Galena.

As he waited for her to answer, he dragged on a pair of jeans and a sweat shirt and jammed his bare feet into his shoes. 'Come on! Come on!' He cursed, then as he heard a sleepy voice answer, yelled, 'Get out of the house, Nikki! There's a fire in one of the outbuildings. I think it's the garage. Fire service is on the way.' He raced down his narrow staircase. 'And so am I. Just get yourself outside.'

As soon as he was satisfied that she was awake enough to understand the danger she was in, he rushed outside and sprinted full pelt up the track. He could have taken the car but he was in good shape and could be there by the time he'd found his keys and manoeuvred his vehicle out of the yard. He knew that Nikki would have sprung into work mode the moment his urgent voice had dragged her from her slumbers. Nikki was not only his neighbour, she was his boss and best friend. Detective Inspector Nikki Galena was the head of his CID team at Greenborough Police Station. She was an outspoken, tough woman who didn't tolerate slackers, but she always led by example, and although her reputation didn't make her the most popular officer on the force, she was fair, and a damned good copper to boot. Most of all, she had earned the respect of her team, and every one of them would have walked barefoot over hot coals for her.

As he sprinted round the side of the old farmhouse he saw Nikki, clad in oversized pyjamas and a towelling dressing gown, spraying water from a garden hose against the garage door.

'Thank God I left the car outside last night!' she yelled across to him. 'That would have gone up like a rocket! She's got a full tank too.' She pointed to the side of the stone outbuilding. 'There are a couple of rain barrels down there. Grab a bucket and help me to damp down the woodwork. If we can just soak everything around it, it'll contain it until the firemen get here.'

Joseph started dowsing the wooden window frames with water. 'It's got a pretty good hold!'

'Damn right it has.' Nikki's face screwed up in anger and concern. 'What the hell happened here? What could have caught fire?'

'It's usually electrics,' called back Joseph. He listened as the crackling inside the old building intensified. 'Nikki! I think we need to get back! Have you got anything in there that could act as an accelerant?'

'Paint cans, white spirit, aerosol sprays, all the usual rubbish that you stuff into your garage.' She jammed the hose through a piece of trellis and left it playing onto the door.

3

'You're right, Joseph. The words discretion and valour spring to mind right now.'

Together they moved back to a safe distance, dragging anything vaguely combustible with them.

'It can't be electrics,' muttered Nikki, as they heaved a decorative carved garden seat to safety. 'I had all the out-buildings rewired just before winter set in.' She looked at him worriedly. 'Remember? I was planning on turning the red-brick store into a home gym?'

Joseph nodded. 'You could still get a glitch. A short or a power surge through a defective connection of some kind?'

'If that's the case, I'll sue the pants off the bloody electrician,' growled Nikki. She looked at him and bit her lip. 'Hell, Joseph, just pray that this doesn't reach the house.' The bite on the lip intensified. 'I don't have much left to hold onto anymore. If my home goes as well, I . . .' She shook her head and her words faded into silence.

Joseph felt a rush of compassion. One so strong that it seemed as if someone had sucker-punched him, and if he had let it, it would have filled his smoke-filled eyes with real tears.

Only two weeks before, Nikki had buried her only daughter, Hannah. Her own mother had died years ago, and her father was in a nursing home suffering from dementia. Joseph glanced up at the beautiful old farmhouse that was her family home, and realised just how much it meant to her. He put his arm around her and gave her a reassuring squeeze. 'Your home will be fine, I promise.'

'And how can you possibly say that?' Her voice was like a small child's, with no trace of the confident grittiness that Joseph was so used to hearing.

He smiled at her. 'Because, my revered and worshipful Boss, I see blue lights! Trumpton are here to save the day!'

* * *

An hour later, Joseph, Nikki and Aidan Barber, the fire chief, stood outside the charred mess that had been her garage.

'How the hell do you guys fathom out how a fire starts?' asked Nikki. 'Look at the state of this place!'

They all looked at the steaming, waterlogged and carbonised junk that puddled and littered the stone floor.

'Oh, this isn't too bad at all.' Aidan laughed dryly. 'It's hardly a conflagration!' His smile disappeared. 'But it could have been. It was damned lucky that you saw the smoke, DS Easter. It wouldn't have taken many more minutes to have spread to the other outbuildings and the house itself. Spark showers have already ruined the exterior paintwork.' He looked at Nikki seriously. 'You had a close shave, DI Galena. And in answer to your question, a good fire investigator could tell you what had happened even if there were only ashes left.' He stepped closer to the gap that had once held two sturdy wooden doors. 'Look. You can see the path that the fire has taken.' He pointed up to the blackened shards of ceiling beams. 'It's called burn-pattern analysis. See, the heaviest area of burning is over there, which is where I believe the fire started, and its direction of travel was towards the door.'

Joseph looked at the burned material on the far side of the garage. 'That's where the fuse box is located, isn't it?'

Aidan nodded. 'Yes, but I'm making no assumptions just yet. I learned a long while ago never to make snap decisions. Only evidence will provide the right answer, and that's why I've called in one of our investigators.'

Joseph nodded. 'Good.' He tried to sound positive for Nikki's sake, but privately wondered if the chief was calling in the investigator because he suspected foul play.

'Is it safe now?' asked Nikki cautiously.

'Don't worry. We'll not leave until we're sure there are no hot-spots.' He threw her an apologetic look, 'But I'm afraid your night is pretty well ruined. I'd prefer it you didn't go back into the house until we've done a thorough safety check. Not that you'd get too much sleep anyway with my boys and girls crashing around.'

'Come back to my place. I think you need a cuppa, or maybe something stronger.' Joseph looked at Nikki's drawn face. Today was to have been her first day back at work after losing Hannah. Now it looked like she would be ordering a skip and trying to clean up the yard.

'Sorry, but what I need is a bloody shower. I look like I've done a double shift at the coal face!'

'I know Knot Cottage is small and full of quaint original features, but strangely enough it does have hot running water.' He tried to lighten the situation. 'And if the chief won't allow you to go in and grab a change of clothes, you can always borrow one of my sweaters and some joggers.'

'I'll take you up on the shower, but as you are well over six foot, I'll pass on the offer of raiding your wardrobe.' Nikki gave him a tired grin. 'But thanks all the same.'

'I'll escort you inside to get some things,' said the fireman. 'Just to be sure you are in no danger.'

* * *

Ten minutes later, Nikki and Joseph were walking slowly down the lane towards the river and his home.

'Thank God for insomnia.' Nikki slipped her arm through his. 'Or have you suddenly developed a talent for clairvoyance?'

Joseph carried a large bulging sports bag that Nikki had hurriedly filled with assorted clothes and toiletries. 'Neither. Something woke me, and the old squaddie reflexes still kick in. I automatically checked the perimeters for incoming rebels.'

'And this time it wasn't a fox making a sortie on your rubbish bins?'

He shrugged. 'I don't know what it was. But I saw the smoke purely by chance.'

The grip on his arm tightened, and he had the feeling that she had just had the same thought as him. What if . . . ? He decided to change the subject.

'There's an awful lot of stuff in this bag. The chief said you'd be back in by morning.'

'I've brought everything I'll need for work, just in case the fire crew are still thundering about in my flower beds.'

Joseph looked at her with surprise. 'You're still going to work? But what about . . . ?' He indicated over his shoulder to the farmhouse.

'You don't think I'm going to clear that mess up, do you?' She gave a short laugh. 'Tomorrow, after I've contacted the insurance company, I'll phone Phil Maynard and tell him to put his son and his mini-digger on red alert. He's always on the lookout for building jobs, and as soon as I get the go-ahead, he can see if it's worth renovating, or whether it will have to come down.' She slowed her pace, then looked up at him. 'I need to be back at work, Joseph. I can't stay at home brooding. Hannah's gone, and I have to find a way to move on.' She ran a grubby hand across her smoke-stained forehead. 'My career is all I have left now. The best that I can do is to give it one hundred per cent.'

'You've always given your all,' said Joseph gently. 'Even when things were close to intolerable for you, you never let the job suffer.' Just for a moment he felt sad, not for Nikki's grief, but for the fact that she had said she had nothing left other than the force. As they walked he realised, somewhat to his surprise, that he felt hurt. Because she had more than her job. She had him. They might not be an item, but they had gone through hell and high water together in the last four years, and they were close. Closer than many of the married couples that he knew. Closer than some families, and certainly closer than work colleagues.

'I just can't believe that I'll never see my girl again.' Nikki was staring out along the shadowy and seemingly never-ending salt marsh. 'I keep thinking that she's still in the hospital, that I should go visit her, that I should ring and check on her. Yesterday I found myself downloading a track from one of her favourite boy bands onto her MP3 player.' She shook her head in despair. 'After all she's been through, after years of fighting for life, I cannot believe that it was something as simple as a cold virus that killed her.'

They'd been over this so many times in the last few weeks that Joseph was scared his replies were beginning to sound like empty platitudes. There was nothing he could say to bring her comfort, so he just squeezed her arm.

'Do you know what someone said to me at the funeral?' Nikki's voice was full of disbelief. 'This woman, some distant cousin, said it must be so much easier for me because Hannah had been in a coma! Easier! Can you believe that? She reckoned I'd lost her years ago, that I'd done most of my grieving when she first collapsed.' She shook her head from side to side. 'I wanted to hit her. And keep on hitting her.' There was raw emotion in her voice now, as anger and pain collided. 'There was not one day, Joseph, in all that time, when I didn't believe that there might be a miracle for Hannah. Not one single day.'

'I know.' There was a lump in his throat, and he hoped that she hadn't noticed. He had a daughter too. One that he believed he had unintentionally let down. Now he was desperately trying to build bridges and discovering just how deep old wounds could go and that healing them wasn't easy. He loved his daughter and would move heaven and earth to make things right again, but he wasn't sure that he could have done all that Nikki had done for Hannah.

'And if I hear the words, *blessed relief,* just one more time, I'll scream. It isn't a relief, its pure agony! Maybe we couldn't go shopping together, or even have a damned good argument like we used to, but at least I could talk to her, hold her hand, run my fingers through her hair.' She kicked angrily at a stone and watched as it skittered down the track ahead of her.

Joseph allowed her to rant. They had an agreement. It had been formed years back when things got uglier than they had any right to be. No secrets, no professional faces, no facades and no lies. He was the only one that Nikki could be Nikki with, warts and all. And the same went for him.

As he opened the door to Knot Cottage he realised that they had found a safety net in each other. The job they did was tough. It could destroy you if you let it, and that safety net kept them sane.

He poured them both a tot of brandy, then sent Nikki in the direction of the shower

As he sipped his drink, he glanced out of the kitchen window and saw that a pale watery dawn was slowly lighting up the strange water-world where he lived.

He wasn't a native like Nikki. He was an incomer. He had been drawn, kicking and screaming into the odd wildness, the solitude, and the beauty of the fen marshes. And very soon he had found that it was just what he needed. The cottage he had rented purely as a stop-gap, became his home after its owner Martin Durham died, and his sister decided to allow Joseph to purchase it. Now the tiny eel-catcher's cottage was his haven, his bolt-hole and his salvation. The bitter, disillusioned spectre of a soldier that still hid somewhere inside the policeman, was finally healing.

He downed the rest of the brandy in one. Now it was Nikki's turn. He just prayed that it would be as painless a process as possible and that she'd come out the other end in one piece.

CHAPTER TWO

Nikki had managed to get into her office without actually having to speak to anyone. The fact that it was an hour and a half before her shift helped somewhat, but she also needed the extra time to lose the memory of funeral flowers and coffins, and get her detective's head back on.

She looked at the pile of reports and memos on her desk, and grimaced. She had left at a bad time. A big case was running, and although Joseph had been a star, quietly shouldering her workload as well as his own, precious little progress had been made.

It was a weird one. It could have been straight from the pen of Agatha Christie, only this case was hi-tech and baffling and as far as she could make out, didn't involve a vicar. 'A real-life, locked-room murder,' she murmured to herself. 'Pity I'm not Miss Marple.'

A knock on the door made her stiffen, but she relaxed again when she saw Joseph nudging the door open and entering, carrying coffees and two white baker's bags.

'Warm croissants and hot coffee.' He looked at her reprovingly. 'We don't skip breakfast on my watch, DI Galena.'

'Oops, didn't think you'd noticed. You'd nodded off in a chair, so I thought I'd make my getaway and let you rest after that horrible night.'

'I was cat-napping, and I heard you go.' He took the lid off his drink and steam rose from the plastic beaker. 'I thought you were probably going to check out what the fire service had done to your property before you left for work.'

She nodded and pulled a face. 'It's a bloody mess, but at least the house itself only needs a coat of paint. I was *so* lucky.' She opened the bag and removed the croissant. It looked good, and she suddenly wondered when she'd eaten last. 'The insurance company are sending an assessor down, and the fire service investigator is already out there. He's going to call in here later and talk to me.'

'Can I sit in?'

'Sure. I'd welcome it.'

'So, what's the plan of action for today, boss?' Joseph looked at her from over the top of his coffee.

'You are going to bring me up to speed on Operation Windmill, then at nine sharp we go to the murder room. I've requested every available officer who is able to, to attend a brief meeting.' Nikki drew in a deep breath. She hadn't planned what she would say to her colleagues, she just hoped that whatever came out organically would be the right thing. Right now she knew she could not cope with a station full of people who had no idea how to react to her. If she put them right from the word go, then hopefully she'd make life easier for everyone, but mainly herself. 'Right. Progress report please, on Magda Hellekamp's murder.'

Joseph grimaced. 'Precious little since I updated you last. We've been in constant touch with Holland, but we can find no reason for her being killed. No record. No enemies. Her business, the Hellecroppen corporation, seems squeaky clean. She's well thought of in her field and has an impressive track record of successes in the world of GPS technology for agricultural machinery. She was single, no known dodgy relationships or jealous exes.'

'And she was rich.'

'Stinking, but it was family money and very much tied up in the business. They are at the cutting edge of technological advances in farming, and that means big financial commitment.' He took a bite of his impromptu breakfast, chewed thoughtfully, then added, 'And as you know, the flat where she was found is an executive rental, all paid for through the firm. It was not a burglary gone tits up. Nothing touched or taken.'

'So, after three weeks, we have no motive and no understanding of how the killer got in or out, completely unseen, from a modern apartment that was covered with CCTV cameras, and locked from the inside apparently by the victim herself?'

Joseph shrugged. 'That's the long and the short of it.'

'Do you think it's another company trying to destroy Hellecroppen? Would her death cause major internal problems?'

'Doubtful. We've talked to both the company and the family in depth. She will be a great loss to them personally, but the business is massive, and it's sound.'

'The king is dead. Long live the king,' said Nikki with a sigh. 'What about her personal life? We must have missed something. Surely a wealthy, striking beauty of thirty-five would have men clamouring around her twenty-four/seven? No intense boyfriends? No jealous lovers? There has to be!'

Joseph puffed out his cheeks. 'None that we can find. The only man she ever sees when she comes to England has an alibi solid enough to build a house on.'

'And he is?'

'Lawrence Carpenter. Fifty-six years old. Divorced. Family friend. Retired early after making a considerable amount of money in the agro-chemical industry. I interviewed him myself, and he was devastated to hear of Magda's death. I could be wrong but if he was faking it, I'd be very surprised.'

Nikki made a grunting sound. 'Well, what about the method? Does it point to a particular kind of killer?'

'Yes,' said Joseph emphatically. 'A damned efficient one! A single, close-range shot to the temple from a gun equipped with a silencer.'

'A professional?'

'No question.'

'I think I'd like to see the crime scene.'

'How about after you've met with the fire investigator? It's still closed up, much to the chagrin of the rental company.'

'I bet! What do they charge for these swanky exec pads?'

'Four grand a month.'

'What! You are kidding me!'

'You wait until you see it.' Joseph grinned. 'It's like nothing I've ever seen.'

'But here in Greenborough? That's a London price.'

'Actually we are considered to be at the heart of British agriculture. It's a short jump across from Holland to the Port of Greenborough in a fast cruiser, and executive jets and helicopters fly in regularly to the Green Fen airstrip. Some of the bigger companies are realising that we are in a pretty good position to base some of their corporate management personnel. Or so the property rental people tell me.'

'How the other half lives,' muttered Nikki. She glanced at the clock. 'Time to go and face the troops.'

'Are you okay with this? I could talk to them if you like?'

Nikki smiled at him. 'I'm not sure quite what I'd do without you, Joseph, but this one is entirely down to me.'

* * *

The room was full to bursting. Officers sat, stood, and gathered in the open doorway.

As Nikki entered, she felt almost smothered by an atmosphere of apprehension, compassion and discomfort, in equal measures. For a moment she wondered if she had the courage to go through with it, but then she saw the face of WPC Yvonne Collins. The older woman officer gave her an imperceptible nod and a warm smile. She looked around and saw the familiar faces of her team: Joseph, DC Cat Cullen and DC Dave Harris. They were her colleagues and her friends. If she was hurting, then they were too.

For once she didn't have to stop the usual banter, because there wasn't any.

'Thank you all for coming. I won't keep you long.' She hoped there was no tremor in her voice. 'As you are all aware, my daughter Hannah died three weeks ago. I have been offered extended leave, but have refused to take it. As far as I know there are no hard and fast rules on how to cope with grief, so . . .' she raised her hands, palms out. 'I can only do what I think is right for me.' She looked at them earnestly. 'I want to make sure that none of you feel awkward or uncomfortable, so I'm saying this to you all.' She took a deep breath. 'I am warmed by your messages of condolence and I truly appreciate them. For that I thank you. But now I am back at work, and it will be business as usual. No tip-toeing around my sensibilities. We all have a job to do, and I wouldn't be here if I didn't think I could do it.' She paused for a moment, savouring the collective silent sigh of relief. 'I don't care if you think I'm a hard-arsed cow. But if you do think that, then you're wrong. I'm just going to be coping in the only way I know how.' She swallowed. 'That's all.'

She took a step back and exhaled, then saw Dave Harris slowly stand up, raise his hands and begin to clap.

It was hard to hold back the tears when the whole room was on their feet and joining Dave in applause, but somehow she managed to hold it together until they had filed out of the room.

'Hell-fire!' She slumped down into a chair and passed a hand across her eyes.

'It's done now, Nikki.' Superintendent Rick Bainbridge made his way toward her. 'I admit to being circumspect, but on reflection it was the right thing to do.'

'Thank you, sir.' She took out a tissue and wiped an escaping tear from her eye. She and Rick went back a long way. This was his last month on the force before retiring, and Nikki decided that whoever copped the post when he left would find themselves trying to fill some very big boots.

He waited until they were alone, then he sat down next to her. Nikki noticed that he winced as he did so. She took in the thick, grizzled grey hair and familiar, craggy face and hoped that whatever was ailing him would allow him a good and active retirement. He'd been a demon of an officer when he was younger, and even in later years had managed to fly a desk with dignity. She would miss him, even if they had had some almighty great dust-ups in the past. But ultimately Rick Bainbridge had believed in her, even when everyone else was ready to stick her on the scrapheap.

She was pleased that she'd been able to pay him back, by making her team one of the best in the Fenland Constabulary.

'Now, as you're back in the saddle, my friend, there's something you need to know.' The deep brows drew together into furrows. 'Intelligence has informed me that there has been a sighting of Stephen Cox in this area.'

Whatever Nikki had expected, it wasn't that. Her jaw clamped, and for a second she did not breathe.

Stephen Cox. Even the name made her feel sick.

Cox was the one that got away. The man was an evil drug dealer, and one who had caused chaos in Greenborough and devastation in her personal life. He was the one that still stopped her sleeping at night, and the one she wanted to see rot behind bars more than anything in the world.

'Where?'

'In a bar in the town, if my source is to be believed.'

'If it were an unreliable source, sir, then you wouldn't have told me. Which bar?'

'Cyn City.'

'Just the kind of dive I'd expect to find him in.' She stood up and began to pace. 'Does Joseph know?' she asked eventually.

'Not yet. I thought I should warn you first.'

Nikki nodded. She had every reason to hate Cox, but Joseph had far deeper cause to want the scumbag put away. Stephen Cox had hurt Joseph badly, and she wondered how he'd take the news.

'With only one unsubstantiated report, I would advise caution, Nikki.' The superintendent looked at her intently. 'We need to be sure it's him before we fly off the deep end.'

'Well, your source is not likely to have confused him with anyone else, is he, sir? With half his face burnt off, he is kind of noticeable.'

'Word on the street says he has had plastic surgery, although as no one we know and trust has actually seen him; that could be part of the great Chinese whisper.' He gave her a doubtful grin. 'And don't forget, we've had sightings before, and they've all been wind ups, specifically designed to get at you. Your determination to take down Stephen Cox has become legend.'

Nikki sat down again. It was true. Every local villain knew that if you want to yank DI Galena's chain, just tell her you'd seen Stephen Cox. Then stand well back and watch her go.

So why did she feel that this time it was different?

Because in her heart she knew it was true. He'd always sworn he'd come back, that the fuzz would not keep him locked out of Greenborough forever. Part of her almost wanted him to; to give her another chance to take him down.

'What are you thinking?'

'Dark thoughts.'

Rick Bainbridge stood up. 'Well, just keep it light until we know for sure, okay?'

'Yes, sir.' Nikki forced a smile.

Bainbridge made to go, then paused. 'Oh, before I forget, uniform have got a promising young lad who has just come back after a shoulder operation. He's shown an interest in CID, and while he's waiting for the doc to clear him for full duties, I wondered if . . . ?' He looked at her with a raised eyebrow.

'Send him down. He can shadow Cat and Dave for a bit.'

The superintendent suddenly let out a loud laugh. 'There *was* a time, Nikki Galena, when you would have told me in no uncertain terms that you weren't a bloody babysitter and perhaps I should contact a crèche before bothering you! I do believe you are mellowing.'

'Don't worry, sir. I'm sure I can revert back, given the right circumstances. What's this lad's name?'

'PC Danny Wilshire.'

'Wilshire? Not Sergeant Bob Wilshire's son?'

The superintendent nodded. 'I forgot you knew Bob. He was a good man, and a very smart cookie. Never knew why he didn't go for CID himself.'

'Because he loved the streets, sir. He never had the slightest interest in being a detective, just good old-fashioned policing.' Nikki smiled when she thought about Bob's funny angular face and the deep brown cow's eyes. 'He was my crew-mate for a while when I was in uniform. I liked him a lot. I was gutted when he got ill.'

'As were we all, Nikki, and young Danny is a chip off the old block. You'll like him.' Again he paused, then threw her a quizzical look. 'Would I be right in thinking that you and Bob were . . . ?'

Nikki's lips tightened. 'I suggest you don't take that line of enquiry right now, sir. I might have to resort to the old "no comment."'

'Thought you were!'

'Sir!'

He grinned and left, leaving Nikki alone in the room.

A whiteboard dominated one wall. The heading on it was "Operation Windmill," and immediately beneath it, a picture of a stunning-looking woman.

Magda Hellekamp was tall, average for a Dutch woman maybe, but tall in Nikki's book. She had flowing rich dark brown hair and a face that would not have looked out of place on the cover of *Marie Claire*.

'So who wanted you dead?' whispered Nikki to the smiling one-dimensional face. She narrowed her eyes. 'You are far too beautiful to be totally committed to satnav guided combine harvesters. What were your other loves, I wonder?'

No answer came and Nikki stood up and made her way back to the CID room.

DC Cat Cullen and DC Dave Harris were both tapping away on their respective keyboards, and staring avidly at the monitors.

'Anything interesting?' she asked them both.

Cat looked up and ran a hand through her spiky rough-cut blonde hair. 'No. I'm bored half to death with all this agricultural stuff. It's bad enough living in the biggest cabbage patch in the world, let alone having to study how to get the ploughed furrows aligned to within two centimetres!' She widened her already wide eyes and added, 'Magda could have been a cat walk sensation, but she chose bleeding brassicas! Can you believe it?'

'I guess Coco Chanel gowns didn't float her boat.'

'Yeah, but tractors? For heaven's sake!'

'Not just tractors,' Dave chipped in. 'I've been looking at some of Hellecroppen's planned ventures and she was heavily into robotics.' Dave eased his large frame back in his chair and shook his head. 'In years to come there will be no one left working the fields. The equipment will be GPS, guided by computers in the farmer's kitchen, and there will be rows of tiny little agribots tilling, weeding and controlling the pests.'

'You've been watching the Sci-Fi channel again, haven't you? And surely that won't happen while we have cheap foreign labour to hand?'

'It will happen. If robots can build cars, they can kill weeds and plant sprouts.' Dave looked at the screen glumly. 'But fascinating as these futuristic farmers are, I'm damned if I can see a connection to Magda Hellekamp's murder.'

'It has to be personal,' stated Nikki.

'Great. Can I please ditch the boring stuff and dig for some real dirt instead?' Cat's eyes sparkled.

'Go for it.' She turned to Dave. 'And you too. Both of you take a look at her relationships again. No one with looks like that has only one friend. And check *him* out again too. What's his name? Carpenter? Yes, Lawrence Carpenter. Joseph thinks he's kosher, but Cat, maybe your famous sleazeometer can pick up something other than a platonic friendship. Grill him, in your own inimitable way.'

Cat looked considerably happier at that suggestion. 'My pleasure, ma'am.'

'And you have a newbie to look after for a day or two. His name is Danny Wilshire. He's waiting for a green light after an operation, and he's keen on CID.' She headed for her office, then called back, 'and do try not to put the fear of God into him. Tell him about some of the good bits, not just the routine crap. We'll need a replacement for Dave here in a year or two, and it'd be nice to have a home-grown baby tech.'

Dave laughed. 'If it's all the same, ma'am, I'm not quite ready for the allotment and the pipe and slippers. Still, an apprentice to pass on all my vast knowledge to would be good. A sort of legacy.'

'Well, just don't bore him to death either.'

Nikki smiled as she closed her office door. The team were doing exactly what she wanted, just being themselves and acting normally around her.

She sat at her desk and pulled a mammoth pile of reports towards her. She really should tell Joseph about the possible sighting of Stephen Cox, but for some reason she was reluctant to do so. Joseph had suffered badly during that disastrous case and she had no wish to stir up bad memories if it turned out to be yet another false alarm. Even Rick Bainbridge had said to sit tight until there was certain confirmation. She opened a file, then closed it again. That wasn't going to work. She and Joseph didn't clam up on each other.

With a sigh she stood up. The reports would have to wait.

* * *

Joseph couldn't concentrate. His mind kept rolling back to the fire, and even though he'd showered thoroughly and washed his hair twice, he could still smell burning.

The sensation wasn't a pleasant one. He associated burning with war. Burning buildings, burning tanks, burning flesh. Even though he was a police officer now, and had been for many years, the soldier's memory still demanded recognition. He hadn't experienced a flashback for many months now, but he knew that they were always there, lurking in the shadows, waiting for a trigger to release them.

He looked at his watch. It was ten thirty, and he knew he would not be able to settle until they had a definitive answer about that fire. He wondered when the investigator would arrive. In the grand scheme of things, when you considered some of the terrible infernos that they had to deal with, a garage fire would be nothing to an experienced man.

'Excuse me, Sergeant? I'm looking for DI Galena and she's not in her office.'

Joseph looked up to find a young uniformed constable peering around his door. He had an unruly mop of dark hair, a strange, angular face and an instantly likable smile.

'I'm PC Danny Wilshire. My boss has arranged for me to spend a few days with you.'

'Good Lord! You look just like your father.' Nikki stood behind him in the doorway, her mouth dropping in surprise.

'So they tell me, ma'am. I'm not sure if I should love him or hate him for it.'

'Love him, Constable. He was a good officer.' She turned to Joseph. 'Bob was before your time, but he was the best beat bobby you could ever wish to meet.' She turned back to the young officer. 'You can shadow DC Harris and DC Cullen. We are working the Hellekamp murder — Operation Windmill. I hope you find it interesting.'

When the young man had gone, Joseph smiled. 'Wilshire? Not your old crew-mate? The one you told me about? And, forgive me for saying so, but you look like you've seen a ghost! How come you didn't know his son was working here?'

'Since when did your cupboard of an office become an interview room?' She gave him a mock frown. 'Actually he's only recently been transferred from Spalding, and apparently on his first day here some drunken shite dislocated his shoulder and tore the tendons. He's been off sick for months.' She gave an amazed little laugh. 'He is the spitting image of his father.'

Nikki flopped down into the only other chair and stared across his desk at him.

Joseph didn't like the expression on her face.

'Changing the subject . . .'

'DI Galena?' A gruff voice interrupted her and Joseph turned and saw a burly, greying man, wearing a fire service ID card around his neck. 'John Carson, Lincolnshire Fire Service. Can we talk?'

Nikki nodded, stood up and beckoned to Joseph. 'One of the advantages of senior ranking is that I get to have *three* chairs in my office. Come on.'

Once ensconced in the DI's room, Joseph closed the door.

'I've completed my check of your property, DI Galena, and I can confirm that the fire started in the fuse box.'

A dark look spread across Nikki's face. Although Joseph felt like heaving a sigh of relief, he was also mighty glad he wasn't her electrician.

'Well, that explains a lot,' said Nikki grimly.

'Not exactly.' John Carson leaned forward. 'As I said, it started there, but it wasn't an electrical fault.'

Joseph felt his expression harden, but the investigator was still speaking.

'The fire was started deliberately. I suggest that whoever did it supposed that the evidence would be consumed by the fire, but that is rarely the case. Sifting through ashes can throw up all sorts of debris.' Carson shrugged. 'It was arson, for sure.'

Nikki threw a worried look at Joseph. 'I've been trying to pretend that that wasn't going to be the outcome, but looks like I'd better shape up and face it.'

Carson exhaled. 'I know that I'm just the *'how'* man, but there are a few questions that I think you *'why'* and *'who'* guys should consider.' He sat back. 'The fire starter was clever. I'll send you a copy of my report, but believe me, he's no amateur. It's not a kid with a can of lighter fluid, I promise you. But if he was planning on killing you, he could very easily have taken that old farm of yours off the map in minutes.'

'But he didn't,' mused Joseph. 'But if he's so clever, wouldn't he have known that an investigator would have seen through his 'fuse box' disguise?'

'He would, and that makes me think that he didn't think I'd be called in.' He gave her a knowing smile. 'But he reckoned without Aidan Barber. The chief has a nose for the causes of a fire. He'd make a good investigator himself. He's certainly curious enough. I doubt any of the others would have got me out for what should have been an unremarkable garage fire.'

'So someone was trying to frighten me?' asked Nikki.

Carson grinned. 'As I said, I'm just the 'how' man.' He stood up. 'Have you got any enemies?'

'You're kidding, right?' Nikki gave a staccato laugh. 'You have *no* idea how many people hate the detective who sent down their father, mother, son, husband, wife, lover, brother, best mate, favourite uncle, second cousin twice removed, pub landlord, bookie. The list goes on and on.'

Carson held out a big, gnarled hand. 'Then the best of luck, DI Galena. I hope you know where to start.'

Joseph watched him go. His shoulders had tensed. This wasn't the news he wanted to hear, even though his gut had warned him of it from the outset.

'Wonderful! Just what I need when we have a murder case running.' Nikki's jaw was set angrily forward. 'Some pillock wanting to get even with me for banging up his granny! Perfect!'

Joseph didn't answer. The aforementioned pillock would have been the kid with the lighter fuel, or more likely with a Molotov cocktail through the front window, not a carefully planned and disguised warning. He glanced across at Nikki and saw another expression cross her face, one of consternation. 'What are you thinking?' he asked quietly.

Nikki heaved a sigh. 'I was about to tell you when the fire guy arrived.' The anger had dissipated and only the troubled look remained. 'The super has had a report that Stephen Cox is back in the neighbourhood.'

'Fuck.'

'I agree, twice over.' She slumped back in her chair. 'It's not confirmed, of course, and we've been here a dozen times before, but . . .'

'But this time you believe it's true.' Joseph felt as if he'd swallowed a large, round rock and it had lodged in his chest.

'I felt that way even before we knew about the fire being started deliberately.'

Joseph screwed up his face. 'Cox isn't clever enough to have set that fire.'

'He was clever enough to outwit half the Fenland Constabulary on the biggest drugs bust we've ever set up.'

'He wasn't clever, he was just lucky to find a sewer to crawl into. And he didn't get away with as much as a packet of Marlboros, let alone his share in the expected street value of three million! He never torched your place, Nikki. I'm certain of that.'

'Maybe not him, but he could pay for a pro, couldn't he?' She sniffed. 'He'd be top of my list of suspects for Galena-hunting, even if I didn't know he was back.'

'*Might* be back. I'd need to see his disfigured little gob personally before I started to worry about Cox.' He didn't feel that way at all, but Nikki needed strength right now, not a mewling wimp who was shit scared of another showdown with that particular villain.

'Superintendent Bainbridge thinks he might have had surgery.'

'So what? The ugliness inside would still seep out. I'd know that shite anywhere, even if he was dressed as Darth Vader.' He summoned up courage that he wasn't sure he possessed and said, 'Sorry, Nikki, we need to forget about Cox, and consider other, more recent, possibilities. Stephen Cox has been AWOL for years. He could have targeted us at any time.'

'Okay, okay, I'll go along with you. I'm just angry. I know we need to keep it in perspective. After all, we have Magda Hellekamp to worry about. She comes first.' Nikki was visibly regrouping. 'Right, I'll inform the super what happened. He needs to be aware of the situation, then we make sure everyone is one hundred per cent red-hot on Operation Windmill. Then you and I will put our heads together on who the hell flambéed my bloody garage.'

CHAPTER THREE

'So your dad was a copper too?' Cat indicated and pulled her car into a space a few doors away from the local bakery.

Danny grinned. 'Yup, and my grandfather. It's in the blood, I guess.'

'Got any kids of your own?'

'One little boy, Connor. He's almost two.' He pulled a small photo from behind his warrant card and passed it to Cat.

'Kids aren't exactly my thing, but even I can see that he's cute with a capital C.'

'He's the happiest child I've ever met.' Danny smiled proudly, then returned the picture to his pocket. 'But I'm guessing that being in the close proximity of a cake shop has nothing to do with Operation Windmill?'

'Too right. We have to get your CID training in order, don't we? As the youngest and most recent addition, you do the bun-run, and you do the tea and coffee-making, of course.'

'Of course. And no doubt I collect the pizzas during my unpaid overtime?'

Cat smiled sweetly. 'I see that policing really does run in the family. You have it perfectly summed up.' She passed him a ten pound note. 'Dave wants two sausage rolls, the boss likes a maple and pecan Danish, the sarge a doughnut, you get whatever you want, and I'll have . . .' she paused. 'Oh, I'll come with you and decide when we get there.'

They slammed the car doors and walked along the pavement. 'We'll go directly to Lawrence Carpenter's office after we pick these up. He's expecting us in fifteen minutes.' Cat looked across to the younger man. 'He's been interviewed before, but I'll be using a different method. It's a bit unorthodox, so I'm told, but you just listen, okay? Listen and learn.'

Cat walked ahead of Danny into the shop doorway, then paused and turned as she heard a throaty, growling engine noise of a large white truck that was making a big deal of pulling out of the space directly in front of the bakery.

Danny stopped and Cat saw him frown as he stared after the clapped-out vehicle that was now moving down the road, crunching gears and back-firing as it went.

'From the look on your face, I'm betting that driver will have a visit from uniform in the next few days,' she said dryly.

'Bald tyres and fit for the scrapheap. I'd definitely PNC the index number, but the plate was too filthy to make—'

A different noise filled the air, one that Cat didn't have time to understand. She just knew that her head had become a kaleidoscope of fragmented reality.

And Danny was gone.

In one blurred second, one screaming moment, he had been hurtled forward through glass and wood and metal. Somehow he seemed to be riveted to the heavy grill of the massive vehicle that had mounted the pavement, and then he was lying at the back of the decimated shop, a limp and lifeless body in a heap of glass, broken display cabinets, blood and a myriad of colourful crushed cakes and pastries.

Instinct made Cat drag herself from the wreckage to see what had rammed them.

But all she saw was black. Everything was black. Paintwork, windows, and the plate where the license number should have been.

'Bastard!' she screamed. 'You bastard!' But the vehicle had already reversed away from the carnage it had caused and was screaming off down the road.

Sobbing, Cat ignored the sea of shattered glass that was tearing into her flesh, and crawled towards Danny Wilshire. She knew it was useless, but she needed to be with him, to beg him not to die, or to reassure him that if he did, the cute kid called Connor would know what a great guy his father had been.

Cat stayed for what seemed like an eternity, then she felt arms around her and a thermal blanket encasing her.

'Bastard,' she whispered, then let go, and allowed the screaming noises in her head to swallow her up, and all was darkness.

* * *

Nikki and Joseph were en route to Magda Hellekamp's apartment when they heard the desk sergeant's urgent voice on the radio.

'We have an incident at a shop on Dock Street, DI Galena. You will want to take this one personally.' His voice was unusually shaky as he explained what had happened from the mixed messages that he had been receiving. 'Hit and run, ma'am. The casualties are already on their way to Greenborough General, but . . .'

They heard the man swallow, and try to get a grip on his emotions.

'PC Danny Wilshire was declared dead at the scene.'

Nikki braked hard, swung the car into a side road and pulled on the handbrake. 'Jesus! Danny? But he was with Cat, wasn't he? Going to see Lawrence Carpenter?'

'Via the bakery on Dock Street,' said Joseph bleakly.

'Oh, my God,' murmured Nikki. She closed her eyes, then snapped them open and turned the ignition back on. 'We're on the way to the hospital. ETA five minutes.'

In seconds they were on the main road and heading for the Greenborough's Accident and Emergency Department.

Neither she nor Joseph spoke. They didn't need to. They were both imagining the same awful scenarios. And how could Danny be dead? He'd been with the team for little more than an hour! And Cat? What of her? Nikki shivered at the thought.

'Are you alright? About going to the General?' Joseph's voice held a slight tremor.

'Of course I'm alright! It's been my bloody second home for years, hasn't it?' The words had been spat out before she could stop them.

'That's what I meant,' he said quietly.

'Sorry. I'm really sorry, Joseph. It's just . . .' she hated herself for snapping at him, but pictures of Hannah in her bed on the high dependency ward had flown into her head. She didn't ever want to see anyone else, especially someone close to her, in that kind of state ever again.

'I'm scared too.' He touched her arm reassuringly. It was a fleeting touch, but it made her feel better.

She exhaled and concentrated on her driving. 'I wonder what the hell happened?'

'Let's pray that Cat can tell us.'

They drove the rest of the way in silence.

* * *

'She's still being attended to, ma'am.' A white-faced WPC Yvonne Collins spoke softly. 'The doctors hope it's mainly superficial lacerations from the flying glass, but she's pretty badly cut about.' In the heat of the hospital's emergency department, Yvonne rubbed her hands together as if she were freezing cold.

'How many other casualties?'

'Three, ma'am. One customer and two shop assistants who were serving at the time.' Her face creased into sadness. 'And poor Danny.'

Nikki shook her head in disbelief. 'What family does he have? I know his father is dead, but other close relatives?'

27

Yvonne's crew-mate, PC Niall Farrow, spoke up. 'A wife and a two-year-old son, ma'am. They live with his mother, out on Amber Drive. Our inspector is already with them and a family liaison officer is on her way.'

'What do we know?' asked Joseph.

'It's not clear, Sarge,' said Yvonne with a frown. 'The witness statements are like you'd expect, pretty varied. Terrified people make rubbish witnesses. Luckily there is CCTV down there and it's already being looked at back at the station.'

'Consensus of opinion is that the vehicle was a Mitsubishi, but with some kind of non-standard grill on the front. That, or maybe a Nissan, whatever, it was a big, black pick-up truck with tinted windows and a blanked-out plate.'

'Blanked out?' Nikki felt a stab of foreboding. 'Which would indicate that it was a deliberate action?'

'It appears that way. Why else would you cover your plates, back and front?' said Yvonne slowly. 'But who would want to hurt young Danny Wilshire? He's the most innocuous young man, apart from Niall here, that I've ever met.' She flashed her younger partner a sad smile.

Nikki tried to see through to the room where Cat Cullen was being treated. It seemed to be a hive of activity. Far too much activity for some superficial cuts. Concern ate away at her gut, and she knew it wouldn't give up gnawing until she'd seen and spoken to the young woman herself.

It was twenty minutes before the doctor came to talk to them. After introducing himself he ran a hand through thinning hair, and let out a little exclamation of relief. 'I'm afraid your colleague scared us there for a moment. She went into shock and we had some trouble stabilising her.' He looked at their worried faces and tried for an encouraging smile. 'It's okay, she's back on track now, and it was hardly surprising, considering the blood loss and the trauma.'

'What are her injuries?' asked Nikki, not liking the sound of extensive blood loss.

The doctor paused before answering. Another thing Nikki didn't like.

'It's the flying glass that has done the damage. It's mainly her legs. She wasn't actually hit by the vehicle and she didn't sustain any other kind of injuries, but we need to take her to theatre to clean her up.' Another pause. 'And we have asked the plastics boys to take a look at her face.'

Nikki felt Joseph tense beside her.

'Why? What has happened to her face?'

'She has a deep laceration that extends from her temple to her jaw-line. Fortunately, it missed her eye.' He raised his own brows. 'By a centimetre.' He looked seriously at them. 'I won't lie to you. She *will* be scarred, although our reconstructive surgeons can work wonders.'

'Then I think we need to hold on to the fact that she wasn't blinded.' Joseph exhaled loudly. 'Does she know about her injuries?'

'Yes. And at this moment in time she's of the same mind as you. Her eyes are safe. But then she's still in shock. I have no idea how she will react when she's had time to consider what has happened to her.'

'Can we see her?' Nikki was feeling sick with apprehension about what might lie behind the screen around Cat's bed.

'Certainly. She is booked for theatre in half an hour's time and she's been given a sedative and pain relief, but she's asking for you, DI Galena.'

Together, she and Joseph walked into the large cubicle. Nikki tried to ignore the bloodied swabs and puddled areas of scarlet that a nurse was hurriedly cleaning up, and looked directly at Cat.

'Can't smile, but hell, I'm glad to see you, guv. And you too, Sarge.'

One side of Cat's slender, elfin face was covered with a large temporary dressing, and her voice was slurred, as if she'd had root canal injections. Nikki saw that the young detective's hands were shaking.

'I couldn't do anything, ma'am, nothing. It happened so quickly. Danny was talking to me, and then . . .' The shaking intensified.

'Hey! Shh, it's alright, we'll do this later. Let's get you sorted first. Then we'll talk.' Nikki took Cat's bloodied hand in her own. 'It's you we need to concentrate on now.'

'No, you need to know what happened. For Danny's sake, I need to tell you.' Cat fought back tears. 'The vehicle drove straight at him, ma'am. It was intentional, I'm sure of it.'

'But that's a busy little street, and people do park there, even though there's a yellow line,' said Joseph. 'How could they be sure they'd be able to carry off such a complicated manoeuvre?'

Cat tried to move, but winced and settled back again. 'I parked in the last legitimate space, three shops away. There was a smallish gap, then there was an old flat-back lorry, a white one. It was pulling away as we got to the bakers.' She halted for a moment and dabbed at a split in her lip. 'It had bald tyres and Danny said he'd like to PNC the index, but it was too filthy to make out.' She shuddered, then sobbed out, 'That's the last thing he said, guv. And then he was hanging there, like some awful rag-doll mascot, on the grill of that black vehicle. Then he was on the floor at the back of the shop.' Cat fought to control herself. 'He's got a little boy, ma'am. A dear little kid called Connor.' Her fight ceased and the tears fell.

'I know.' Nikki wanted to cry with her, but for the young woman's sake, she knew she had to keep strong. 'Cat? The black vehicle? What do you remember about it?'

Cat swallowed and said, 'Mitsubishi L200 Barbarian long-bed. Plates covered. Black windows. Approached from the docks end of the road, and took off towards the main road out of town.'

'Hey! I see your memory is not impaired! Good work, detective.' Nikki smiled at her. 'Now let's concentrate on you. Have they called your mum?'

'I told them not to. She's on holiday with her sister. She hasn't been away for years. I'll be out of here by the time she gets back, and . . .' she paused, 'my mum's nerves aren't too good. I'd rather tell her myself, in my own way.'

'Anyone else we could call for you?' asked Joseph.

Cat looked at him with a weird twisted grin. 'Other than mum, you guys are my real family.'

Joseph leaned forward and kissed her forehead. 'And we'll be here for you, okay?'

'The doc said my face is a mess.' She gave Nikki an apologetic look. 'Sorry, guv, but I think my undercover days could be over. A bloody great scar would be something of a giveaway.'

Cat Cullen was the best undercover detective Nikki had ever known. She had the ability to blend in and assume other identities in a strangely chameleon-like fashion. For some reason, scar or no scar, Nikki got the feeling that she wouldn't lose that talent. 'You're not getting out of it that easily, young lady! A smart plastic surgeon and a bucket of make-up will see you back with the low life in no time!'

'Goody,' murmured Cat sleepily. 'I can hardly wait.'

'I think the sedative is getting the better of her,' said Joseph.

'Which is lucky,' said a voice from behind them, 'because theatre is ready now.' A nurse and a porter approached the bedside and smiled down at her.

'Hope you've got plenty of cotton and a really sharp needle. I feel like one of those teddy bears that's all patches and sewn up bits.'

'Well,' the nurse laughed. 'I hope you come out looking a bit better than that, or you'll be suing our surgeons!'

'Hang on in there, kiddo!' Joseph grinned at her. 'Your adopted family needs you back.'

'Ditto.' Nikki gave her hand a gentle squeeze.

As Cat was wheeled away, Yvonne and Niall moved forward.

'We've checked the other casualties, ma'am. Luckily, no one is critical. They were at the far end of the shop and missed the worst of it.' Yvonne stared after Cat. 'Other than Danny, DC Cullen took most of the fall-out.'

'She did, didn't she? And for that reason, I want you two to stay here with her. When she's back from theatre,

31

don't leave her alone.' Nikki gave them a worried stare. 'It's probably not necessary. It could have been a hit and run, a scared idiot who didn't stop, but until we know more, we have to assume it was intentional. Then we should consider that Danny Wilshire might not have been the target. It could have been someone else altogether, like the bakery owner, or it could have been Cat. Okay?'

Niall and Yvonne nodded in unison. 'That nasty thought had already gone through our minds, ma'am. Don't worry, we'll look after her.'

Nikki knew that to be true. She had worked with them often enough to be able to trust the two uniformed officers completely.

As they walked down the corridor to the car park, the knot in her gut began to unravel. Cat was a strong woman. She would make it through.

Outside, she threw Joseph the car keys. 'Right. Back to base, my friend. It's time to go see the super. Something very unpleasant is happening in Greenborough, and I've a horrible feeling it's just the beginning.'

CHAPTER FOUR

'The bakery has been sealed up. And I've asked DI Jim Hunter to take over the investigation.' Superintendent Rick Bainbridge looked hollow-eyed and gaunt. 'You've got enough on your plate with Operation Windmill, and anyway, this is too close to home for you guys.' He gave a small shrug. 'Of course there's always the chance that it was a tragic accident, and when the driver saw what he'd done he panicked and drove away.'

Nikki shook her head slowly. 'I thought that initially, sir, but we've just seen the CCTV footage.'

Joseph agreed. 'It was carried out like a military exercise, Superintendent Bainbridge. Timed perfectly. The lorry moved out and the Barbarian moved in. They were helped by the fact that the bakery is the last shop in the row and close to the corner of the road.'

'No one parks on the corner,' added Nikki, 'so when the old lorry had vacated its space, there was easily enough room for the manoeuvre.'

The older man sighed loudly. 'Uniform are pulling out all the stops to find the vehicle. And as you can imagine, every officer in this and all the surrounding counties, are out looking for it. There's not a man or woman that wouldn't like to be the one to get their hands on him, or her.' Rick glanced at his watch. 'I'm giving a statement to the media in an hour's time. Apart from the villains, the general public will be devastated at the news of such a promising young policeman being killed in such a sickening manner.'

'*And* an attractive young woman CID officer having her face half sliced off,' added Nikki vehemently.

'I know, I know.' Rick looked as if he were aging by the minute. 'Why would anyone want to hurt either of them?'

'And how did anyone even know they'd be there?' Joseph frowned. 'It's not a regular thing they do at a specific time of day. Cat was only showing Danny where we pick up cakes from because most of uniform go to the baker in the High Street.'

'Maybe you've just answered your own question,' said Nikki pensively. '*We* always go there, so do quite a few others from the station. The High Street bakery is in a pedestrianised zone, hence a no-go area for this type of attack.' Nikki rocked to and fro on the back legs of her chair. 'I think our killer was after police officers, simple as that, and Danny and Cat were the unlucky choice.'

'So are we looking at a cop-hater, or was it a revenge attack?' Joseph's eyes narrowed, and he turned abruptly to Nikki. 'Have you told the superintendent about the fire at your place yet?'

Nikki drew in a deep breath. 'It seems rather insignificant in the light of what has just happened.'

'Fire? What fire?' asked Rick, his craggy furrows deepening even further.

'Someone torched my garage last night, sir. The fire investigator confirmed arson.'

'Bored yobs?' He pulled a face. 'But then it wouldn't be, would it? Considering the remoteness of your farmhouse on Cloud Fen. Few people know it's even there.'

'He's certain it was a professional job, sir.'

'Add that to what has just occurred and I'm beginning to worry even more.' Rick stood up and began to walk around. 'Should we connect the two?'

'Not yet,' said Joseph firmly. 'There are too many unanswered questions to jump to conclusions, don't you think?'

'True.' The superintendent perched back on the edge of his desk. 'Like I shouldn't be thinking that all this is happening the moment we hear a rumour that Stephen Cox could be back in Greenborough, but I really can't help but wonder.'

'You and me both,' muttered Nikki and looked across to Joseph, but he said nothing.

'Nikki?' Rick Bainbridge stared at her. 'Would you mind keeping the thing about your fire being deliberate to yourself for the present? The whole station is in shock right now, but they naturally think that it is an isolated incident. Let's allow things to settle before we suggest that our officers are possibly being targeted.'

'Certainly, sir. Meantime, I'm fully aware that our investigations must go on unimpaired by what has happened. Operation Windmill isn't going to solve itself, so as soon as we can get our heads around what has happened today, we'll press on with that. If it's all right with you, we'll also surreptitiously check out any known fire starters in the area.'

'Good idea, but right now I have to go.' He stood up and adjusted his collar and tie. 'I need to decide exactly what to say to the press. As PC Wilshire's family have all been informed, I want to be the one to tell the national media what happened, before the tabloid sensationalists get hold of the story and twist it beyond recognition.'

* * *

Nikki was staring at some memos that had been left on her desk, but not really seeing them. Danny's death and Cat's terrible injury seemed to have sent her usually well-ordered mind into free fall. Right now it was playing back old memories, some of Hannah, and others of Bob Wilshire. Her funny-faced Bob. Always bright, the eternal optimist, and totally on the ball when it came to policing. As crew-mates went, they were a shit-hot team, but just as they were tentatively taking things one baby step further than that, she had met another Robert. Sometimes Nikki wondered how she could ever have fallen for Robert Galena in the way that she had. Soon after Hannah had been born, she had known without a doubt that they had made a terrible mistake. She had mistaken raging hormones for love, and he had never understood how important her career was to her. He had wanted to come first in all things, and she simply couldn't comply. Then one really bad case had torn Nikki apart, and that was the final straw for Robert. She had always believed that he would leave her one day. She'd been right about that too.

Nikki turned over some of the paperwork. She wanted to ponder on what life would have been like as Mrs Wilshire, but that would mean there would have been no Hannah, and no Danny, so she ditched that particular hypothetical scenario.

She pushed the reports away and walked out into the silent CID office. 'Someone should go back to the hospital, to be there when Cat wakes up.' She spoke generally.

'Can I go, ma'am?' asked Dave Harris. 'I was going to go when I finish work anyway. I haven't seen her yet and I really need to.'

'Of course you can, Dave.' She took in his haggard features, and mentally agreed that he did need to see her. Cat was his partner on the team, and although he was old enough to be her father, they bounced off each other perfectly. He would be imagining terrible things until he knew the truth. 'In fact, as I can't concentrate on anything, I'll come with you. Give me five. We'll take my car.' She walked over to Joseph's tiny office.

He looked up from his screen. 'How are you doing, Nikki?'

'Can't get my head around it.' She shook her head as if to make the point. 'Got the attention span of a gnat, and I keep trying to imagine what that poor kid went through seeing Danny killed just inches away from her.' She gave him a wan smile. 'Hold the fort for me? I'd like to get back to see Cat.'

He nodded. 'Tell her I'll go down after my shift finishes. And tell her I'll take the obligatory grapes, then sit and eat them myself.'

'I'll do that.' She looked at the screen on his computer. 'What's that?'

'A list of known arsonists. I'm checking out their methods of starting fires.' He looked at her earnestly. 'I'll let you know if there are any similarities. And how about I call into Cloud Cottage Farm on my way home from the hospital, with a Chinese? I know if I don't, you won't eat anything.'

'As I said before, I don't know what I'd do without you.'

'Starve, probably. See you just after eight.'

* * *

Nikki and Dave walked across the station car park to the corner where Nikki liked to park her silver 4x4 X-Trail.

She flipped the central locking and opened the front passenger door. 'Hold on. I'll just throw all my gym stuff in the boot.' She hauled out a red and black sports hold-all and a pair of training shoes from the front seat. 'I'm always hoping that I'll make it to the gym or the pool after work, but it rarely seems to happen.' She smiled ruefully at him. 'Good intentions, huh?'

'I'll get the tailgate, guv.' Dave moved quickly around to the back of the vehicle as Nikki juggled the car keys, her shoes and the grab bag.

'Thanks, I—' The bag crashed to the ground. 'Jesus! What the hell . . . ?' She stiffened and stepped back away from her vehicle. 'Don't touch anything, Dave! Go in and get the desk sergeant. Now!'

As Dave raced back to the station building, Nikki stared at the interior floor of her boot. She had lined it with rubberised matting to protect it. Now it had been decorated, graffiti-style, with three words: CRASH AND BURN.

Nikki's heart raced as she stared at the message. It wasn't just the words and the implications they held, it was the smell that had hit her when the back door had lifted. She knew instantly that they were written in blood.

She drew in a long shaky breath, then her professional hat slid back into place.

How had it been possible to do this? The station staff car park was monitored from every angle by cameras. Anyone seen going near her car would have been dragged into the nick in seconds. So where else had she been? Immediately she thought about the hospital. That was the most likely place, but what about the smell? Had she noticed anything odd as she drove back here? She decided that she hadn't. She had a good sense of smell, and a boot smeared in blood would have registered warning bells before she'd driven out of the hospital gates.

'Guv? Dave's just told me what happened.' Joseph stared down into her car. 'Hell!'

'Apart from the blindingly obvious message to me . . .' she kept her voice low, 'i.e. the method of Danny's murder and my garage fire, what does *crash and burn* actually mean?' Her eyes hadn't left the three words.

'In slang I guess it means a spectacular fall from grace.' He frowned. 'It's also a great album by Savage Garden, a sci-fi film and a book, amongst other things.'

'Mmm.'

They were still staring into her boot when the sergeant and two constables arrived.

'We need to look at our CCTV straight away, and I want a SOCO called in, with a camera.' The sergeant sent one of his officers hurrying off and spoke quickly to the other one. 'Stay here. No one comes near or touches the Inspector's vehicle until forensics have been over it.' He turned to Nikki. 'Sorry, ma'am, but they could be working on it for some time.'

'They must do whatever they need to.' She glanced at Joseph. 'I don't think I'll ever feel quite the same about this vehicle again.'

'I could arrange a pool car for you,' said the sergeant.

'I think I'll organise something myself, Sergeant. Thanks all the same, but I've seen the pool cars.'

Joseph smiled. 'A load of junk.' He looked at Nikki. 'Don't worry. If you don't want to hire a vehicle, you can car-share with me until you get yours back.'

'Actually I can use my Dad's old car. I'd planned to sell it after he went into the nursing home, but like most things, I haven't got around to it.'

Dave walked over to them. 'Is it alright if I still go to the hospital, ma'am? There's not much I can do to help here, is there?' He was staring at the bloody words as he spoke. 'And what the hell does that mean?'

Nikki had no intention of keeping Dave in the dark about the arson attack at her home, but decided to leave explanations until the next day. 'We've an idea, Dave, but I'll fill you in in the morning. You get over to the hospital and see that girl of ours. Give her our love and tell her we'll take it in turns to visit, okay?'

Dave nodded, smiled a tired smile that faded quickly. Then he said, 'Ma'am? You've seen Cat, haven't you? Is she, well, is the poor kid going to be badly disfigured?'

'I don't know, Dave. She was covered in dressings when we saw her. The doctor warned us that she would be scarred, but how badly? I don't know.'

'I wish it had been me,' he said softly. 'I'm an ugly old sod anyway, it really wouldn't have mattered that much, but Cat, well, Cat is a lovely girl.'

Nikki reached out and touched his arm. 'Go see her. Let her know just how much we care, okay? And more than anything try to keep her spirits up. You never know how someone will react to a traumatic experience like that when it all sinks in.'

As Dave walked away, Nikki called, 'And ring me later. Let me know how she is.'

'Will do, ma'am.'

* * *

Back in her office she looked at Joseph anxiously. 'Little doubt now about the connection between what happened to Danny and Cat and my fire, is there?'

Joseph ran a hand through his thick, light brown hair. 'I'd like to disagree, but I can't. No way could the wording on that bloody message be coincidence.'

'What I want to know is, is this personal? Or a general attack on police officers?'

'I'd also like to know if those words are written in animal or human blood.'

'I've asked the sergeant to ring me when the SOCO gets here. I'll make quite sure that we get an answer to that one ASAP.' She sank down in her chair. 'What a piss-poor day! I just cannot believe that Danny Wilshire is dead.' She paused for a moment. 'Don't get me wrong, Joseph. I'm not for one moment understating the severity of what has happened, but what do we actually know about PC Danny Wilshire? Because what if he *was* the intended target?'

Joseph screwed up his face. 'Okay, I'll play devil's advocate. You state the known facts and I'll put a different slant on them.'

'Right. So he was very well liked.'

'By us, but not necessarily by the criminal fraternity.'

'Highly thought of by senior officers.'

'A brown-nose?'

'Excellent arrest rate for one so young.'

'That will certainly not make him flavour of the month with the villains.'

'Comes from a family of police officers. Bob was old-school, but he helped put a hell of a lot of people away. So did his father before him.'

'Ah, well, that means he could have *inherited* an old feud, some bad blood festering away from years ago.'

Nikki leaned back in her chair. 'Perhaps we should check out his service record?'

'And perhaps we should let the dust settle first?'

Nikki's face hardened. 'We don't have the time for niceties. I've been labelled a hard-hearted bitch many times before. I can cope with that. Something nasty is going on here and I don't want to wait until another officer gets killed or maimed. I want to know everything there is to know about Danny Wilshire, and as soon as possible.'

'And Cat? What if the killer was intending to kill her, but hit Danny instead?'

'Cat's different. Her past is an open book. Her enemies are our enemies.' She raised her shoulders in a small shrug. 'And we can talk to Cat. Danny can't explain anything anymore, can he? If for no other reason than to give his wife some answers, we need to discover if his death was a tragic random killing, or something deliberate.'

Joseph nodded. 'Agreed. Shall I get onto that?'

'Please. Then get yourself over to the hospital and relieve Dave.'

'Our Cat could be looking at major life changes.' Joseph bit on his bottom lip. 'I hope she copes with what has happened to her, *and* what she witnessed. It's a wicked double whammy of trauma for her.'

Nikki rested her chin in her cupped hands and leaned forward to face Joseph across her desk. 'I think Cat will cope very well. She has a philosophy that says, Shit happens, so let's deal with it.'

'True. And with the team behind her, she has a better chance than most of getting through this undamaged.' Then he added, 'Mentally, that is.'

As Joseph stood up to go, Nikki said, 'Did you have any luck with that list of arsonists?'

He exhaled and shook his head. 'Not yet, but I'd barely started. I'll get back on it as soon as I've looked at Danny's service record.'

'Right, and talk to his friends too. We need to know if he had any worries or secrets.' She looked at him earnestly. 'As soon as Dave knows the score it will be easier. He can help chase down anyone capable of starting a clever fire.'

As Joseph closed the door behind him, Nikki had the feeling that no matter what they did or how hard they worked, they wouldn't be fast enough to find whoever was behind all this before he struck again.

CHAPTER FIVE

Cat woke up to find Dave fitfully dozing in the chair next to her. She would have smiled if she could.

Even after all that had happened, his presence there made her feel safe. She couldn't remember her own father, so she couldn't make comparisons, but there was something about Dave Harris that always gave her a feeling of being looked after, watched out for, in a protective, fatherly kind of way. Not that she would have told him as much.

'What does a girl have to do around here to get a drink of water?' she croaked.

Dave jumped up from his chair and instantly reached for the water jug from her locker. 'Maybe I should check that it's alright for you to have a drink?' He held the glass hesitantly.

'Give me the bloody water, Harris! It wouldn't be there if I wasn't allowed.'

Dave leaned over and put the bendy straw to her lips. 'Good point. How are you feeling?'

'Like I'm in someone else's body.' She sipped the water and sighed. 'Half of me is numb, and the other half feels like it's run the Sea-bank Marathon.'

Dave sat back down, leaving his hand draped reassuringly across her arm. 'I'm just so glad to see you safe.'

'Safe and remarkably in one piece.' It was hard to talk when half of your face was dead and unresponsive, but she was alive. Unlike Danny.

Cat's whole frame gave an involuntary shudder. She saw again the look of shocked horror on the young officer's face as he was hurtled forward and through the glass window. For a moment she wondered if that image would ever leave her.

'The surgeon is very pleased with you,' said Dave quietly. 'And he told me that you had a piece of incredible luck. Apparently a shard of glass in your leg missed the femoral artery by a cat's whisker. If it had pierced it, you would have bled out before the ambulance arrived.' He squeezed her arm very gently. 'So, my friend, when you consider that your eyes are also unharmed, I think we can safely say that you have a charmed life. And your Uncle Dave can breathe again.'

'Great. Now let's get down to the really important stuff, like did the doctor say when I can get back to work?'

Dave gave an inappropriately loud laugh. 'No, he did not! You have a lot of healing to do before you will be allowed back.'

'I can heal just as easily behind my desk as I can at home.'

'Much as we will miss your gobby little self, Cat, I'm afraid it's one step at a time.'

Patience was never her big thing. Still, as soon as she no longer looked like Frankenstein, she knew that DI Galena would have her back on desk duties. There was a murder enquiry running. The team needed her.

She looked across to Dave. 'I know I talked to the guv'nor before I went to theatre, but everything's a bit fuzzy now. I seem to have forgotten a lot about what happened.' Other than Danny's death-mask face, she thought silently. She halted, not knowing how to ask the question that was eating away at her. 'Dave? Was it an accident? Or were we deliberately run down?'

Dave heaved a long sigh. His face was haggard as he said, 'It was no accident, Cat.'

She closed her eyes. 'I'm cold, Dave.' She began to shiver.

A few minutes later, a chubby-faced nurse with kind brown eyes was placing an extra cover over her and checking her stats. She had a smile that reminded Cat of the cartoon mama on the Dolmio advert. 'It's shock, sweetheart. Just try to relax. I'll go get you something to help you sleep for a while.'

Cat wanted to answer but her teeth were chattering. She didn't want to sleep. She didn't want to be in hospital. She wanted to be back in the office, in the safest place she knew, with her friends and workmates.

'It's reaction,' she heard someone say. 'Surgery and anaesthesia has that effect on a lot of people, and that's apart from the trauma she's suffered in the accident.'

Cat felt something cold go into the cannula in the back of her hand, and a heaviness descended over her. As she slipped into sleep, she wondered for the first time what she would see when she next looked into a mirror.

* * *

Dave rang Nikki just before her shift ended.

'Cat's asleep, ma'am, but someone really should be here when she wakes up.'

'Joseph is already en route. He'll be with you in ten.'

'Good. I think it's really starting to hit home now.'

Nikki thought that would be the case. 'I hate to go against her wishes, but I really do wonder if her mother should be contacted.'

'Give her until tomorrow and let her make the decision, ma'am. I get the feeling her mother is pretty fragile. I think Cat knows how to deal with her better than anyone. You wouldn't want to send the poor woman off the rails.'

'True. Okay, I'll talk to her in the morning. I'm assuming the operation went well?'

'She's pretty well patched up, but the doctor said that she will need another operation on her face . . . maybe more than one.' He gave a short laugh. 'But, as you can imagine, she wants to get back to work.'

'I'd expect no less.'

Dave rang off and Nikki went back to looking over the crime scene photographs from Operation Windmill. She still hadn't seen the apartment. She glanced at her watch. It was only a ten minute walk to the Waterside Quay. She could check it out, then walk back and get a patrol car to run her home. Now was as good a time as any to acquaint herself with the place where Magda Hellekamp had died.

She tidied her desk and pulled her jacket from the back of her chair. She felt tired. Actually she felt totally wrung out, but she knew that if she stopped, she'd start seeing floral tributes, orders of service and crematoriums in her head. 'Oh Hannah,' she whispered. 'The world isn't the same without you in it.'

* * *

Ten minutes later, she arrived at the gated entrance to the apartments. A few words into the intercom system had the gates opening, and she saw a tall, well-built man beckoning to her.

'My name is Courtney, Don Courtney. I'll take you up and let you in, DI Galena.'

'I'll wait for you.'

She had to practically scamper to keep up with his long stride. 'Were you on duty the night Ms Hellekamp died, Mr Courtney?'

'No. I generally do day shifts. Grant Lawson was working that night.' He looked at her with a slightly puzzled expression. 'But you have all this on file. He was interviewed at the time.'

'I've just come back after leave, sir,' said Nikki. 'This is my first trip to the murder scene. I need to get a feel for the place.' She smiled at him. 'And put some faces to the names in the records.' She looked around at the manicured gardens and elegant design of the three-storey apartment blocks. 'This place is something else, isn't it? Straight from the pages of a glossy magazine.'

'The standards here are very high, DI Galena. But then the owners pay for it.'

'So I hear. Rather out of my price bracket, I fear.'

'And mine.' He waved a card at an entry lock and the door swung silently back. 'Top floor. There is a lift, but it's worth walking up as there are some lovely views across the gardens to the river.'

'Then let's walk.'

The view from the third floor landing area was stunning. The gentle curve of the wide tidal river and the older red-brick buildings of Greenborough glistened and glowed in the evening sunshine. From this angle you could not see the docks, the Carborough Estate, or the main roads, and for once, Greenborough looked entirely pretty, peaceful and serene.

'This is it.' Courtney pointed to a door with a shiny highly-polished brass number 37 on it. 'Any idea when it will be freed up? Surely there's nothing left to gather from it? The letting agency is anxious to get it cleaned up and back in use.'

'At the prices they charge, I can believe it.' She shrugged. 'But it will only be released when I understand how the killer got in and out of a locked apartment.'

Courtney pulled a face. 'Then they can kiss goodbye to their rent for a long while, can't they? I've been trying to work that out ever since I came back on duty the day after the murder.'

'And your thoughts?'

'It's impossible.'

'Sorry to tell you this, but someone found it all too possible.'

'But how?' The man's voice was exasperated.

'Talk me through all the ways you could legitimately gain entry here.'

'Right. If you are staying here, you have a special pass key. Well, they aren't keys as such, they are called intelligent key cards and they use contactless technology. The locks and door furniture might look elegant, but they are state of the art

RFID, that means Radio Frequency Identification.' He held up his card in front of the brass handle plate and Nikki heard a click. Courtney turned the handle and the door opened. 'The sensor in the lock recognises your card, and only your card.'

Nikki thought about it. 'And if you are a visitor?'

'Intercom allows you to give access to visitors, but there's a computerised record, and no one visited Ms Hellekamp that night.'

'So what if the killer arrived with her when she entered the flat?'

Courtney shook his head vehemently. 'Sure he could have gone in that way but, according to the log, he never left.'

'And what log is that?'

'Audit log. In and out. Every time a door is used, the action is recorded. There was only one recorded entry and that tallied with Ms Hellekamp's arrival home. End of story.'

Nikki pursed her lips and whistled. 'Mysterious.' She looked through into the apartment. 'I'll be about ten minutes. Is that okay?'

The man nodded. 'I'll be outside taking in the view. Take your time, DI Galena.'

Nikki walked into unadulterated, decadent luxury. 'Here in Greenborough?' she said to herself, taking in beautifully worked wood, Italian marble, the softest leather, and massive glass picture windows with panoramic views. 'I had no idea.'

Magda Hellekamp had been shot in the huge open-plan lounge area. Nikki had already studied the photographs of the scene, but the blood stains and splatters still remained to show her that Magda had been seated on one of the leather couches. After the shot hit her, she had slumped forwards to the floor.

Nikki narrowed her eyes and pictured it.

Sitting calmly, Magda either knew her killer very well, or was totally unaware of his presence. Nikki decided on the latter. He took her by surprise. One shot, perfectly placed. She was dead even before she hit the pure wool carpet.

No doubt, this was a professional hit, another thing that you didn't expect to find in the fenland market town of Greenborough.

Nikki walked slowly through the apartment and wondered what it would be like to live in comfort like this. She sat down on the huge king-sized bed and sighed. 'I'd feel constantly on edge,' she told herself. 'I'd never relax with all this technology and wildly expensive furnishings.' She thought about the warmth and comfort that her old farmhouse offered. Well-trodden carpets, old armchairs with huge cushions that swallowed you up, weathered stone and scrubbed pine. 'Sorry, Waterside Quay, you just lost out in the popularity contest to Cloud Cottage Farm.'

'Are you okay?' Courtney stood in the doorway.

'Sorry, talking to myself. Comes with the territory, I'm afraid.' Nikki threw her bag over her shoulder. 'I'm done, thank you.'

'And no closer to solving the problem, I assume?'

'Well, a few things are swimming around in my head.' Her tone was non-committal.

The man ushered her out and checked the locked door. 'Well, if you find an answer to this mystery, I'd really love to know what it is.'

You and me both, sunshine, thought Nikki, but she said, 'Thank you for your help, Mr Courtney. Oh, and I'm certain we will be releasing the apartment very soon.' As Nikki jogged confidently down the stairs, she knew without turning round that the man had a surprised expression on his face.

Although it was very satisfying, it was actually quite sad that she was conning him. She had no clue whatsoever as to how the murderer had left the room.

Oh, Miss Marple, where are you when you are really needed?

CHAPTER SIX

Joseph was in an uncharacteristically sombre mood when he arrived at Cloud Cottage Farm.

As Nikki spooned out the food onto plates, he opened a bottle of rosé wine and sighed. 'She was pretty tearful when she woke up. I've never seen Cat like that. I don't know what I expected, but it was kind of shocking.'

'And what was she like when you left?'

He poured wine into their glasses. 'Better, I guess. Joking about her injuries, but there was an undertone. She's scared, Nikki.'

'Of course she is.' Nikki handed him a knife and fork and sat down. 'Scars may look very dashing on a bloke's cheek, but she's a pretty young woman. Hey, I'm no spring chicken, but I'd be shit-scared at what I'd look like.'

Joseph gave her a half grin. 'You're far from being an old boiler yet. I have actually heard it said that you are a very attractive woman.'

Before she could remonstrate, he sat heavily on the old pine chair, then picked up his glass and raised it in a salute, 'Here's to Cat, and her swift recovery.'

Nikki touched her glass against his. 'To Cat.'

As they ate Nikki told him about her trip to the Waterside Quay apartments. 'I see what you mean about luxurious. Everything was operated by remote control, even the curtains.'

'You could easily become a great fat slob, just sitting on your nappa leather couch, pressing buttons for everything.' Joseph took a forkful of beef and black beans. 'But you'd have no history, or the living warmth of a crackling log fire, would you?'

'Could we not talk about fires?' Nikki frowned. 'When I got home tonight I felt really weird, just imagining someone skulking about in my garage with intent to destroy.' She shivered. 'Crash and burn. I know it's only a phrase, but it sounds horribly threatening, doesn't it?'

'Considering what's happened, yes, it does.' He gave her a concerned look. 'I don't think you should stay here alone.'

Nikki shook her head dismissively. 'It was a warning, and I've taken it on board. I'll be mega-careful, Joseph, but I'm not being driven out of my home by that shite!'

They continued eating in silence, until Nikki's mobile rung.

'Ah, my favourite detective inspector! I *do* hope I'm interrupting your supper.'

Nikki smiled and pressed the loudspeaker button on her phone. Professor Rory Wilkinson, their forensic scientist and Home Office pathologist, had entered Nikki's brief list of friends some five years ago after a particularly harrowing case. Rory was a sensitive man, considering the work he did. He managed to combine high camp and black humour with compassion. And that, Nikki reckoned, was no mean feat.

'Perfect timing, Rory. Joseph and I are just sampling the Sichuan peppercorn shrimp.'

'How simply lovely! Did you know that there was a fascinating study done regarding prawns and shrimps feasting around sewerage outlets?'

'One more word about that, Wilkinson, and I'll hang up.'

'But it's *so* interesting! Still, onto the serious stuff . . .' His tone altered. 'First, I am so sorry that one of your boys bought it today, but he's safe with me now and as you know, he'll be shown every respect and kindness here.'

He wasn't being facetious, and Nikki knew it. 'Thank you, Rory. We appreciate it.'

'My pleasure. It's the least I can do. Now the second thing is about the person who used your car boot to write his memoirs. Sorry to tell you, but it *is* human blood.'

'Oh shit!' She looked across to Joseph, who was deliberately taking a long, slow swallow of wine. 'Any clues as to who donated it?'

'Give me time. I've sent a sample off for DNA analysis, then we'll run it through the data bank to see if we can find a match. I'll keep you posted. Now go back to your Chinese. And by the way, I lied about the shrimp.' The line went dead.

Nikki closed her phone and shook her head. 'Impossible man!'

'But a clever, no, a *brilliant* and highly intelligent man too," said Joseph.

'Add infuriating to that list.'

'Oh yes, and he's the best wind-up merchant I've ever met.'

They stopped almost mid-sentence. Nikki said, 'Human blood, huh?'

'Worrying.'

'Very worrying.'

They ate in silence for a while, each wrapped in their own thoughts. Joseph suddenly said, 'Hey, before I drink too much, what about your father's car? Do we need to go collect it from somewhere?'

'Relax. It's here. I brought it back for safe keeping months ago. It's under a tarpaulin in the big barn.'

'Then we better check that it starts.'

'It should be fine. I turn the engine over every so often, and it was serviced only recently.'

'What is it?' asked Joseph, helping himself to more jasmine rice.

'A right old workhorse. A Montego Countryman estate. Dad bought it new in 1994, and he never bought another car after that.' Nikki smiled at a sudden memory. 'Actually he did buy one more car, but that was an old VW Beetle that he bought for a bit of fun as a renovation project. He loved the Countryman and he used it for absolutely everything. I should have got rid of it ages ago, but now I'm glad I didn't.'

'How about tax and insurance?'

'I think they are all up to date. I'll check it as soon as we've eaten.' She gave Joseph a sad smile. 'Dad is a stickler for everything being done by the book, typical ex-RAF, and I guess I just kept it going so as not to let him down. I reckoned that while I still owned the car, it was down to me to keep it in order.' She grimaced. 'It was lucky the fire starter didn't choose the barn instead of the garage for his little escapade.'

'I get the feeling he knew exactly what he wanted destroyed, and the barn is a bit too far from the main house. There would have been less threat to you, and as he wanted to scare you, he chose the garage.'

Nikki sipped her wine. 'You're probably right.' She placed the glass back on the table. 'I can't help but wonder what will come next, because I'm sure he has a plan.'

'I'm certain he has, but as we have little or nothing to go on yet, I don't know how we are going to stop him.'

'I'd feel happier if I knew the whereabouts of Stephen Cox. The thought of him skulking in the background won't leave me.'

Joseph stabbed a prawn with his fork. 'Where did you say he'd been seen?'

'Cyn City.'

'Then why not call in and have a word with Cynthia. She owes you one as I recall, after that pervert kept threatening her clientele as they were leaving the premises. You nailed him a treat. I've never seen the inscrutable Madame Cyn so happy.'

'Good idea.' She looked at Joseph thoughtfully. 'How much have you drunk?'

'One glass, why?'

'And I've hardly touched mine. Let's go into town after our meal, and catch Cynthia when we know she'll be at the club. And we can give the old bus a run to clear away the cobwebs from its crankshaft.'

'Hey, a retro ride! Yeah, I'm game.' He turned back to his meal. 'And by the way, why aren't you eating the shrimp?'

* * *

Nikki always referred to it as a dive, but Cyn City was actually one of the most expensive clubs in the area. The decor was opulent South East Asian, with massive pictures of the Bangkok skyline lining the walls. They varied from the incredible futuristic tall buildings at night, to a huge reclining golden Buddha, and the ornate, gilded temples along the Chao Phraya River.

It was not the kind of club that police officers frequented, and both Nikki and Joseph took perverse delight in walking brazenly through the door.

'Inspector! And Sergeant Easter! What a surprise! Are you trying to get my club a bad name?'

Cynthia Changtai did not look the part. She could have been a highflying business woman, some kind of executive, or an anchor-woman for a TV news channel, but she was Cyn City's owner and manager, and she ruled it with both panache and a rod of iron. She was around five foot three, had glossy black hair and the darkest of almond-shaped eyes. Tonight she was wearing an elegant navy suit with a pure white silk shirt underneath.

'Sorry.' Nikki gave her an amused smile. 'I thought I heard an intake of breath as we came in.' She glanced around. 'My, it's just like looking through the pages of our mugshot gallery.'

'Let me get you both a drink. Over here.' Cynthia led them to a secluded seating area to one side of the bar.

'Get us neatly out of sight, huh?' Joseph was also enjoying the visit.

'Well, I do have my reputation to think of.' Cynthia raised a beautifully shaped eyebrow. 'What can I get you?'

'Just a fruit juice for me, thank you. I'm driving.' Nikki slid into the banquette and sat down.

'A bottle of Singha would be great, Cynthia.' Joseph moved in opposite Nikki.

'Cheap round.' The woman called across to the bartender, then sat down next to Joseph.

'I can guess why you are here.' Her voice was clear and precise with only the slightest hint of her Thai ancestry.

'I need clarification of the rumour.' Nikki looked at the other woman intently.

'I'm sure you do, Detective Inspector.' She held a finger to her lips, and waited as the barman placed their drinks in front of them.

When he had gone, she carefully poured Joseph's beer into a sparkling tall glass, passed it to him and said, 'He was here last week.'

Nikki felt an icy stab of cold between her shoulder blades, and she shivered. 'You saw him yourself?'

'I spoke to him.' Her eyes narrowed. 'He's not a man I encourage to drink here. You know very well, Inspector, that my clientele are, well, somewhat varied. But he and his kind are not welcome. I made sure that he realised that fact.'

'You threw him out?' Joseph's voice rose an octave. 'Respect!'

'What did he say to you?' asked Nikki, sipping tentatively at her drink. 'Did he say why he's here?'

'I gather he has business to attend to. Although what that is, I don't know.' She looked directly at Nikki. 'You should know that he does not look like he did before.' She touched the side of her face. 'Extensive and *expensive* surgery I should think. He still looks disfigured, but he would no longer scare children and small animals.'

'Was he alone?' Joseph asked.

'No, although the two men he was with were not known to anyone here. One of them was foreign, either German, or Belgian or maybe Dutch. He didn't speak much so it was impossible to tell. The other was English, with that distinctive accent of the North East.'

'Geordie?'

She nodded and took a delicate swallow from the high-ball glass that she held. 'That's right. I did not like them, Sergeant. Not one bit.' She smiled at Joseph. 'And in my business I need to be able to read people very well.'

'I'm sure you do.' Nikki gave a cold laugh. 'As most of your punters have criminal records.'

'Everyone needs somewhere to go to relax, to unwind, even criminals, Inspector. And my clients and I have a very clear understanding. No drugs. And partly because of that, we have no trouble here, as you guys are fully aware. They play by my rules, and they are very well looked after. They cross me, and they find somewhere else to drink.' She gave a little laugh. 'And there aren't too many places like this.'

And that was true. Cynthia had once told Nikki that she offered access to a wide range of services for her regulars. "Sometimes people need something to make their lives a little more pleasurable, but they don't know what it is." Cynthia had smiled knowingly. "They just want organising, and because of the hedonistic streak in my Thai genes, I know exactly what they want. And I'm a very good organiser."

Nikki found it hard not to like Cynthia Changtai. She was a powerful woman, totally in command of her little empire. And it was true, they never had calls to disturbances at Cyn City. Other than the problem with the weirdo that Nikki had swiftly sorted out for her, Cynthia and her very able employees took care of most things in-house.

'I doubt he will come back, Inspector. I'm certain that he understood my warning, but . . .' She shrugged. 'If he does, would you like me to contact you?'

Nikki nodded. 'Anything you hear or see, please ring me. I'd appreciate it very much.' She finished her drink and stared at the empty glass. 'We should go, so your patrons can breathe easily again.'

Cynthia smiled at them. 'They'll survive.' Her smile faded. 'You need Stephen Cox out of your life, Detective Inspector. Until that happens you will never move forward.' She stood up and gave them a small and courteous nod of the head. 'I must go now. I have a lot to do.'

Nikki thanked her. But they walked out with no amusement in their expressions and no swagger in their step. The knowledge that he was back had draped a dark pall over their town. Cynthia had been correct. Nothing would be right again, until he was gone forever.

CHAPTER SEVEN

The edges to the marsh lanes on Cloud Fen were a lush green mix of grasses, reeds and nettles, delicately decorated with clouds of tiny white lacy flowers of Queen Anne's lace or, as the locals said, kecksie. Usually this would have brought a smile to Nikki's face, but this morning, even though the day promised to be clear and sunny, the drive into work had been tinged with sadness. As soon as she had started the old car, Nikki had been enveloped in memories. Memories of her father as a younger man, and of Hannah.

Her dad had been a rock when Robert had left them. She had never had to worry about Hannah getting to and from classes or trips, or any of the fun things that kids wanted to do. When the police force had thrown a spanner in the works for Nikki, her dad was always there for her. And that made it even harder when the dementia had taken hold. Suddenly she had to be the rock, and as things got worse for her father, Nikki had felt as if she had two children to care for.

Right now she wasn't sure how she had ever managed to hold down her job and juggle her dad and her child. Nikki didn't want to remember those distressing, anxious and exhausting days before her father went into fulltime nursing care. And now when she visited, he hardly ever recognised her, and that broke her heart. So, she preferred to recall the happy times. Like

58

those when her father would turn up at the weekend, picnic packed in the back of the car, and they would drive off, anywhere and everywhere, all singing their hearts out as he drove. He called them "Granddad's Misery Tours" because young Hannah always mispronounced the word *mystery*. Sometimes he would ring and tell them to pack a bag, they were going north. That meant they were going to the holiday cottage for a couple of days. It belonged to an old RAF buddy of his, and was close to the beach at Runswick Bay, just north of Whitby. It was Hannah's favourite place, and they spent long, happy hours on the beach hunting for shells and ammonites.

Nikki knew she should be grateful for having such happy moments in her life, but remembering them now made her loneliness and grief seem even worse.

As she drove into Greenborough, she tried to channel her emotions somewhere different, and she thought instead about Robert. Her jaw tightened. Her wonderful ex-husband had let them down more times than she could count. She had become immune to it, although she never stopped feeling hurt for Hannah. But she would never, *never* forgive him for not attending Hannah's funeral. She gritted her teeth. He had sent flowers, a huge, vulgar and totally unsuitable tribute to his 'beloved' daughter, but had declined to make the trip. According to his email, it would be "far too distressing for him to fly in all the way from the States, knowing that he would never see his beautiful child again."

'What bullshit!' growled Nikki. Robert Galena had seen Hannah only once when she first went into the coma, and had never returned. She had dealt with the whole horrible process without one iota of support from the girl's father.

Nikki pursed her lips and blew out air. She was glad it was all over. She had nothing to thank him for and now, finally, he could be permanently relegated to the place where he belonged — in her past. Nikki would never have to see his handsome, horrid face again.

For the first time that morning, she smiled.

* * *

'You are going to need another officer, Nikki. With Cat out of action and Operation Windmill ongoing, I'm going to have to find you a temporary detective to fill the gap.' Superintendent Bainbridge rubbed hard on his chin. 'Problem is . . . I don't have one right now.'

'Can I make a suggestion, sir?' Nikki asked hopefully. 'Could uniform spare two constables? I was thinking of Yvonne Collins and Niall Farrow. We've worked together before, they know exactly how my team operates, and it won't be for long. Cat was hardly out of theatre and she was asking if she could come back in as a desk jockey.'

'I believe it, although in reality her sick-leave will be considerably longer than that.'

Not if I can help it, thought Nikki. For Cat's sake and for our own.

Rick nodded slowly. 'I can arrange that for you. I'll speak to their duty officer.'

'Thank you, sir. I'd appreciate it.' Nikki looked at her old boss and saw his tired, deep-set eyes and the grim droop of his mouth. 'I bet you'll be glad when the day arrives when you can hang up your handcuffs, sir.'

'I never thought I'd say it, Nikki, but it can't come soon enough.' He shook his head. 'I've seen the best years, times when we were looked up to and respected, but now . . . ?' The shake of the head continued. 'Policing has changed beyond all recognition. Now young men and women can't walk down the street and know that they are safe. Those two young officers yesterday were buying cakes, for heaven's sake. Now one is dead and the other in hospital. No, I've got three weeks left and I'm damned glad I'm going.'

'I'll miss you.'

Rick smiled at her. 'At least you don't need someone to remind you of why we do the job. You have good values, Nikki. Don't let the budget-jugglers and the civilian administrators knock them out of you. Without tough 'proper coppers' like you, the force would disintegrate.'

'Remind me to ring you every week for a pep talk.' She grinned at him. 'Or will you be too busy with your runner beans and double-digging potato trenches?'

'I'm going to buy a camper van, my friend. My wife and I are going to throw a whole load of clothes in it, oh, and the dog of course, and we're going exploring. The kids all have lives of their own now, so if we take a week or a month, or six months, we won't care. Lovely!'

'Good for you, sir. And as a leaving present, I'm determined to have Operation Windmill sewn up before you go.'

'Then I'd better get hold of those two extra officers for you.'

'One last thing, sir. Your intelligence on Stephen Cox was correct. Joseph and I had it confirmed last night by Madame Cyn herself. He's back.'

The superintendent gave a long sigh. 'Do you know, Nikki, all of a sudden that camper van is looking *really* good.'

* * *

As Nikki entered Joseph's office, she saw him replacing the phone into its cradle. There was a slightly bemused expression on his face.

'Worrying news? Or just constipation?'

He looked up and gave a little laugh. 'Hardly. Well, not after eating your prawns as well as my own.'

'Pig.'

'Ah, now generally it's some spotty oik calling me that, not my boss.' The smile faded. 'That was Lawrence Carpenter on the phone. He wants to talk to us about Magda Hellekamp. He's driving in now.'

'Any idea of what he wants to tell us?' asked Nikki.

'He said it may be nothing, but when he had the call from Cat asking if she could visit him, he said he had another think about his last meeting with Magda, and he's remembered something.'

'I assume he knows about Cat's injury?'

'Yes. Dave rang him as soon as he heard about the incident.'

Nikki nodded, then turned and paused in the doorway. 'Good. Give me a call when he arrives. We'll talk to him together.'

She headed back to her own office, then stopped. A stocky older detective was just entering the CID Room. He had a round, moon-shaped face and a deceptively benign smile, one that she knew masked a razor-sharp mind.

'Jim? Anything on the vehicle from the hit and run?'

DI Jim Hunter walked towards her, shaking his head. 'Sorry, Nikki, but we believe it's been spirited away to some dodgy workshop, either for a paint job or to be carved up and dumped.' He leaned back against an empty desk. 'CCTV followed it to the edge of town, then it disappeared out towards the marsh villages, and we all know there are no cameras out there.' He pulled a face. 'And not a soul saw it after it crossed the river out of Greenborough. One day it'll probably get hauled out of a mere or a pit, or a derelict barn, but our chances of finding it are about as remote as the villages it was heading for.'

'I expected as much. It was too well-planned,' said Nikki sourly.

'CCTV and a string of witnesses would agree. Everyone said it drove at the two officers deliberately.' He paused. 'My only question is, was it aiming for one of them in particular?'

'We'd like to know that as well.' She gave him a tired smile. 'Keep us up to date?'

'Will do.'

'Guv!' Joseph's voice rang out. 'Lawrence Carpenter is downstairs.'

'Gotta go, Jim.' She turned and called to Joseph. 'Take him to an interview room and I'll be down directly.'

'Something helpful on Operation Windmill?' asked Jim, eyebrows raised.

'I hope so. This particular bloody mill seems to have ground to a halt.'

'Then good luck.' Jim walked away. 'I'm mighty glad you got that case and not me. Locked room mysteries belong in crime novels, not on the streets of Greenborough.'

'Thanks a lot. I feel *so* much better hearing that.'

* * *

Lawrence Carpenter was a far cry from the suave business man Nikki had expected. He had the rusty, leathered hue of a man who had worked most of his life in the great outdoors, and his clothes were more 'field' than 'boardroom.' It would take an enormous stretch of imagination to pair him up with the sultry good looks of the elegant Magda Hellekamp.

'I still can't believe she's dead.' His voice was deep and educated, even though it still held a hint of the local accent. 'I've known her since she was a youngster.'

Nikki looked at the man's intensely sad expression, and immediately believed that Joseph was right about him. Lawrence Carpenter looked crushed.

'You said that you'd thought of something?' asked Nikki.

He leaned back in his chair. He seemed unbothered by the sombre, windowless room equipped only with a table bolted to the floor, four chairs and a rubber strip panic button running around the blank walls. 'There are two things, possibly irrelevant, but considering the terrible thing that happened to Maggie, I wanted to tell you.'

Joseph held a pen poised above his notebook, and looked enquiringly at the man.

Carpenter exhaled. 'The last time I spoke to her was at my office, and she sounded both elated and angry.' He frowned. 'I've thought about this ever since I had the call from your detective . . .' He stopped mid-sentence. 'Oh, how is she, by the way?'

'She's made of strong stuff, sir. She'll pull through.' Nikki hoped she was right on that score.

'Good, good.' He paused then continued, looking at Joseph. 'It never occurred to me when I first talked to you,

Sergeant. It had only just happened so I suppose the shock numbed things. Now I've had time to remember, she was not quite her usual self.'

'In what way?'

'Before I answer that there are some things that perhaps you should know about Magda. I doubt very much the family will have said anything, so I will take it upon myself to fill you in.' Another pause. 'When she was much younger, Magda attracted a stalker. The young student, little more than a boy really, was not suffering from puppy-love, as she had believed, but was an obsessive neurotic, with the capacity to be very dangerous indeed.'

'Why didn't the family tell us this?' asked Nikki in amazement. 'Surely he would be a number one suspect?'

'No, Inspector. He is in a secure institution in Holland. He was incarcerated for attempted murder.'

'He tried to kill Magda?'

'No, he attacked her cousin, Daan. Poor kid had simply offered to walk her home one night because she was so afraid of her stalker. He was beaten so badly he never recovered full health.'

'And you are certain that this stalker is still locked up?'

'Absolutely.' He tilted his head to one side. 'I only tell you this to explain Magda's personality. She never got over the fact that, because of her, her cousin had been so badly injured. And she never trusted men after that.' He sighed. 'She was very clever, almost a genius, and after the court case she threw herself into her studies. I'm sure she would have become a recluse had her inventions and her scientific discoveries in the world of agro-technology not been so ground-breaking. She was more or less forced to present her findings to the industry and, for the family's sake, to help market them.'

'So Magda was one of the brains behind these agro-bots and computer generated farming equipment?'

'She was.' His eyes narrowed. 'And when I saw her last, I'm certain she had something that she wanted to tell me about a brand new development she was working on. Sadly, although she was clearly excited, she said that she was waiting for someone to provide what she called "the last piece in the jigsaw."'

'Did you ask her what she meant?' asked Nikki.

'I did. She said I'd never met him, although if his expertise was everything she thought it was, then his name would soon be on everyone's tongues.' He furrowed his brow. 'And I'm certain she would have told me more had she not been so angry about her car hire company.'

'Sorry?'

'Magda didn't drive. She used a chauffeur when she was over here, and the company always gave her the same man. As I said, she didn't trust people, so when a different driver turned up, she said she went ballistic.'

Joseph glanced at Nikki. This could be the lead they were looking for. Something small, but out of the ordinary, a minute change in the normal day to day running of things.

Nikki frowned. 'So what happened exactly?'

'The day before she came to my office, she had a meeting in Lincoln. The car arrived, with a new chauffeur. Apparently she was so upset that the temporary driver got her to ring her usual man's mobile, and he assured her it was all quite kosher. He said he had a severe migraine but had personally arranged his substitute.' Carpenter bit on the inside of his cheek. 'The new man was Dutch-speaking, and eventually he did calm her down. She told me that he was actually quite charming and a very good driver. The next day the old driver was back, full of apologies, but because of the way she was, it had really upset her, and she wanted to offload on me.'

'She trusted you implicitly, didn't she?'

'Sometimes I think I was the only one she ever trusted.' His voice was full of sadness. 'She was a brilliant, beautiful woman, but her life had been ruined. She was as damaged as her cousin. Daan was hurt physically, and Maggie psychologically.'

Nikki tried to think. 'I wonder why she didn't ring the car company's office? If I was going to complain, I'd ring the business number, wouldn't you?'

Carpenter nodded. '*I* would, but possibly not Maggie. She had a long and good relationship with her usual driver, and she was comfortable with him. First name terms, private mobile numbers, in case of emergency. I can kind of understand her thinking.'

'Have we spoken to him?' she asked Joseph.

'Yes, I did.' He flipped back a few pages in his pad. 'Ted Brookes. He seemed very upset and extremely shocked.' He sucked in air. 'But according to my notes, he made no mention of any migraine or substitution of drivers.'

'Another chat seems required, don't you think?'

'Oh yes, just as soon as we are through here.'

They talked for a little longer, then Carpenter looked at his watch. 'I have to go. I hope what I've remembered helps. I should have thought about it before, but Maggie and I had spent well over an hour together that day. We talked about all sorts of things, about her family and the industry in general. Her excitement over a new project was quite normal. She was always passionate about her work. Her ranting over a substitute cab driver, well, it's something most people wouldn't bat an eyelid over, isn't it?'

They both nodded.

As Carpenter prepared to leave, he looked back to Nikki enquiringly. 'Is that young policeman's death and your detective getting hurt connected to Magda's murder?'

Nikki shook her head. 'We are not considering that at present, sir.'

'Maybe you should. Think about it, Inspector. She rang me and asked to talk, then half an hour later there was an attempt on her life.'

'If the attempt had been on *your* life, sir, I would agree. But taking Cat out of the picture has not stopped us talking, has it?'

Carpenter shrugged. 'I suppose I just hate coincidences.' He gave them a weary smile. 'Please find Magda's killer. She didn't deserve to die like that.'

After he had left, Nikki leaned her elbows on the desk and looked intently at Joseph.

'Well, that explains why there were no traces of other people other than the cleaners in her apartment. If she was that scared of men, she would hardly be partying every night.'

'And certainly not holding small intimate soirees,' agreed Joseph.

'And another thing . . .' Nikki nibbled on the side of her thumb. 'She was in contact with an unknown man regarding a new scientific development. Now, reading through the notes, I never saw any mention of her working with someone whilst she was here, did you?'

'No one. And all her colleagues, family and work associates on her phone, computer and in her diary have been checked out. And if it was someone unknown to Lawrence Carpenter, it might have been someone unknown to everyone, except Magda Hellekamp.'

'Someone she would let in to her apartment?'

Joseph bit on his lip. 'Maybe, but even if she didn't, it is someone we haven't accounted for. We now have a Mr X to locate and interview.'

'Don't we just.' The corners of her mouth twitched into a cold smile. 'I suddenly feel that odd, sneaking suspicion in my gut, don't you?'

'The one that says, something feels all wrong?'

'That's the one.' She abruptly stood up. 'Let's go investigate.'

CHAPTER EIGHT

Before they could leave the station to question Magda's regular chauffeur, Joseph heard an urgent voice call out his name.

'Sergeant Easter! There's a call for you. It's Kent Police.'

'Kent?' He looked at Nikki blankly. 'I'd better take this.' He hurried over to the desk and took the phone. 'DS Joseph Easter. How can I help you?'

There was a woman's laugh at the other end. 'It's the other way round, my friend. It's us who could be helping you. I'm DI Steph Beauchamp. Having read your request on the Police National Computer, you might be pleased to know that I've got a certain gun in my possession, one that I believe you are looking for.'

Immediately Joseph straightened. There was only one gun that he was interested in right now, and that was the one that killed Magda Hellekamp. 'Tell me more.'

'Well, I'm reliably informed that it is a SIG-sauer P220, 45 calibre semi-automatic pistol. It's Swiss, and the bullets in the magazine would appear to be a match for the gun you are looking for regarding Operation Windmill.'

'How the devil . . . ?'

'Don't ever say that God doesn't move in mysterious ways, DS Easter. We had an RTC last night, on the main A2 Dover road. Car versus concrete bridge, one fatality.'

'The car driver.'

'Correct. But here's the twist. Our traffic boys found a gun concealed in the wrecked vehicle and the driver turns out to be on the most wanted list of Interpol *and* the Serious Organised Crime Agency. He has several names, but the one he's used on our patch is Aaron Keller. Ring any bells?'

'Phew! Does it! That's one hell of a turn up for the books.' Joseph's mind was turning somersaults. Keller was suspected of being a hired killer, no, an assassin would be a better term. Police forces across Europe had been unsuccessfully hunting him down for years. 'Now he's dead,' he whispered, almost to himself.

'As a dodo, detective. And I'm guessing that you'd like to run some forensics on my firearm?'

'I certainly would. But can I ask, were there any prints on it?'

'It had been thoroughly cleaned, oiled and wiped. It was looked after like a cherished baby. So, sorry, DS Easter. You can't have it all.'

'The gun is enough. Can you get it to us, or shall I send someone to collect?'

'This is vital evidence so, as we need continuity, I'll get one of our motorcyclists to bring it up to you, together with all the relevant paperwork. He'll be with you in around four or five hours.'

'Can't thank you enough, ma'am. We are really grateful.'

'Oh, no problem. We love solving other forces' investigations for them.'

Joseph turned and saw Nikki's impatient look.

'Okay, so what was all that?'

He told her as briefly as he could, and watched her expression change to one of stunned amazement.

'So Magda *was* killed by a professional hit man.' Her eyes narrowed. 'And to use that particular executioner, someone wanted her out of the way very badly indeed.'

'And that someone would have parted with a lot of money. Aaron Keller wouldn't come cheap.'

Nikki smiled at him. 'This is great news, but we can't get ahead of ourselves. We still have no actual proof that it was him. We need to place him in the area at the time of her death.'

'And we need the forensic report on the gun. If we know for a fact that it is the murder weapon, at least we know it was Keller.'

Nikki nodded. 'Let's get some mugshots of Keller run off. And we still need to talk to Magda's driver. We'll show him the picture and see if he recognises Keller, or saw him hanging around prior to the shooting.' She gave Joseph a friendly punch on the arm. 'Hey! The super is going to be so chuffed when he hears this.'

'Yeah, he could do with some good news. Why don't you go bring him up to speed while I get some photos of Keller printed off?'

* * *

Half an hour later they were entering the offices of the Fen-Elite Luxury Car Hire Company. The young man who welcomed them looked as if he had got up at six in the morning in order to style his hair. Joseph looked at it with enormous interest and decided that every gelled strand had been carefully guided in a different direction to all the others. It wasn't long and it was spotlessly clean, but it was certainly wild. Strangely, thought Joseph, it worked. Perhaps it was the crisply ironed shirt and perfectly centred silk tie that made it acceptable, or possibly the straight white teeth and welcoming smile.

'I'm so sorry, officers, Ted Brookes is off sick today. Can I help at all?'

Without taking his eyes from the boy's intricate haircut, Joseph thanked him but said it was a personal matter. Then he asked for Brookes' home address.

'He lives in Fenny Bridge Village. If you'll just wait for a minute, I'll get the full address for you.' The young man stood up and went into a back office.

As he did, Nikki's phone gave three short rings.

'Text message.' She flipped open her phone then looked at the screen for a few moments before closing it again. 'That can wait until we've finished.'

Joseph found himself looking at glossy pictures of Mercedes Benz limos, and wondering why they did nothing for him. Maybe he'd spent too long looking at tanks and armoured personnel carriers. Anyway, immaculately valeted executive vehicles didn't sit well in their muddy, agricultural landscape. For life in the Fens, he'd rather have a tough off-road vehicle.

'Here we are.' The young man handed Nikki a sheet of paper with an address written on it.

She took it and thanked him. As they turned to go, she said, 'Tell me . . .' and looked at his shiny silver name badge, 'Nathan. Was Brookes off sick a few weeks back?'

'Not to my knowledge. I've been here for two years and he's never taken time off for illness.'

* * *

There was no answer at 3 Croft Cottages, but Ted Brookes' elderly neighbour took delight in telling them that Brookes was definitely indoors. She had heard him turn off the "very loud" TV when their car drew up outside.

Joseph immediately disregarded the bell and the knocker, and hammered on the front door with his clenched fist. 'Police! Open up, Mr Brookes!'

On his second, even louder attempt, the door was tentatively opened.

Ted Brookes was clearly off work for a reason. He looked ghostly white, red-eyed and sick as a parrot. 'Migraine,' he whispered.

'Nasty.' Joseph held up his warrant card, as did Nikki, and said, 'But I'm afraid so is murder, and we need to talk.'

Brookes reluctantly held the door back and at a shuffling pace, led them through to his lounge. He pointed to a dark brown leather sofa, then eased himself into a matching reclining chair. 'I'd offer tea, but I've run out of milk.'

'We are fine, sir.' Nikki leaned forward and slapped a large portrait photograph of Aaron Keller on the coffee table in front of Brookes. 'Know him?'

Brookes' already pasty face turned a sickly grey.

'I'll take that as a yes, shall I?' She smiled smugly at the chauffeur.

To Joseph, Nikki sounded calm and unimpressed by the news that the driver had seen the killer, whereas he was totally gob-smacked. He had had no idea that Keller would be identified so quickly. So, they more or less had the '*who*-dun-nit', and now, in the words of the fire investigator, they just needed a 'how' and a 'why.'

'Time to talk to us, Mr Brookes. And I'd make it an honest, clear and concise account of everything you know' Nikki gave him an icy stare, 'because you are going to need a very good reason for not coming forward with evidence when Magda Hellekamp was murdered.'

At the word 'murdered,' Brookes flinched. 'Oh God! I knew you'd find out. I knew I'd been lied to, but I didn't know what to do.' He looked at Nikki beseechingly. 'He seemed so official, so straight. I had no reason to doubt him.'

Joseph watched as the man's eyes constantly strayed to the photo of Aaron Keller. 'From the beginning?'

'Well, see, I always drove Ms Hellekamp, every time she came to the UK. She was a really nice woman, and I liked her.' He shivered a little then, hugging himself, went on. 'Then a few nights before she . . . uh, died, *he* visited me.' He jabbed a finger viciously at the photograph. 'He showed me all these credentials and identity cards. I would have sworn he was the real deal.'

'What kind of identity cards?' asked Nikki.

'National Fraud Authority. He said he was working for the Home Office.' Brookes screwed up his face. 'I even went online and checked the logos on his ID card, and they were the same.'

Joseph puffed out his cheeks. 'What brass-neck nerve!'

'What was his name, Mr Brookes?'

'Kershaw. Arthur Kershaw. And he does exist! I Googled him to check him out.'

'With no picture available, I'll bet,' murmured Joseph.

'No.' Brookes sighed. 'No picture available.'

'Okay, so what did this guy want you to do?' asked Joseph, although he was pretty sure he already knew the answer to that.

'He said that his department was keeping a close eye on some competitors of Ms Hellekamp's company, Hellecroppen, in connection with serious fraud — some massive money-laundering organisation. They needed to speak with her privately, but believed that she was under surveillance. They also believed that she was in danger, and there was a chance that the threat came from somewhere inside the police force.'

'Oh, very neat! I'm beginning to see why you got sucked in.' Nikki's words might have given the impression that she was softening, but her tone did nothing of the sort. 'So you took a sickie, and *he*,' her stare moved down to Aaron Keller 'spent the day with Magda Hellekamp.' Her gaze snapped up. 'How much did he pay you?'

'Uh, well, two grand.' At least Brookes had the grace to look crestfallen.

'Funnily enough, government agencies don't generally pay for your services. They expect patriotic loyalty. Didn't that give you a tiny clue as to the fact that you were being played?'

'Not the way he put it.'

Nikki gritted her teeth. Joseph saw a flash of the fiery old-model Nikki straining to get out and bite this moron's head off.

'Right, Mr Brookes, so what happened on the day you feigned your illness?'

Brookes stared at his hands that were twisting and turning in his lap. 'He knew all about Ms Hellekamp and her problems with strangers. He said that he would ask her to ring my mobile number, and I was to put her mind at rest and assure her that everything was okay.'

'Which you did.'

'Yes.' He swallowed noisily. 'And I must tell no one. Not even my company, as the Home Office had no idea where the threat was coming from. God, he even told me that he was a high ranking officer, but he was taking charge of Magda personally because he was of Dutch descent and could talk to her in her native language.' He reached forward and picked up the photocopy. 'Who is he?' His voice was shaky and full of emotion. 'What have I done?'

'He's not who he said he was, Mr Brookes,' Nikki stated. 'And I'm afraid that's all we can say at present.' She stood up. 'We'd like you to come to the station and make a written statement, and we will have more questions for you.'

'Are you arresting me?'

'No. But you *are* going to help us voluntarily, are you not?' Joseph threw the man a warning glance.

Ted Brookes nodded fervently. 'Absolutely.' He let out a relieved sigh. 'I thought you'd be arresting me for perverting the course of justice.'

'Don't worry, there's still time.' Nikki growled. 'But you've been right-royally conned by a master, so at present, all you are really guilty of is being a gullible prat, and I can't actually think of a section number or an act that covers that.' She moved towards the door. 'Be at the station this afternoon at three p.m., okay?'

'I'll be there.'

'Good.' She hesitated. 'Was your Mr Kershaw alone when he came to see you?'

'He was the only one I spoke to, Inspector, but I saw another shadowy figure in the driving seat of his car.'

'No description?'

'I wouldn't even have known if it was a man or a woman.'

'And the car?'

'Big, silver, maybe a Toyota Highlander SUV? I couldn't be certain, but it was that kind of vehicle.'

'Okay, thanks anyway. And remember, three p.m. on the dot.'

As they walked back to the car, Joseph recalled what he had pulled off the computer about Keller's RTC. 'Aaron Keller was driving a silver Mazda CX-9 SUV when he totalled himself. And that could easily be taken for a Toyota at night.'

'But he wasn't alone, and that worries me. From past history, I don't recall Keller ever working with a partner.'

'Well, not one we know of. But he was always something of an enigma. Perhaps Interpol can give us some extra info on his methods.'

'Mm. Follow that up when we get back to the nick.' Nikki glanced at her watch. 'Would you mind if we just called in at Cloud Cottage Farm? It's only five minutes further on from here. That text I had earlier was from my handyman, Phil Maynard. He and his son are at my place doing a visual check of the damage. He can't get inside the remains of the garage until I give him the go-ahead, and he wants a word, if that's all right with you?'

'Fine. We aren't expecting the Kent Police motorcyclist until mid-afternoon. We've got plenty of time.'

* * *

Phil Maynard and his son, Luke, were the epitome of like father, like son. Both were built like heavyweight wrestlers, and both sported thick thatches of white-blond hair, cut in the original 1950's pudding-bowl style. Whenever Nikki looked at them, she had a vision of Mrs Maynard, pinking shears in hand, wielding an ancient Pyrex bowl.

'We don't want to disturb anything, Mrs Galena. We saw the tape was still wrapped round the doorways.' Luke looked at the striped tape in awe. He was clearly hoping that if he waited long enough a gorgeous red-lipped CSI with long blonde hair and high heels would arrive.

'You can get a good look tomorrow. Someone is coming out this afternoon to double-check for evidence.' Nikki looked gloomily at her wrecked garage. 'What can you do with it?'

Phil clapped a large hand on her shoulder. 'It's not so bad, Mrs G. I reckon we could rip out all the timber, take a high-power jet washer to the remaining brickwork to clean it up, then repoint it. We can skim the floor, wang a new roof on, bung in some smart new windows and doors, and Bob's your uncle.'

'So simple.' Nikki gave a little laugh.

'Dad always says, "Why make a drama out of a crisis?"' said Luke, nodding sagely.

'Will I need to order a skip?'

'No, no. We'll bring my brother's truck down.' He looked across to his son, 'And Luke here can play with his new toy, can't you, son?'

'Bobcat.' Luke's watery grey eyes ignited with enthusiasm. 'Dad's invested in a compact excavator. I can rip out all the damaged roof timbers and clear the whole area in no time.'

'Nice one,' added Joseph, wondering what that would have cost.

'Tired of paying the plant-hire people,' said Phil philosophically, 'so I thought I'd get a loan and pay the bank instead.' Phil looked around. 'Could we use one of your outbuildings, Mrs G.? To store our tools and our gear while we're working here?'

'Of course.' Nikki took her keys from her pocket. 'Now I'm using my father's car for a bit, you can use the barn.' She unclipped the key and walked across the concrete yard. 'It's padlocked and there's only one door, so your stuff should be okay.' She halted at the big double doors. 'I'll show you, then you keep the key until you're finished, okay?' She unlocked the heavy padlock, then threw the key to Phil. 'All yours.'

Nikki pulled open the doors, then gasped in horror.

In front of them was an ugly, black, flat-back truck. The paintwork was scratched and gouged and the license plates had been ripped away.

The grill faced them. It was dented and twisted and stained with a congealing brownish fluid.

'Get back!' Nikki screamed. 'Touch nothing!'

It took Joseph only a moment to understand what he was looking at, and then his phone was in his hand and he was requesting DI Jim Hunter to get there immediately and to bring some uniforms and a forensic team. As he stared at the big Mitsubishi Barbarian, he decided that Luke was going to get his CSI after all, even if they were a middle-aged, motley crew in all-in-one paper suits and masks.

He moved to Nikki's side and together they stared open-mouthed at the vehicle that had killed one of their officers and injured their friend. 'What the devil is going on?' he breathed softly.

Nikki looked up at him and he saw both distress and intense anger in her expression.

And then her phone was ringing. She stared at the display and her brow wrinkled slightly. It was obviously not a number she recognised, and very few people had her private mobile number. As she answered it, she glanced at him and pressed the loudspeaker button.

'DI Galena,' she said tersely.

'I assume I now have your full attention?'

Joseph stood rooted to the spot.

The voice was odd, and it made the hairs stand up on the back of his neck. It sounded strange, cold and inhuman. All he could think in that fleeting moment was that it was full of hate.

Nikki's eyes were riveted to her phone. 'Who is this?' she hissed. 'And what do you want?'

Joseph strained to hear the answer, even though he didn't want to listen to that creepy, sinister voice again.

'Compensation.'

The line went dead.

'Turn your phone off, Nikki.' Joseph spoke quickly. 'We need to get it to IT immediately. Hopefully they will be able to tell us something about the last number that rang.'

Nikki straightened up, then shook her head. 'We won't trace him, Joseph. You heard it. That was a state-of-the-art voice distorter. Not the old kind that makes the speaker sound garbled and hard to understand. That was one of those new generation voice changers. If he's into all that, then he'll not allow a trace on his phone, will he?'

Joseph knew she was right, then he realised that Phil and Luke were still standing, like two frozen giants, just behind them. He indicated with a little jerk of his head, and Nikki nodded.

'Sorry, Phil. The job is on hold until this has been sorted out.' She smiled wanly at the man. 'You'd better go now, and I'll need that key.' She pointed to the small key, dwarfed by the big clenched fist. 'And I'm afraid we'll need to get your fingerprints for elimination. They'll take them down at the station, if you don't mind? I'll ring you as soon as we're finished here, okay?'

The two men nodded dumbly, then slowly made their way back across the yard to their ancient Land Rover. Opening the door, Phil paused and called back, 'We'll go straight to the nick, Mrs G., get it over with.'

Nikki waved in acknowledgement. After they had gone, she whispered, 'What does he want? Compensation for what?' Her face tensed. 'Joseph, do you think it's Stephen Cox?'

Joseph didn't rush into his reply. He looked out over the fields towards the marsh and thought carefully. Cox certainly hated her enough. Hated her for losing him a fortune in drug money, hated her for getting half his face destroyed. In fact he hated her for everything bad that had happened to him. But none of this seemed to fit around Stephen Cox. The dealer was nasty, vicious, and as close to evil as it came, but all this? Could he organise something so calculating and so mentally destructive? He would have to say no, because the planning was too devious, too sophisticated. But as Nikki said, he could have paid for help.

Joseph wanted to give Nikki a definitive answer, but he couldn't, because he didn't know. He really didn't know.

CHAPTER NINE

'One thing is for sure, you are not staying in your home alone.'

Nikki knew that this time there would be no negotiation. But as it was, she was feeling far from her usual confident self. The shock of opening her barn to see the blood spattered bull-bars of the Barbarian had shaken her far more than she would admit. She just didn't like the idea of being driven out of her own home by someone's twisted mind game.

'I have a spare room,' said Joseph. 'And from Knot Cottage we can keep a close eye on Cloud Cottage Farm.'

'My guest room is empty too,' added Dave. 'It doesn't have the quaint and rural charm of the sarge's place, but I am only minutes from the police station.'

'Thanks, Dave, but I think I'll accept Joseph's offer this time. As he says, we can watch my home for any more unwanted visits, and if I need anything, it's only a few minutes' walk up the lane.'

'Excellent. That's settled,' said Rick Bainbridge, pulling a pile of papers towards him. 'Now, we need to decide how we proceed. Nikki? Your thoughts?'

Before she could answer there was a knock on the office door, and Yvonne and Niall, both dressed in civilian clothes, walked in. 'We are at your disposal, ma'am, for as long as you need us. I think our sergeant is relieved to get rid of us for a while.' She grimaced. 'But I don't feel right without my uniform.'

'And I miss my utility belt already,' added Niall miserably.

'I insisted on civvies, Nikki,' said Rick Bainbridge. 'Considering everything that's happened, I think your team needs to keep a low profile until we know what we are dealing with.' He leaned forward against the desk, pressing his palms together, prayer-style. 'So where do you intend to go from here?'

Nikki pulled herself together and went back into work mode. 'Obviously we need to liaise with Jim Hunter's team regarding Danny Wilshire's death, but we must still work on bringing Operation Windmill to a conclusion. The gun will be here shortly and we'll get it straight down to ballistics. We can now tie Aaron Keller into Magda's murder. Not just because of the pistol, if it matches, but because Magda's regular chauffeur, Ted Brookes, fingered him as the man who swapped places with him as her driver.'

'Has he given a formal statement?' asked the superintendent.

Nikki checked her watch. 'He'll be here in an hour, sir.'

'Magda Hellekamp's death is undoubtedly connected to some huge corporate organisation. We have only scratched the surface, but it looks like she and an unknown male were on the verge of some kind of scientific advance, something monumental by the sound of it.'

'Something worth killing to get hold of?' asked Niall.

'Or something worth suppressing,' said Yvonne darkly.

'Good point.' Nikki went on. 'Joseph is going to contact Interpol to find out more about Aaron Keller's methods. I have to say that the way he duped the chauffeur was mega-impressive. I've given the guy a hard time about it, but to be honest, I think Keller could have convinced the sharpest sceptic into believing he was a security agent.' She eased back in her chair. 'Three things really bother me. One: Keller had an accomplice, a man who was driving Keller's car on the night he visited Ted Brookes. Why? What was this other person's role? Two: Who was the mystery brain-box helping

Magda? And three: That damned locked room at Magda's apartment. I have been assured that there was only one key-card issued to Magda, and the computer access record and CCTV shows no other activity other than Magda herself. Even if Keller spent time with her, there was no way he could have either entered or left surreptitiously.'

'I have another niggle,' added the superintendent. 'Why was she killed with a .45 calibre pistol? I thought the professional hit-men preferred a smaller calibre, like a .22 for an execution-style shot to the head?'

Joseph answered. 'Apparently Keller always used a .45, even though it caused tremendous tissue damage to his victims. It was his weapon of choice because its stopping power was tremendous, and the shot was always fatal, unlike the smaller calibres.'

'*Nice* guy,' murmured Niall.

'*Dead* guy,' corrected Yvonne grimly. 'Ironic really. He lived by the sword, and died by a blow-out throwing him into a concrete stanchion.'

'And good riddance,' said Joseph. 'At least the taxpayer won't have to look after him at Her Majesty's pleasure, because we would have caught him one day.'

Nikki looked around her. At least she was back on track as far as staffing levels were concerned. Cat was invaluable in certain fields, but Yvonne and Niall were excellent coppers and she had no doubt that they would commit totally. 'Okay, guys, here's the plan. Dave, I want you to try to find the mystery scientist. Use Lawrence Carpenter to get names and contacts in Hellecroppen. We need to know who she was working with. Yvonne and Niall, go back to that apartment, talk to the security men and the maintenance people. Tackle them on staff pass keys and see if there are any loopholes that we might have missed.' She looked across to Joseph. 'You sort out the weapon when it arrives and get onto Interpol, and I'll take Ted Brookes through his statement.' She stood up. 'So get to it.'

After they had filed out, Rick Bainbridge looked at her long and hard. 'Are you alright, Nikki? I'm very aware that this business with the Barbarian in your barn must have been very unpleasant for you.'

'It shook me.' Nikki struggled to find the right words. 'I can't quite explain how I felt when I saw it. It was right there, slap bang in my face, and in my own barn to boot. Apart from being an outrage, it was a kind of personal invasion. It was a cruel thing to do, sir.'

'It certainly was, and whereas I'd usually say we have a psycho at work here, there's nothing crazy about the way this was organised. It's wicked, but meticulously ordered.'

'When he spoke to me, even though he was using a voice changer, there was a precision in the few words he used. And so much anger, but anger that was held in check. It was creepy,' she gave a little shudder, 'and very scary too.'

'I can imagine.' Rick indicated the chair that she had just vacated. 'Sit for a moment.' He looked at her soberly. 'If you lived in the town, I'd get one of our crews to keep an eye on your home, but living where you do, I'm afraid that's not possible. You can't do a casual drive-by right out on Cloud Fen.' He gave her a worried look. 'But it hasn't escaped my attention that to get the padlock key to your barn, the intruder had to get into your home to both take and then return the spare.'

'I know, sir. The only other key to the barn is on the fob that I carry with me. And the padlock hadn't been forced. The only explanation is that he broke in and took it from my key cupboard.' Nikki suddenly recalled that Magda's flat had also been accessed without disturbance.

'We could leave a man on watch for a while. I know we are pretty thin on the ground, but I'm sure I could authorise it.'

'Thanks, but no thanks, sir.' Nikki shook her head vehemently. 'If this bastard is out to get at coppers, whoever was left out there would be your proverbial sitting duck. I don't want to feel responsible for another officer being injured.'

'You are right, of course, and at least you won't be sleeping there for a while.' He looked at her thoughtfully, 'You say he said one word when you asked him what he wanted, and that was "compensation?"'

Nikki sat back in her chair. 'Yes, sir, just that.'

'So that would imply something bad has happened to him in the past, and he wants some form of recompense.' Furrows formed around his eyes. 'Another word for that would be damages.'

'And Stephen Cox had plenty of bad things happen to him, all of which he blames me for, whether or not I was even involved.'

'He is certainly our number one suspect, but I need you to think carefully, Nikki, about who else bears a grudge deep enough to terrorise and kill over.'

'That narrows the list down to a few hundred, I suppose.'

'No, it doesn't.' He shook his head slowly from side to side. 'Yes, aggrieved parties will shout abuse and threaten us with every kind of mutilation and torture, in both this world and the next. I wouldn't like to think how many times I've been told that someone would see me burn in hell for banging up their son or their spouse, but they rarely intend to see it through.'

Nikki knew he was right. She'd had dog dirt through the letter box, abuse and threats, her car had been keyed and she'd received some most innovative hate mail, but they hardly ever went further. Maybe it was just a way of feeling better, making a show of their indignation to look good in their loved one's eyes.

'Make a list, Nikki. Serious cases. Dangerous cases. Cases that made your gut churn away long after the prison gates had been locked.' He watched as she nodded, and then added, 'By the way, I chased up the officers who were checking our own CCTV footage from the car park, and there was no activity around your vehicle at any point from the time you arrived to when you made the discovery of the blood in your boot.'

Nikki groaned. 'How's that possible, sir? If it had happened at the hospital I would have smelt it as I drove here.'

83

'I had the hospital car park cameras checked too, Nikki, and nothing there either. Are you absolutely certain that you didn't stop anywhere on the way back here?'

Nikki threw him a withering look, but simply said, 'Absolutely certain, sir.'

'So, you have another mystery to add to your locked-room scenario.'

'Lovely. Just what I need right now.' She moved to the door. 'Better get on, sir.'

'Nikki?'

She glanced back.

'Take great care, won't you?'

* * *

It was a little after three thirty. Nikki was still in one of the interview rooms with the chauffeur, Ted Brookes, and Joseph was the only one left in the office. His talks with Interpol had been interesting and now he was skimming through reams of information that the international criminal police organisation had forwarded to him. When he considered some of the terrible crimes that Keller had committed, Joseph was still amazed that his death-dealing career had been brought to a sudden halt by a ton of concrete, and not the police.

He picked up a report of a recent investigation carried out in France, then laid it down and compared it with another, this time in Portugal. He sifted through a small pile of different cases, then frowned. Apparently their previous info about Keller had been wrong. He was not the loner that everyone believed he was. Yes, the executions were done solo, but to get to that point, it seemed that he used a carefully selected logistics team. And that would account for his 'driver' when he went to visit Ted Brookes.

Joseph wanted to know more, and after scrutinising some of the cases again, he found one that had taken place in Northern Ireland, and it featured a name he knew.

Liam Feehily was a detective with the PSNI based in Belfast, and Joseph had spent a few weeks working alongside him on a combined operation a few years back. He was a wiry, dark-haired, pale-eyed gypsy of a man, and one of the shrewdest police officers Joseph had ever worked with. With a smile, Joseph pulled out his notebook and turned to the back page. Liam's number was scribbled in the right-hand corner with the nickname, 'Dr Feelgood' written above it.

The phone was answered on the second ring and a lilting voice asked, 'So, would you be ringing to ask after my health, or to join with police officers everywhere in rejoicing at the news?'

'Hi, Doc. You heard then?'

'Good news travels fast, my little Brit friend, and that slimeball's death is very good news indeed.'

'It certainly is, but sadly, before he shuffled off his mortal coil, he left a dead woman on my patch.'

'How sweet! A parting gift? Don't take it personally.'

'I am taking it very personally, because for the love of Mike, we cannot fathom out how he did it.'

'That sounds like Aaron Keller alright.' Liam paused. 'But how can I help? Or were you really ringing to book a weekend in my beautiful city drinking some of the black stuff with me?'

'Believe me, that sounds like heaven. But right now I need to know more about the dearly departed, and I think you might be the man to talk to.'

A long sigh echoed down the line. 'And here was me thinking that I would enjoy my day off with a little fishing in Belfast Lough.'

'I won't keep you long, I promise. Just a few points?'

'Fire away, I'm all ears.'

They talked for around fifteen minutes, then Joseph saw Nikki going into her office.

He thanked his friend, promising to take a few days out when the case was over and spend it with a rod and line in a peaceful Irish river, and hung up.

'How did it go with Brookes?' he asked as he closed her door.

'Our Ted was one terrified witness, until I told him that Keller, or as he knew him, Home Office special agent Arthur Kershaw, was road-kill.' She smiled harshly. 'And then he developed verbal diarrhoea. It's all on paper, signed and sealed, just how we like it.'

'Excellent. I was a bit worried that he might do a runner, although admittedly he didn't seem the type.'

She sat back. 'And how have you got on?'

'Good, I think.' He pulled up a chair. 'I've discovered a lot more about Keller and how he worked.' He stopped and gave a satisfied grin. 'Oh, how gratifying it is to use the past tense when referring to that evil son of a bitch!'

'Isn't it just? So go on.'

'Well, it seems that for every hit, he used a handpicked team on the ground, to assist him in the preparation, then he went in alone and finished the job. I've just spoken to a friend who knows his MO very well, and he reckons the plan never varied.'

'And was it the same team each time?'

'No, there were undercover groups set up all over. Abroad and here, and here's the interesting bit. My friend Liam was certain that the hub for Central and Eastern England was in Peterborough.'

'That's close!' Nikki whistled. 'And what did this back-up team provide exactly?'

'Local intelligence and logistics. They were, well, still are, I guess, ghosts that checked the location, planned the routes, studied the victim, provided cars, fetched, carried and generally supported Keller until kill-time. Then they disappeared.'

Nikki leaned on her desk, her chin in her hands. 'That makes me think that Keller was working for a big criminal organisation, because no one could afford to have a set-up like that for occasional use. I mean to say, how many contract killings have you ever heard of in our area?'

'I agree, and so does Liam. He thinks that someone is running a multinational "temping" agency for anything and everything illegal.'

'What, like a sort of Rent-a-Crook?' Nikki grinned.

'Exactly. Liam uncovered a small cell operating out of Londonderry, but although he knew it was all part of something much bigger, everything closed down on him. He's left with suspicions and rumours and little else.'

'Interesting. But I'm guessing that kind of outfit would cost a fortune to use, so we'd have to be looking at either someone with money to burn, or a big corporation.'

'And I'd go for the latter. Let's hope Dave has some luck in hunting down this mystery man that Magda was in cahoots with.'

The more he thought about that arrangement, the more confused he became. If Magda was so frightened of strangers, and traumatised by men she didn't know, how had she become involved with someone that no one else seemed to have any knowledge of? How would you win someone's trust if they were shit-scared of meeting people? 'Of course!' he murmured. 'The Internet!'

'Am I missing something?' Nikki looked perplexed at his sudden statement.

He puffed out his cheeks. 'I need to talk to Dave, and one of our techies. I think I've just found something we might have overlooked.'

Nikki raised her eyebrows and waited for him to fill her in.

'Right, well, we checked all her emails and all her correspondence on her laptop, but we were looking for personal stuff — threats, abusive mail and jilted boyfriends, all that crap, but we only skimmed over all her technical and scientific work. It didn't seem relevant, and frankly it was so far above our heads, it could have been Greek.'

'And you think the mystery man will be found somewhere in her work files?'

'That's the only way someone could have developed a close relationship with Magda without scaring the pants off her. They used the Internet.'

'Where is her computer?'

'In the evidence store. I'll get it brought over. This time we'll concentrate entirely on professional data and its source.'

'Do that.' Nikki nodded. 'That's good thinking, Joseph.'

He went to stand up, then saw her face, and noticed the anxiety. He sat back. 'If it helps, I keep hearing that awful voice too.'

'*Compensation.* That word is bugging me to the point of distraction.' She gnawed on her bottom lip. 'I'm certain it's Stephen Cox. If anyone in the world truly hates me, it's him. We need to pick him up.'

'There's been only one sighting, Nikki. Maybe his "business" here had nothing to do with you and it's taken care of. He could be a hundred miles away.'

'And he could be two streets away, making threatening calls to my number.'

'Cox could.' Joseph rubbed at his eyes. 'But for some reason, I get the feeling that although the man we're looking for wants your attention, it's not actually you he's after. I think his grudge is bigger than going after just one person.'

'Joseph, for heaven's sake! He's got my private mobile number. He knows where I live, because he's kindly barbequed my garage, and he's used my locked barn as a short-stay car park for a bloody great murder weapon!' She glowered at him. 'Correct me if I'm being neurotic, but it feels damned threatening to me!'

Joseph was forced to agree with her, but deep down he was certain their man was just using Nikki to get their attention. And whatever he wanted compensation for, was going to turn out to be something completely different to anything they might suspect. He looked at the clock on Nikki's wall. 'That gun will be here shortly. At least we can get a step closer to winding up Operation Windmill. For once, I think I need to work with facts and forensic proof, rather than conjecture and guess-work.'

'Sorry about the outburst.' Nikki looked grey. 'I guess this is all a bit much after losing Hannah. When I said I'd return to work, I never dreamed I'd get thrown in at the deep end in such a horrible, personal way.'

Joseph felt awful. Things had suddenly got so intense that he'd almost forgotten that it was only a matter of weeks since her daughter had died. 'You could back off. Take a break, a long way away from here, somewhere hot, with turquoise pools and cool drinks served by hunky waiters. No one would think any the less of you.'

Nikki turned up one side of her mouth. 'No matter how attractive those hunky waiters sound, do you actually think I'd do that?'

'Not in a million years, but I thought I'd give you the option. Will you settle for a strong coffee served by me, instead of a bronzed Adonis?'

'You'll do, I suppose. And make it two sugars.'

CHAPTER TEN

Cat lay back on the uncomfortable bed and waited for the painkillers to kick in. Her dressings had just been changed and she felt as if she had had a run-in with some malevolent Edward Scissorhands. She knew that the team were up to their necks in work, but she still watched the door hopefully.

All in all, pain apart, she wasn't feeling too bad. That was what she tried to tell herself anyway. In truth, she felt like a terrified child, alone in the house when a storm broke. No matter what she did, she couldn't forget the look of total shock on the face of Danny Wilshire. It had happened so fast that her mind seemed to need to play it over and over again in order to make any kind of sense of it.

Since this morning Cat had begun to recall everything, and she was not liking her memories. Twice she had begun to shake uncontrollably, and on one occasion her blood pressure had soared, setting off an alarm buzzer at the side of her bed.

'Perfectly natural,' the nurse had said calmly. 'Early days. It will pass, I promise.'

Cat wanted to believe her, but she wasn't sure that she did.

She had been in some pretty hairy situations in her time in the force. Several were when she was undercover, with little or no back-up, but this was in a different league altogether.

She didn't know why it had happened to her and Danny, but it had. Someone had deliberately and viciously tried to take their lives. It wasn't like the normal good guys v. bad guys scenario — light versus dark, best man wins. There was something predatory and inhuman about the attack. They never saw it coming. Now Danny was lying in the morgue three floors below, and she was facing a life with shredded legs and a different face. A tear eased down her good cheek and settled in the corner of her mouth, leaving a salty tang on her lips.

'Here.'

She hadn't even noticed the superintendent come into her room. Cat accepted the folded tissue and dabbed her face. 'Sorry, sir, you caught me with my guard down.'

'So to ask you how you are feeling would be pretty stupid, wouldn't it?'

'I have had better days.' She attempted a smile, gave up and gently touched the dressing on the side of her face. 'Still, I can always look forward to auditioning for a part in a zombie movie. I might even have an advantage over some of the other hopefuls.'

'Not funny, Detective.'

'Far from it, sir.'

'Actually I've been asked to come in by the chief constable.' He smiled at her. 'I was coming to see you anyway, you understand, but he gave me a direct order.'

Cat hadn't been expecting good wishes from such lofty heights. 'I appreciate it, sir.'

'He wants me to assure you that whatever treatment you need, you'll get. He is fully aware of your good record and your high standing within your team, and he doesn't want you worrying any more than you have to. You'll get the very best care, Cat, I promise.'

'Oh, I can't complain about my treatment, sir. They haven't let me see my face yet, but I'm seeing the facial surgeon later today to talk about further surgery. I trust him, sir. I wouldn't want to go anywhere else.'

'Okay, but any problems and you speak to me, alright?' He pulled a chair up close to her bed. 'And so, apart from your obvious injuries, how are you coping?'

'Not too good, sir. But I'll be fine as soon as I get out of here and back to work.' She looked down at her heavily bandaged legs. 'They should heal quite quickly. I was lucky that no major blood vessels were involved. They say there will be scars, but hey, I hate swimming, and thank God, miniskirts are well out of fashion. A nice pair of jeans and I will back in the murder room in no time.'

'You come back when the FMO says you are fit, and not before, young lady.'

'But I'm bored already, sir,' she said.

'So read a book, do a crossword, chat up a doctor.' He looked at her fondly. 'Heal. Get well. I'm sure your team miss you very much, but they'll want you in good shape before you get back in the saddle.'

Cat knew there would be no arguing with Rick Bainbridge. She'd save that for the DI. She had a much better chance with Nikki Galena.

'Is there anything you want?' asked the superintendent. 'Joseph is coming in later, and he asked me to check with you.'

'No. Yvonne Collins has stocked me up with toiletries and nightwear, oh, and lots of chocolate.' She looked at him hopefully, an idea suddenly springing to mind. 'But my iPad would be good. If I give you my door-key, do you think Joseph would mind calling in and picking it up on his way in?'

'I'm sure he won't mind at all.'

She eased herself closer to her locker, opened the drawer and removed her key.

'Tell him it's on the kitchen table, and the charger will be plugged in on the work top, next to the toaster.' This time she did manage a half smile. 'That would be really great, sir. Help to pass the time.'

She edged her way back into a comfortable position. The painkillers were working now and moving her legs felt less like she was sticking them in a shredder.

'Sir? Can I ask you about the accident? Although it was far from being an accident, but you know what I mean. It had to be random, didn't it? I mean, no one other than a few people in the office knew where we were going, and even they didn't know whether we would call in at the bakers before or after our appointment.'

'We think the hit was made on you because of the fact that Danny was in uniform, that's all. It was most likely someone who hated police officers. Some kind of revenge, Cat. And for you, it was a case of very bad timing. We think you were targeted because of *what* you are, not *who* you are.'

'So if Danny had been in civvies, it might never have happened,' she mused.

Rick Bainbridge looked at her with a steely glint in his eyes. 'We'll get to the bottom of it, Cat. I guarantee that. We'll get who hurt you, and we'll get the answers that you need.'

Cat nodded slowly. She knew it was true. DI Nikki Galena might be juggling another murder case right now, but she would never rest until she'd put the driver of that vehicle behind bars. As far as Nikki was concerned, someone had hurt one of her family, so God help him!

* * *

Nikki stared at the blank sheet of paper in front of her. Joseph was seeing to the receipt of the murder weapon from Kent Police, and she had decided to try to make the list that the super had requested. She had thought it would be far from easy, but as she considered some of her past cases and old incidents, faces and names came rushing back. She began scribbling some of them down, then crossed most of them through. Okay, they were all villains and some of them were capable of a lot of very bad things, but killing police officers and threatening detectives was outside their remit. Even for the hardened criminals, it was one step too far.

Soon the white paper was full of hastily written and scratched out words. But although the name Stephen Cox was still central, clear and underlined, Nikki was surprised to see that three other major players had crept into her top ten of cop-hating suspects. She looked at them carefully. Strangely, none of them were actual criminals. 'Well, well. Windsor Morton, Jeremy Bow and William French. There was a time when you guys had us quaking in our boots.'

She frowned. Each one of them, for very different reasons, had caused mayhem in Greenborough, and although it had been some time since she'd heard their names mentioned, Nikki knew that they could all fit the bill.

William French blamed them for his father being murdered whilst on the witness protection programme.

Jeremy Bow blamed them for his teenage son's death after a high-speed chase.

Windsor Morton believed that the police had falsified evidence against his daughter and son-in-law, resulting in their going down for murder.

Nikki sucked in air. Were they still as bitter and full of hatred as they had been, even if they had not been seen around for some while? With a little grunt of annoyance, she pulled out her phone and selected the number for Cyn City. All three needed checking out, but right now her money was on Stephen Cox. He was still her numero uno and he was the one she'd start with.

'I'm afraid she's with her accountant right now.' Cynthia's assistant sounded more like a big company PA than a dodgy club receptionist. 'Can I get her to ring you?'

'Would it be possible for you to interrupt her and ask her just one question for me?'

There was a short pause, then the voice said, 'I suppose I could.'

'Tell her it's DI Galena, and ask her if she's seen our mutual friend again. She'll know what I mean.'

Nikki waited for a while, then a voice that she recognised came on the phone.

'Hello, Inspector, Cynthia here. In answer to your question, I haven't seen him. I've asked around, just a few people who I trust, and there have been no sightings of him since he visited us the other night.'

Nikki thanked her, then added, 'If you could continue to keep an ear to the ground for me, I'd be grateful.'

'I will. I'm secretly hoping that he was just passing through and now, like the vermin he is, he's crawled back into his hole again. I don't want my clients upset by the likes of Stephen Cox.'

And that, thought Nikki, sums him up a treat. Even crooks don't want to associate with him. But right now Nikki wanted to know exactly where that particular hole was, so that when the time came, she could set her rat trap.

'Ma'am?'

She looked up to see Yvonne and Niall in her doorway. Yvonne clasped a coffee mug in her hand. 'You look like you need this, guv.' She placed it on Nikki's desk.

'Life-saver.' She looked up at them. 'So how did you get on at Waterside Quay?'

'What, apart from having to physically drag our Niall away from the place?' Yvonne grinned. 'He's decided he's going to give up the Police force and learn about big tractors, then maybe he can live in a place like that.'

Niall shook his head. 'It looked like a film set, ma'am.' He spoke dreamily.

'Yeah, a horror movie, and it even had the obligatory bloodstains and brain matter on the floor and up the wall,' said Yvonne. 'But we've been over the place with a fine-tooth comb, guv. We've spoken to her neighbours and security, but they are as puzzled as we are. According to them, it couldn't have happened.'

Niall dragged himself away from his dreams and added, 'So we contacted the security company who installed the lock system. We went over to their offices just outside town, and they were all running round like headless chickens.'

'The system is supposed to be fail-safe, and we got the feeling they are looking for a scapegoat to stick the blame on. We've got the name of the guy they've brought in to find the error, but he has nothing to tell us yet.' Yvonne placed a business card on Nikki's desk. 'He'll contact you immediately when he finds the gremlin.' She glanced at the card. 'His name is Alan Brady and right now, he is one very busy and very worried man.'

'Okay. Well, that's about as far as you can go with that.' Nikki stared thoughtfully at Yvonne. 'Would you two mind doing a bit of off the record sleuthing for me?'

'Your wish is our command, ma'am.' Yvonne looked back with interest.

'Stephen Cox.'

Both officers stiffened.

'Please don't tell me he's back?' Yvonne said. Her face had set like hardening cement.

'One sighting, but it was confirmed.' Nikki lowered her voice. 'I need to know what the word is on the streets. Can you have a word with a few of your snouts? See if they know more than we do.'

'You got it, ma'am.' They looked at each other soberly, then turned and left. As they did, Dave entered the room. 'I've contacted as many people in Hellecroppen as I can, and they all categorically state that Magda was working alone. Only when she was at home in Holland would she collaborate with her own specialist Dutch team.' He shook his head. 'Not one of them knew anything about a work colleague in Britain. They are as nonplussed as we are.'

Nikki felt frustration eat its way into her. More dead ends. Still, there was one hope. She told Dave about Joseph's idea regarding the Internet, and saw his face begin to lose its miserable expression.

'That's a really good point, ma'am. And for a woman with Magda's phobias, cyberspace would be the safest place to liaise with someone. Is the sarge getting hold of the laptop now, or shall I request it?'

'He's already done it. And he's asked one of the techies to lend a hand sifting through the data.'

'Good. That will make the job a lot easier and faster.' He pulled a face. 'Without Cat around, I feel a bit like a fish out of water with the old computer skills.'

Cat had spent a whole year doing advanced computer studies in her spare time. She had always been something of a wizard with the keyboard and now she was fast becoming invaluable to the team. She had cut down the use of the IT techies by half, and as that particular department had been 'civilianised' and it cost money every time they enlisted their help, her new talent made even top brass pleased.

Nikki thought about that fact. It could be a major blessing that Cat now had another string to her bow. If her injuries precluded her going back into the field for a while, she would still have a valuable place in the team, even if she was tied to a desk.

After Dave left, Nikki found her mind wandering back to her three other candidates, three men who might still be bitter enough to wage war on the police. Each one made her feel cold inside when she remembered them.

Windsor, Bow and French. Very different animals, but all three had expressed intense emotions that had escalated rather than waned as time passed. And in each case their hatred went far deeper than organising demonstrations, setting up petitions and obtaining the services of lawyers. They had all showed a level of unbalanced animosity that had had local police officers watching over their shoulders and fearing for the safety of their loved ones.

But still, other than vile threats, nothing had ever come of their intimidating behaviour, and now Nikki wondered how many officers serving in Greenborough would even remember them.

'William French, Jeremy Bow and Windsor Morton,' she whispered to herself. 'I think it's time to make a few discreet enquiries as to whether you are still living locally, and see how you feel about a visit from the police these days.'

CHAPTER ELEVEN

It was almost ten in the evening when Nikki and Joseph finally arrived on the track that led up to Cloud Cottage Farm. They had agreed to go there first, collect some of Nikki's things and check the place over before locking it up.

They had driven in convoy across the darkening fen, and Nikki had felt a growing dread as they made their way across the marsh lanes towards her home. For the first time in her life, Cloud Fen looked sinister, full of unseen menace. She had spent the whole journey worrying whether the faceless killer had returned. And if he had, what the hell would they find this time?

The famous scene from the *Godfather* had flashed unbidden into her mind. The horse's severed head nestling on golden satin sheets in Jack Woltz's bed. Suddenly it had lost its cinematic distance, and seemed all too possible.

They parked close together and Nikki looked uneasily across to her barn, dreading that the bloodied bull bars of the Barbarian would still be lurking in the shadows.

Thankfully by the time they got there, the vehicle had long since been placed on a low-loader and taken back to the police yard for forensic examination.

They crunched across the gravel, both grateful for the bright security lights. They glanced apprehensively at each other as Nikki pushed the key into the lock, but neither said a word. She couldn't recall ever feeling so edgy, so powerless. They didn't know who was threatening them and they didn't know why. He had given them no indication of what he wanted from them. And the word "compensation" meant very little. Compensation for something that had happened to him? Or to someone else? Or for some kind of incident that he blamed them for?

'Whoever he is,' murmured Joseph, his voice low and steely, 'he has certainly succeeded in getting to us.' He moved in front of her. 'I'll go in first.'

The house was quiet. There were no lights on that shouldn't be, and nothing appeared to be out of place.

Joseph looked around suspiciously. 'Maybe you should change the locks.'

Nikki didn't think that would do any good. 'I think I'd be wasting my money. If he got in once, he could do it again.'

'I guess. I'll check upstairs.'

He led the way and searched each room carefully.

As Nikki watched, she saw the soldier in him, still vigilant, still on duty. Every area was meticulously checked and cleared, and then he visibly relaxed.

'All clear.'

'For now,' said Nikki uncomfortably. 'But I can't help wondering what the beast's next move is going to be.'

'He will tell us what he wants before long. This kind of terrorist always has an agenda and he'll have demands to be fulfilled.' Joseph gnawed on his lip. 'I wonder what we are dealing with?'

'I dread to think.' Nikki started gathering her things together. A selection of clothes, nightwear, wash-gear, phone charger, laptop. She looked at Joseph. 'Grab my duvet and pillow from my bed. They are all freshly laundered and it'll save you washing and ironing after I've left.'

'No way.' Joseph shook his head. 'That's no problem. The guest room is always made up ready, just in case.'

Ah, his daughter, thought Nikki. The 'just in case' was for Tamsin, if she ever wanted to visit. Not that Nikki could remember it ever actually happening. Tamsin had gone to live with her mother after the divorce, and for years had refused to see or talk to Joseph. She blamed him for everything bad in the world. Even as a tiny child Tamsin had been a pacifist, a mender and a healer, and her father was a soldier. He killed people. And that, in Tamsin's eyes was not acceptable. But now she was an adult, and things had apparently eased into a bearable truce. But even though Joseph had tried his hardest, they were not yet on "dropping in" terms.

She took a pair of trainers from the bottom of the wardrobe and decided not to argue with him. It was good of Joseph to let her share his tiny cottage. She didn't want to offend him before she'd even set foot in the place.

She bundled the shoes into a bag and suddenly realised how much she needed his company right now. It was bad enough trying to come to terms with Hannah's death, let alone find her home besieged, and Nikki and her friends stalked by an unidentified killer. In fact, there was no one else in the whole world that she'd rather have by her side right now.

'That should do.' She looked around, then picked up a framed photograph of Hannah from beside her bed and pushed it into her grab bag. 'And if I've forgotten anything, we are only minutes away.'

Together they went through the house again, this time checking that all the windows and doors were closed and secured. Nikki saw that a red light was flashing on her answerphone and found one new message. It was Phil Maynard telling her that he and his son had been to the station and had their fingerprints taken. Before hanging up, he offered their help if she needed anything. Nikki smiled. They were a good old fen family, not perhaps the brightest academically, but hard workers and always swift to lend a hand.

She cleared the message and looked around. 'I guess that's it. Time to go.'

'I was going to ask if you had any food in the fridge that needed using up,' Joseph grinned at her, 'then I remembered it was Nikki Galena that I was talking to.'

'Don't be facetious. I cooked something last week.' She pondered for a moment. 'Or was it the week before? I forget.'

'I rest my case.' He held the door open for her. 'And when we get to my cottage you will find homemade beef and mushroom cannelloni. I'll get it together while you unpack your things.' He smiled at her, a gentle, thoughtful look in his eyes. 'Knot Cottage is yours, for as long as it takes. Help yourself to anything. Open the cupboards, look in the drawers, I have no secrets. Just make yourself at home.'

She squeezed his arm with her free hand, and they walked out into the darkness.

* * *

Joseph eased his vehicle into a space close to the cottage, leaving plenty of room for Nikki and her big old estate wagon. As the noise of their engines died away, he heard the evening sounds of the marsh and the estuary drift around him. Late birds still called, water trickled and gurgled, and the breeze rustled the reeds and the grasses. There was a salty smell of seaweed and ozone, and, as always, it welcomed him home. This was the point in his day when he allowed the job and all its myriad of worries to slip away, and he could just be a very small part of the countryside that he had come to love. Knot Cottage was like a giant battery, and after the day had drained him, his home powered him up again.

Only tonight was different. There would be no letting down of his guard, not until he knew their adversary and knew exactly what he wanted from them. And then, of course, there was the fact that Nikki was going to be here with him, in a very small space.

Oh well, they'd cope somehow. He smiled in the shadows. If the circumstances were different it might even be fun.

He loped across to the door, unlocked it and they both stepped into the kitchen.

It smelt of cooking. The night before he had stayed up late doing the one thing that really relaxed him — Joseph Easter's personal therapeutic cookery. He had made pasta for the cannelloni, cooked a delicious sauce and baked some olive bread, then the next morning he had ground fresh coffee. There was a wonderful Italian bistro aroma to the room.

'You do realise that I could stay for some time.' Nikki let out a sigh of contentment. 'That smells *so* good . . . my kitchen never smells like this.'

'That's because the only food it ever sees is a takeaway.' Joseph threw his keys into a wooden bowl on a shelf close to the door. 'Now, let's get you settled. Follow me, ma'am. Your suite awaits you.' He opened the door into the sitting room, then ushered her up the narrow staircase that led directly from behind the open fireplace.

'You know the layout, Nikki.'

On the landing, he opened the pine door and carried her grab bag inside.

Although he had done all the work himself, the room was decorated in a rather feminine way. He had chosen everything with his daughter in mind, but in case her tastes had changed over the years, he had not made it too flowery. The result was a warm and inviting room in soft pinks, pastel greens and dusty lilacs. He'd found a couple of watercolour prints, a landscape that could easily have been Cloud Fen, and a seascape that he chosen simply for the muted evening colours that merged sea and sky into a haze of soft greys and pinkish lavender. And finally, the crowning glory, was a handcrafted patchwork throw over the antique pine bed. He'd seen it in a bijou little shop in Stamford and it had cost him a small fortune.

He looked around appraisingly. It would do. He silently wished he'd known earlier that Nikki would be staying, because he would have picked a few flowers for the dressing table.

'I'll go prepare dinner.'

'This room is lovely, Joseph. I thought so when I stayed over the night of the fire. If you ever decide to give up police work, you could take up interior design.'

Joseph pulled a face. 'I don't think so. I'm not camp enough. And anyway, renovating this cottage was a labour of love, and a way of getting my head back together after that bad case.' He didn't have to say more. Nikki knew exactly what he meant. The bad case was Stephen Cox. Although their team had managed to stop him getting away with a fortune in smuggled drugs, Joseph had been left fighting for his life. It made her go cold when she thought about what happened, but now was not the time to dredge it up again.

She placed her bag on the bed and turned to him. 'I'll do this later. Come on, I love to watch you cook, and I'm really good at opening wine bottles.' She produced a bottle of Chablis from her bag. 'See, there was something in my fridge after all.'

'I stand corrected.' He took the bottle from her and they went down the steep wooden staircase and into the sitting room.

As he stepped off the last step he saw the red light flashing on his telephone. He pressed it and switched on the loudspeaker as he moved towards the kitchen.

'You have one new message. Message received today at twenty-two hundred hours.' There was a click, and then Joseph froze.

'I suppose you're thinking that there's safety in numbers, huh, Detective Sergeant Easter? Sticking together? You and the boss? Well, it's certainly cosy. But safe? Are you sure about that?' There was a pause, then the weirdly distorted but now familiar voice added, 'Compensation, Joseph. I want compensation.' A longer pause, then, 'Sleep tight.'

There was another click and the recorded voice cut in with its infuriating list of options. Joseph turned slowly and saw Nikki standing stock-still behind him. 'Play it again,' she said.

He pressed the number to hear it again. When it had finished he realised that his jaw had clamped tight enough to break his teeth. The bastard, the sick bastard! Anger threatened to tear him apart. What right did he have to intimidate them like this? He controlled his breathing, then said, 'Nikki, I want you to go outside and wait until I call. I need to know what he meant about not being safe. I have to check the cottage and I'd rather you were not in here.'

Nikki's face drew together, fierce, tight-lipped. 'Bollocks! We look together, Joseph. I've done the training too, not to your level admittedly, but if you think I'm standing outside while you risk life and limb, think again!'

There was no point in arguing. This was the Nikki of old, and even if he thought her foolhardy, he still admired her guts. He threw up his hands and said, 'Okay, but I'm thinking it's a hoax. I believe he's playing with us. I know my home and I don't believe he's actually been in here. But we can't risk it. We'll do inside first, then the garden, although that won't be easy in the dark.'

It took them twenty minutes to feel certain that the cottage was safe, then armed with powerful battery lanterns they slowly searched the area around the cottage.

'This is ridiculous,' growled Nikki as she shone the beam around the interior of a big old shed. 'There's more rubbish in here than the local tip.'

'I've not got around to clearing the outside yet. All this belonged to Martin.' He said no more because Martin Durham had been the previous owner and a great friend of Nikki's. She had taken his untimely death badly and although she was delighted that Joseph had bought Knot Cottage, he had the feeling that sometimes she felt nostalgic for how things used to be.

He moved close to her and tried to see if anything had been disturbed. 'I'm loathe to throw it on a skip, there's some great old rural memorabilia here.' He pointed to an eel trap. 'This is local history.'

'And that? What is that?' Nikki was pointing to the dusty floor of the shed. 'Your shoes are at least two sizes larger than that footprint.'

Joseph drew in a breath. He hadn't been out here for months, and the print was clear and new. 'Nike Air Max training shoe. I recognise the sole pattern.'

'And you don't have a gardener or a handyman, do you?'

'No, I don't.' He stepped carefully into the shed and moved closer to the footprints. They stopped at a rough work bench towards the back of the old, dilapidated building.

Joseph shone his torch along the bench and gave a little gasp.

A box sat centre stage. It was about a foot square and was wrapped in multi-coloured foil gift paper. It glistened brightly in their torch beams.

'Oh shit,' whispered Nikki. 'That does not look like the kind of present I'd like to receive.'

'And this is where we should carefully tip-toe out and call in the relevant units to deal with it.'

'Should?' asked Nikki quietly.

'I still believe it's a hoax.'

'And your gut feeling is enough to go on?'

'I'm sure of it, even though I know he is more than capable of killing. But I don't want to risk you too.' He looked at her beseechingly. 'Please? Let me do this alone.'

'Have you *ever* won an argument with me, Joseph?'

'No, but maybe it's time I did. Back off, or I call the bomb disposal guys and we'll be sat out in the middle of the bloody marsh until morning.' He tried to look masterful, although he knew it wouldn't work, so he added, 'And besides that, they'll send my precious shed and all its lovely contents to kingdom come!'

'Joseph, open that damned box, or I will. I've had enough of this maniac's games.'

She stepped towards the bench.

105

'Okay, okay.' He held an arm across to prevent her getting close to the package. 'Just get behind me.'

What if he was wrong?

Joseph drew in a long slow breath and stared at the box. He was a professional, and he knew what to look for. This was not a serious threat. This was theatre.

He swallowed, then leaned forward and carefully stripped away the wrapping paper. He then eased open the lid of the cardboard box, and stared inside. It was half full of soil to give it some weight, and on top of the earth lay a note.

Joseph lifted it out with his fingertips, touching only a corner of the sheet of paper.

There was a question printed on it in large neat letters:

DID YOU LOCK THE DOOR WHEN YOU CAME OUT HERE?

CHAPTER TWELVE

It was midnight by the time they felt able to get some food, and then they realised they were famished.

'He underestimated me if he thought that I'd check my cottage from top to toe, then walk out and leave it unlocked,' muttered Joseph, tearing another piece of olive bread from the loaf. 'Although I suspect it was just another scary little trick to make us doubt ourselves.'

'I'm just so *angry*.' Nikki forked in a mouthful of cannelloni and chewed aggressively.

'Me too,' agreed Joseph, gulping back a long swallow of wine.

Nikki felt that whoever their stalker was, he was stealing away everything that was precious to her. Her home was off limits, her friends were all under threat, and he'd even taken away her right to have some quiet time to grieve for her beloved daughter. And now Joseph was in the bastard's sights too, and she felt for him. He had spent years looking for order and peace. His life had been chaos since his time in the military, and Knot Cottage and Cloud Fen had finally offered him a place of safety. Now that sacred space was in danger. As she ate, Nikki decided that in the long run, his loss could be even more damaging than her own.

She bit her lip and decided that it was time to think of something else. 'Why were you so certain that the package was a con?'

'Everything about it was wrong. And let's face it, if he took us out of the equation, it would be game over. We, well more correctly *you*, are the linchpin. If you are mincemeat, where does he go from there?' He looked at her over the top of his glass. 'I hate to say it, but you could well be his intended final move, Nikki, the taking of the queen. But I get the feeling this game has barely started.'

'But if we are going to play, we need to know the rules and get ourselves a plan, which we can't do when he has us scurrying around like frightened rabbits.'

Joseph wiped a piece of bread through the remainder of the pasta sauce and cleaned his plate. 'I want to know how he knows where we are at any given moment.' He wiped his lips with a sheet torn from a kitchen roll and looked at her pensively. 'I think we are under surveillance. And tomorrow I'm going to call up an old buddy of mine and get him to sweep both our properties.' His expression changed to one of determination. 'And then we'll play him at his own game. Vinnie Silver was in my regiment, but now he's on Civvy Street and he specialises in hi-tech security. If the killer can watch us, then maybe we can watch him.'

Nikki raised her eyebrows. 'Nice one. I like the thought of that. And I was thinking, let's do what the villains do and buy a handful of throwaway pay-as-you-go phones. He won't have the numbers for those and we could keep in touch in an emergency without him listening in.'

Joseph nodded. 'Excellent idea. I'll call in at the supermarket on my way in to work.' He stood up, collected the dirty plates and placed them in the dishwasher.

'How are you feeling after that little fiasco?'

Nikki thought about it. 'Furious and helpless.' She sniffed, then added, 'and I hate to admit it, but frightened.'

'We all like to know our enemy,' said Joseph. 'The sniper in the trees or on the roof is always the most dangerous and insidious opponent.'

'Ah, I've been trying to find a name for this perverted git. And as sniping is a cowardly way of attacking people, that will do nicely. We'll call him Snipe, until we know the name he was born with. Okay?'

'Perfect.' Joseph drained his glass and washed it up. 'We should turn in, but . . .' He looked at her, an anxious expression marring his good looks.

'For all you've said about him not finishing me off yet, you are worried about leaving me alone behind a closed door, aren't you?'

He raised his shoulders and let them fall. 'Can't help it. It's the not knowing what we're up against.'

'Then we both stay down here. You've got a perfectly comfortable sofa. One of us can doze, and the other can keep a watchful eye open. We can take shifts, then at least we'll get a bit of rest.' Nikki wasn't too keen on that closed bedroom door either.

Joseph went upstairs and brought down a huge soft, fleecy blanket and a couple of pillows. 'I'll take the first watch. You sleep.' He placed the pillows at one end of the sofa and indicated for Nikki to lie down.

'I'm not sure I can, after everything that's happened. My head is spinning. Come and sit with me for a while.'

Joseph sat down close to her.

She leaned back into the soft pillows. 'You haven't told me how Cat was when you visited her earlier this evening.'

'That seems like an eternity ago.' He relaxed and gave a little yawn. 'She was a bit fretful, but she brightened up a treat after I gave her her iPad. And I got the feeling that she will not be playing *Angry Birds* on it. She didn't say as much, but I reckon our Cat is going to be doing a bit of undercover sleuthing, cyber style.'

'She could find that difficult without the PNC. I'll go see her tomorrow.' Nikki closed her eyes.

'She'd like that.'

'She idolises you,' he said. 'And she wants back in as soon as you'll have her.'

'Good, and I'll make that happen, the moment I believe she is reedy.' She shifted to get comfortable, but dangerous things still played in the background of her mind.

'Come here.' Joseph nestled into the corner of the sofa and held an arm out. 'I don't think it's against police procedure to give your boss a hug if she needs one, do you?'

Nikki's first impulse was to push him away and laugh it off. Then she found herself moving towards him, leaning against his broad chest and tucking her legs up underneath her. Right now she didn't feel like the intrepid and fearless detective. She felt like a woman who had just lost her only child, and all she really wanted was to be held by someone who cared about her. In a small voice she said, 'On this occasion, no. But remember to wake me up for my shift.'

'Of course I will,' said Joseph, pulling the blanket over them both. Nikki failed to notice his crossed fingers.

Then the adrenalin dispersed and exhaustion hit her. With a long sigh, Nikki slipped into a deep, dreamless sleep.

* * *

She awoke at six thirty, briefly wondering where she was. She pushed back the blanket, ran her fingers through her tangled hair and looked around for Joseph. She smelt coffee and bacon. So much for his promise to wake her up.

Nikki stretched her shoulders, rubbed at her stiff neck and yawned. How the hell had she managed to sleep right through?

'You have ten minutes to grab a shower, then breakfast will be on the table.' Joseph stood in the doorway grinning at her. He had a tea towel draped over his shoulder and was obviously washed, dressed and ready for anything.

'You bum! You let me sleep!'

'You needed it. I spent years learning how to make one half of me cat-nap, while the other half was still on full alert. That's probably why I survived all those years on active duty.' The grin widened. 'And now I'm fresh as a daisy, and you'd better hurry up or I'll eat your breakfast as well as my own.'

Ten minutes later Nikki ran down the stairs and into the kitchen. The old pine table was set for a full English. She gazed at it in amazement. 'How the hell do you do all this? I can barely manage to burn some toast and drink a black coffee before I leave for work.'

'Priorities. I like my food, and when I'm at home, I like routine.' He placed a piping hot plate in front of her. It contained egg, bacon, sausage, tomatoes and a fried slice. 'I guess it's because our working lives are pretty random. We eat on the hoof and never know where we're going or what we are doing next. When I'm here, I can be in charge of what I do and how I do it.'

'And is this hotel on Trip Advisor? Because the food would get a five-star rating.' Nikki ate with relish, almost forgetting what had happened the night before.

Almost, but not quite. Her face clouded over.

'So. I wonder what Snipe has in store for us today?' said Joseph, reading her mind.

'Some rules of engagement would be good.' She placed her fork on her plate and stared across the table at Joseph. 'Surely it's no fun for him, when all the cards are stacked in his favour? It would be like a seasoned poker player having to play happy families with a three-year-old. You can hardly be a proud winner when you are the only one who knows the rules.'

'Maybe he just gets his rocks off watching us running scared and tearing our hair out.'

Joseph spread butter carefully over a slice of toast. 'It could be a power thing.'

'But he is asking for this damned compensation. We *have* to know what the hell he's talking about before we can negotiate, pay up, or tell him to go to hell.'

'Maybe we are paying already. Danny Wilshire certainly paid the highest price, and Cat has paid dearly too.'

'But what *for?*' exploded Nikki. 'He's doing my head in!'

'If it's any consolation, I think we'll hear all about it very soon. As you say, if he's a true game player, then he needs an opponent to pit his wits against.' Joseph took a sip of hot coffee. 'By the way, I've already contacted Vinnie Silver and he's motoring up here this morning.'

'I bet he loved you, calling him along with the dawn chorus.'

'We went through a lot together, Nikki. He knows I'd never bother him if the situation wasn't serious. He's dropped everything for us.'

'Where does he have to come from?'

'Chislehurst in Kent. He reckoned by the time he's picked up everything he needs, he could be on the road by eight and here around eleven, M25 providing.' He took a forkful of food and chewed it. 'He's a top-flight guy. If any-one can spot Snipe's covert surveillance equipment, he will.'

'It'll be nice to have an expert on our side.' Nikki sat back. 'I guess we'd better make a move soon. The super will need to know about last night's drama and I should prepare the morning briefing.'

Joseph took her plate, placed it on his and walked to the dishwasher. 'Yes, and I have a pile of things to put into motion too. I'm anxious to hear from ballistics about that gun. If we could just put the Magda Hellekamp case to bed we could really get to grips with finding out about your three other possibilities, French, Windsor and Bow.'

Nikki nodded. 'You're right, we need to track them down sooner rather than later.' She stood up and pushed her chair under the table. 'Thank you for that, Joseph. It's the best start to the day I've had in years.' She patted her stom-ach. 'Fuelled up and ready to go.'

'That reminds me. I've checked both vehicles to make sure that no one has tampered with them overnight. You are safe to drive.'

'You think of everything.'

'We aim to please.' He gave a small bow, but his smile was forced.

They both knew that the joking was superficial, a way of coping, because the reality was that a simple slip-up, an accidental oversight, could cost them their lives.

CHAPTER THIRTEEN

Cat had barely slept. Her night had been riddled with dark dreams filled with shadows and hidden menace. At one point she had found the anxious face of a male nurse hovering over her, trying to gently prise her from the grip of a nightmare.

She eased herself up in her bed and stared at the other patients on the small ward.

There were no open eyes, and that meant no one to talk to. There was a uniformed officer outside, but she knew not to distract him from his duty.

She sighed. She had been offered a private room, but although she had not yet been particularly friendly with any of the other patients, there was usually lots going on. Things to distract her. A quiet room would mean spending too much time in her own head, and listening to her thoughts was not something she relished right now.

Cat swung her legs carefully over the edge of the bed and braced her arms to ease herself up. For a moment she felt pretty well okay, then pain pulsed through her lacerated legs, making her gasp and swallow back a scream.

'Come on, Cat. Deep breaths,' she muttered to herself, drawing in air. And slowly the pain calmed down to a dull, throbbing ache. 'Just a blood rush. Get over it.'

She shuffled off towards the toilets, watching the nurse's station as she went, hoping that she would not be seen. They had insisted on gentle exercise, but only when accompanied, and her surgeon had stipulated that the bathroom, with its big mirrors, was out of bounds until he said otherwise.

And that was why Cat was hobbling in that direction so furtively.

It was no call of nature that drove her there, just curiosity, and the memory of a nightmare.

Cat closed the door behind her and cursed the lack of a bolt.

She had dreamed about seeing her damaged face for the first time.

The doctors had sat her on a wooden chair in a room with mirrored walls, ceiling and floor. She was suspended in a place that reflected her white-gowned self and the hard wood seat. Then they had peeled off the dressing and stepped back, leaving her to behold her new face.

In the dream, Cat had started to scream. The face that stared back at her, mocking and full of evil intent, was that of Stephen Cox.

One whole side of her face was burnt into a melted mess of disfigurement. The skin was puckered, burnt, twisted and raw. And terror consumed her, until the nurse had brought her back into the real world.

Cat stood in front of the mirror. Nothing she saw now could be as bad as the nightmare. She eased a finger nail beneath the adhesive edge to the dressing and began to pull.

'Morning, Cat. Up to no good, I see.' Her personal nurse had opened the door and was beaming at her.

'Ah, Angie.' Cat let her hands fall to her sides. 'Oh well, it's a fair cop, guv. I'll come quietly.'

'Want to use the facilities while you're here? Make your wasted trip worthwhile?'

Cat gave the woman a lop-sided smile. 'Why not?'

'Then I'll wait here, and escort you back.'

'Thought you might.'

Back on the ward, Angie helped Cat into her chair.

'When can I go home?' Cat asked.

'In a day or so, as long as your blood pressure stabilises.' Angie picked the medical chart off the end of the bed. 'Today we'll get you more mobile, and I understand someone from the counselling service is coming to talk to you this morning.'

Cat wasn't looking forward to that. She knew it was routine and all officers who had suffered trauma, mental or physical, were offered counselling, but to her, that made it more real. It made her a victim, and she didn't want to feel that way. Not now. Not ever. 'And my face? When can I see it?' She tried a smile. 'I'm a police officer, Angie. Getting injured is always on the cards at some point. I won't freak out, and I won't threaten litigation, honest!'

'I'm sure you won't, but right now there is a lot of bruising, a lot of swelling and the surgery hasn't had time to heal at all. It will look far worse than it really is, so,' she raised her eyebrows, 'it's time for patience, I'm afraid. The surgeon is really pleased with you, and after the second op he has every confidence that scarring will be minimal.'

Cat nodded. 'He told me the same.' She sat back. 'Okay. I don't do too well with that "P" word, but I'll try to be a good girl.'

After Angie had gone, Cat reached for her iPad, turned it on and waited for the Wi-Fi to connect. She moved the cursor to Messages and found one from Travis. She opened it immediately.

It was short and to the point. *'Hi there, Old bag! Wanna visitor today?'*

Cat replied *'Morning, Nerd. You just want to gloat, don't you?'*

'Me? How could u? I'm insulted. I shall phone the florist and cancel the get well bouquet.'

Cat gave a soft laugh and wrote. *'OMG! I didn't know you owned a wallet! How about this afternoon for that visit?'*

After a while the answer came back. *'CU at 4.'*

Travis Taylor was one of the IT guys from the station. She had recognised a passionate and real talent in the odd young man and had spent a lot of time with him, trying to unlock the secrets of computer technology. In turn, Travis had seemed to like her company, and they had struck up an unlikely friendship, based on techno-jargon and good old-fashioned insults. Cat reckoned that you really have to like someone to slag them off to their face.

She decided that a visit from Travis would be just the kind of lift she needed. Considering he spent most of his time on another planet anyway, looks meant nothing to him. He was a cerebral person, and things like fashion, make-up and hair styles passed him by completely. Sadly, that often reflected in his personal appearance, which was usually retro, and not in a cool way.

Cat knew that there was a very good chance that Travis wouldn't even notice her dressings but dive immediately into a conversation about some new anti-malware tool that he'd designed. And that would suit her perfectly. Plus she had a few ideas of her own to put to her little computer wizard friend, and if he decided to help her, then maybe she would have something to keep her mind away from scarred faces, crashing cars and dead police officers.

With a painful but determined smile, Cat sat back and waited for breakfast.

* * *

At thirteen hundred hours, Nikki called the team into her office. The morning had been a head-spinning rush of information pouring in from all directions and she needed to collate everything they had.

'Fast track ballistics report came in, boss.' Joseph looked down at the document he was holding. 'The striation pattern comparison between the bullet that killed Magda and the barrel of Aaron Keller's gun are a match. So, although we cannot yet prove he pulled the trigger, we do know his precious .45 semi-automatic was the murder weapon.'

'And as he spent a whole day driving his unsuspecting victim around in the guise of a chauffeur,' added Dave, 'I don't think we need to look further for our killer. We just need to know how he got in and out of that bloody locked room.'

'Well, I can't answer that yet,' said Joseph, 'but the techies are trying out a hunch. Stuart and Travis are down at the Waterside Quay now, testing out some wacky theory about the security system. I didn't understand a word of what they were saying, but they were pretty hyped up and they refused to clarify anything until they'd seen the place first hand.'

'That's encouraging, at least.' Nikki sucked in air. 'But what worries me is the fact that we may have earmarked the killer, but who paid him to do it? Anyone got anything on Magda's mystery Internet play pal?'

Dave nodded. 'Not much admittedly, but IT have managed to isolate a series of emails that have been made using something called a distorting proxy server.' He raised his eyebrows. 'Apparently that means that the IP address is hidden so we can't trace it back, and however the sender managed to do it has our guys and girls foxed.'

'But we can read the messages?'

'Oh yes, and if you have a deep interest in robotics and genetic engineering, you'll probably find them absolutely fascinating.' Dave handed her three printouts. 'I've passed them on to an expert to decipher for us.'

'Who?' Nikki asked suspiciously.

'I spoke to Lawrence Carpenter and he suggested a local man, an agricultural specialist. He said he was trustworthy and he certainly seemed the DB's when I saw him. I'm going back to pick his brains as soon as we're through here.' He gave her a reassuring smile. 'It's all right, guv. I ran him through the system first. Clean as a whistle *and* a golfing buddy of the ACC.'

Nikki relaxed, then grimaced, 'Oh well, at least we know who to blame if he sells Magda's secrets to the opposition.'

'Do you think that's what this is all about, ma'am?' asked Yvonne thoughtfully. 'Industrial espionage?'

'It seems that way. Who else could afford a professional hit-man? And Magda was a long-term loner. It's hard to think of her making such a dangerous enemy.'

'I wish we didn't know about her maniac stalker,' mused Joseph. 'I don't like to think about such a dangerous psychopath being attracted to her in that way. If he was incarcerated at the time he couldn't have been involved in her death, but he's still there, skulking in the background, and it gives me the creeps.'

For a moment the group were silent, all trying to imagine how traumatised Magda had been by her stalker and his vicious attack on her cousin. For someone's actions to leave you with a life-long phobia, it had to be truly terrifying.

'I think we should leave things there, until we hear from your two techies, Joseph, and your expert, Dave. There's not much more we can do until then.' She looked gravely at her team. 'Now, we need to talk about the threats made on us by Snipe.'

She sat back and in an emotionless voice, filled them in on the previous night's activities.

'Bloody hell, guv!' Niall looked shell-shocked. 'Whoever this Snipe is, he's really got us by the short and curlies!' His expression darkened. 'Jeez! I'd like to get my hands on him.'

'You and a station full of officers,' growled Yvonne. 'So how on earth do we go about finding his ID?'

Joseph answered. 'Just between us, I've got an old army mate helping out. He's at Cloud Fen now, posing as a surveyor. What he's actually doing is checking whether our adversary is using covert surveillance equipment to watch us, and researching the possibility of using counter surveillance to get a fix on him.'

'Mm, set a thief to catch a thief,' murmured Dave. 'I like it.'

'*If* that's how he's working. Not that I can see another way to keep such close tabs on people.'

'If my friend finds anything, I've asked permission for him to check out the external perimeters of the police station.' Joseph looked grim. 'Snipe might just enjoy his new hobby of copper-watching enough to keep an eye on here too.'

Nikki nodded. 'Good idea. Now, moving on, do we have any reports on our three old cases that might have festered into someone taking revenge into their own hands? I'm talking about William French, Windsor Morton and Jeremy Bow.'

'I've checked out Morton.' Dave flipped over the pages of his pocket book. 'He's moved away, ma'am, to a small Moors village somewhere north of Pickering. He's turned into a real Billy No-Mates, and everyone I spoke to said he'd given up his crusade and wanted nothing more to do with society. Hence the remote cottage surrounded by heather and sheep shit.' He flipped over a page. 'The local bobbies say that that they've had no dealings with him, other than a few complaints about him being aggressive to anyone who attempts to call at his cottage.'

'And I tried to trace William French,' stated Niall. '*Tried* — until I discovered that he was dead. He moved about a bit for a few years and was discovered lying dead on his father's grave on the coldest night of winter. The alcohol levels in his blood were off the scale, and the inquest brought in death by misadventure. The coroner did not believe it to be suicide, although there were rumours that he had threatened to take his own life.'

'And Jeremy Bow?'

'Still around, and still causing a bit of trouble, but on a much lesser scale. His neighbours say he's "gone a bit odd,"' said Yvonne. 'I thought the name rang a bell. We've been called out to a few disturbances where he was involved. Nothing that would have meant bringing him in, but he's had several warnings over the last two years.'

'But nothing to worry us? Nothing that indicated a serious change of mental condition?'

'No, ma'am. Popular opinion has him as a right pain in the butt, not dangerous and not a real threat.'

'We'll need to speak to both Bow and Morton, and maybe have a word with the remaining members of the French family. You never know. If two of the family have died, there could be a close relative still harbouring a grudge.' Nikki stretched, then looked again at Yvonne. 'Now the million dollar question. Any luck with Stephen Cox?'

Yvonne glanced at Niall, then said, 'We spoke to our snouts, ma'am, and Cox has been seen on the Carborough Estate.'

'That was Monday of last week and he hasn't been seen since,' added Niall quickly.

'The Carborough,' Nikki almost whispered the words. Memories poured back. Bad ones. She glanced across to Joseph and he gave her a sombre nod.

The Carborough Estate had been the bane of their lives for years, a rat-hole of criminal activity and drug-dealing. But now it was changing and thankfully for the better. There had been riots a few years back, but after calm had been restored, some sort of normality had begun to creep in. People started to take a pride in their homes, and with encouragement from a tireless group of enthusiastic residents, the Carborough was now becoming a regeneration project. So what was Stephen Cox doing there? Who would he be visiting?

'Where on the estate, Niall?'

'Eastern Street, guv. He was seen leaving the Fisherman's Knot, just before closing time.' Niall shrugged. 'That fleapit is the last stronghold of the old guard.'

'It's the only place left where low life still hangs out.' Yvonne turned up her nose.

'Did your snout say who he met?'

''Fraid not. Cox was getting into a car by the time he was spotted.'

'So his trip to Cyn City wasn't a one-off. He's hanging around.' Nikki felt a sinking feeling inside.

'Or was,' Niall said flatly. 'If he's still here, he's keeping a very low profile.'

'We've left word with a few trusted souls to keep their eyes peeled, ma'am. If he shows, then we'll know about it.' Yvonne tried to look confident. 'He's a pariah in Greenborough. No one wants him here, believe me.'

A knock on the door interrupted her reply, and as she looked up she saw the chubby figure of DI Jim Hunter entering the room.

'Sorry to interrupt but I thought you'd like to know that the vehicle that killed Danny had been reported stolen three weeks ago. There were no prints as the whole interior had been steam-cleaned and scrubbed with some powerful cleanser.' He leaned back against the door frame, his body language speaking volumes. 'Forensics have taken soil samples from the tyres and pollen and plant material from beneath the interior flooring for scientific analysis to try to pinpoint a location of where it had been kept, but . . .' He shrugged. 'I don't hold out too much hope, and those tests take time.' He gave her a helpless look. 'Sorry it's not better news.'

'I didn't expect anything else, Jim. Our guy is as slippery as they come. He's hardly going to leave a handful of prints on the steering wheel for us.'

Jim nodded, straightened up and moved back through the doorway. 'I'll keep you posted, whatever.'

Nikki thanked him, then returned her attention to the team. 'Well, guys, I hate to say this, but right now we seem to be in the hands of the IT department. I suggest we get together again as soon as Stuart and Travis are back from Magda Hellekamp's apartment.' She halted, then added. 'And I'm sure I don't have to remind you of this, but watch your backs, and watch each other's too. We have no way of knowing where or when Snipe will strike again.'

* * *

Joseph hung back after the others had filed out. 'Do you think maybe it's time to go visit an old friend of yours? An old Carborough friend?'

In his mind, Joseph saw thick greying hair, piercing and intelligent eyes and the impressive straight-backed frame of Archie Leonard, one-time godfather of the Carborough. In his time Archie had controlled everything illegal in Greenborough, but he had done so in a strangely old-fashioned way. He had fought with Nikki more times than she could remember, but over the years they had formed an alliance, built on a grudging respect. Archie didn't like the drug-fuelled, mindlessly violent misfits that tried to rule the estate any more than the police. Hence, on occasions he had helped Nikki, and one time in particular, helped her big-style.

'No. I don't think so.'

Joseph blinked in surprise. Nikki's negative reply shocked him, and he looked at her in confusion. 'Why? If anyone could help us to find Stephen Cox, it's Archie.'

'Not this time, Joseph. We need to sort this out for ourselves.' She threw him an odd look, but one he knew not to question.

'Right, then I'll go see if Vinnie Silver has finished out at Cloud Fen.'

She nodded and left it at that, saying only, 'And I have to see the superintendent with an update. Let me know about the techies and what they find.'

It was Joseph's turn to nod, then he left, closing the door behind him. There was still puzzlement on his face.

Sitting at his desk, he suddenly had a vision of Hannah Galena's funeral service.

At the back, keeping a respectful distance away from the sea of police officers, sat a smartly dressed man and woman, with a teenage boy crammed uncomfortably between them. It was one of Archie Leonard's sons and his wife. But it was the boy that Joseph knew best. Mickey was one of the few success stories to come out of the Carborough, proof that a leopard could change its spots if it was given the right opportunities and shown love and care. Peter and Fran Leonard had taken him in to save him from social services, and the boy had blossomed. Joseph had grinned at the lad from where he sat close to the front of the chapel, and the boy had responded with a bigger grin and a cheeky salute.

Joseph smiled. It had been good to see the kid again, and from the few words they had grabbed after the service, Mickey clearly remembered Sergeant Joe from the days when the Carborough was in turmoil.

The smile faded. He had believed that Peter and his wife were there as a token representation of Archie and his whole family. But thinking about it, even if the entire Fenland Constabulary had been in attendance, nothing would have stopped Archie turning up in person. Unless he hadn't wanted to.

He frowned. If Nikki had fallen out with the old man, surely he would have known about it? But there had been a definite blanking of his idea to go visit. He leaned back, tipping the front legs of his chair off the floor. So why hadn't Archie been at Nikki's daughter's funeral?

Joseph suddenly lurched forward, and his thoughts dispersed instantly into the blue.

Funerals. Chapels. Crematoriums. Oh shit! If Snipe were trying to get at them in ways that would hurt, he would know about Nikki's daughter's death. Hannah's passing had been too recent for Nikki to organise a proper stone memorial yet, but she had arranged for a temporary engraved plaque to be hung on the wall of remembrance.

Joseph flipped his computer awake and brought up Google. In seconds he had contact details for the Greenborough Crematorium.

He briskly introduced himself and asked the young receptionist if she would be kind enough to check on one of the memorial plaques for him. He gave her the name of Nikki's daughter then added, 'and should there be any damage, vandalism, or anything at all out of the ordinary, please be sure not to touch anything, but come back and tell me immediately.'

The woman, who told him her name was Hayley, seemed delighted and full of self-importance to be given a task that meant helping the police. 'I can take the telephone with me, Detective Sergeant Easter. It's cordless with a good

123

range, and the Garden of Remembrance is not far from the office.'

He heard the click-clack of her heels on concrete and her short breaths as she hurried across the paths.

'I'm here now. I just need to check the location number of her plaque.' There was a moment's silence, then she came back, 'Ah, yes, here we are, number 238, Hannah Galena.'

Joseph waited anxiously, hearing only the whisper of a breeze as it passed over the mouthpiece of the receiver. 'Is everything okay?' he asked.

'It looks fine to me.'

Joseph let out a sigh of relief.

'Although . . .'

He tensed again. 'What's the problem?'

'I'm not sure, sergeant.' The voice was soft and a little uncertain. 'There are flowers here, red roses, with the young woman's name on. I know that shouldn't sound unusual, but flowers are always left in the chapel's ante-room. These are wall plaques, so there are no vases or containers for plants or flowers here.' She paused. 'These are propped up against the wall, and I think there's a written card on them. Shall I . . . ?'

'No! Don't touch it!' Joseph shouted.

'Oh dear, uh, well, what . . . ? Oh no!'

The last stunned cry sent a spike of fear down Joseph's back. 'What's happened? Are you alright? Hayley?'

From the other end, Joseph heard a whimper, then a sob. 'My hand! Something sticky . . . oh, it hurts! Help me!'

'Okay, Hayley. Just hang on, I'll get help and I'm on my way.'

Joseph grabbed his mobile and phoned for an ambulance. He had no idea what had happened but he knew it wasn't good. He then looked back at his computer screen and thankfully saw a second number for the crematorium. He swiftly briefed them of what had occurred and asked for their help. 'An ambulance is on its way for Hayley, and don't let anyone near those flowers! No one must touch them or the card. It's imperative, okay?'

He closed the phone and yelled across to Niall, who was just about to take a bite out of a triple-size sandwich. 'With me! Now.'

* * *

They reached the Garden of Remembrance in less than ten minutes, just a moment or two after the paramedics. Together they ran to where they could see a small crowd gathered around a hunched figure sitting on the ground and rocking backwards and forwards with pain.

One of the green-clad ambulance crew was trying to calm her, while the other endeavoured to attend to her injured right hand.

'Acid burns by the look of it.' The puzzled paramedic looked around. 'Was she attacked? What on earth happened?'

Joseph didn't answer. He moved swiftly to where a sombrely dressed young man was standing staring down at an innocent-looking bouquet of flowers that lay on the concrete path. 'Okay, son, stand away now. I've got it.' He pulled out his phone and rang for assistance. 'I need specialist help and a SOCO, as fast as you can, and tell them we are dealing with a deliberate attack using a small quantity of a Hazchem Class 8 corrosive. I have no idea what it is, but it's dangerous.'

He turned to Niall. 'Go grab an armful of those metal stands with name cards on them and put them around the flowers. Form a temporary barrier and don't let a soul get close, okay?'

Leaving Niall in charge of the lethal bouquet, Joseph ran back to the sobbing girl and the paramedics. After telling her who he was, adding a few soothing words and a promise to follow the ambulance to the hospital, he turned to one of the paramedics. 'Do you know what she touched?' he asked.

The medic looked at Joseph with real concern on his face. 'Hell, I'm hoping I'm wrong, but I've seen something like this before, an industrial accident with something called hydrofluoric acid. It's wicked bloody stuff and we need to get her to the emergency department fast.' He lowered his voice so that the young woman couldn't hear him. 'My partner is beginning irrigation and we'll keep it up all the way to the hospital, but the thing is, once this stuff starts burning through tissue, it doesn't stop.'

Granite-faced, Joseph stood back and allowed the medics to get their patient into the ambulance. He gritted his teeth together tightly and wished to high heaven that he had not asked the girl to check the memorial. He should have come himself. After all, he knew they were dealing with a bloody psycho. What was he thinking? He should *never* have put that kid in such a position. He let out a groan of frustration. Now there was every chance she would be scarred for life, and if the acid was as dangerous as the paramedic had suspected . . . he didn't allow himself to think any further.

As soon as help arrived and the Garden of Remembrance was sealed off, Joseph gave Niall his car keys and as they drove to the hospital, he rang Nikki. It was not the easiest thing to explain, and not least his reason for getting the crematorium staff to go look for signs of vandalism in the first place.

'Are you trying to think like Snipe?' asked Nikki, her voice cracking with emotion.

'Not at all. I was actually thinking about Archie Leonard and Hannah's funeral.' He gave up trying to explain, knowing it wasn't working. 'Oh, it doesn't matter now, it was a shot in the dark and I happened to hit on something that Snipe would consider hurtful to you.'

'Just a lucky guess?'

'I'd call it a very unlucky one for Hayley, the kid who got burnt. And now I'm going to have to live with the fact that I handled the situation unbelievably badly. Like a total bloody imbecile.' He looked miserably out of the windscreen. 'We are just approaching the hospital now. I'll ring you when I know how the girl is.'

'Don't bother. I'm on my way. I'll meet you in A & E.'
The phone went dead.

* * *

Twenty minutes later, while Niall was endeavouring to make the vending machine work, Nikki and Joseph sat outside the emergency department. To his surprise, Nikki had not laid into him with all guns blazing. If she had, he would have accepted it without question. He believed that he deserved the bollocking of the century. Instead she had asked him exactly what he had said to the receptionist and listened carefully.

'You are certain that you made it perfectly clear that she should touch nothing, just report what she saw?'

'Absolutely. But even so, that's no excuse, I should have gone myself.'

'Why? You were only working on a vague hunch and asking the officials there to check for . . . for what? What did you expect they might find? Something dangerous?'

'Of course not. Just graffiti, I guess. I think maybe I expected the word "compensation" to be daubed across the plaque in spray paint.'

'Exactly. So you had no idea that there was any danger there.' She shook her head. 'For heaven's sake, Joseph, you are the last one to put someone else at risk. You aren't a bloody clairvoyant. Plus you didn't ask the girl to look at the card, did you?'

'I expressly told her not to.'

'Well, there you go, and finally, you did it because if you were right, you were fearful that I'd have to face seeing my lovely daughter's memorial plaque desecrated. Am I correct?'

Joseph didn't answer. He didn't have to. Of course he wanted to save her from any more pain.

'So stop beating yourself up and get a grip.' Her words were brusque, but he detected the undertone of another softer emotion beneath them.

'I wonder how Hayley is?'

'Looks like we're about to find out.'

Joseph looked up and saw a tall, thin man with a hooked nose and narrow glasses approaching them. He was somewhere around forty, and wore khaki chinos, a navy shirt and a worried expression. He hurriedly told them that he was a speciality lead consultant. 'The medics were right about the acid. It is hydrofluoric, and it's one of the most powerful acids we ever have to treat.'

Joseph's heart sank, but the doctor was still talking.

'We've set up an IV line and are using special solutions to try to neutralise it, but once the flesh has begun to disintegrate, the damn stuff eats down to the bone.' He looked at them angrily. 'Our job has been made worse by the fact that whoever did this secreted the stuff in a sticky gel base, making irrigation almost impossible.'

'So how is she? Can you help her?' Joseph asked miserably.

'She's in a lot of pain. Luckily she only grasped it with her thumb and forefinger, although in trying to get rid of it she spread it to her palm and the fingertips of her other hand. I'm sorry, but she will have a lot of scarring and loss of function in the hand that is worst affected.'

'What the devil is this evil stuff used for?' asked Nikki. 'I've never heard of it.'

'Etching metal amongst other things. Hell, it can etch titanium, so can you imagine what it does to human flesh? Thank God she didn't touch her face, poor kid.' He frowned at them. 'What kind of person does something like this?'

'The same kind of person who spikes baby food with broken glass,' growled Nikki.

'Can I see her?' asked Joseph, not knowing what the hell he was going to say to her.

'Not just yet. The pain relief hasn't really kicked in and she's badly shocked. The thing about hydrofluoric is that initially it seals off the nerve endings. Some patients feel no pain at all when they first come into contact with it, but later . . .' He gave a long, low whistle. 'Later, it's pure agony. Anyway, her fiancé and her mother are on their way in, but I'll let you have a few minutes before they get here.' He tilted his head in a birdlike fashion. 'Sorry, but I have to get back in there. I'll call you when she's more comfortable.'

They spent another ten minutes sitting, drinking coffee and trying to get their heads around what had happened. Then they saw the consultant beckoning to them.

'Just a few minutes, officers. She's calmer now, but still very upset.'

I bet she is, thought Joseph, and she probably hates my guts!

'I'm so sorry, Sergeant'

Whatever he had expected, it was not an apology.

'You told me not to touch anything. But I did.' She stared at her hand, which was mercifully covered with sterile dressings. 'Now look what's happened.' Tears filled her already sore, red eyes.

Joseph made to reassure her that it wasn't her fault, but Nikki gave him a cautionary glance. He changed his words for a promise to catch who ever had hurt her.

Nikki spoke gently to her, reassuring her that she had done nothing wrong and that they had suspected nothing more than graffiti or minor vandalism.

After a few more words, Joseph promised to visit later that evening to see how she was, and they turned to leave.

'Sergeant Easter?'

Joseph looked back at the pale figure lying on the trolley.

'I wouldn't have touched them at all,' she looked imploringly at him, 'but they were only flowers.'

CHAPTER FOURTEEN

Joseph left his car for Niall to drive back and went with Nikki. Before he climbed into her vehicle he said, 'I've just had a text from Vinnie on my disposable phone. He wants us to meet him, but not at the police station. I've suggested the cafe car park on the junction of Washdyke Road.'

'So he's found something?'

'I suppose he has.'

Five minutes later they pulled into the rough parking area that backed the transport cafe known simply as Susie's Place. Joseph saw a familiar figure leaning against the side of a mud-splattered Land Rover.

'Vinnie! Don't you ever clean that thing? It hasn't rained for two weeks.'

'No time, mate. I keep getting calls from neurotic coppers asking for my help.'

Joseph went up to his old army comrade and gave him a bear hug. Vinnie responded by clapping him heartily on the shoulders.

'Good to see you, man, and we appreciate you making the trip.' Joseph turned to where Nikki stood watching the reunion with mild amusement.

'This is my boss, DI Nikki Galena. Boss, this is Vinnie Silver.'

Vinnie smiled appreciatively at Nikki and raised an eyebrow to Joseph. 'Why didn't any of *our* senior officers look like that? They were all hairy arses with bad breath, as I recall. I see now why you joined the police force.' He gave Nikki a wide, white smile and said, 'Pleased to meet you, ma'am.'

Nikki was far from being disapproving of Vinnie's outspoken comments, though they verged on being offensive. She smiled back and stuck out a hand. 'Likewise. But I'll pass on the man-hug bit if it's all the same.' She turned towards the back entrance to the cafe and all trace of humour fell away. 'Let's go get a coffee. Right now, we need to talk.'

* * *

Vinnie Silver was around six foot four, strongly built and obviously took care of his body. He wasn't quite muscle-bound, but the seams of his denim shirtsleeves were taut and clearly in danger. His face epitomised the word rugged, and Nikki decided that he would look good on the back of a horse, or maybe felling a giant Redwood with a small axe.

She stared at him while Joseph paid for the coffees, and decided that the best thing about Vinnie was that he looked honest. Through and through. And although he was obviously a silver-tongued rogue where women were concerned, it was almost impossible to take offence.

Vinnie accepted his drink and looked up. This time his face was serious and his voice was low. 'I'm not sure what you guys have done to warrant it, but you are being monitored by one mother of a surveillance system. It's not super-sophisticated, but it's certainly clever.'

'The thing is,' breathed Joseph quietly, 'we don't know what we've done.'

'Then I guess you are in big trouble.'

'One officer is dead, one badly injured, a civilian has been acid-attacked, and we have been threatened by both fire

131

and a dummy IED.' Nikki threw her hands in the air. 'Big enough for you?'

'Shit,' murmured Vinnie.

'Indeed.' She stared at him. 'So, tell us about the surveillance bugs.'

'I think they are originally American, but heavily adapted by someone who knows what he's doing. He's listening, he's watching, he's almost touching you, every minute of the day and night.' He smiled grimly. 'Well, actually I'm talking about you, DI Galena. For some reason, he's not so keen on Joseph. I've only located two small devices at Knot Cottage and they are basically coming and going trackers, one back door and one front.' He gazed at her intently. 'It's you he's interested in.'

Nikki shivered. When she glanced up, she saw how tight Joseph's facial muscles had become.

'The thing is . . . what do you want me to do about them?' He held up a hand. 'And before you say strip them out and stamp all over them, remember that if I remove them, you won't be able to use them against him in any way.'

Nikki thought hard. The fact that some evil bastard was watching their every move made her blood boil. And they *still* didn't know what he wanted. She ripped the top off three sugar sachets and tipped them into her coffee. 'Okay, Vinnie. What would you do?'

'Fight fire with fire. But I'd need to spend some time here with you, and in some guise that won't alarm him. Because unless I'm very wrong, the moment I step into your cop shop, he'll know about it.'

Joseph stirred his coffee and without looking up, said, 'You really think he's got the station wired as well?'

'Exterior for sure, but the interior?' He shrugged. 'I very much doubt it. But I still don't want to roll up into your car park and get eyeballed by matey-boy.' He sipped his drink. 'Keep my presence here discreet. Tell no one other than your close team about me. I need to be your secret weapon, and by the sound of things, you need one.'

'I can't deny that,' said Nikki wearily. 'We are like little ducks sitting on a fence just waiting to be picked off, one by one.'

'Then it's time we stacked things in the ducklings' favour.' He looked across to Joseph, a steely glint in his pale grey eyes. 'Just like old times, Bunny-boy, although there's one major factor missing before we can go to war, isn't there?'

'Know your enemy.' Joseph, whose army nickname had been Bunny, because of his surname, pressed his lips together so tightly that they almost disappeared, 'And that's something of a problem.'

Vinnie sat back and folded his arms across his chest. 'First things first. I think I'll stick with being the surveyor. I have a vehicle full of appropriate-looking stuff: tripods, Hi-Viz jackets, hard hats etc. And you, ma'am,' he stared at Nikki, 'have serious drainage problems that are hampering your plans for a new . . . uh, oh, a new water feature. Something fancy with a big Koi pond and a Japanese bridge.'

'Just what I've always wanted.' She grimaced. 'I don't think.'

'Nonsense, you've dreamed about it for years.'

Nikki nodded. 'Oh yeah, of course I have.'

'So I'm going to have to spend a bit of time on your property. It's old and I should think the drainage plans are missing, aren't they?'

'Long gone.'

'Excellent. So here's my card.' He reached into his pocket and produced a brightly-coloured business card with a picture of a house on it. 'Got them done at a service station on the way up. Dead cheap and very useful. If you need to talk to me or make plans to meet, the number on it is safe, as long as you use one of your pay-as-you-go phones. Give me a few hours to formulate something and I'll contact you.'

'Where will you stay? Under the circumstances we can hardly offer to put you up.'

'I'll find somewhere low-key, don't worry.' He took a long swallow of his coffee. 'I can tell you one thing. From the way he has modified his equipment your man has a great interest in spy gadgets and technology. I wouldn't be surprised if he's worked with them, either in sales or the security sector. Cutting-edge spy gadgets are big business.'

Nikki looked nonplussed.

'It's not so surprising these days. Corporations, governments, investigative companies all use top-range equipment, and it's easy to come by.'

Nikki had a picture in her head of Stephen Cox. 'This just doesn't fit with the man we are thinking of.'

'Then either think of someone else or ask yourself if he's paid for an expert's services, because your adversary is a tricky one, no two ways about it.'

'And ruthless.'

'Then I'd better get my arse into gear.' Vinnie drained his mug and stood up. 'I'll sort out some lodgings and be in touch tonight, okay?' As he pushed his chair under the table he leaned towards Nikki and whispered, 'Thought for the day. Consider that both your vehicles will have trackers in them somewhere. Choose one car, find the tracker and disable it. They can dislodge quite easily, so your man won't be duly alarmed if one goes down, and it'll give you a bit of freedom.' He moved away from the table and in a louder voice said, 'Thanks for the coffee, and I'm sure we can sort out that *beautiful* water feature for you.' He winked at her and left.

Nikki exhaled. 'Wow!'

'He's good at what he does.' Joseph pushed the mugs together in the centre of the table. 'The best covert communications officer I've ever served with, not to mention one hell of a good man in a tight situation.'

'I believe you.' Nikki stood up. 'But he's still a cheeky sod.'

'True.' Joseph grinned. 'Always was.' Before he could say more, his mobile phone rang. 'DS Easter.'

He listened for a while then gave a little exclamation of excitement. 'Good work! We'll be there in . . .' he took a quick look at his watch, 'ten minutes.' He closed the phone and raised his eyebrows. 'Would you believe we have some good news?'

'Tell me first, then let me decide. Who was that?'

'Stuart Broad from the IT Department. He and Travis Taylor are with the security company trouble-shooter, Alan Brady, the man whose job it is to find the glitch in the security coverage of the Waterside Quay. Well, they think they've solved the locked-room killing of Magda Hellekamp!'

* * *

Nikki and Joseph eased their way into the dimly lit room that housed the monitor screens. There must have been ten others in there, all wide-eyed and eager, and chattering like baby jackdaws waiting to be fed.

'Can we downsize the audience?' Nikki frowned, hoping that some code of discretion existed amongst the group. The last thing she wanted was for a possible breakthrough to be leaked before she'd had a chance to brief the superintendent.

'These guys all have high level clearance.' Stuart stood beside them. 'They were responsible for building the system, so they really need to know how someone managed to exploit a weakness in their program.'

Nikki moved towards the front of the gaggle of technicians, and found Travis sitting at a keyboard. His fingers flew across it so fast they were blurred.

'Explain, please, in words that a woman who thinks a typewriter is cutting edge would understand.'

Stuart Broad placed a hand on his colleague's shoulder. 'Travis here suspected what had happened, and as soon as we got into the system we spotted the anomaly. Can you run it for the inspector, Travis?'

'Coming up.'

Screens flashed up, and Nikki and Joseph recognised the CCTV footage from outside Magda's apartment.

'Watch the digital clock, especially the second countdown in the right-hand corner of the screen.' Travis pointed.

'I'll freeze it at the right moment, then you'll see where the black hat has infiltrated.'

'Black hat?' asked Nikki.

'Criminal hacker,' Stuart chipped in. 'Sometimes we call them crackers rather than hackers. We are the white hats because we only hack ethically, if you get my meaning.'

'Like the cartoons?' asked Joseph.

'I guess. But look.' He pointed to the screen.

Nikki stared at the view along the corridor outside Magda's front door. She saw the shiny polished wooden floor-ing, the entrances to the two top floor apartments, and the landing window at the far end of the corridor. Nothing moved, except for the time-log numbers that flashed continuously.

'Here.'

Nikki peered at the big screen, but saw nothing. 'Where? What?'

Travis gave a little laugh. 'I'll run it again.'

The screen backtracked, then Travis moved it forward frame by frame. 'Up until this point, the system was oper-ating perfectly, but . . .' He paused, and stopped the screen and pointed to the fractions of a second. 'Here, it has been accessed by black hat.' He leaned forward and Nikki and Joseph saw a slight tremor and the tiniest change in the dig-ital numbers.

'What happened?'

'A new system has taken over from the original. It operates for exactly one minute, and then the old system is reactivated.' Travis looked up at Nikki. 'For one minute the cameras were locked. And in that minute, we suspect your killer entered the apartment block completely undetected.' He moved the screen forward. 'The same thing happened fifteen minutes later, a one minute hold on the cameras. In that time, he could easily have exited the apartment and disappeared.'

'The thing is, DI Galena,' Stuart rubbed the side of his nose thoughtfully, 'black hat disabled the whole system for those two individual minutes. That's why the entrance key card recording log showed nothing.'

'And,' Travis looked really excited, 'we found a security weak point in the layout of the residential complex. A black spot where the cameras do not cover and there are no windows looking out from the side of the apartment block. There is one wall, easily scaled, that drops into some shrubbery. Stuart did a trial while I timed him. It is perfectly possible to get from the road, over the wall, through the front door and up the stairs in exactly one minute.'

'The return trip was even quicker, as going down the stairs is a damned sight easier than running up them.' Stuart looked well pleased with himself. 'Not all us nerds are unhealthy you know. I did the Sea-bank Marathon last year in three hours fifty-seven!'

'Then you're a fit lad. That's seriously impressive,' said Joseph. 'But regarding those minutes where time stands still, wouldn't the gate security man have noticed something?'

'Black hat left the entry gate and the road cameras active,' Travis explained. 'I'd say whoever did this is an elite hacker and he's done a lot of research in order to get the timing so good.'

'Where calculated murder is concerned there's no room for error.' Nikki turned to Joseph. 'I'm supposing that Aaron Keller isn't this black hat?'

Joseph shook his head. 'No way. But don't forget he used a crack team for logistics. Black hat is just one of the team of enablers that he used.'

'Bloody Rent-a-Crook,' muttered Nikki.

Joseph was staring at the screen. 'How did you find it, Travis?'

The young man swung round on his chair. 'Well, we look at programs differently to the way you police officers look at CCTV, sir. With software there are all sorts of crazy anomalies going on behind the screens, so to speak. You basically just look for weird computer code.'

'But in this case Travis actually did see something on the screen as well, didn't you?' Stuart added.

Travis laughed. 'Yeah. After I'd got the warning bells, I saw this.' He went back to the shot of the corridor just prior to the time when the system was interrupted.

'Watch the window.'

They all stared at the window at the far end of the corridor.

'See that tall tree on the perimeter of the estate?'

Nikki nodded. It was massive old oak, obviously ancient and probably had a conservation order stuck on it. The evening breeze moved the high branches gently around in a lazy dance.

'And now.' Travis touched his index finger to the screen. 'The seconds are still ticking, but guess what? No wind. No wind at all, not a whisper.'

They waited for one minute and the tree instantly began its swaying motion.

'Voila!' He grinned smugly. 'I know we get some strange weather in these parts, but that's something else.'

'Good work, boys.' Nikki allowed a smile to spread across her face. 'Another part of the puzzle is complete. We now have the *who* and the *how*. All we need is the *why* and we can stamp "closed" on Operation Windmill.'

Joseph paused as they prepared to leave. 'Stuart? When that other software was running, would there be a record of what was really occurring anywhere? I mean, would your black hat guy have the killer on camera somewhere?'

Stuart looked at Travis and they both pulled faces. 'No, I don't think so. He more or less just pasted a picture, a still frame, into the system. I think recording what really happened would have been counter-productive, don't you?' Stuart asked his friend.

Travis nodded. 'Definitely. He was protecting the killer, allowing him the time he needed to come and go. Keeping some kind of video log on Keller's movements could incriminate them.' He sat back. 'No. Sorry, Sergeant, but I think this is all you're going to get.'

'It's good enough, Travis. One last question. Can you trace him? This black hat.'

Travis puffed out his cheeks, 'We're going to give it our best shot, sir, but as I said before, this guy is elite, and I'm guessing there will be no finding him.'

'Okay. Well done, you two. Great job.'

'Absolutely. We'll see you back at the station for a debriefing?' said Nikki.

'Ma'am? Would it be alright if I called in at the hospital on the way? It was my afternoon off and I'd promised to go see Cat. I don't want to let her down.'

Nikki nodded. 'No problem, but get back ASAP so that we can get all this into a report. And tell Cat I'll see her when I finish, whenever that might be.'

'DI Galena?' Alan Brady blocked her exit. 'Would it be in order for me — well, my company — to ask your technicians to go over all this with some of our top people?' He was still looking worried out of his skin. 'This should not have happened, and there's a chance your chaps could throw a few pointers our way.' He looked at her imploringly. 'Something to help protect future projects?'

'I don't see why not. But it can't be on our time, Mr Brady, and only if their company agrees, okay?' She looked at his pasty and deeply etched face and added, 'Have a word with them before they leave.'

'Thanks a lot, Inspector. Much appreciated.' He scurried off.

'Can we draw a line under this now?' asked Joseph, as they exited the building. 'I mean, stop chasing 'elite' black-hatted shadows, and get back to hunting Snipe and his very real threat to us all?'

'Maybe.' Nikki walked slowly across the car park. 'Magda's probable time of death, according to the pathologist, corresponds pretty well with the CCTV freeze. There are still a few grey areas, like how did the killer get hold of a duplicate keycard for Magda's flat? But there is no doubt that it was Aaron Keller who murdered her.' She halted, some way from her car. 'Considering the pressure we are under with Snipe, I could throw Operation Windmill upstairs and let another section tie up the loose ends. But . . .' She paused.

'But that's not your way, is it?'

'I've never passed the buck before. I'd like to think we've done a thorough job. But under the circumstances, maybe I'll talk to Rick Bainbridge and be guided by him.' She looked across the concrete to her father's old car. 'Now, before we go back to the station and Snipe's blasted covert surveillance cameras, what say we go bug hunting?' She walked slowly towards the old Countryman, her face screwed up in thought. 'Do you know what we are looking for, Joseph?'

'Oh yes, ma'am. I do.' He grinned and rubbed his hands together. 'Easy-peasy! Let's get the little bugger, shall we?'

Nikki watched as Joseph slipped into the car, turned on the engine and cranked up the radio. 'Just in case it's voice sensitive and not just a location tracker.' He opened the back and ran deft fingers around the interior of the boot. Happy that it was clear, he walked to the front and lifted the bonnet. He kept his voice low and said, 'Expensive GPS tracking devices are sometimes hard-wired to the battery and then hidden almost anywhere, but,' he slammed the lid closed, 'not this time.' He eased himself down to the ground and slipped his head and shoulders under the vehicle. His voice was muffled but she heard him say, 'Signals are well received near the road surface. Under the car is a favourite, or,' she heard a chuckle, 'tucked into the wheel arch!' He dragged himself out, stood up and checked his watch. 'Two minutes. I'm getting rusty.' He showed her a small black coin-shaped object, then he dropped it onto the concrete and crushed it beneath his heel. 'Oops, butter-fingers!' The grin broadened. 'Shall we go?'

CHAPTER FIFTEEN

Cat had been right in believing that a visit from Travis would lift her spirits, although it wasn't in the way she had envisaged. For the first fifteen minutes he regaled her with his and Stuart's first mega-success at cybercrime fighting.

If he told her once how pleased DI Galena had been, he must have mentioned it six times. 'And we have to go in later for a debriefing with her and Sergeant Easter,' he finished off self-importantly. 'Cool, isn't it?'

'Very cool, techno-freak. I bow to your superior brain power.' She gave him a look like that of a long-suffering parent towards a pretentious child. 'But don't forget, we detectives do that sort of thing on a daily basis. And we don't crow about it for weeks either.'

'I'll remind you about that next time you have a . . . oh, what do you professionals call it? A blinding good collar?'

'Do that. Now . . .' Cat tried to drag his attention away from his CCTV footage and back to her present predicament. 'I'm going quietly barmy in here, Travis, and apparently I've now got an infection in one of my leg wounds.' She broke off. 'You have noticed the odd dressing, haven't you?'

Travis blinked, as if seeing her properly for the first time. 'Oh, uh, sorry, old bag. Do they hurt?'

'Only when I laugh.'

'Does anyone really say that?'

'Only when they're talking to a moron. Of course it bloody hurts! And I need to take my mind off it. So . . .' Cat produced a sheet of paper. 'I need your help. Can you upload these to my tablet? Then I can do some proper work, even if I am incarcerated in this stinky place.'

'Most people would prefer to spend happy hours trying to get to a higher level on a gaming app. Speaking of which, knowing how much you liked Temple Run, have you tried Vector? Now that has you testing your parkour skills to the limits. I suggest—'

'And I suggest you belt up and look at the files I need.'

Travis looked at the list and frowned. 'Mm, very interesting, but sadly neither legal nor possible. Ever heard of data protection?'

'Look, if I was behind my desk, I'd be accessing them myself. Help me out here, Travis. Please.'

'I'd love to, but none of this can be accessed outside the nick.' His look was disparaging. 'You know that, venerable baggage.'

'For heaven's sake, Travis, what I've asked for isn't sensitive and I'm sure I'm not asking for anything that will get you the sack. We have two big cases running. I just want to pull my weight, even if I am hospitalised.'

He nodded. 'Understood. But any sleuthing you need to do will have to be done through the private sector. I'm not having either of us getting oiked out of our jobs for being total prats.' He looked at her sternly, then smiled furtively and added, 'However, I do happen to know a few interesting and informative sites that might allow you to dig a little deeper than simply Googling names and places.' He turned her piece of paper over and wrote down the names of two internet sites. 'I'll send you another in an email, so look out for it. It needs password access, so use this.' He scribbled a word and three numbers on the paper. 'Use them only when all else fails. Stuart and I find them well tasty. They have no connection to the police or any other official computers. Let's just say that they use pathways that are not well-trodden.'

Cat tried a relieved smile. It wasn't what she had hoped for, but it was better than nothing.

'And this is one of my spares.' Travis handed her a leather laptop case. 'It should give you more power than your tablet.'

Cat took the computer. 'Thanks, my geeky little friend. I appreciate that. Now, tell me again about your amazing CCTV discovery.'

* * *

When Joseph stepped back into the police station he could feel a difference in the atmosphere. Nothing else of note had happened, but the usual noisy banter and general sense of organised chaos was somehow muted. Danny's death hung over everyone and he decided that the whole building felt depressed.

He knew that Nikki felt it too, even though she tried to keep up the impression of determined confidence.

'I need to see Rick. Put him in the picture regarding Operation Windmill.' She pressed the button on the lift. 'And get his opinion on how we should proceed.' She looked at Joseph as they waited. 'I think I'll do it now and get it over with.'

'Then I'll chase up all the outstanding reports and see if anything else has come in from forensics.'

She nodded. 'Good, and ring Rory Wilkinson and ask him to give us the low-down on the bouquet of flowers as soon as he can. Plus see if uniform have found anything yet on the crematorium security cameras. The bloody thing didn't just drop from the sky. Someone put it there.' She shivered. 'And they had to do it very carefully, unless they wanted to get burned.' She shook her head in disbelief at the killer's cold-blooded action. Then she added, 'By the way, I've said I'll visit Cat later tonight. Will you come with me?'

'Of course I will. I miss her. It doesn't seem right in the CID room without her and her gobby streetwise wit.' He stood back as the lift door opened. 'Poor old Dave looks like a fish out of water. You don't realise just how much you rely on your partner until they aren't there.'

They stepped inside and the doors closed. Joseph felt the urge to thank Nikki for not balling him out over Hayley's injury, but he stopped himself. He was still aching with guilt and self-reproach, but she seemed to have dealt with it differently, so maybe he should let sleeping dogs lie. And, as there was nothing he could do to physically help Hayley, maybe he should direct all his thoughts to catching the man responsible. The man who was also responsible for Danny Wilshire's death, Cat's injury and all the other outrages that were being heaped upon them.

The door whispered open and he got out. Nikki went up another floor to the superintendent's office. At least the IT boys had given her some good news to give him.

Back at his desk Joseph was suddenly reminded of the thoughts that had led him to the debacle at the crematorium. And the main focus of these thoughts was Archie Leonard.

What had happened there? Nikki should have been high-tailing it around to Archie long before she even considered speaking to Cynthia Changtai at Cyn City. But she hadn't mentioned him once, not even when Stephen Cox was seen on the Carborough Estate. Archie had very good reason to hate Cox, and as the one-time King of the Carborough, it was ten to one that nothing went on, even now, that the Leonard family didn't know about.

Joseph leaned back in his chair and chewed on the end of his pen. He saw again the look she had thrown him when he suggested a visit. It had been one big, fat, "don't go there!" He had wanted to press her, but it was clear that the subject was off limits. She'd tell him in her own time, he knew, but when?

He sauntered over to where the office manager sat behind a desk piled high with files. Sheila Robbins was a civilian who did a brilliant job in driving the office. She was PA, secretary, filing clerk, Agony Aunt and Mother Superior all rolled into one.

'Anything from forensics yet?' asked Joseph hopefully.

Sheila flashed him a reproving smile, and pushed a swathe of greying hair behind her ear. 'Now wouldn't you be the first person I'd tell if they had come in, Sergeant Easter?'

He made small apologetic noises and returned to his desk. Then he'd have to ring Professor Wilkinson direct.

The pathologist answered. 'Joseph, dear boy! Why ring when you could have called in person? My mortuary gets so very few visits from anyone who's capable of holding a decent conversation.' He paused. 'Actually, most of them are incapable of any conversation at all.'

'I promise to drop in next time I'm passing, Rory, but right now DI Galena has asked me to contact you about the flowers.'

'Ah, the deadly bouquet! But having studied it, I suspect you will trace where it came from quite easily.'

'Really?'

'The floral trade is much belittled by the uninitiated, my friend. Considerable skill and expertise went into making that bouquet. It certainly didn't come from a garage forecourt or a supermarket. It was carefully made by a very good floral designer using highly perfumed top-quality flowers and specialist florist sundries.'

'So we need to check florist shops to see who placed that particular order?'

'And look for a left-handed florist. You can tell by the direction of the binding. And I would think said florist is no youngster. The balance of the bunch was perfect and the positioning of the individual blooms shows an artistic talent that has been honed over years of practice.'

Rory stopped speaking and waited. Joseph knew that it was his cue to make a suitably impressed comment. 'Excellent, Rory. That certainly gives us something to follow up on.'

'Oh, but I have more.'

Joseph smiled into the receiver. No matter how dark and sombre his mood, Rory Wilkinson had the ability to lift his spirits. 'Why am I not surprised?'

'Because I always leave the best to last, don't I? When you go hunting for your fabulous florist, make sure her name is Gillian, that the bouquet cost forty-five pounds, was paid for in cash, and came from a flower shop located next to a local hostelry.'

Joseph let out a small exclamation of surprise. 'How the hell . . . ?'

'I wish I could tell you, but my lips are sealed.'

'Rory, for heaven's sake! Time is of the essence here.'

'Spoilsport. Oh well, actually a dear friend of mine, sweet Piers — a lovely boy — he works in the most divine florist in Greenborough. I rang him, described it, and he told me that his boss, a southpaw called Gillian Bayliss, had made up something similar yesterday. I emailed him a photo of it, and hey presto!' He gave a sigh. 'The shop is called the Flower Garland, and it's in Roper's Gate next to the Roper's Arms.'

'Thanks, Rory. I'll go round there immediately.'

'I'm not sure you'll get much more than you already know, but say hello to sweet Piers for me, won't you?'

'Of course. But Rory, how and when did the acid get into it?'

'Added by the killer just prior to placing it in the Garden of Remembrance, I should think. It wasn't a bona fide florist's greeting card. It was purpose made, soaked in that insidious stuff and placed in a strong, clear, plastic envelope. The top was left open and as soon as it was touched, it oozed the gel base and the acid upwards and out of the sachet. Very, very nasty. It could easily have squirted up in her face, especially if she was bending down to try to read it.' He paused, the joking manner gone, 'She could have been blinded or terribly disfigured. I don't know what you've been told about hydrofluoric acid, Joseph, but the burns are a unique clinical phenomenon. The tissue destruction and necrosis is horrific, often involving the underlying bone. Severe burns can result in systemic fluoride ion poisoning and sudden death. In brief, it's treacherous stuff and I'm relieved that it's in another lab right now being disposed of.'

'I'm sure.' Joseph scratched his head. 'But if this lethal acid can etch metal and glass, and human tissue, why didn't it eat through the sachet?'

Rory gave a tight laugh. 'Ironic, isn't it? It can eat through a steel plate or a glass bottle, but can be safely stored in a plastic container.'

Joseph thanked the pathologist and replaced the receiver. He looked at his watch and realised that he could just make it to the flower shop before they closed. 'I'm going to this address, Sheila.' He scribbled down the florist's name and handed it to her. 'Tell the DI where I am, or if you need to get away before she comes back from her meeting, if you'd be so kind as to leave a message on her desk?'

'You got it, Sergeant, and my favourite flowers are freesias, by the way.'

* * *

Half an hour later Joseph left the florist shop. Sweet Piers had turned out to be a likeable and inoffensive young man who had introduced Joseph to the owner of the shop and between them they had told him all they knew, which as Rory had predicted, was precious little.

It had been a phoned order, collected by a young woman who Piers had seen hanging around with a small gaggle of youths and girls outside the pub at lunchtime. She had said that she was picking them up for her employer who was too busy to come himself. And whatever, she had paid the £45 cash and carefully carried her tied bouquet away with her. Joseph had known immediately that they would get no further than that. A crisp note for a few minutes' work could bring on terminal amnesia in most of Greenborough's out-of-work youths.

He retraced his footsteps back across the town bridge over the Wayland River and headed for the police station. Just as he was about to enter, he saw the familiar figure of Sheila Robbins hurrying through the front door.

'Sheila! Hang on a minute.' He loped across to where she stood.

'Ah, Sergeant Easter, I'm glad I've seen you.' Sheila moved a little closer and spoke in a soft voice so as not to be overheard. 'Uniform wants you to know that the CCTV footage from the crem was corrupted. They will try to get it cleaned up, but they don't hold out much hope. And DI Galena said that she is going to be tied up for at least another hour. The superintendent has set up a Skype call with our counterparts in Holland. Apparently they have some exciting new developments on Operation Windmill too, so considering what your team came up with earlier, they need to confer. She asked if you would wait for her so that you can visit DC Cullen together.'

'Of course. No problem.'

'Give our Cat my best wishes, won't you?'

'I will.' Joseph smiled at the older woman, then produced the bunch of flowers that he had been hiding behind his back. 'You did say freesias, didn't you?'

Sheila's mouth fell open into a small round 'O' as she stared at the pretty bouquet of yellow and white flowers. 'Sergeant Easter! Oh, now I feel dreadful! I was only . . . well, I never meant . . .'

'It's my pleasure, Sheila. I don't tell you often enough just how much all your hard work is appreciated. We get all involved in things and we forget to say thank you. I'm not sure how the CID office would run without you, but I suspect very badly indeed.' He flashed his very best smile. 'So, thank you.'

He watched as she walked down the road and noticed a spring in her step. That was what flowers were supposed to do, make you happy, not burn and scar you for life.

Joseph halted at the front door and wondered how he could utilise the next hour constructively. Unless some more reports had come back, he was pretty well stymied. Unless . . . ? Joseph turned around and walked in the direction of the staff car park.

There was one thing he could do. It probably wouldn't win him any brownie points with the boss, but it would certainly put his own mind at rest.

He pulled his car keys from his pocket and his identification card from his wallet so that he could exit the yard's security gates.

The Carborough was only a few minutes away, and there was a man there he badly wanted to talk to. He just hoped that Archie Leonard would want to talk to him.

CHAPTER SIXTEEN

Joseph stood on the doorstep to Archie's house and looked around. It was a sign of the times that he hadn't needed to interview someone from this part of the Carborough Estate for ages, and since his last visit the change was incredible.

Before, he would never have left his car unattended, not if he valued the wheels and its entire contents.

Before, he would have looked around warily before his feet even landed on the pavement.

Before, graffiti, broken glass and the remains of burnt out dustbins would have been the first thing he saw.

But now he saw freshly painted front doors and window frames, and . . . hell-fire! Window boxes! Okay, they would not make a feature at the Chelsea Flower Show, but even the few straggly petunias and valiant geraniums made a difference that was hard to believe.

A slender-faced woman with tightly drawn back hair answered the door and pulled Joseph from his reveries.

'Joan, isn't it?' He flashed a bright smile, recognising her as the wife of one of Archie's sons. 'I'm Joseph Easter. Is Archie around?'

The woman looked at him suspiciously, then glanced past him up and down the street. Apparently regeneration had not stopped the embarrassment of finding the Old Bill on your doorstep.

'I know who you are, Detective Sergeant. You better come in.' She almost dragged him into the hall. 'But I'm not sure if he'll want to see you . . .' Her voice trailed off. 'Wait here.'

Joseph watched her walk down the hall and into a room at the end of the corridor.

He'd been here before, many years ago. He felt a niggle of worry. Why wouldn't Archie want to see him? Years ago they had supported each other through a bad time, and they'd become . . . Joseph wondered what exactly. He could find nothing that quite covered their odd copper/criminal relationship. He settled for friends. And he'd done nothing in the last year to change that.

He drew in a breath. But maybe Nikki had. And Archie might consider them an inseparable duo. What was good for one, was good for the other.

'Joseph?' Joan Leonard was beckoning to him. 'Come down. But I'd appreciate it if you didn't stay too long.' She stood back and opened the door, then padded back down the corridor.

The sight that met him in that small claustrophobic room had him taking hold of himself to suppress a gasp of surprise.

The once tall, straight-backed Archie Leonard sat hunched in an upright armchair. An oxygen cylinder secured in a metal trolley stood slightly to one side of him, and a plastic tube snaked its way to the clip that was fastened to his nostrils. His chest rose and fell as he breathed.

'Hell! Archie? How long have you been like this?' Joseph knew he could not hide the shock, so decided not to try. 'I never knew.'

'Few do,' Archie rasped. 'But it's good to see you, Joseph.' He indicated another chair. 'I hope your unexpected, although very welcome, visit doesn't mean that there is something wrong with Nikki?'

Joseph almost sighed with relief that there had been no acrimonious falling out. 'No. Well, physically she's fine, but—'

'I know. Mentally exhausted and still grieving,' finished off Archie. 'And now worried sick over rumours of the return of a particularly disgusting piece of detritus. Am I right?'

'You are.' He looked at the old man and saw that, sick or not, the eyes were still the same. Intelligent, thoughtful, a piercing bright blue, and the message in them was, *Sod the illness, I'm fighting back*. 'Seriously, Archie, how long have you been so poorly? And does Nikki know?'

'I've been ill for years, Joseph. Always hidden it as best I could.' He gave a heavy guttural cough that seemed to be dredged up from the depths of his body. 'But a couple of months ago the bastard thing decided to up its game.'

'I'm so sorry.' Joseph meant it. Criminal or not, he had always harboured a sneaky respect for Archie and his old-style morals.

'Mea culpa, my friend. Too many hours in smoke-filled rooms plotting how to make a million and get one over on you guys.' He tried to laugh, but the coughing took over, sending Joseph hurrying for the water that stood on the table next to him.

'Don't talk. Just rest for a moment and I'll tell you why I'm here.'

Archie shook his head, coughed again then whispered. 'I know why you are here. This will pass. Just give me a minute.'

Joseph watched as the man fought to control his failing lungs. In his mind's eye, Joseph imagined them, blackened, like two old and decrepit inner tubes. Two pieces of perished rubber straining to hold in the precious air that seeped noisily out through ragged holes and worn patches.

As Archie began to recover, Joseph looked around the room, and suddenly realised where they were. His first distressing sight of the older man had totally blanked out everything else, but now he realised that the small room was a teenager's bedroom. And as soon as he saw the fading pink wallpaper and old photos of laughing girls and tanned, good-looking young men, he knew that he was in Lisa Jane's room.

Lisa Jane, Archie's niece and ward. Until she was murdered four years ago.

'Don't worry. I don't sit here all day every day and think morbid thoughts.' Archie was more in control of his voice now. 'I just come here sometimes to remember. She was so beautiful.'

Joseph knew, although he had only met her after she became a temporary resident in the morgue. 'She was.'

Archie sat back. 'Now, let's talk about Stephen Cox, shall we?'

Joseph nodded. 'We have come under threat from someone with one serious grudge.' He told Archie everything and watched as the man's face darkened. 'Nikki is convinced it is Cox. I'm not so sure.' He paused. 'We know he's back, and he's been seen at Cyn City and here on the Carborough . . . and I find that puzzling.'

'Because of the Leonard family and our threat to tear his balls off if he ever set foot here again?'

'Absolutely. Surely, if he had any sense at all, he'd avoid Greenborough, and your backyard in particular, like the plague?'

'You'd have thought so, wouldn't you? But he's certainly been here.' Archie gave him a tight smile. 'The family try to keep things from me these days, but I have an ally. One who keeps me very well informed of absolutely everything. A friend of yours, as it happens.' The smile widened.

'Mickey.'

'Mickey. My eyes and ears.' Archie gave a contented smile. 'He's not blood, you know that, but I couldn't love him more if he were my true grandson.'

'I saw him at Hannah's funeral. He's a credit to Peter and Fran.'

'And to you. If Sergeant Joe hadn't believed in him, then my son and his wife would never have had the chance to take him in.'

Joseph gave Archie an enquiring glance. 'At the funeral? They were there representing you?'

'I had a bad day. And with a cough like mine the vicar would probably have thought he was cremating the wrong person.' His hands were folded in his lap, and he looked down at them. 'I wanted to go, to be there for Nikki. But in all honesty I think she's seen enough illness and death recently, don't you?'

'So she doesn't know about your health?'

'She does, and she visited me a few days after the funeral. It upset her badly, so I told her to stay away, until we were both stronger.'

'I wish she'd told me.' Joseph hoped there wasn't a peevish tone to his voice.

'I told her not to, Joseph. Good Lord, I'm old news around here, and we've all got to go sometime. You young ones have busy lives.' A sudden frown ate up his face. 'And now you are being threatened?'

Joseph nodded.

'I heard about that young policeman dying. I talked to Mickey about it, wondering if there was some connection to Cox. Mickey said he'd heard that Cox was back to settle something. The moment he arrived in that flea-pit of a pub, the Fisherman's Knot, the slimeball was sent a message, one he would have had no trouble understanding. My eldest son, Raymond, gave Cox two hours to get out of Greenborough, or he would never leave here again, well, not on two feet.' He gave a little shrug. 'Most of the family, especially Peter and Fran, wholeheartedly support the regeneration scheme. They are sick of the old ways, the feuds, the jail sentences, and the constant looking over your shoulder, but not Raymond. He remembers the old days, he misses the way things were, and if I'm honest, he resents the change.'

'And has Cox been seen since?'

'Mickey reckons he's gone to ground. He's certainly not been seen around, but he hasn't been seen leaving either.'

'Do you know who he met in the pub?'

Archie gave a short rattle of a cough, then said, 'Two strangers. Not locals. Mickey was told they had sharp suits and shoes that would have cost enough to feed a small starving nation.'

Joseph exhaled. 'Not sure I like the thought of that. Sounds like a deal, or a meeting set up to plan something unholy.'

'And Nikki Galena would be the only person that I know of who could draw that son of a bitch back here.' His eyebrows drew together. 'Despite our warnings.'

'What's your gut feeling, Archie?'

The older man sat back and rubbed thoughtfully at his chin. 'In truth, I'm not sure. But watch that woman like a hawk, Joseph. Stephen Cox hates her and he's risked everything by showing his ugly face on the Carborough. Whatever business he has here, it's worth dying for.' He pulled in a shaky breath. 'So, as I said, watch her like a hawk.'

CHAPTER SEVENTEEN

As the evening shift began to settle in, Nikki sat in her office, wondering what the night would bring and staring at the notes she had just made. From what she had just heard from Holland, Operation Windmill was approaching the dénouement stage. It was all there and coming together fast. Which had sounded really good, until they realised that their combined efforts had opened an even bigger can of worms. Nikki's joke about Rent-a-Crook was turning into something very unfunny indeed, and much bigger than one execution-style murder. The Dutch police had just told them that they had had a crack squad looking into the possibility of an international network with 'specialists for hire,' for almost a year.

She now understood how frustrated Joseph's friend, Liam Feehily, must have felt, knowing that he was onto something huge, and then hearing the doors closing on him.

Nikki looked at her report. The two IT guys, Travis and Stuart had confirmed in their debriefing that the system used by the killer's support team had been highly sophisticated. "Awesome" was their word for it.

She looked out of her open door and across to the CID room. Joseph was standing at his desk, pointing to his wrist watch and then waving a set of car keys at her. He mouthed the word, *Cat.*

Nikki nodded. Her head ached and she craved a long shower, a decent drink, and an even longer sleep. Not that she expected to get all three. It rarely worked out that perfectly. And she did want to see Cat. 'Two minutes,' she called back.

He gave her a thumbs-up and began tidying his desk.

Ten minutes later they were walking across the car park to where her father's old car sat waiting. Thanks to Joseph it was now bug free, but just in case Snipe really had found a way to watch the peripherals of the police station, they played out a small charade for his benefit.

Joseph walked to his car and made to unlock it, then Nikki called out to him and pointed to the Countryman. 'Leave yours here tonight. We don't need two vehicles for one journey. Let's take mine.'

Joseph nodded emphatically, then checked that his vehicle was locked and strolled across to her. Inside he said, 'When exactly are the BAFTA awards?'

She threw him a disparaging look and said, 'Sorry chum, but you're not quite Hugh Grant.'

As they drove she told him about her meeting with the super, the Dutch Skype call and the debriefing of the IT team.

'Regarding Holland, they've also discovered some emails on Magda's main works computer. Same thing, blocked IP address, so no way of tracing them.' She smiled. 'I think they were a bit miffed that we were already following the same line of enquiry.'

Joseph wiped a smear from the side window with a finger and said, 'Mind if I pass on what we know about this Rent-a-Crook thing to Liam? I'm sure he'll have no problem liaising with the Dutch police and sharing what intel he's gathered. I don't like the thought of some sinister underground network springing up with cells in and around major towns and cities, do you?'

'No, and especially not if the damned organisation is mega-big, like worldwide, and we have an established cell right here in the Fens. No, go ahead and talk to him. I can give you the name of the Dutch detective in charge of the investigation. He sounded like he could do with a bit of help.'

They were almost at the hospital when Joseph told her that he had been to the florist who supplied the deadly flower bouquet, and afterwards called in on Archie Leonard.

On hearing his words she clamped down on her jaw and bit back rising anger. Then she realised how stupid it was. Why shouldn't he visit Archie? She was more in the wrong than he was, for not telling him that the old man was ill.

'I suppose you think I've been underhand, about Archie being sick.' She pulled into the main gates of the hospital. 'I should have said something, I know. It's just that . . .' She stopped, not knowing how to finish the sentence.

'I understand, Nikki. You've had enough on your plate recently. You don't have to justify anything.'

'I do, because we're a team and we don't have secrets. It was stupid, but . . .' She shook her head. 'I couldn't handle it. I'm sorry, Joseph, but I don't think I'd cope if I lost someone else who is important to me.' Nikki felt, and was sure she looked, wretched. She parked and pulled on the handbrake. 'And Archie *is* important. Maybe he shouldn't be, but he is.'

Joseph nodded and she knew that he felt the same. Okay, it was something of an unholy alliance, but they had been in some tough situations over the years and it had forged a bond, one that was hard to describe.

'Come on.' He gave her a smile and placed his hand on the door handle. 'Enough of this, let's go see our Cat, shall we?'

* * *

They stayed for half an hour. The visit began with tears, and ended in hilarity.

Totally against her wishes, Cat had been moved to a private room and was being barrier nursed. Not because she had contracted something nasty, but to protect her wounds from incoming infections. Seeing how low she was, Joseph used the gown, mask and gloves to do some very bad impressions of a demonic doctor hell-bent on stealing as many of her vital organs as he could. It did not take long for the tears to disappear.

When it was time to leave, Cat said, 'I had another visitor just before you came in. Professor Wilkinson called in for a chat. He wondered if you'd go down to his department before you go home. He's working late and might have some new results ready for you.'

'Then we'd better get a move on.' Joseph looked at his watch and frowned. 'I'd like to get back to Cloud Fen before nightfall.' Visions of what Snipe might have prepared for them suddenly crossed his mind and he became acutely grateful that they had Vinnie Silver close at hand.

They said goodbye and hurried down to the lower level of the hospital where Rory Wilkinson attended to the less fortunate inmates of Greenborough General.

Rory looked tired and exasperated. 'Sorry, my dear little friends, but I've got you here on a wild goose chase.' He stared at his computer as if he hated it. 'I was faithfully promised the DNA result on the blood found in the boot of your car, but you can trust no one these days.' He put on a peeved expression. 'They've probably all gone home to a delicious cooked dinner, a cool glass of Chablis and a soft comfortable bed.' He threw up his hands dramatically. 'And here am I, starving to death, and up to my armpits in someone else's entrails and gastric juices! Sometimes I think that life's not very fair!'

'Ditto,' said Nikki with feeling. 'But entrails apart, don't worry about our wasted trip. It's good to know that those results are imminent.'

'You will have them the moment some lazy sod gets off his pretty little arse and sends them to me, I promise.' Rory yawned. 'And now I'm giving up the ghost and going home, before I get too tired and mix up my post-mortem findings.'

Joseph grinned. 'Ah, not a good idea.'

'Certainly not when you have two guests on your slabs, one a twenty stone, ninety-year-old above-knee amputee, and the other, a stick thin woman who'd been knocked over and killed whilst running for a bus.'

Nikki winced. 'See your point. Maybe it *is* time to throw in the towel.'

* * *

It was an uneasy drive back to Cloud Fen, and as they drew closer, anxiety began to gnaw at Joseph's guts. Snipe was devious, and there was no telling what his twisted mind had conjured up for his next vile surprise. Luckily, just as they were approaching Knot Cottage, Joseph had a text message from Vinnie, telling them that he had done a late recon of the area and as far as he could ascertain, all was quiet on the Eastern Front. He would ring them later on their safe phone and discuss his proposed plans.

Joseph unlocked the front door and put on the lights. He was naturally suspicious of what might lurk there, but it was as Vinnie had said, all quiet.

Joseph still erred on the side of caution and insisted on doing a careful walk-around check of every nook and cranny, something that fortunately didn't take long in his small cottage. 'Safe,' he breathed. 'For now.'

And then the house phone rang.

Every muscle in his body suddenly tensed to snapping point.

Snipe? He looked swiftly at Nikki and she seemed to have been carved from stone. A wide-eyed and hardening expression set on her face.

He moved across to the table and slowly lifted the receiver.

'Dad?'

Relief flooded through him. 'Tamsin?'

'You have more than one daughter?'

He laughed out loud. 'No, sweetheart, I'm just surprised to hear your voice.'

'I hope that's not a knock about how little I phone you?'

This was going to be tricky. Already she had him on the defensive, but that was hardly surprising, considering he had been expecting a psychotic killer.

'Of course not. Hey, how are you?'

'In a bit of a jam, actually.' She gave an irritated snort. 'That's why I'm ringing. Oh, and I tried your mobile, is it switched off or something?'

Joseph's earlier delight at hearing his daughter's voice faded rapidly. 'It's an iffy signal, that's all. What's wrong?'

There was a short delay, then she said, 'Can I crash at your place for a couple of days, Dad? I know it's short notice, but I don't have anyone else to turn to.'

Confusion and alarm swept over him. How could he let his only child walk into a situation as dangerous as this? Well, he couldn't. Simple. But how the hell did he tell her, without her mind screaming one word, over and over. Rejection! Again.

After years of tearing down the wall of hurt, brick by brick, their relationship was slowly healing. Whatever happened now, he couldn't afford to jeopardise it.

'I'd love to see you, Tam. So tell me what's happened?' He spoke quickly so that she didn't detect a 'but' in his voice.

'Massive cock-up in my travel plans.' She paused. 'Look, Dad, can I explain when I get there? I'm on a friend's PAYG mobile and there's not much money on it.'

Joseph felt a stab of panic. 'Where are you now?'

'In a service station on the A1M. There's some numbers on the wall. I'm going to try to get a cab.'

'No. Don't do that. Tell me exactly where you are and I'll pick you up.'

'Sorry . . . can't hear y . . .' A crackling noise filled his ears.

'Tamsin! Listen!'

Through the static he heard something that sounded like, "See you in an hour."

A dozen scenarios flashed through his brain, and none of them was good.

Joseph dialled 1471 and pressed recall, but there was no service. He lowered the phone and looked helplessly at Nikki. 'What do I do now? She can't come here.'

Nikki looked at him nervously. 'I know that. This place is about as safe as a haystack in a bushfire. But frankly, I'm more worried about something else.'

He felt a shiver as he saw her staring directly at the telephone. 'Oh, shit! Tamsin rang on the house phone, didn't she?'

Nikki nodded. She didn't need to say any more, because they both knew that Snipe could still be listening to every word that was said.

And if he was, then he knew that Joseph's precious daughter was on her way to Cloud Fen.

CHAPTER EIGHTEEN

As Joseph tore himself to shreds worrying about Tamsin and their fragile relationship, Dave Harris was also worried sick.

He sat at his kitchen table and stared at the three opened letters that lay in front of him. One was a demand for settlement on an outstanding credit card account, the second was a polite reminder from the residential nursing home where his wife was being cared for, and the other, far less polite, was from a finance company that dealt with a hire purchase agreement that he had taken to buy a new three-piece suite.

He did what he always did in a crisis, and sipped at his mug of tea. As he did he decided that it had to be a horrible bank error. He had funds to pay for everything, and he was a stickler for paying his bills immediately they came in, especially where his wife's care was concerned. It had to be some glorious bloody mistake.

Dave got up and walked through to the dining room where an old desktop computer sat on one end of the dining table. He hated doing this, but Cat had assured him that it was perfectly safe and had helped him set up online banking. At least he could check his bank account, even if it was almost eleven o'clock at night.

He logged on and waited for the PC to load. As he waited he slipped a small white card from under the tablecloth and stared at his details. Ridiculous, wasn't it? He was an old-fashioned copper, and one with a pretty good memory, all things considered, but when it came to his own passwords and memorable dates, he was rubbish.

After what seemed like an eternity, the machine stopped chuntering and he was good to go. Dave accessed his bank site, then carefully followed the onscreen instructions to log in to his account.

He always felt huge relief when he was finally in, but tonight his relief was short-lived. He had three active accounts, a current account for utilities and day to day stuff, and a saver reward for bigger things like holidays or emergencies, and an account that held their savings, and as he watched the screen, he saw that they were all almost empty.

He stared at the monitor for a full minute before it sunk in. When it did, Dave let rip with a string of swear words and scrolled down the page to the Contact Us *emergencies only* number.

Getting through was a nightmare, but after listening to recorded messages and tapping number after number, he finally found himself talking to a human.

Somehow he managed to get his befuddled mind back into police mode and explained that he was a detective constable with the Fenland Constabulary, and gave the operator the details of what had occurred as clearly and concisely as he could.

'There have been significant online transactions recently, sir.' Dave could hear the sound of the young man's fingers on a keyboard. 'Are you sure that you haven't made any transfers of large sums in the last few days?'

Dave gritted his teeth. 'In the last few days I have written only two cheques, both under fifty pounds, and used my debit card twice, once at Sainsbury's and once at the petrol station. I have made no transfers.'

'And no large withdrawals?'

'Bloody hell! I've just told you! No!'

Dave didn't want to bawl out the kid. He didn't want to be shouting down the phone at anyone. But he was scared. Shit-scared. And he had every reason to be, because police officers cannot have debts. The bottom line was that he could lose his job. He swallowed hard. He understood why, and he'd always agreed that it was quite right. An officer with money problems could be open to bribes. A broke officer could easily become a bent officer.

Dave let out an exasperated sigh, then tried to concentrate on what the young man was saying. It was all a bit of a blur. His account would be frozen and his cards all cancelled. The bank's fraud division would contact him.

After a few minutes, he replaced the phone. He needed to talk to the sarge and the boss. He glanced at the ornate mantle clock that he hated but kept only because it had belonged to his wife's mother, and saw that it was half past eleven. No way could he ring them now.

Dave slowly dragged himself up from the chair and switched off the computer. It was going to be a very long night.

* * *

Cat was also suffering, but her discomfort was purely physical. She was now on intravenous antibiotics for the infection in her leg, and she was feeling wretched. Earlier she had phoned her mother, and for fifteen minutes had had to keep up the pretence of the whole thing being blown out of proportion and that she was fine really, just in for observation.

The well-meant farce had drained her, and being in a small room with a closed door was slowly sending her stir-crazy. She was still desperate to see her face, but at the same time, scared to death to know what was under the dressings. For two hoots she would have discharged herself. The thought still lingered in her mind, but she knew that she would be letting her specialist down and also diminish her chance of that vital second operation, the one that would

165

change her from John Merrick into Keira Knightley in the flash of a skilled scalpel. Well, that was the plan anyway.

She pulled Travis's laptop closer to her. Maybe he was right. She should play games. Catapult angry birds and stupid zombies. Move brightly coloured candy into rows and watch them disintegrate into even brighter showers of colour. She sighed. The pain in her leg was making concentration almost impossible. She needed more than just mind-numbing games.

She looked at the piece of paper that Travis had left, and decided to take a look at one of his iffy info sites. It was part of the dark web and first she had to download a Tor browser. Then Cat tapped in the URL address and waited. For a while there was only a dark screen, there was obviously a lot of data being downloaded, then a box appeared mid-screen. It opened very slowly and flame-coloured letters spilled out. As they landed, they spelt out the words, *Sophia's Key. Wisdom at your fingertips. Press to enter.*

Cat pressed. All that came up was a plain black screen with a centralised white search box. 'Ah,' she whispered to herself, 'What do I really want to know about?' She thought for a moment, then remembered something that the sarge had told her earlier when he and the boss had visited her. Apparently Lawrence Carpenter had filled in some more background on the beautiful victim of Operation Windmill.

She stared at the keyboard and then typed in *Man jailed in Magda Hellekamp Stalker case.*

She had barely lifted her finger from the Enter button, when a massive list hit her screen. Discussion boards, blogs and God-knows-what trailed down the page. 'Wow!' This was impressive, although some of the site names made Cat's warning bells jingle a little tune. Maybe she should tread carefully.

After an hour Cat had forgotten about the pain in her leg. It might have been the painkillers, or it could have been the fascinating journey that she had just taken around the Netherlands' cyberspace (fortunately the sites were either in

English or Google translate did the job, with a bit of cutting and pasting).

I need a damned printer, she cursed silently, as she scribbled down some of the best sites, then murmured, 'This is extraordinary stuff. And this is only the first of Travis's alternative sites. What the hell are the more sensitive ones like?'

'Talking to oneself is not a good sign. I think maybe you should endeavour to get some sleep, don't you?'

Cat had not even heard the door open, let alone one of the night nurses approaching the bed.

She looked up at the wall clock. It was almost one o'clock. 'Sorry. The pain was getting to me so I tried some distractions.'

The man looked at her with interest. 'You're the detective, aren't you?'

Cat nodded. This was a new nurse, and his uniform was different to the others.

'It's alright.' He seemed to read her mind. 'I'm agency. My name is Todd. Is there anything I can get you?'

My old face back, thought Cat. Or maybe two strong legs to chase the bad guys with. 'No, I'm fine, thanks.' She closed down the laptop, placed it in her locker and eased herself gently down the bed. 'You're right, it is late. Good night.'

* * *

It had taken Nikki a good five minutes to bring the distraught Joseph to his senses and get him refocussed.

The first thing they did was go outside to the car and phone Vinnie on the safe phone. They told him what had happened and, unlike Joseph, Vinnie was instantly geared up.

'Right, there are nine services on the A1M, and if you think she said she was about an hour away, that would make it either Baldock, or more likely Peterborough. Get one of your guys to ring them and ask . . . oh hell, you don't need me to tell you what they should ask.' He paused for a moment. 'I think you two should stay put, in case she calls again. Meanwhile I'll drive up to the junction of Cloud Fen

Lane and the main road in. It's late for a cab to be out this way. When I see it turn off, I'll flag him down and check all is well, okay?'

Joseph nodded, and Nikki said, 'Thank you, Vinnie, we appreciate it.'

'No problem. And tomorrow we strip out everything the bastard put into your places, and sod the fact that we will be giving away our hand. It'll piss him off, but at least I can rig things up so he can't spy on you again.'

'Let's talk tomorrow when we've sorted out this scare with Tamsin.'

'Will do. And, Nikki? Tell Joseph I don't think Snipe will hurt his girl. Don't ask me why, but I get the feeling that if he is involved with what has happened to Tamsin, this is a scare tactic not a real threat to her life.'

'I'll do that, and thanks again.'

Joseph then called the station and asked them to make all relevant enquiries and ring him back on his temporary number.

The call came in less than five minutes. A young woman fitting Tamsin's description had been at the Extra Service Station at Peterborough and had been picked up by a local cab company. The company was kosher, and the uniformed sergeant had asked their control to radio the cab in transit and make sure that the driver stopped for no one, other than the man with the Land Rover stationed at the Cloud Fen turn-off.

Knowing that, Joseph visibly began to unwind.

Nikki felt for him. He had been treading on eggshells with both Tamsin and his ex-wife for years, and just when things were beginning to come together, this happened. She knew for a fact that since being injured on duty, Joseph had made a mammoth effort to make Tamsin understand that he was no longer the dedicated career soldier who put Queen and country before wife and daughter. He was a very different man to the one who went away to fight. But things like that took time, and the slightest upset could tip the balance and destroy all that he had done.

'If I'd told her not to come here over the phone, at the one time when she needed me, I'm willing to bet I'd never have seen her again.' Joseph ran a hand through his hair and shook his head. 'It'll be bad enough doing it face to face, but at least she can't slam the phone down on me.'

'So where will you take her?' Nikki asked.

'I'm still trying to work that one out. First I need to know what happened to her "travel plans," and why she's in this area at all. Her mother lives in Edinburgh now, and Tamsin shares a flat with two other uni students in Exeter, so what she's doing in Peterborough, I have no idea.'

Nikki gave it some thought then said, 'I think we should take her to the nick.' She stared at him. 'Would you say she's a sensitive girl?'

Joseph nodded vehemently. 'That's why we are where we are now. Unlike other kids in army families, Tamsin took every tour of duty as a personal rejection of her and her mother. Plus, in her world, killing people does not make you an acceptable human being. Whenever her dad came home, while all the other fathers were hailed as heroes, I was just a killer who put my vile job before my family. '

'That must have been pretty tough.'

'I can't tell you how much it hurt. But I love her. I always have.'

'Then I think maybe I should shoulder some of the blame for what you are going to have to tell her. And if you say she's sensitive, we'll give her a chance to notice the photos on the whiteboard, so she can see that Greenborough is not exactly Shangri-la at present. She's no kid anymore. She needs to know that keeping her safe is your one and only directive.'

'Even so, I predict a riot.'

'Then allow me to wade in with my two-penny worth. I'm sure I can make her see reason.' She gave him a Machiavellian smile. 'One way or another.'

Joseph gave her a wan smile. 'Best of luck. As you say, she's no kid anymore, but she's still a feisty one.'

'How old is she now?'

'Coming up to twenty-three.'

Nikki thought about Tamsin. She had met her only twice and was struck on both occasions by the resemblance to her father. Tamsin was tall and willowy, had the same fair hair, and had inherited Joseph's incredible eyes. Eyes that could have belonged to a poet or an artist. Or, just as easily, an Olympic gold medal winner or a soldier. Whatever, they were always full of commitment. For Joseph, that meant loyalty to his work, his team and his daughter. Apparently, in Tamsin's case, it meant saving the planet and righting all the wrongs in the world.

'Is she still fighting for the rainforests and snow leopards?'

'Oh yes, but now you can add the polar ice cap and every known endangered species.'

'I don't remember Hannah having such high ideals.' Nikki felt a lurch in her chest when she thought about her daughter. 'She was an emotional and driven teenager, but sadly most of her energies were wasted on trying to impress the wrong people.' Anger and a feeling of being cheated out of Hannah's best years threatened to overwhelm her, but she pushed them away. Hannah was gone, but Joseph's daughter was still very much alive, and right now she was heading into dangerous territory. This was no time for morbid thoughts and recriminations.

Joseph looked at his watch. 'They should be here in half an hour and I agree about going to the police station, but where then? I want her as far from Greenborough as possible.' He chewed anxiously on the side of his thumb. 'But I want her to trust me, and not think that I'm just trying to get rid of her because I'm too busy with work.'

'Leave that to me.' Nikki adopted a firm expression. 'She'll understand, when I tell her what happened to Cat and the young copper who was standing next to her.'

'I'm sure you're right, but I'm just terrified of rocking the boat. I want my daughter back.' Joseph's face creased up into a mask of pain. 'Oh, Nikki, I'm sorry! That was one hell of an insensitive thing to say to you. I didn't think before I opened my stupid mouth.'

'It's alright. I know how important it is for you to heal the past with Tamsin.' Nikki smiled gently at him. 'And *you* have the chance to do it. It's too late for Hannah and me, but that doesn't mean I resent you getting it right with your girl.'

'I just can't believe how bad the timing was for her to ring me. You know how long I've waited to have her stay with me, even just for a day.'

Nikki stiffened. It really was one heck of a coincidence. She exhaled noisily and tried to quell the thought. She was in danger of becoming neurotic about Snipe. It would be very easy to blame everything that happened on him and forget that life had its own way of throwing spanners in the works, without the aid of a vengeful psycho. She sighed. 'I know. She couldn't have picked a worse time.'

For the next twenty minutes they talked about anything and everything in an attempt to keep from wearing a track in the sitting-room carpet. To say that they felt jittery was an understatement, and in the end they fell into a silence, one that was loaded with tension.

'Let's wait outside,' said Nikki, anxious to lose the feeling that the walls were closing in on her.

Joseph was at the door in three strides, then paused. 'Don't forget Snipe still has surveillance on the front and back doors.'

'Then he'll see her arrive no matter what.' That's if he didn't organise the whole shebang in the first place, she thought. 'And we are not staying, are we? As soon as we see that Tamsin's safe, it's into the car and off to the nick.' She stood beside him and listened to the hushed sound of the night wind off the estuary. 'I think we should all stay at the station tonight. There's a futon in my office. Tamsin can have that, and you and I, well, we can doss down somewhere, can't we?'

Joseph sucked in air. 'I guess that's best. And it would give us until the morning to sort something out for her.' His voice fell to almost a whisper. 'It's in my head to put her on a train up to her mother. As Snipe is so busy terrorising us, he won't want to take time out to travel to Scotland.'

'Let's find out why she's here in the first place, before you pack her off to the glens. She may not take kindly to being bundled out of the way and back to Mummy. She's old enough to decide for herself where she'd like to go, within reason.'

Joseph straightened. 'My phone.' He slipped the mobile from his pocket and pressed the loudspeaker button as he answered it.

'She's safe, mate.'

Vinnie's voice and what he said was the best they could have hoped for.

'Thank you, Vinnie.' Joseph let out a little whoop of relief. 'I can't tell you how glad I am to hear that.'

'She'll be with you in no time, Bunny, and you can see for yourself. And hey! She's a cracker, isn't she? Even if she did give me the evil eye for flagging down her taxi.'

'We'll see you tomorrow, Vin. I'll ring you early, okay?'

'Sure thing. We'll talk then.'

'Thanks again. I owe you one.'

'The bill is going up by the day, mate, but you're welcome.'

The phone clicked off, and as it did Nikki heard an engine. 'She's here.'

Together they walked to the edge of the drive and waited beside the road. Soon the two bright headlights turned into the dark shape of a big old Toyota. A second or two later, it ground to a slow halt and the driver cut the engine.

'Blimey! Where is this? World's End?' A short, stocky man with a bald head and a badly moulded face got out and opened the rear door for Tamsin. 'Give us your bag, love. Apparently this is home sweet home!'

The young woman stepped out and again Nikki was amazed by her looks. The girl was simply stunning.

Joseph was paying the driver, and from the wide-eyed expression on his funny face, giving him the kind of tip that doesn't come along too often.

As the car turned and drove back up the lane, Tamsin looked around in surprise.

'What's going on, Dad? Who was that tall man who stopped us? And . . .' she looked at her watch, 'Inspector Galena? Why are you here? It's almost one in the morning.'

Before Joseph could answer, Nikki grasped Tamsin's hand. 'We're really glad you're safe, Tamsin, but something has happened, something serious, and we can't stay here. We are going back to the police station, then we'll get you some food and explain, okay?'

'No, actually it isn't.' The girl stood up straight and used her inch or two of extra height to look down on Nikki. 'Look, I'm totally knackered. I've had a dreadful day, and if it's all the same, I'd like a shower and a bed, not a drive to a police station.'

Nikki caught Joseph throwing her an "I told you so" look, before he said, 'We have an ongoing situation here, sweetheart, and as Nikki just said, we can't stay. The cottage is not safe. Now . . .'

A baleful look flooded Tamsin's face. 'Oh, that's absolutely perfect, isn't it? Just when I thought the day couldn't get any worse.'

Nikki had a sudden picture of Cat's face. Then she saw a hospital trolley and blood-soaked dressings. 'I don't know why you've had such a piss-poor day, girl, but we have one dead officer, smashed to a pulp by a truck, and one of our team, a pretty kid, will never look quite the same again. So forgive me, but I'm betting that your day isn't half as bad as ours.' She returned the look with a blazing one of her own. 'Now, into my vehicle. Before we go any further with this, we are getting to a place of safety, understood?'

Tamsin turned pale. Then she nodded.

Joseph looked as if he were about to have a go at Nikki for her harshness, then suddenly he turned away and locked the cottage door. 'We'll explain en route,' he said quietly. 'I'm really sorry, Tam, but I promise we'll explain everything.' He forced a small smile at his daughter. 'And we do have facilities at the nick. They tell me the women's shower room is really very nice.'

The atmosphere in the car was frosty, but at least there were no more outbursts and in twenty minutes they were in Nikki's office.

On the way there she had ordered takeaways for the three of them and sent one of the night shift officers to get them hot drinks. She drew two chairs close to her desk and pointed to them. 'First things first, Tamsin. What happened to you? From the beginning.'

'Don't you generally use interview rooms and leather straps to grill your victims?' The attempt at sarcasm fell flat.

Nikki smiled. 'Sometimes. But you are not a victim. And it's because we don't want you to become one that we are here.' She looked up as the coffees arrived and indicated the desk. 'Just there, thanks.'

As the door closed, she passed a drink towards Tamsin. 'Now, tell us what happened.'

It seemed as if the girl suddenly knew that there was no getting out of this. She clasped her drink to her, as if for warmth, sat back and said, 'All right.' She blew on the hot drink for a moment, then said, 'Actually it was really weird. Gemma, a uni friend of mine and I were going up to Edinburgh.' She looked almost apologetically at her father. 'Mother has organised an interview for me with a big company in the city. A real chance for when I finish uni. And as Gem had always wanted to see Edinburgh and she has a faster car, we thought we'd make a holiday break of it.'

Nikki glanced at her one small travel bag, but the girl saw her. She said, 'I suppose detectives have to be suspicious, but it's the truth. I have plenty of clothes at Mum's house. I can afford to travel light when I go to Scotland.' She sipped her drink then carried on. 'Gem's not keen on the M1, so we decided on the A1M and we'd share the driving. We left later than we'd planned so we decided to stop overnight in York.' She paused and pulled a face. 'But we never got that far. We pulled into Peterborough Services to fill up and some bastard stole my phone.'

Joseph's face darkened. 'Your smartphone?'

She nodded. 'With all my contacts on it.'

'Did you report it stolen?'

'I was going to, but then it all went wrong.' Her face had lost its aggrieved look. Now she just seemed tired and upset. 'Gem got this call from her parents' home in Dorset. Her mother had collapsed and been rushed to hospital. Apparently it was serious.' She gave a little shrug. 'What could I do? I didn't want to miss my interview, and I knew that Dad lived about an hour away, so I told her to go, that I'd make my way to Dad's place, and liaise with Mum from there.'

'So what was so weird about it? It sounds very sad, but not actually weird,' Joseph asked. 'Expensive phones get nicked all the time, and people get bad news,' he raised an eyebrow, 'and usually at the most inopportune moments.'

'That's not the weird bit.' Tamsin looked at him anxiously. 'Gem has a phobia about being out of touch, so if she's going anywhere, she always takes a spare phone, a PAYG throwaway. She lent it to me when mine got stolen, and she rang me on it while I was in the cab on the way here.' Her voice dropped and she looked from Nikki to Joseph. 'When she got down to South Mimms service station, she pulled in for a wee and rang the hospital. They had never heard of her mother.' She swallowed. 'Then when she rang home, her mother answered the phone. She was fine. It was all a hoax, Dad. Just a hoax.' She looked at Nikki. 'And now I feel as if I've landed in the middle of a Cold War film. What's all the secrecy? What *is* going on here?'

Over the next twenty minutes, Nikki and Joseph told her all they deemed necessary.

And when Joseph went out to refresh their drinks, Nikki made quite sure that Tamsin understood the distress her father had been feeling, knowing that she would be walking into a virtual siege situation, but not wanting to turn her away.

'I know I'm a first-class bitch sometimes.' Tamsin looked at Nikki and gave her a rueful smile. 'I'm sorry. When I phoned, I sensed he was less than thrilled to hear from me, but I thought it was going to be just another "job comes first" situation. Now, well, I understand why he was so worried.' She drew in a breath. 'I'll ring my mother in the morning. Perhaps Dad would be able to put me on a train? Then when this is all over, I'll try to come and stay for a few days, spend some time with him for once.' She gave Nikki a warmer smile. 'I think it's time I tried to see our past history from his point of view. No promises that I'll understand, but I'll try.'

'He'll be so pleased to hear that, Tam. It's all he wants.' She looked at the familiar-but-different eyes. 'And I'm sorry I was so hard on you back at the cottage, but you can see now that I was concerned for your safety.'

'Forget it. I deserved it, flouncing in like some prima donna when you guys have a killer running loose.'

'You weren't to know that.' Nikki stopped, then suddenly said, 'I had a daughter too. She was a bit younger than you.' She swallowed. It was probably too early to be talking like this but she felt that, for Joseph's sake, it needed to be said.

'*Had* a daughter?'

'She died a few weeks ago. But the thing is, we didn't see eye to eye either. Now she's gone, I realise that instead of fighting, we should have made an effort to find a little bit of common ground, some neutral territory, and make some time for each other.' She fought back tears, and said, 'When she was young, we had some wonderful, magical times, but later things changed, and now I can't turn back the clock and do things differently. Your dad loves you very much, Tamsin, and he'll never give up trying to make things good between you.'

Tamsin stared silently down into her lap.

'And the young officer who was killed, he was around your age too. I keep hoping that when he left for work that morning, he kissed his wife and told her he loved her.'

176

Tears formed in Tamsin's eyes. 'I hear what you are saying, DI Galena.'

'Nikki. Call me Nikki. And Tam? I know a little about your issues with your dad. While I have no idea what kind of soldier he was, I do know that he's a damned good policeman. He has the respect of every officer on this station and I'd trust him with my life.' She paused. 'Although, come to think of it, I already do that every day that I work with him.' She took two tissues from a box on her desk and passed one to the young woman. 'Remember, just find some common ground, and start to build on it.'

She looked up as the door opened and Joseph appeared carrying another tray of drinks and several bags of food. 'What have I missed?' He looked in surprise at the tissues and the two sets of red eyes.

'Girl stuff,' murmured Nikki, sniffing hard.

'Absolutely,' added Tamsin, snorting heartily into the tissue. 'Now, when we've finally got to eat this takeaway, perhaps you'll point me in the direction of those fantastic shower rooms that you were telling me about?'

CHAPTER NINETEEN

At around six in the morning Joseph drove out of Greenborough and across the fen lanes to a spot on the marsh where he knew there were old wooden bird-hides. He'd been there before when things got tough, just to sit and think.

The narrow single-lane track was lined almost to shoulder height with grasses, spiked broad-leaved reeds and brilliant yellow rapeseed that had self-sown after the last harvest. He knew that the wall of gently waving greenery and flowers concealed a deceptively deep ditch, one that he was anxious to keep out of.

He carefully steered the big vehicle around the long winding lane, knowing that when the mist lifted, it would be a stifling hot day.

As he got close to the route of the wide tidal river, he pulled into a small roughly concreted area surrounded by stubby trees and shrubs, and parked the car. Opposite him was the mud-caked Land Rover belonging to Vinnie Silver.

He locked the car, offered a swift prayer that it would still be there when he returned, and set off through the treeline and down the grass path to the copse that housed the hides.

Vinnie was waiting for him. He was sitting on the rickety wooden steps to one of the disused hides, and staring out across the watery landscape of shallow lagoons and marshy wetland. 'Reminds me of Vietnam, although hopefully we aren't about to get ambushed by the Cong.'

'You never fought in Vietnam! That was the sixties!'

'Well I've seen *The Killing Fields* a dozen times.' Vinnie gazed lazily around the lonely place. 'It has a strange feel to it, don't you think? Kind of old, no, more like primeval.'

'Sometimes it feels that way, but when the dawn light glints off the water and everywhere is bathed in a green/gold hue, it seems almost like Eden.'

'Bloody hell! Wordsworth lives! Reincarnated in the body of a copper.' Vinnie gave a mighty laugh, and a surprised pheasant took off with a noisy clatter of wings. 'So, why here?'

'I needed to feel that we were completely alone. No distractions, no surveillance and no listening devices.'

'Fair enough. And?' Joseph's friend knew him very well.

'And this morning I looked at my daughter, sleeping on a futon in the boss's office, and it nearly broke my heart when I realised that I'd missed all those years of her growing up, changing from a child to a woman.'

'So instead of drinking that moment in, and savouring it like nectar, you wanted to run away to a boggy mire and watch geese flying by with an ageing squaddie? Bunny, I frankly doubt your sanity.'

'Put like that, I'm inclined to agree.' Joseph sat down beside him. 'Tamsin is going up to Scotland this morning. Her mother is going to meet her in Edinburgh.' He drew in a long breath. 'She says that she'll come back when this is over, but . . .' He pulled a face.

'Then she will.' Vinnie turned and squeezed his shoulder. 'If she has anything of you in her, she'll have appreciated the deep shit you guys are in right now. She'll want to talk to you when things calm down, I'm bloody certain of it.'

'I hope so.' He forced a smile. 'But now, what plans do you have regarding Snipe?'

Vinnie straightened up. 'Plenty. But first, I'm going to strip both your places out of everything he's set up. Forget alerting him to what we know. I'll sweep again for bugs and any other form of hidden surveillance equipment and then I'm going to set up a bit of technology of my own, something that will warn the bastard off setting foot on Cloud Fen again, unless he wants us to see his pretty face as wallpaper on our laptops.'

'And the station? What about his watching the nick?'

'If he's got cameras in there, and I'm sure he will have, you can consider them gone. And I won't even have to set foot in the building.' He grinned maliciously. 'I can find them, block them, and destroy them with a nasty little bug of my own. My company has some very bright youngsters working for it right now and I'm *very* glad they are on my side.'

'Can we help you at all?'

'No. I'm better working alone. And as you have no idea who Snipe is, it's best I remain in the background. I'll ring you when I'm through, and we'll organise a command post so that I can monitor anything that Snipe endeavours to do electronically.'

'Great.' Joseph watched as a pair of oystercatchers coasted into the lagoons to feed. 'I must get back now. I'm going to pick up some breakfast and hopefully get back before Tamsin wakes up. Plus I have the feeling that today is going to be hellish busy.' He looked anxiously at Vinnie. 'And you? What about your own business?'

'It's in good hands, Bunny. Fear not, I'm with you until the fat lady sings.'

* * *

Tamsin looked at the McDonald's box with a worried expression on her face, then she opened it and smiled down at the toasted bagel. 'You remembered.'

'Hope it's okay? It's got Philadelphia on it. There's not too much choice for a veggie around here at this time of the morning.' Joseph passed her a beaker of black coffee. 'Did you sleep?'

180

'On and off.' She nibbled around the edge of the bagel, then placed it back in its cardboard tray. 'I kept thinking about the photos on that board in the CID office.' She gave a little shiver. 'There's so much of that kind of thing on the television that you think nothing of it, until you see something for real. How could anyone do those terrible things?'

'Sadly, all too easily,' said Nikki, tipping a sachet of ketchup onto her bacon and egg McMuffin. 'But we'll get him.' Her face hardened. 'Oh yes, we'll get this one alright.'

'I certainly hope so.' Tamsin turned to her father. 'What time is the train, Dad?'

'10.15 from Peterborough. We have a squad car arranged to take us to the station, and your mother will be at the other end. It's a fast train, only four hours.'

'Oh God! Four hours with no iPhone,' groaned Tamsin.

'You could try a book . . .' suggested Nikki. 'But maybe not a crime thriller.' She broke off to answer the desk phone.

'I do love family reunions, don't you, Detective Inspector? Oh, sorry, I forgot, with a mad father and a dead daughter, you don't have much in the way of family left.'

The distorted voice made Nikki drop her food and, placing her hand over the receiver, she mouthed, 'Joseph! Trace this!'

'And don't bother with the trace. I'm not silly enough to stay on here long enough. I just have a message for the sergeant. Well, it's more of a question really. Ask him if he's sure that sending such a pretty young woman off on a long journey all alone is wise? Oh, and tell Tamsin her phone was most useful.'

Nikki drew in a breath, about to speak, but all she heard was a howling noise and then silence. She swallowed, then stood up and walked to the door. 'Tam, excuse me, I won't be a minute. I need to report that call.' She hurried out into the CID office and saw Joseph at Niall's desk, replacing a receiver and shaking his head.

'No chance, boss. He was only on for a matter of seconds.' He looked at her expectantly.

'We have a problem,' she whispered, then told the two men, word for word, what had been said.

Neither of them spoke for a moment, then Niall gave Joseph a determined look and stood up. 'If that's the case and you still want her to go to Edinburgh, then you can't put her on that train, Sarge. I'll drive her. I'll take her directly home to her mother. She'll be safe with me, I promise you. I won't let her out of my sight.' He gave his boss a boyish grin to lift the taut atmosphere, 'Even if she does have to wee in a bottle rather than leave the car.'

'Women can't do that, numpty, but I do appreciate your offer.' Joseph looked at Nikki. 'What do you think, guv?'

'All the time she's here we are going to be on tenterhooks. We have to get her to a safe place, no question. But isn't she still vulnerable at her mother's house? Snipe knows everything about us, and that probably includes where your ex lives.'

'I'm still certain that *we* are his main targets, that he's just using Tamsin to scare the shit out of me. It's all about fear, isn't it? About what scares us the most.' He bit on his lower lip, then looked up determinedly. 'I'll talk to her mother, tell her the whole situation and get her to take Tamsin away for a few days, somewhere safe where no one would know her. She'll hate me for it, but tough. I want Tamsin as far away from Greenborough as possible.'

'Then yes, do it, as soon as possible.' She narrowed her eyes. 'And I suggest we disguise her in some way to get her out of the station, just in case we really are being watched.'

'What about one of Yvonne's spare uniforms, ma'am?' Niall offered. 'She always keeps a change of clothes in her locker. Seeing a WPC going out wouldn't alert him to anything.'

'Good thinking. Is Yvonne in yet?'

'No, but she won't be long. I'll catch her and we'll sort something out.' He hurried off, leaving Nikki and Joseph in the empty office.

'So the son of a bitch *did* orchestrate Tamsin's "detour" to Greenborough,' growled Joseph.

'I think we'd already worked that one out when we heard about the hoax on her travelling companion.' She glanced back towards her office. 'Now, what do we tell Tamsin?'

Joseph shrugged. 'Change of plans? It's too dangerous leaving her alone on a train. We are going to get her chauffeured to auld Reekie, courtesy of the Fenland Constabulary, etc. etc. etc.?'

'Okay, let's get it over with, and I suggest you ring Midlothian Police and put them in the picture too.'

Joseph nodded and together they went back into the office and closed the door.

* * *

Cat was back online and barely managed to find time for breakfast. Travis's sites had opened a whole new world for her, one that just might make her a useful part of the investigation, even if she had to stay in hospital a bit longer.

She gave a little grunt of excitement as another batch of answers spewed out of the search engine, but hell, she really needed to talk to the sarge. Some of the stuff that she was picking up didn't tie in with what he had told her, and she was pretty certain that the info she had dredged up from the dark side of the Internet was true. Well, in essence, at least. One thing she was sure of, Magda Hellekamp's life was not what it originally seemed. Posted comments, underground articles and discussion boards were throwing up alternatives all the time.

She let out a loud sigh of frustration. She wanted some help from the CID office, and she wanted a bloody printer. She also wanted some relief from the pain in her leg. It seemed to be getting worse, even though she was being given brain-blasting amounts of analgesics.

If only she could get home. It would be so much easier.

She put the laptop to one side and closed her eyes. When her doctor arrived for the daily ward round, she would ask about getting out. She was sure that she had less chance of picking up an infection in her own home. And she could work from there. She was absolutely certain that the team could use some of the information she had in her head and on the dozens of scribbled scraps of paper that were strewn across her bed.

She let out a soft curse, knowing that there was no one there to hear her. It was such a bloody unbelievable thing to happen. In the middle of a big murder enquiry, she gets hurt and completely cut off from her team, and that was without the trauma of seeing a colleague murdered right in front of you.

The sight of Danny Wilshire flying forward on the grill of the Barbarian still came to her in flashes and, depressingly, she knew they probably always would. All she could hope for was that the passing of time would make them less vivid, and the emotions tied inextricably to them, less raw.

She opened her eyes. Right now the best she could do was to keep working.

With a heavy heart, she pulled the laptop back towards her and, trying to push the pain away, stepped back into the secret world of Magda Hellekamp.

CHAPTER TWENTY

At just before 9 a.m., "WPC" Tamsin Easter and PC Niall Farrow walked purposefully across the car park, got into Niall's car and drove quickly from the police station. Joseph watched from a first floor window and decided that there was nothing about their departure to give the slightest cause for suspicion. His daughter, her hair pushed neatly beneath the borrowed uniform bowler, and wearing a Hi-Viz vest complete with radio, and black trousers with an equipment belt, looked every inch the regular young beat bobby. Joseph looked after the departing car and felt a rush of love sweep over him. He had tried hard in the past to make things right. Now he would try even harder. A little more effort and he might . . . he might just get his daughter back.

'Joseph?' Nikki dragged him back to the present. 'The super wants us in his office in ten.' She watched over his shoulder as the tail end of Niall's car disappeared from view. 'Now we just have to wait for the call to say that she's safe with her mother.'

'Don't worry about that. I've made them promise to check in with me on the throw-away number every hour.' He gave her a lopsided smile. 'I swear she only agreed to go because Niall said she could use his new Air Gesture Galaxy S4 Smart phone.'

'What the hell? Air what?'

He raised an eyebrow. 'Don't ask me. Technology is getting beyond me too.'

'Technology.' Nikki's voice was little more than a whisper. 'So much of this case comes back to technology, doesn't it? Maybe we should run covert checks on everyone on the staff or affiliated to us who has expert knowledge in that field? What do you think?'

Joseph puffed out his cheeks. 'Maybe we should, although everyone within the station, both police officers and civilians, are vetted at the highest level.'

'It won't hurt to double check. I'll tell Jim Hunter and maybe he could get his team to put that in motion.' She picked up the phone and after a few moments, thanked her colleague and replaced the receiver. 'He agrees and he's going to check everyone from the cybercrime unit and the IT specialists, to the guys who installed the security cameras. It might be a waste of time, but on the other hand . . .' she shrugged. 'With Snipe, we can't afford to leave anything to chance.'

'DI Galena! Got something for you.' Sheila Robbins, the office manager, called across, waving a large brown envelope. 'It's marked urgent and it's from Professor Wilkinson.'

Nikki hurried over and took the envelope, tearing it open almost before it had left Sheila's hands. 'It's the DNA report on the blood found in the boot of my car.' She read the report, then looked at him, her expression a mixture of disbelief and shock.

'Well? Is it anyone known to us?' he asked urgently.

'Not in the sense you mean. I mean, it's not a criminal. It's . . .'

Joseph realised that she was having trouble coming to terms with what she was reading. He reached out and took the report from her.

DNA analysis has identified a match from records already on our database. Blood from crime scene belongs to Brian Anthony Faulkner. No present details on file.

Joseph looked at Nikki and frowned. The name that had drained the colour from her face meant nothing to him.

'He was my first skipper, Joseph. He retired years ago with poor health. He's a highly decorated officer.' She looked at him with sadness in her eyes, but anger on her lips. 'He's one of us, Joseph, and his blood was in my boot.'

* * *

Rick Bainbridge stood behind his desk and stared down at the DNA result. It was several moments before he spoke.

'I haven't heard from Brian in years. He was sick for a long while.'

'Sick in what way?' asked Joseph.

'He was dealing with a bad case, Sergeant. A very bad case, and he probably did himself no favours by working on when he should have backed off.' Rick lowered himself down into his chair. 'He took early retirement and,' he shrugged, his face a mask of regret, 'I'm sad to say, we lost touch. I heard that he became something of a recluse, and I have no idea where he is now.'

'Me neither,' added Nikki. 'Yvonne is running a search for me. Hopefully we'll track him through the electoral roll or utilities.'

'Is there anyone left at the station who remained friends with him that you know of? Someone who may know where he lives?'

Nikki shook her head. 'The only one that I know of who kept in contact for a while was Bob Wilshire.' She drew in air. 'And of course, he's dead.'

'And so is his son, so we can't even ask him.'

Nikki's face tightened. 'Ironic, isn't it? Brian is one of our own. *We* don't know where he is, but bloody Snipe does.'

Rick nodded gravely. 'I'm forced to think that whoever Snipe is, he knows you very well, Nikki. 'Few people would recall Brian, and that he was your uniformed sergeant.'

'*And* he was Bob Wilshire's too,' said Joseph slowly. 'I wonder if there's something in that.' He looked thoughtfully at the superintendent. 'Like a connection to a case that DI Galena *and* Bob Wilshire were involved in?'

'Then get one of your team to look into it.' Rick ran a hand over his deep-set, craggy brow. 'I don't need to tell you how urgent it is that we identify this Snipe. I am very troubled that he knows so much about us and we know sod all about him.'

'Aren't we all, sir,' muttered Nikki.

'What is most frightening is his complete lack of compassion. He is brutal and merciless, and he knows our weak points too damn well. He's playing a vicious game and only he knows the rules.' He stood up again and began to pace his office. 'I notice that when he rang you this time, there was no mention of this *compensation*, was there?'

'None. He said only what I told you.' She stood up. 'I'd better go and see what Yvonne has found. And we need to go visit Windsor Morton, Jeremy Bow and the French family. I'll tell you the minute we know something.'

As they left, Joseph glanced back and saw Rick Bainbridge sitting stock still, staring at some point in the distance. His eyes were filled with worry, and also something Joseph decided was reproach. Maybe the super and Brian Faulkner had been buddies? But everyone knows that as time moves on, some old friendships falter.

As he closed the door, Joseph thought that perhaps that particular friendship had not faltered but failed, and Rick Bainbridge was suffering because he had failed too.

* * *

Nikki approached her office door and saw Dave hurrying towards her. At first she thought he had some news about one of the cases. Then she noticed the pallor of his face and that his clothes looked as if they had been slept in.

'Sorry, I'm late in, ma'am, but I need to talk to you urgently.' He glanced around, 'and sarge as well if he's available.'

Nikki beckoned to Joseph who was just about to check his computer for messages.

Once inside the office she closed the door. 'Whatever's wrong?'

Dave slumped into a chair, then leaned forward and handed her a sheaf of papers. 'This,' he said wretchedly, 'this is what's wrong.'

Nikki took the papers and saw that they were bank statements. She looked at them, realised immediately why the man was so distraught, then passed them to Joseph. 'When did you discover this, Dave?'

'Last night. I received a couple of letters asking for payment of outstanding bills, and I have no outstanding bills, ma'am. Never.'

Joseph let out a low whistle. 'This big account, Dave, what was it?'

'My wife's parents left her their house when they died. Because my wages were sufficient for our needs, we sold it and banked the money into that high-interest account.' He looked miserably at them. 'We've never needed to touch it, but I know that because of my wife's care home bills, I'll be dipping into it pretty soon.' He paused, then added, 'We were going to use it for our retirement, for some fun. I don't know why, but we never once considered illness, let alone poor Margaret succumbing to Alzheimer's.'

Nikki shuddered at the word Alzheimer's, and wondered how often that happened. That wonderful planned retirement, nipped in the bud for one of a dozen awful reasons. 'You've reported this, Dave?'

'I phoned the bank immediately.'

'And now you need to log it as a crime.' Nikki looked across to Joseph, 'It's Snipe, isn't it? He's played another dirty hand in his poxy game.'

'Almost certainly.' Joseph handed back the paperwork to Nikki. 'But hang on in there, mate. We'll get it sorted.'

'But, Sarge, he's taken everything I have. And what about Margaret? I can't pay the nursing home, I can't pay the mortgage, I can't even fill my car!'

'I'm going to tell the super.' Nikki stood up, clasping the statements. 'Come with me, Dave. He'll get things moving for you.' She gripped Dave's arm as she moved towards the door. 'Try not to panic. As long as you can prove that you keep your computer up to date with security protection, most banks will ensure that you don't lose your money. But Rick Bainbridge will know exactly what to do.'

* * *

As Nikki and Dave hurried towards the lift, Joseph returned to his computer. The first thing he saw when he accessed his emails was a message from Cat.

Hi Sarge. Need to see you. Can you come and visit? Have found some interesting info on Windmill. Make it soon, please! Cat.

Joseph skimmed through the other stuff in his in-box but nothing needed immediate attention so he pulled out his private phone and rang her mobile.

She answered almost immediately. 'Sarge? Brilliant! Can you get over here?'

'I'll try, but things are pretty fraught here.' He told her about Dave's problem.

'Shit! That's awful! Poor Dave, he must be beside himself.'

'He's well cut up about it, and so would I be.'

'Listen, Sarge, tell him I have some money, not a fortune, but enough to tide him over until the bank sorts things out for him.'

Joseph smiled to himself. That was Cat for you. No hesitation. A mate needed help and there she was. 'I'll tell him as soon as he's back from the super's office.' He stared at his monitor as they spoke, and noticed a new message from Ireland. He opened it and saw a request to ring Liam Feehily.

'Look, Cat, can you tell me what it is you've uncovered?'

'Not over the phone, Sarge. We need to talk face to face. And I need a notepad, a big one. A4 size, with lots of pages.'

'What exactly are you doing? This doesn't sound like rest and recuperation to me.'

'As good as. I'm trying to stay sane.'

'And your injuries? How are they coming along?'

There was a sigh from the other end. 'They are not coming along anywhere near fast enough for my liking. The doc should be here soon and I'm going to tell him I want out, but until this infection in my leg backs off, I can't see it happening. That's why I need to see you.'

'Okay, I'll get there. I just need to clear it with the boss, and I have a call that I'm expecting, from Tamsin. I'll take that, then I'll see you, okay?'

'Thanks, Sarge. Much appreciated. And it'll be worth it, I promise.'

After he hung up, Joseph smiled. He had known from the start that she wouldn't be using her iPad for playing Candy Crush Saga.

'How is she?' Yvonne Collins walked up to his desk.

'Impatient. Bored. In pain. Frustrated. You name it and Cat is suffering from it.'

'And she will until she gets back here where she belongs.' Yvonne shook her head. 'I think we'd all feel the same.'

Joseph agreed, then added. 'Any luck on tracing Brian Faulkner?'

'That's what I need to talk to you about, Sarge. It's nothing definite, but I do have a hunch where he is.' She walked over to a large wall map of their area. 'There's a cottage, way out here on Silent Fen.' She stabbed her finger on a remote part of the marsh, 'It's tucked away down a lane that used to lead to the old Dredger's Quay, but that place was demolished years ago when the new docking area was built nearer the estuary. It's a real ramshackle cottage that still uses well water and has an outside karzy. Know the kind of place I mean?'

He nodded and looked at her with interest. 'Why do you think Faulkner is there?'

'Well, according to the records, the place is owned by a Mrs Marion Weir, but I know for a fact that it is inhabited by a single man. Niall and I had to go out there a couple of months back when some kids burnt out a stolen car on the marsh. I saw him then, although he didn't want to talk to us.'

'You think it's him?'

191

'I've just checked the archives and found his service record and his personal details, Sarge. His mother's name was Marion, and after her husband died she married again, to an Arthur Weir. She is now dead, and I guess Brian is living in his mother's old place.'

Joseph grinned at her. 'Well, I'd say you've located him. Well done, Yvonne.' He stood up and pushed his chair back. 'I'll get uniform out there immediately.' He paused. 'I think you should go with them. You can show them where the cottage is, then you can report back what you find.'

Yvonne nodded quickly. 'Of course, sir. I'll go check with the duty sergeant.'

As she hurried away, Joseph's phone rang. 'Dad? WPC Easter reporting in. Niall says to tell you that we are making good time with no problems to report.'

Joseph allowed himself a sigh of relief. 'That's excellent. Where are you?'

'Somewhere near Wetherby, or so I'm told by my chauffeur, or should I call him my crew-mate? Which reminds me, Dad, could you ask Yvonne if I can keep the uniform? It would be *so* useful!'

'And *so* against the law. The answer is an emphatic no.'

'Spoilsport.'

'Ring again in an hour, okay?'

'Okay, Dad. Now, stop worrying, we're fine. Speak later.'

Joseph rang off and glanced across to Nikki's office, but it was still empty. He wanted to get over to the hospital but as he'd just sent Yvonne out, and Dave was temporarily indisposed, felt he should hold the fort until he'd spoken to Nikki.

The name Liam called to him from his monitor screen. Joseph dialled his number.

'Ah, my favourite Brit! Thanks for phoning back.'

'It's just a quickie, Doc. I'm up to my proverbial in muck and bullets. So what's happening?'

'Quite a lot, as it happens. And I'm really grateful to you for putting me on to that Dutch police officer regarding my evil syndicate in Derry.'

'Any progress?'

'Our combined intel has already brought in two suspects in Holland, and one arrest on my home soil.'

'That's good news indeed.'

'Isn't it? And for once the timing was perfect for my arrest. My man had just held his first baby son in his arms and strangely, his view of the world has suddenly changed. We might just have a supergrass, if we play our cards right.'

Joseph could feel Liam's excitement pouring down the phone to him. 'Excellent! You don't often find that kind of luck on your side, even if you are Irish.'

'Very true, my friend. Anyway, I thought you'd like to know a few little nuggets of information that have come our way.'

'Any crumbs from your table would be gratefully received.'

'One. Although this network of criminals is multinational with a heavy presence in the UK and Northern Ireland, we now know its HQ is based in Amsterdam. And two. Aaron Keller was the numero uno hit man, and they are very worried indeed by the news of his sad demise. It has been intimated that there are certain jobs that only he could have undertaken, and some of their clients are less than happy bunnies.'

'Ah, trouble at mill?'

'Big trouble. And they are not going to find it easy to replace him. Thankfully, cold-blooded executioners with his years of expertise are not two a penny.' Liam gave a chuckle. 'Oh, my heart bleeds!'

'Ditto.' Joseph saw from the corner of his eye that Nikki was entering her office.

'Well, thanks for that, Doc, and good luck with your grass.'

'I'll keep you in the loop. Stay safe, Brit.'

Joseph stood up but as he did so his safe phone rang, so he flopped back in his chair. 'Vinnie?'

'Just thought I should warn you that Snipe will now be seeing sod all of Cloud Fen on his surveillance system. Best you know, just in case he decides to contact you.' Vinnie gave a little snort. 'Because if it was me, I'd be pissed as hell.'

Joseph considered that. 'In which case, you should keep a careful watch yourself. He might decide to go out there and check out the damage.'

'I doubt that very much. He'll know that whoever disabled his eyes and ears would have done a good job on them. I'm betting he'll move onto something else. Oh, and I'll be out here for some while, setting up a bit of counter-surveillance and protection for you. Of course, I can't stop him driving onto the marsh with a missile launcher, or poisoning your water supply, but other than sticking a platoon of squaddies on watch, it's the best I can do.' He paused for a moment, then added, 'And when I'm through here I'll be over to the nick to check out your backyard.'

'That's great, Vinnie. I'll tell the boss.'

'Ah, now, speaking of your DI . . .' Vinnie hesitated for a moment. 'Is she married, Bunny?'

Joseph stiffened. 'Divorced, why?'

'So is she . . . ? Well, is she seeing anyone?'

Joseph tightened his grip on the phone. 'Look, mate, I wouldn't suggest that you . . .'

'Oh, say no more! Sorry, I wouldn't tread on your toes, you know that.'

'No, Vinnie, you've got it wrong. It's not like that, we're not . . .'

'Yeah, yeah.' Vinnie laughed. 'A great-looking woman like that, and you do still have a pulse, don't you?'

'Honestly, Vinnie, it's just that she's been through a lot recently, that's all, and well . . . it's complicated,' he added lamely.

'What a shame this isn't a video call, cos I'm pretty certain, Bunny Easter, that you're turning red.'

Joseph absentmindedly touched a warm cheek and silently cursed his friend. 'Look, I've got to go, Vinnie. Ring me when you're through on the Fen and we'll meet somewhere out of Snipe's earshot.'

'Said he, neatly changing the subject.' Vinnie chuckled. 'But yeah, I'll ring. Bye.'

Feeling acutely uncomfortable, but having no idea why, Joseph walked across to Nikki's office and knocked on the door. 'How's Dave?'

'Still with the super, who's already contacted the cyber-crime boys. At least Dave knows that no one is suspecting him of running up debts. Poor guy has been worrying himself sick all night.' Nikki sank down onto her chair. 'You know what Dave is like with money.'

'Yes, I do.' He knew that Dave had been brought up in a family with very little money to spare, and he was very careful with it. 'Snipe knows exactly where to hit us so that it hurts.'

'And he's causing chaos too.' Nikki gently rubbed her temples with her middle fingers. 'I'm beginning to wonder if that is all part of the plan. I mean, look at us! Dave is tearing his hair out trying to salvage his life savings, Cat is in the hospital and Niall is ferrying your daughter to bloody Scotland. Talk about divide and conquer.'

'You missed out Yvonne. She's yomping around the Fen looking for our retired Sergeant Brian Faulkner.'

'Ah, she's got a trace on him?'

'Most likely. She's off on one of her famous hunches.'

'Excellent. So what do *we* do now?'

He told her briefly what both Liam and Vinnie had passed on for her attention, then added, 'and I've had a call from Cat. She was excited about something she's discovered regarding Operation Windmill.'

'And she didn't say more?'

'Wants to see me in person.'

'Then go. I'll use the time to make a surprise call on Jeremy Bow.'

Joseph immediately looked worried. 'Alone? With his past history? Is that wise?'

'Don't worry. As everyone else is committed elsewhere, I'll take a uniform. Bow still lives in Greenborough, so I won't be gone long.' She pulled her jacket from the back of her chair. 'You go see Cat, and we'll tie up back here in an hour, okay?'

He reluctantly agreed. As he got to the door, she called out, 'Have you heard from Tamsin?'

He nodded. 'She sounded in good form now she's on the road and heading north.'

Nikki crossed her fingers and held them up. 'She'll be fine, Joseph. At least she's out of here and far away from Greenborough.'

* * *

When the door of her room opened and the gowned figure of Joseph stepped inside, Cat gave an audible sigh of relief. With everything that was going on, she had not been sure he would make it.

'Sarge! I'm so pleased to see you. Sit down.'

Joseph pulled a chair closer to the bed and flopped into it. 'Sorry, but this is a really swift visit. So, how are you doing?'

'Let's skip the pleasantries. We'll talk about me when you have more time.' She gathered up a small sheaf of papers and turned the laptop around so that Joseph could see it. 'I need you to read this and tell me what you make of it.'

Joseph read silently, then drew in a long breath and said, 'Well, I'm damned! So this was not the first attempt on Magda's life?'

'Nope. According to some very interesting accounts that I've dug up from some of the far reaches of the Internet, this was actually the third.'

'So someone really wanted her dead, didn't they?'

Cat nodded and, using her notes, logged in to a different site. 'And that "someone," though never named or even hinted at by the Dutch police, has been thrown around in speculation by a lot of interested parties.' She tapped on the screen. 'Look at this online conversation from an underground anti-police chatroom. It's translated'

Joseph read out loud.

'Wolfdog: 'If the authorities really want to know, they should look closer to home.'
Bliksem: 'Blood close?'
Wolfdog: 'Of course. It's been in plain sight for years. They just interpret what they know incorrectly.'
Bliksem: 'I'm thinking revenge? Retribution? Compensation?'
Joseph faltered as he read that last word, then shakily finished *Wolfdog's* final comment.
Wolfdog: 'Got it in one, my friend. Who else?'

He looked at her, his head to one side.

'Sorry to just throw that at you, Sarge. I've had longer than you to work it out. And based on what I surmise, I've come up with some very interesting material.' Though Cat knew she shouldn't take up too much of his time, she was certain that she had nailed Operation Windmill once and for all.

'Surely these sites aren't your average search engines? You didn't get that from Google, did you?' Joseph stared at the site name — *Judicium Keus* — and decided that it must mean some sort of rough justice.

'Stuart and Travis from IT use them all the time. Travis reckons that if you know where to look, you don't need the PNC.'

'Apparently not.' Joseph raised an eyebrow in surprise, then pushed the laptop back to her. 'So, tell me what you discovered.'

'It's all connected to the stalker. If she'd only realised it, Magda had little to fear from him. He simply idolised her. There was someone else out there who was far more danger-ous.' She paused for effect, then remembered the sarge's tight time schedule. 'Remember that Magda was not the only one damaged by the stalker?'

Joseph's eyes narrowed. 'The cousin? The one who was actually attacked by the love-struck student?'

'Absolutely. The cousin, Daan. I've checked out what injuries he sustained, and believe me, they were life-changing. His back was broken and he had a severe head trauma.'

'But he's still alive?'

'Oh yes, and although he is disabled, he holds a powerful position in a major agricultural company.'

'Hellecroppen? Magda's company?'

'No, their sister company, owned and managed by Daan's father's side of the family.'

Joseph closed his eyes and tried to follow what she was saying.

'Listen, Sarge, you need to read some of this stuff, but the bottom line is this, okay?' Cat leaned forward closer to Joseph. 'Daan hated Magda for what happened to him. She wasn't the only bright light in that family.' Her voice became more urgent. 'Daan Hellekamp was the real genius, but together with the unbelievably clever Magda, he was heading for great things — prizes, awards, money. Lots and lots of money — and fame. He was good-looking and very fit, in a sporty way I mean. At least, until Magda's lovelorn disciple almost killed him.'

'Why blame Magda? It wasn't her fault, surely?'

'Well, she was indirectly the cause, and I did say he'd suffered a head injury. I can't find the exact details, but it's suggested that it had a considerable effect on his brain. It certainly didn't mess up his high intelligence, but it could have screwed up his emotional side.'

'Phew!' Joseph sat back and looked in awe at her. 'That's amazing!'

'Not bad for a night's work with limited resources.' She tried a painful and somewhat awkward grin. 'But Travis needs to take a little of the praise for providing me with such unconventional search sites.' She shifted around uncomfortably as the pain began to nag at her leg. 'One more thing. I think I know about Magda's secret Internet "friend," the one who was "helping" her with her big new discovery? It was Daan, contacting her under a false name. He bounced his IP address to make it look as if the messages were coming from England, when they actually originated in Holland. He knows as much, maybe more, about agro-engineering as she did. I reckon he fed her titbits about new innovations to hold her attention and gain her trust.'

'Of course! And he knew all about her phobias, so disguising himself via the Internet would have been perfect.' His face darkened. 'But why?'

'To ensure that she would be at the Waterside Quay apartment, waiting patiently for him to contact her, at the exact time when . . .' She gave him a sad smile. 'When the killer came to call.'

'So after two failures, he invested in the best executioner that money could buy. Aaron Keller. He hated her *that* much?'

'That's how I see it.'

'You little beauty!' He grasped her arm and squeezed it. 'The boss is going to be so pleased!' He stood up. 'Can I take your notes, so I can get this confirmed formally?'

'Be my guest.' She handed him the relevant papers. 'Did you bring those notebooks that I asked for? I've decided that I can use those sites to delve into a lot of things that are still unanswered on other cases too.'

Joseph passed her a plastic bag. 'From Sheila Robbins. She sends her love and says whatever you need in the way of stationery, just shout, okay?'

'She couldn't cough up with a printer, could she?'

'Don't push your luck, Detective.' He leant forward and kissed her gently on the cheek, then turned to leave. 'I'll be back ASAP.' He stopped at the door. 'Well done, kiddo! Now, we can put all our energies into finding out who hurt you.'

'Why do you think I did it?' She fought back tears. 'Only not for me. For Danny Wilshire and his little kid, Connor.'

CHAPTER TWENTY-ONE

As the two speeding squad cars made their way towards Silent
Fen, Yvonne Collins began to worry about what they might
find. Organising the team and getting underway had hyped
her up. Now, sitting in the car looking out over miles and
miles of flat crop fields the adrenalin drained, leaving her
jittery.

Silent Fen had a bit of a reputation. Nothing too spooky,
but the place was strange. Which was the best word Yvonne
could come up with. It was different from Cloud Fen in a way
she could never quite explain. They were both remote spots
with no proper village to speak of, just a scattering of isolated
homes and small farms. But Silent Fen always seemed somehow lifeless, whereas the place where DI Galena and Sergeant
Easter lived was brimming with nature — waterfowl, skylarks,
butterflies and hares. Yvonne was sure that those creatures
must live on Silent Fen too, you just never seemed to see
them.

'Along the next road on the right, then take the lane sign-
posted Dredger's Quay.'

She hoped she was right. Everything pointed to this
place being where the retired policeman lived. She'd gone
through his file, and she knew that when he left the force,

more than anything he had craved anonymity and peace. The bad case had been his last, and she suspected that, had he lived in town, it would have haunted him every waking hour and every sleepless night. Silent Fen, his mother's old home, with no fast roads, no drunken boy racers and no school buses, would suit him perfectly.

As the officer driving carefully manoeuvred the car onto the track that Yvonne had directed him to, she felt herself tense up. She had described Silent Fen as strange, and that was exactly how she felt. Today, she was not "one of the boys," there was no Niall beside her. Most of all there was no uniform, and it felt all wrong. For the first time she realised exactly why she had never had a hankering for a position in CID. She knew she had the brain for it, but she didn't have the heart. There was nothing Yvonne liked more than walking into a bad situation and diffusing it. She was a doer, an organiser, a visionary in a stab-proof vest. She could take one look at an ugly crowd and instantly work out the logistics of speedy dispersal. She knew which drunks to bang up, and which ones to get off the streets and home to their family. She knew the street kids and what made them tick. She could tell the really bad guys from the confused teens who had taken a wrong turn. Yvonne was more than happy to give DI Galena all the support she needed — after all it was a common cause. But as soon as it was over, she'd be back in her uniform where she could continue to do the job that she loved.

'Never been down here — well, not that I can recall,' said Jimbo, the driver.

'You'd have no need to.' Yvonne squinted into the sunlight blazing through the windscreen. 'I'd never have seen the place either if it hadn't been for the burnt-out vehicle.' She pointed to an area surrounded by trees. 'There it is, on the left.'

Both cars parked on the verge and Yvonne took in the scene. Further down the track was the sea-bank, a raised high path that edged the river, the marsh, the wetlands and the mud-flats. It stood in front of them, barring their way, its banks massed thickly with glowing yellow wild mustard flowers and the fluffy purple heads of thistles. A narrow track ran parallel with the bottom of the bank and led alongside a silted ditch to the now deserted Dredger's Quay.

Yvonne looked at the dried mud of the track and saw that no one had driven down to the quay for some time. There were no tyre prints and the lane was so overgrown in places that it was almost impassable. It gave the impression of being disused and forgotten.

Which could also be said of Dredger's Cottage.

'Oh dear,' said Jimbo quietly. 'What a shithole.'

A feeling of intense sadness flooded over Yvonne. She had seen Brian Faulkner's name on the wall at HQ, up on the honours board. He had been a brave man with an exemplary career behind him. It seemed all wrong that he should end up alone in such a depressing place.

The cottage sat in a hollow. The small area was enclosed by a thorny barricade of hawthorn hedging and a thick mat of stinging nettles and brambles. Tall spikes of reddish-brown sorrel fought with pink rosebay willow herb to add a touch of colour to the tangle of green.

'And how exactly do we get in?' asked one of the other officers.

'Around to the right. There's a broken-down gate.'

Yvonne looked at the desolate old building. It could have been pretty once, but that was a very long time ago. Weathered wood, peeling paintwork and crumbling brickwork was not pretty at all. Even the small trees that held the cottage in a snug, protective embrace were scrubby and distorted, bent into arthritic shapes by the constant attentions of the east wind.

'Okay, let's see what we can find.' Her voice was low. 'And be careful. We have no idea what we're walking into.'

The smell hit them as soon as they pushed open the unlocked door. But it wasn't what Yvonne had expected. There was no cloying metallic stink of shed blood, merely that of rotting food and damp decay.

The sadness that she had felt earlier intensified as they moved from room to room and found nothing but the trappings of a frugal and lonely life. She saw a faded photo of a passing-out parade, proud young officers in immaculate uniforms, all that was left of years of loyal service. Tarnished memories, she thought sombrely. All destroyed by one bad shout.

It took only a few minutes to ascertain that Brian Faulkner was not there, and by the condition of the food in the larder, hadn't been for a while.

Outside, the four police officers gave each other puzzled looks.

'Odd,' said Jimbo, staring around. 'Where's his car? You couldn't live out here and not have a vehicle.'

Yvonne had already thought of that, but as there was no garage and no barn, she could only conclude that he had driven it away, or been driven away in it by person or persons unknown.

As the other three poked around the yard and the overgrown area that had once been a vegetable garden, Yvonne perched on the edge of the stone well and thought over what she had seen.

Nothing added up. Although the place was rundown, the duvet on his bed had been clean, so had the blanket in the plastic dog basket that sat under the bedroom window. But there had been no dog food in the cupboards and there was no collar or lead hanging on the hooks inside the back door. So where was the dog? Was it with him? And where was he?

She shook her head and tried to think. His blood had been used to send DI Galena a message, but there was no mutilated body here. And there was no blood anywhere in the cottage. She puffed out her cheeks. There was only one answer to this puzzle. Abduction.

* * *

Nikki sat opposite Jeremy Bow. A uniformed officer stood beside her. She had deliberately picked a young PC, a slender, fine-boned lad called Matthew Boyd. She had chosen him over some of the more intimidating men and women available because she had no desire to threaten the mercurial Bow in any way. Matthew would have looked at home in a white surplice and carrying a hymn sheet, and posed minimal threat to the cop-hating Jeremy Bow. Only she knew that beneath the choirboy exterior was a competitive kickboxer holding more trophies than Seabiscuit.

The room they sat in was dark and smelt of stale whisky and staler smoke. But they had been allowed inside, which was more than Nikki had expected.

She glanced around and saw a mess of newspapers, empty spirit bottles, dirty mugs and plates — all the detritus of a lone man living in conditions that were nearly squalid. It was the kind of room she'd seen a hundred times on the Carborough Estate in the bad old days, but this was not the Carborough. It was a big Victorian semi-detached three-storey property that had once been a proud family home. But the proud family had been ripped apart by Jeremy's son's death, a death he still blamed on the police.

She turned her gaze to the man himself. Bow's clothes hung on him. He was skinny and undernourished, close to emaciated. His hair was colourless, worn too long and lank, and his eyes were sunken, shot with unhealthy colours and seemed unable to stay focussed on anything for more than a few seconds at a time. Her first thought was drugs, but then after listening to him talk, she altered her diagnosis to untreated mental illness and a crap diet. His friends — she used the term loosely — had all said he'd gone weird, and now she was inclined to agree. But she was there to make an assessment. Could he be Snipe? She looked at him thoughtfully. If his demeanour was a front, some sort of elaborate cover for his true self, then it was a bloody good one. For one thing, she didn't think he'd have the strength, physical or mental. Years ago it would have been a different story. Then Jeremy Bow had been a college lecturer, a highly intelligent man and his teenage son, Adrian, had been destined for a similar academic life, until he hit a bad patch and went off the rails. His final action was to get drunk and go joy-riding with a couple of mates. Sadly there had been very little joy around that evening and after a high-speed chase, Adrian lost control of the stolen vehicle, killing himself and his best friend and severely injuring another boy.

But right now Jeremy Bow was lecturing her about insidious police cover-ups and the wicked actions of corrupt officers and secret undercover operations to discredit honest innocent members of the public. Nikki listened without making comment. She noted that, although his speech was educated, there was also a lot of stuttering, repetition of words and an unstable wildness in the accusations.

'I'm sure that much of what you say does go on,' she stated, taking advantage of a small break in the tirade, 'but not here in Greenborough, sir, and not on my watch. If I thought one of my officers was corrupt, he or she wouldn't have time to draw breath before they were facing an internal investigation.' She leaned forward, anxious to hold the floor for a bit longer. 'Someone has killed a young police officer, Mr Bow. A good, promising lad, like your own son was. It's a terrible waste.' She looked over to the mantelpiece where there was a photograph of Adrian, a handsome youth with bright intelligent eyes and a warm smile.

'*You* killed my boy.' Jeremy hissed. 'You terrified him, hounded him into driving faster than he was capable of and then you deliberately ran him off the road.' His eyes flashed maliciously. 'I found witnesses, but the law closed ranks, didn't they? They protected their own.' The eyes became slits in his thin face. 'I don't care about your dead policeman. In fact that's just how it should be. An eye for an eye.'

Nikki felt Matthew tense up beside her, but she had warned him about what he might hear and to her relief, he did and said nothing.

She was angry too, but part of her almost felt sorry for the man. He had been so eaten up by grief that he had chosen to deny the fact that when he crashed the car, Adrian had enough drugs in his system to stock a small pharmacy. Jeremy hadn't even been there, so his allegations were completely without substance. And he had found no "witnesses," other than bewildered passers-by that Jeremy had actively sought out, trying to convince them that they had "seen" an innocent lad killed by the police. The law had got it right, but because he wouldn't let it go, the press took Bow's side. His school chose to highlight the boy's dashed hopes and dreams and extolled his virtues, not his failings. The media, following other recent high-profile cases, were happy to scratch away at the already tarnished veneer of the police force, and made sure that they were made out to be the villains.

'I'm sorry about your son, Mr Bow, truly I am. I know what it's like to lose a child.' The words stuck in her throat. 'And I'm sorry that what happened broke up your family, but if you know anything about what happened to our colleague, I beg you to tell us.'

This time he didn't spit back accusations, instead he stared at her, as if trying to make some kind of connection. Maybe the conviction, the truth in her words about knowing how he felt, had affected him on some level. After a while he said, 'My wife took my younger son, my lovely little Sean. He was nine at the time and . . .' his hands moved constantly, winding and unwinding his fingers. '. . . I haven't seen him since. I lost two sons because of your actions.' The vicious belligerence had melted but bitterness still tainted the man's sorrow. 'I think you should go now.'

Nikki stood up. 'Thank you for your time, sir.'

Outside in the car, Matthew let out a low whistle. 'I don't know how I didn't deck him after that comment about Danny's death.'

'Don't worry, Constable. You held it together very well. Did you get a chance to check out the other thing I mentioned earlier?'

'Yes, ma'am.' Matthew nodded. 'He does have a computer, quite a hi-spec one too. It was set up in an alcove just off the kitchen. I saw it as you were talking to him when we went in. There were also two printers and heaps of printed hard copy lying around, plus a laptop carrycase.' He looked at Nikki earnestly. 'I don't think he's as barking as he made out.'

'He *looks* a wreck. He clearly doesn't eat properly and from the scattering of Scotch bottles, he drinks far too much.'

'I agree, ma'am, but I was watching him carefully, and I didn't like the way he looked at you. Sure his eyes were all over the place, but every now and again, especially when you looked away from him, they were stuck on you like laser beams. I don't trust him, ma'am, and I don't think you should either.'

CHAPTER TWENTY-TWO

Back at the station Nikki listened in total amazement to what Joseph was saying about Cat's discovery. Soon her stunned expression broke into a smile. Joseph decided that it was the first full-blown smile he'd seen on her face for a long while.

'And she managed all that without access to a police computer?'

'Thanks to Travis, one of his old laptops, and some very unorthodox sites. She said he left her with several ways to track information without going out of the public domain.'

Nikki's eyes darkened slightly. 'You don't think he gave her anything he shouldn't, do you? They seem quite fond of each other, and he's a clever young man, and Cat can be very persuasive.'

'No, guv. She showed me the actual sites. The way Travis explained it to her was this: using the old term, Information Superhighway, or Infobahn, you could compare Google to the M1 and his sites to a back alley in Bethnal Green. They call it the dark web.'

Nikki sat and leafed through what Cat had uncovered about Magda Hellekamp. 'We need to get all this verified through official channels as quickly as possible, then sent across to Holland. I'll contact them now and give them a brief outline.' She raised her eyes to Joseph. 'This is seriously good work and one hundred per cent commitment from Cat, especially since she's so badly injured. It won't go unnoticed.'

'I'm sure it won't, ma'am.'

Before Nikki could lift the receiver, the phone rang.

'Yvonne? It's a bad line, can you speak up?' Nikki screwed her face up in concentration as the signal faded in and out. After a while she said, 'I've got the gist of that. Keep me posted. Oh, and ring from a better area next time, this is impossible.' She hung up, then rubbed her chin thoughtfully. 'It seems that Brian Faulkner does live at Dredger's Cottage, but he's not there, and as far as I could understand, neither is his dog, and that is puzzling Yvonne. She's had some idea of how she can check it out, but I'm not sure what it was. She'll ring again later.' She glanced up at Joseph. 'Which reminds me, any more news from Tamsin?'

'Not yet.' He lifted a wrist and checked the time. 'I should hear soon though.' He exhaled. 'I just keep telling myself that every minute that passes is another minute travelling away from Snipe, but hell, now I'm not one hundred per cent sure that she'll even be safe across the border.'

Nikki knew what it was like to have a daughter under threat, and empathised totally. His mind would be in turmoil and his heart would be in purgatory until he knew that Snipe was behind bars. But he would also know that if he didn't keep working at full throttle, Snipe's capture would not happen. And she had better stop daydreaming and shift herself. 'Right, I'll go report this to the super, then contact Holland. And after you've talked to your girl, I suggest you get everything together pertaining to Operation Windmill because, thanks to Cat, we have something concrete to give to the Dutch police and we can concentrate on finding Snipe.' She paused. 'And we have to get up to Yorkshire and talk to Windsor Morton face to face. I know the local lads have nothing on him, but we need to see that man personally.'

'We do, but what about Jeremy Bow?'

209

Her face darkened. 'I was dead sure we could cross him off the list, but the young PC who accompanied me has given me the heebie-jeebies about him.'

'Who did you take?'

'Matthew Boyd.'

'Ah, the little Ninja. Good choice.' Joseph grinned at her. 'He doesn't look like a martial arts pro, but I'm telling you, I'd think twice before I tangled with him. Plus, that lad has extremely good powers of observation. So what was it about Bow that spooked him?'

She glanced at the clock. 'Let me go see the super, then I'll tell you about it. I'll be interested to see what you think.'

* * *

Yvonne walked along the top of the sea-bank. Sun blazed down on her and she began to think that although her idea might have shown results early morning or late evening, she was unlikely to find dog-walkers when the temperature was this high. She and Jimbo had branched left, and their two mates had taken the right-hand path.

They had walked for over ten minutes when she saw a parked vehicle down at field level. It was clearly some kind of official Land Rover, because she could make out lettering and an insignia on the side door.

'Looks like waterways maintenance to me,' said Jimbo. 'Shall I shin down the bank and have a word?'

Yvonne nodded. The bank was steep with no footpath and she was in smart civvies.

She watched Jim almost enviously as he slipped and skidded to ground level, then strolled over and began to talk to the driver.

A few minutes later, he was scrambling back up again, puffing and out of breath. 'Steeper than it looks!' Jimbo laughed. 'Still, that bloke reckons if we walk a couple of hundred metres further on, there's a slipway that leads down to two land-workers' cottages. He said they both own dogs so, if anybody is in, it'd be worth a chat.'

The woman who answered the door was in her late twenties with long hair caught back in a ponytail and a wiry figure. On seeing the police at her door, her face became drawn, making her look thinner than ever. 'Oh my God! Is it Bill? Has something happened?'

Yvonne smiled at her and said, 'No, nothing's wrong, so please don't worry. We just need your help,' adding, 'as a local.'

The young woman forced a smile. 'Thank goodness for that. My Bill works with that big farm machinery, and I'm always afeared he'll have an accident one day.' She stepped from the dark doorway into the sunshine. 'I'm Doreen Lucas. How can I help you?'

'We need to speak to Brian Faulkner. He lives some way back along the sea-bank, on the lane to Dredger's Quay. Do you know him? Would you know where he is?'

Doreen gave a weary smile. 'Oh, Brian, oh dear . . . well . . .' She paused for a moment and looked hard at Yvonne. 'I think he's ill, officer. I mean, not sick as in something physical, but poorly in his mind.'

'He has had a lot of problems,' said Jimbo, 'but what makes you think he's ill?'

'I don't know him well.' She stared down at her feet. 'I don't think anyone does, but the other day he arrived on my doorstep, and he looked terrible. Pale and sickly, and he'd not shaved or anything.'

'When was this?' asked Jimbo.

Doreen considered the question. 'A week yesterday. Around six thirty in the morning.'

'So what happened?' Yvonne coaxed.

'He asked me to look after Marti. That's him you can hear barking out back. Marti is Brian's cocker spaniel.' She gave a half smile. 'Called him after Marti Pellow, because he spends most of his life wet, wet, wet.'

Yvonne grinned. She had always liked the Scottish group. And she could certainly hear the sharp bark of a dog. 'Did he say when he'd be back?'

Doreen shrugged. 'He gave me food for a fortnight, one of the little dog's beds and his lead and some toys.' She pursed her lips. 'To be honest I thought he'd be back by now, and although he never said where he was going, I suspected it was the hospital.'

'That would make sense.' Yvonne was thinking out loud. 'And if it were about a psychological problem, he most likely wouldn't mention it.'

'He gave me some money too. Far more than I would have expected. Marti's no trouble and luckily he gets on with Scrappy, my Jack Russell. To be honest, they are company for each other, because I work part-time in the food processing plant on the Greenborough Road.'

Yvonne reached into her pocket and pulled out a card. 'You've been really helpful. Would you mind ringing me when Brian returns? We are very worried about him.'

'He hasn't done something wrong, has he?'

'Far from it, Doreen. He's a good man. It's his safety we are concerned about.'

As they walked back up to the sea-bank path, Jimbo contacted the other crew and asked them to return to their vehicles. Yvonne rang the station and asked Sheila Robbins to ring round the local hospitals.

They were just driving along the main road into town when the answer came back.

Sheila confirmed that one week ago Brian Faulkner was booked into the psychiatric unit of Greenborough General for a full mental health evaluation, but he had never turned up. Sheila had been asked if she knew whether they should send him another new date for admittance.

Yvonne closed her phone and gloom descended upon her. Somehow she was sure that, new appointment or not, Brian never made it to the hospital, and Scrappy would have company on a permanent basis.

CHAPTER TWENTY-THREE

Dave checked his watch. The boss had called a meeting in the CID room at twelve sharp, but all he could think about was the state he was in financially. Since the day he joined the force he'd always been in the black. He and Margaret had never lived beyond their means and, having no children, their money was their own. They had budgeted, invested, scrimped and saved to get their own home and make it comfortable. They had even taken advice on how best to save the money left to Margaret by her parents, and after years of watching every penny, they had finally felt secure. Wonderful! That had lasted for a single year, then Margaret had begun to show signs of dementia. Now some evil bastard had stolen every penny.

As Dave walked slowly along the corridor to the murder room he felt deep resentment and bitterness welling up inside him. The bank had assured him things would be sorted out, but right now he had a wife in an expensive care home and not a brass farthing to his name. If he ever got hold of Snipe, he would kill him. Plain and simple. He'd put his hands around his throat and choke the life out of him. And it wasn't all about the money, although that was bad enough. The most important people in his life, apart from Margaret, were the team. And Snipe was taking each one of them in turn and crucifying them.

He entered the room and felt a cold determination descend over him. His own situation was out of his hands, and Margaret was beyond his help, but hunting for Snipe was an action he could take. He would give his all to the search.

Dave sat down and willed his mind to concentrate on every word the boss was saying. He had a job to do and he was bloody well going to do it.

'I know you will all be pleased to hear that Operation Windmill is going to be taken over, mainly by Holland. Thanks to DC Cat Cullen, and her back-up crew, Travis and Stuart from IT who put her on the right path, we are now pretty sure that Magda Hellekamp's death had nothing to do with shady business deals, money, or industrial espionage. The motive seems to have been hate, a purely personal vendetta. Our contract killer, the late Mr Keller, was hired by her cousin Daan, who had been terribly injured by Magda's stalker, and who blamed her for his misfortune.' DI Galena leaned against the edge of a table and added, 'Obviously it's too soon to have received official confirmation from Holland, but *unofficially*, using Cat's pathway, the Dutch officers have already traced the emails that Magda received back to the cousin, and he is now helping the police with their enquiries. I'm reliably told that he is "cooperating."' She gave a wry smile. 'I am also told that he is as mad as a box of frogs.'

'What about the gang Aaron Keller used to set up the hit?' asked Joseph. 'Will we have anything further to do with hunting down the local cell?'

'Oh yes, but at this moment we need to prioritise.' Dave noticed the boss's eyes narrow slightly before she went on. 'Right now, our main aim is finding Snipe and bringing him in. Nothing else takes precedence. That is our prime target. So settle back, folks. We'll assess everything we know to date, then formulate a strategy.'

She took it from the top and Dave scribbled bullet points in his notebook as she spoke.

1) The fire at her home.
2) The killing of Danny Wilshire and injuring of Cat Cullen.
3) The stolen vehicle that was used was left in her barn, steam-cleaned of all evidence.
4) The bloody message in her car boot: "crash and burn." The blood identified as belonging to retired police officer Brian Faulkner, now missing.
5) The bogus "bomb" in Joseph's garage.
6) The acid attack at the crematorium.
7) The stealing of Joseph's daughter Tamsin's phone and the engineering of her visit to Cloud Fen.
8) And the surveillance and the phone calls. Calls that had made it clear that Snipe was watching them and threatening them all in turn.
9) And finally, Dave's bank accounts being stripped.

On writing that down, Dave tried to remain apart from the raw anger that had almost consumed him earlier. Somehow he managed it. He had a good head when it came to sussing out villains. He must not allow this vile individual to render him useless. The team needed him firing on all cylinders, and if the boss could do it after losing her beloved daughter, and Cat could solve a crime after being injured, then he could damn well do it too.

He raised his hand. 'Ma'am? I was thinking, if we assume that Snipe was actually after Cat in the hit and run, that would mean he has targeted you, the sarge, Cat and me. Is it possibly about a case that we've worked on as a team? Or do you think he's lashing out at all and sundry around you?'

She drew in a long breath. 'If I knew the answer to that one, Dave, I'd be in a better place right now. Gut instinct says it's the team he's after . . .' she glanced across to Yvonne,

215

'but that doesn't let Yvonne and Niall off the hook, because we've all worked together before.'

'So, are we going to join forces with DI Hunter on this?' Yvonne asked.

'Yes, I've already talked to him, and although the super thought it was too close to home for us, he's finally agreed. And as it was Jim Hunter's case originally, I've agreed to let him take the reins.' She looked towards the door. 'He'll be here shortly to update you on the present status.'

The door opened, but it wasn't Hunter. A civilian apologised for interrupting and asked for the sarge. 'Someone downstairs to see you, Sergeant. Says it's urgent.'

'Name?' asked Joseph, standing up.

'Mickey Leonard, sir.'

Dave saw an amused look flash across the sarge's face before he looked at the boss for permission to leave. The DI nodded and Dave saw the hint of a smile on her face too. He wondered what had brought one of the infamous Leonard clan into the enemy's lair.

* * *

As Joseph ran down the stairs, he glanced at his watch. Tamsin's third call was due in ten minutes, and with luck and a fair wind behind them, they should be in Edinburgh in two and a half hours' time. He'd already spoken to Lothian and Borders Police and given them a rundown of the situation. They had promised to do what they could, although in the last two days they had found themselves with a murder enquiry that was draining resources. It had not been what Joseph had wanted to hear, but there was nothing he could do — other than catch Snipe and put an end to the nightmare.

He found Mickey sitting in an interview room, playing an arcade game on his smartphone. Joseph smiled to himself. There was a time when the only way that Mickey Smith, as he had been before Peter Leonard adopted him, would have had a hi-tech phone like that, was if he'd nicked it. Now he knew that the phone would be legitimately bought and paid for. Peter might have stemmed from an infamous family of crooks, but he and his wife were straight as a die.

'Mickey?'

The boy jumped up. 'Sergeant Joe! Great to see you.' He offered a hand and Joseph grasped it.

'You're looking very cool, my friend. Life must be treating you well.'

'Too right.' Mickey grinned broadly. He was dressed in a dark red-and-white striped Breton T-shirt with charcoal grey denim jeans and a pair of dark red canvas high tops. His hair was fashionably long and wavy. Joseph suddenly had a flashback to the first time he ever saw the boy, and mentally shuddered. This was no longer the sullen teen who communicated in grunt language, adolescent angst seeping from every pore.

'You've come a long way, kiddo.' Joseph felt a lump in his throat.

'Thanks to you.' Mickey sat back down. 'I didn't like to mention it at the funeral, but maybe we could meet up one day and talk?' He looked at Joseph hopefully, then went on. 'But right now I've got a message for you from Grandfather, and he'll kill me if I don't deliver it fast.'

Joseph pulled up a chair and sat opposite him. 'Okay. Well, it's a yes to meeting up, just as soon as the present case is over. Meanwhile, fire away with the message.'

'Archie said to tell you,' he lowered his voice, 'that Stephen Cox is still in Greenborough. We know that he's found someone who is not afraid to let him stay with them, although we're having big trouble finding who and where. My Uncle Raymond has put the frighteners on him alright, but for some reason, Cox is not going anywhere until whatever business he has here is done.'

Joseph gritted his teeth. Was it Cox all along? He thought about what Dave had said about a case that involved the whole team, and that would fit. Years ago, the team had gone after Cox, and sent him on the run. He *could* just hate them enough.

'Archie also said to tell you everything I'd heard on the streets.' He leaned forward closer to Joseph. 'There's a rumour on the grapevine that Cox mentioned Inspector Nik by name. I don't think it was an actual threat, but whatever, your boss is on his mind, and knowing that scrote, that's not good news.'

If it hadn't been so serious, Joseph would have laughed at hearing Mickey's old nickname for DI Galena again. Sergeant Joe and Inspector Nik.

'Anything else?'

'Yeah, the other thing I picked up was that he's got a lot of dosh. And I mean a *lot*. Sure he's a dealer, but he's either made a real killing somewhere along the line, or his old granny has kicked the bucket and left him a small fortune.'

So if he also had the money to pay for professional assistance, their theory that he was not bright enough to pull off some of Snipe's tricks was rendered null and void. Maybe Rent-a-Crook even did rates-for-mates. Joseph felt a sinking feeling inside. This wasn't looking good at all. He rallied a smile. 'Well done, my friend. That's certainly given me food for thought.'

'Oh, there's one last thing, Joe.' Mickey looked worried, as if he were about to break a confidence. 'It's not about Cox.' He fidgeted in his chair. 'Look . . .' His head snapped up. 'I never said this, alright? But . . . not all the Leonard family are on your side. You know I'm not talking about Peter or Fran, and certainly not grandfather, but just be careful around some of the others, okay?'

Joseph looked thoughtfully at the teenager. It couldn't have been easy to say that. The Leonard family had thrown him a lifeline. A reprieve from a future where his home would have been either a young offender institution or a secure training centre. It must have felt like he was grassing up his own, but then he also had an obligation to Joseph. He decided not to press the boy further. He knew exactly who

Mickey meant. Raymond Leonard had never made a secret of his hatred of the police, or his disgust that in the past his father had chosen to work with them. 'Thank you, Mickey. I hear what you're saying, and it'll go no further, I promise. And I really appreciate your help.' He stood up. 'Keep your ear to the ground for me, huh?'

'Sure will.' The boy gave him his signature salute, then added, 'Catch you?'

'For sure.' Joseph placed a hand on his shoulder and walked him down to the foyer. 'As soon as we have our killer locked up, we'll hit the town, okay?'

Mickey walked through the front door, waved and stuck a thumb in the air. 'Don't forget!'

Joseph called out that he wouldn't, then hurried back upstairs to the CID room. The minute he entered he knew that he'd missed something vital. He was greeted by stunned expressions and pale faces.

'He rang again, Sarge.' Dave's voice was shaky. 'The boss put it on loudspeaker. We all heard him.'

Joseph moved swiftly to Nikki's side. 'What did he say?'

'He said he's disappointed in us. He'd expected more.' Her voice was a monotone. 'That we are no match for him and maybe he should up his game.'

Joseph exhaled through gritted teeth and growled, 'Oh God! What next?'

'I dread to think.' Nikki rubbed at her forehead.

'Did he say anything else?'

'Just that it was no wonder people had so little faith in the police these days.'

Joseph stared at Nikki and knew that she was keeping something from him. 'And?' he demanded.

Her eyes looked straight into his, then she dropped her gaze and said, 'Okay, I know I have to tell you. Just before he hung up, he said, "Do tell the sergeant that his daughter looks amazing in that uniform, really hot."'

Joseph felt his blood freeze in his veins. 'Did he say *looks*? Or *looked*?'

Nikki's voice was a whisper. 'He said *looks*.'

Joseph spun round and stared at the wall clock. It was ten minutes after the time when they had arranged to speak. With his heart hammering in his chest, he rang Tamsin's number, waited impatiently, then punched the red 'off' button. 'No damned signal.' He knew his voice was little more than a croak.

'Don't worry. I'll try Niall.' Yvonne already had her phone in her hand.

He watched her as she closed her mobile and mutely shook her head. The kind of fear that you read about in horror stories gripped him. Was this what Snipe meant by upping his game?

'Sorry to interrupt again.' The same civilian stood in the doorway, seemingly unaffected by the looks on the detectives' faces. 'This time the message is for DC Dave Harris?'

Dave stood up. 'Yes?'

'Two officers from the cybercrime unit are outside. They would like to speak to you immediately. Can I bring them in?'

Nikki seemed to suddenly spring awake. 'Yes, do.' She nodded to Dave. 'This could be important. Let's see what they want.'

The two officers, a man and a woman, hurried in through the door. They were both in a state of intense excitement, and began speaking in unison. 'Only ever seen this once before!'

'Yes, amazing! Look!' The man pointed urgently to the woman.

She nodded, opened a laptop and punched in a load of numbers. 'We are using the passwords that you gave us, Dave. Now take a look at this!'

Joseph, despite his terrible concerns for his daughter, could not help but join the others around the computer.

'This is a copy of your accounts prior to the cyber theft.' The man passed Dave a sheet of paper. 'Is that right?'

Dave nodded glumly. 'It is.'

'Now we all know the accounts were stripped to zero balance on all three accounts, but . . .' She turned the screen slightly. 'Does that look like a miracle, or what?'

They all stared dumbly at the screen, then Dave looked as if he were going to give the woman a bear hug before bursting out with, 'You've got it back! However did you manage that? You guys are incredible!'

'My friend, we've done nothing. This started to trickle back in about half an hour ago.' The woman grinned broadly. 'And look closer at the figures.'

Dave looked then stepped back. 'I don't understand.'

'This is one of the cleverest scams we've ever seen.' The man looked at Nikki. 'This is elite stuff, honestly.'

'Where did the money go? Can you track who stole it?'

'It wasn't stolen, that's the beauty of it. Someone accessed the account and sent Dave's money halfway round the world, into other accounts and out again, into shares, then minutes later the shares were sold and the money was moved on. It's so complex that we'd never track it if we live to be a hundred.'

'And it's come back with interest!' The woman laughed. 'We reckon you've made around twelve per cent.'

Joseph looked at Dave's white face and saw his panic. 'But couldn't he take it again? Like he did before? How can we protect it? Should I withdraw it?' The questions poured from his open mouth.

'No way! We've set up a new generation fraud detection system. He won't dare try again on the same accounts.' The man looked more confident than Dave. 'Honestly, if he did try, he'd recognise the system and know not to touch it. And if he did, we'd have him.'

Dave looked shell-shocked. And if he hadn't been so worried, Joseph would have laughed at the wide eyes, the parted lips and the cheeks flushed scarlet. And then his phone rang, the throwaway PAYG phone. He grabbed it and as he did so, he realised that the whole room was silent.

'Dad? I'm so sorry my check-in call is late. We've just spent ten miles in the longest cellphone dead zone in Britain.'

Joseph wanted to cry. He wanted to laugh too, but all he did was say, 'She's okay,' to the officers that had gathered around him. Then he listened to his daughter explain their location and how drop-dead embarrassing it had been when Niall had insisted on standing guard outside the ladies loo in the service station.

'And he made five poor women who were busting to pee queue in the corridor until I was out again! Can you imagine it?'

'Sorry, but he acted exactly as I would have expected. Your safety is his only concern. The distressed bladders of others come second, I'm afraid.' He tried to sound casual, but his heart was still racing and his head was a mess. 'Can I have a word with Niall before you hang up?'

'Sure. He'll be back in a minute. I'm locked in the car and he's paying for fuel.'

Joseph swallowed. Snipe's words, placing his daughter within eye-balling distance, echoed around in his brain. Come on, Niall, and get your arse back in that car . . . He needed to keep hearing her voice. 'So how long does Niall think it'll take to get to your mother's place?'

'He reckons just over two hours, traffic allowing.' She paused for a moment, then added, 'He's nice, Dad, isn't he? I mean he's really thoughtful.'

'He's certainly one of the good guys, Tam.'

'How old is he? I don't like to ask in case he gets the wrong idea.'

Joseph gave a small smile. 'Not absolutely sure, but his crew-mate is here. I'll ask.' He called across to Yvonne, who threw him a knowing look, grinned and told him that Niall was twenty-six and available.

Joseph passed the information on, and heard a little murmur of appreciation from Tamsin. 'And he's not attached,' he added helpfully.

'Dad! I was only thinking he looked quite young to have been working at the station even before you went there. Don't start making something out of nothing.'

Yeah, yeah, thought Joseph, but said, 'Of course not.'

'Here he comes. I'll pass you over, and no matchmaking, okay, Father?' she hissed.

Joseph heaved a sigh of relief when he heard Niall's voice, and he swiftly told him what had happened. 'Don't alarm her, Niall. But keep your wits about you and don't let your guard down for one second.'

'Wilco, Sarge. We'll ring again in an hour.'

Joseph closed his phone and stared at Nikki's concerned face. 'I don't know what to think.'

Her face darkened. 'Well, I do. I think Snipe is showing us just how clever he is. He has us by the balls. He knows our weaknesses and the things that wind us up quickest. He's playing us for fools and loving every fucking minute of it.'

He could hardly dispute that. In the last few minutes he had been to hell and back, and probably for nothing. More than likely it was just another little diversion, courtesy of their wicked trickster. He sank down into a chair. Nikki did the same.

'I had a text while you were talking to Tamsin.' She tapped her phone a couple of times and passed it across to Joseph. 'Read it.'

Cop-shop exterior now clean. 3 live spies found, all dealt with, permanently. ☺

Joseph handed the phone back to Nikki. 'Thank God for Vinnie.'

'Ditto.' She leant forward resting her elbows on the desk. 'Let's call a powwow. Just Yvonne, Dave and the two of us.'

'And Jim Hunter?'

'Not yet. He's been delayed by the super and right now, I want to keep this in-house.' She looked at him pensively. 'They say that to know the perpetrator of a crime, you have to know the victim. It all stems from them. And from where I'm sitting it seems as if the team is the victim, so we need to look more deeply at the people we've collectively and royally pissed off.' She stood up, determination strengthening her voice. 'I'll disband the meeting, and you get the other two and bring them to my office. This has gone on long enough. If we don't nail this bastard soon, he's going to tear this team apart and destroy us all.'

CHAPTER TWENTY-FOUR

At two o'clock, Nikki closed her door and looked around her. Dave and Yvonne were seated and Joseph was leaning against the wall. The frightened look they had been wearing was replaced with something far more suited to a group of hunters.

Nikki perched on the edge of her desk. 'As I see it, we've concentrated so hard on the stingers that Snipe has thrown under our tyres that we haven't spent nearly enough time trying to discover who Snipe really is.' She slipped off the desk and began to pace. 'Someone hates us. Someone wants to hurt us. Someone wants us dead. That takes a lot of energy, a whole lot of pent-up vengeance. And my God, he's planned this carefully. No way is it a spur of the moment thing. This is a vendetta that has been germinating for years, festering and boiling in his blood.' She looked at them intently. 'We are looking at older cases here. Who hates us that badly?'

'Stephen Cox. He's still here in town, even though he's been warned off, and he's mentioned you by name,' Joseph stated.

'Ah, little Mickey has been padding the backstreets looking for titbits, has he?'

Joseph nodded. 'And he's discovered that Cox is in hiding, and he's loaded.'

'Ah.' Nikki stopped pacing and stared down at the floor. 'Then he really is still in the frame, isn't he?' She looked up, exhaled, then said, 'But who else? We can't afford to put all our eggs in one basket, and let's not forget Snipe's initial request at the start of all this.'

'Compensation,' said Yvonne gravely. 'I've been wondering about that, and apart from the obvious, Stephen Cox, we really need to look further into the lives of your three original possibilities, William French, Jeremy Bow and Windsor Morton. If you check their reactions at the time of their respective 'injustices,' they were all *way* over the top. And I'd kick off with William French. He was incandescent over his father's murder whilst on the witness programme.'

'But he's dead. That was confirmed without a doubt,' said Dave. 'Why start with him?'

Yvonne blinked a few times. 'Because it was a dramatically sad case, his dying on his father's grave in the depths of winter. Lord, it's positively Dickensian!'

Nikki gave a tight smile. 'I see where you're going, Yvonne. Was someone close to him badly affected by his death?' She nodded. 'We need to know about his family and if one of them, or maybe more than one, blamed us for his demise.'

'And Windsor Morton only lives in the Yorkshire Moors. That's not far away. At the time his rage knew no bounds. Maybe he has been spending the long lonely nights plotting cold-blooded revenge?' added Joseph.

'And even though I've just spoken to Jeremy Bow, I can't remove him from the frame. He may have stopped active heckling, but he's severely damaged by what happened to his boy.' Nikki nibbled on a thumbnail. 'So, we need to get into these guys' lives and shake things around a bit. We'll do it in pairs. I want no one going it alone, it's too dangerous. We'll have Niall back by the morning, and since our Cat is so bloody good at searching on the underground Internet, she can lend a hand as well.'

'Oh yes, she'd like that. She'll feel she's not being left out of the investigation. And thinking about computers, could Stuart and Travis help as well?' suggested Joseph. 'If Cat is going off-piste, then they can pitch in using the official channels.'

'Why not? Jim Hunter has just given me the all-clear on their company's security status and they both checked out. We'll sort them out some specific enquiries to run with, and see what they come up with. But to begin with, Dave can work with me, and Joseph, you work with Yvonne.' She looked at the other woman. 'And as you have a gut feeling about French, you guys start with him. Go see those relatives — and dig deep, okay?' She looked at Dave. 'Fancy a flying visit to the Moors? We can be there in two-and-a-half hours, so plenty of daylight left. We'll see what we can drag out of that lovable recluse, Windsor Morton.'

Dave nodded enthusiastically. 'Now I can breathe again after my recent financial scare; that would be fine.'

Nikki felt immediately better that she was about to be doing something concrete. 'Is Cat's mobile phone operational?'

'Signal varies,' said Joseph, 'but you can email her. At present she's permanently plugged in to either her precious iPad or her laptop.'

'Right, I'll fill her in on my chat with Bow then give her some homework to do regarding his background and recent activities. Then when we have a better idea of what kind of searches we need to be doing, we'll rope in IT and the PNC.'

As the others left, she saw Stuart Broad approaching her office. 'Could I have a word, please, ma'am?' As usual, his long hair was caught back in a smooth mini ponytail and he was wearing his signature UCLA sweatshirt. What was unusual about him was the troubled expression.

'Actually you are just the man I want to see. We have some extra work for you and Travis, if you are not too stretched?'

Stuart nodded. 'No problem. Now the Hellekamp enquiry is being tied up, we'll have more time.' He shuffled from one foot to the other. 'Um, well, that's what I wanted to talk to you about.'

'Close the door, Stuart.' She pointed to a chair. 'Sit. Tell me what's wrong.'

'Nothing's actually wrong, Inspector Galena, but do you recall the security boffin in charge of the Waterside Quay apartments? His name is Alan Brady.'

Nikki saw in her head the man's tight lips and fraught expression. 'Yes, I remember him. He was the headless chicken. He asked if he could grill you and Travis with regard to the glitches.'

'And he did. And we gave him a couple of hours of our expertise, but he wants more and neither of us is happy about that.' Stuart rubbed his hands together nervously. 'Thing is, ma'am, their system is flawed. Not just the couple of anomalies that we identified, they have major problems and they want us to help sort them.'

'And you don't feel comfortable taking that on?'

'Our company has us contracted to you, first and foremost. If the security company's system needed an overhaul, it would have to be other staff, not us, and Brady specifically wants us. He's offered us a very substantial amount of money to take it on privately.'

'Has he indeed?' Nikki frowned. 'Not that I'm belittling your skills, Stuart, but surely all your colleagues are competent enough to tackle the task?'

'Most of them. Although without bragging, Travis and I are probably top of the league, and I'm sure that's because of the nature of the work we do for the police.'

'Do you want me to tell him to back off?'

'No, ma'am, I can do that, but we wanted you to know the situation first-hand.'

'Thanks for that. I appreciate it. And I appreciate your loyalty.' Nikki had always rather liked the two amiable, if somewhat oddball eggheads, and now they had risen even higher on her merit board. The offer of cash in hand can be very tempting, although with these two guys, it would most likely have been the kudos of finding the ghost in the machine that would have floated their boat, not mega amounts of money.

Stuart stood up and nodded his thanks. 'Just send us anything you want us to work on for you, Inspector. We'll be waiting.'

* * *

Joseph replaced the phone. The French family would see them in an hour's time, but as he had not been in the area when William French's father had died, the intricacies of the case were not known to him. He logged onto his computer and waited. The one thing that he did know, and so did every other officer in the Fenland Constabulary, was that there had been one glorious cock-up over the security surrounding the witness protection programme. It had failed James French miserably. His place of safety had become a trap, and when two balaclava-clad gunmen broke in and opened fire, it was one he didn't make it out of.

Joseph leaned forward in his seat and brought up all of the relevant background material that was available. It was the son, William, that interested him most. His grief had to have been truly something to send him off the rails in the manner that it had. Joseph skimmed the reports. It seemed that when his violent anger and fury at the police had diluted down to a seething mass of depression, William had taken to drink and any other mind-numbing substance he could get his hands on. It was no surprise that he died in the manner that he did. It was the location and the temperature that turned his passing into a Victorian melodrama.

Joseph stared at a forensic photograph of the frozen body curled up in a foetal position on the cold stone of his father's grave, and instantly thought of Little Nell.

A tiny shiver darted across from shoulder blade to shoulder blade and Joseph decided that Yvonne was very likely right to start with this case. It certainly had enough horrors attached to it to unhinge a sensitive mind. Was there someone out there who blamed them for *both* deaths? Not just

James's murder, but William's untimely passing as well? It was possible.

He beckoned to Yvonne, and explained his thoughts to her.

Yvonne smiled grimly. 'I've been thinking exactly the same thing. We need to check out those who mourned William more than those who were close to the father, James. Up until now it would have been easy to disregard the French case, because the main instigator of all the anti-police threats had himself died, but it could have been *his* death that sparked off Snipe to plan his vendetta. I checked who found him that night, but it was an anonymous call.' She shrugged then glanced at the wall clock. 'At least we know what questions to ask of the remaining members of the French family.' She pulled a face. 'Not that I'm expecting this interview to be easy.'

Joseph grimaced in return. 'Frankly I expect a total disaster, but we can only do our best and hope that someone gives us something to work on.' He paused. 'As Snipe is not exactly playing fair, we could do with a bit of luck falling our way.'

'Right, but I wouldn't count on it, Sarge.'

* * *

As Nikki and Dave drove over the Humber Bridge and on towards the Yorkshire Moors, she began to feel uneasy. There was no way of knowing if they would even get to see Morton, let alone talk to him. She had notified the local police that she was intending to see the man, but their response had been less than encouraging.

'They reckon he's more likely to chuck bricks at us than to let us in. Apparently no one has set foot across his threshold since the day he arrived. Any dealings that the local lads have had with him have been conducted from the far side of a high gate.'

'I know,' said Dave. 'Let's just hope that he'll respond to you better than some of the tooled-up uniforms that have been sent out to him in the past.'

'They have offered to escort us to his cottage. It's not easy to find. No signposts, no numbered roads, and satnav doesn't recognise it.'

'So his little moorland "Dunromin" isn't quite the idyllic, roses-round-the-door kind of cottage?'

'The locals call it Alcatraz, if that helps.'

Dave threw her a half-smile. 'Lovely. Can't wait to see it. Do you think he does holiday lets?'

And an hour and a half later, they did see it.

'Scrub what I said about the holiday cottage.'

'Bloody hell!' Nikki swallowed. 'I expected something somewhat uninviting, but this is more like a fortified compound than a home. Is he totally off his rocker?'

The uniformed constable that was their guide gave a humourless laugh. 'When we said he's a recluse, we meant it, ma'am.' The man shifted from foot to foot as they surveyed Morton's "cottage." 'And there's a book open on the fact that you won't even make it to the front door — if there is one. I haven't got past the seven-foot-high gate yet.'

Nikki looked around her. The wild moors stretched out for miles all around them. Thick carpets of heather and huge clusters of lush green bracken covered the ground, and small rivulets of water trickled and flowed down the steep rocky slopes. It was breathtakingly beautiful, and a complete contrast to the ugly, bastardised cottage that belonged to Windsor Morton.

Dave shook his head. 'I saw something like this on an American documentary once. It was a homestead that had been turned into an impregnable stockade to protect a cult that lived inside.'

Nikki suddenly wished they'd stayed in Greenborough. If Morton did not want to communicate, they'd never get to see him. Not in a month of Sundays. They would need a wrecking ball to get through the outer perimeter fence alone.

With a grunt she leaned back into her car, turned on the ignition, pressed her hand firmly on the horn, and kept it there.

The harsh sound echoed through the valley, disturbing a clutch of black pheasants and sending them clattering into the air. Nikki let her hand drop, then called out the man's name several times.

'That's odd.'

She turned and looked at the local officer. 'What's odd?'

'No dogs barking.' The man's eyes narrowed. 'Last time I was here they scared the life out of me. *The Hound of the Baskervilles* had nothing on that lot.'

'How many dogs does he have?'

'I don't know for sure, but I'd guess at three or four and they sounded big too.'

Nikki strode towards the thick wood-panelled gate and hammered on it with a clenched fist.

When no answer came and the valley fell quiet again, she looked at Dave. 'Something's not right here.' She walked a little way along the perimeter until she came to a thick post with wire fencing attached and, checking its strength, began to pull herself up.

'Wouldn't do that, ma'am!' the constable called out in concern. 'Those dogs are vicious, and if he's got them holed up in the house and lets them go, you'll be in big trouble.'

Nikki continued to climb. At the top she felt the breeze ruffle her hair and looking around she saw that she had an uninterrupted view of Morton's cottage. It still wasn't pretty. Balanced carefully against the sturdy post, she looked hard at the forlorn and loveless place. The original building was old, made of thick stone, and probably built some two hundred years ago, but it was the jerry-built additions that made it such an eyesore. There were shutters at the windows, a metal cover to the front door and a big handful of ramshackle outbuildings. A haphazard conglomeration of sheds, containers and dog-kennels looked as if they had been dropped into the yard and left where they fell. Not one single flower bloomed anywhere. 'Home sweet home,' she murmured.

'Anything?' Dave called up to her.

'It looks deserted.' She gazed around. 'Even the dog mess on the concrete looks old.' The place had that odd air of being uninhabited. It was a bit like when you looked at a dead body. It just felt empty, a shell, and you knew that all life had gone. 'I'm willing to bet he's not here, but where are the—' She stopped mid-sentence. 'Oh shit.' She gritted her teeth.

'What's wrong?' asked Dave anxiously.

Nikki didn't answer immediately. What she had seen had made her feel nauseous. Nauseous and bitterly angry.

One of the kennels had no door, and inside she could just make out a huddle of dark shapes, and without confirmation she just knew that the animals were not drugged or sleeping. Nikki drew in a breath and began her climb down. She jumped the last two feet. 'We're going in. Get the enforcer from my boot, Dave. We are going to need it on that bloody gate.'

'I'd really advise caution, ma'am, and we have no warrant.' Their guide's voice was full of anxiety.

'Your concerns are noted, officer, but I believe that someone inside is in mortal danger, so that negates the warrant. Now, get the enforcer, Dave. I need to see inside that building.'

The gate did not give up easily, but finally, between the two men the padlock area splintered and then the wood shattered. Nikki gathered herself, but anger at what she had seen over the fence made her aggressively kick the gate wide open and stride into the yard.

Dave was right beside her and the other policeman, baton drawn, brought up the rear. Suddenly she felt a hand on her arm.

'Wait, ma'am. Don't go any further.' Dave was tensed up, and looking around almost furtively. 'The sarge told me a few things about when he was in special ops, and this place is giving me the willies.' He pointed to a single, almost invisible thin wire that seemed to circumnavigate the cottage. It was carefully threaded through short pegs with loops at the top and was only some six inches from the ground. 'If it had been dark, we would never have seen it.' His hand was still on her arm, holding her back. 'I could be wrong, but I think he's set traps. This is potentially a very dangerous situation.'

'It wouldn't surprise me,' the constable's voice had a slight tremor, 'considering his mental state. He's no recluse, ma'am. He's a raving nutter.'

Nikki thought about what was lying in the dog kennel and was forced to agree. 'I need to know if he's in that house, and if he's still alive. I'm certain he's killed his guard dogs. But has he also topped himself?'

'I'll radio for back-up, ma'am.'

There was nothing Nikki could do but agree. It was not her patch, not even her county. With no one to call on she had little choice. The local man spoke hastily into his radio, then turned back to her. 'Twenty minutes, ma'am, and in the meantime, just in case this cottage is rigged, my boss has suggested that we wait back at the cars.'

It seemed to Nikki to be the longest twenty minutes of her life. Even the beautiful surroundings of the North Yorkshire Moors did nothing to ease her growing dread at what they were going to find.

Finally a team of officers arrived with a couple of specialist men in thick protective flak jackets and helmets. She watched helplessly as they painstakingly traced the wires and tested every entry and exit to the miserable place. It took a further forty-five minutes before it was safe to go in.

'So you were right, Davey-boy.' Nikki stared at him thoughtfully. 'And I was so heated about what he'd done to his animals that I'd have stalked straight in. I have to thank you for saving my life.' In truth, she would have been spread halfway across the county if she'd marched in blind. Morton had set up every kind of booby-trap known to man. Nothing professional, just nasty schoolboy surprises, but all souped-up enough to be lethal. Then he'd added a few homemade incendiaries for good measure.

'Thank the sarge, guv. He's the one who put me wise on things to look out for.'

'Then I thank you both.' Nikki looked at the team of men and women who were exiting the house.

'It's all clear, DI Galena, but Morton's gone. We know his vehicle and we've already circulated the license number.' A tall, thin sergeant with close-cropped hair and a weathered complexion was addressing her. 'Problem is, from the rotting food, I'd guess he's been away for a week or two.'

'And his dogs?'

The sergeant drew in a long breath and shook his head sadly. 'Poor little sods. I'd really like to get my hands on the evil son of a bitch. There was no need for that. There are enough charities who would have taken them. Hell, there's even a pet sanctuary just west of Pickering.' His face creased into anger. 'If you're an animal lover, as I am, this side of the job really sucks.' He shrugged then looked at her hopefully. 'If he should show up in your neck of the woods, would you take him somewhere private and have a quiet word with him from me, Inspector?'

'It would be my pleasure, Sergeant,' growled Nikki. She thanked him for his help and they made their way back to the car. 'This was not what I had in mind, Dave.' She stared at him apprehensively. 'Far from crossing Morton off the list of suspects, he has just moved up the ladder. I might not have liked the thought of him sitting there plotting terrible revenge, but it was a damn sight better than not knowing where the hell he is.'

Dave took the keys from her. 'I agree, and there's another thing I'm not happy about. Thinking about what you said about Snipe using technology, I asked one of the local guys about Internet access way out here, and guess what? It's surprisingly good, and Windsor Morton has a router and a printer in one of the rooms, but the computer is missing.'

Nikki felt her heart sink. 'Let's get home, shall we? Before things get any worse.'

CHAPTER TWENTY-FIVE

It was almost ten in the evening when they arrived back at the station. In the CID office, they found Joseph and Yvonne picking their way through a bucket of Kentucky Fried Chicken.

'Have you eaten?' asked Joseph, wiping his lips with a piece of kitchen towel.

'Grabbed a burger on the way back, thanks, but I could kill a strong coffee.'

Yvonne stood up. 'On its way, guv. I hate to say this, but you both look out on your feet.'

'Harrowing trip, wasn't it, ma'am? Everything considered.'

Dave looked exhausted, and Nikki suspected the long drive and the booby-trapped cottage had less to do with it than the recent scare over his stolen savings. 'I think you should get home, Dave, and catch up on some sleep. I'm willing to wager that you got no rest last night.'

'In a nutshell, I never thought I'd sleep again when I saw those empty accounts.' He gave her a weak smile. 'But I'd rather hear how the sarge and Yvonne got on before I quit for the night.'

Yvonne brought the drinks and placed them on the desk in front of Nikki. 'Actually we didn't do very well at all, did we, Sarge?'

Joseph shook his head. 'I think the French family only agreed to see us in order to let us know that they have long memories.' His shoulders slumped forward. 'They really let us have it with both barrels. The phrase "to vent one's spleen" has never seemed so appropriate.'

'And making us wait an hour for the appointment enabled them to gather the troops.' Yvonne puffed out her cheeks. 'We walked into a lounge stuffed with relatives, all ready to take us on.'

Joseph nodded. 'Thing was, we couldn't help but feel for them. Hell, the man was executed whilst in our care. No wonder the son fell apart.'

'So, apart from escaping as quickly as possible, did you manage to get any leads? Any feelings about any of them in particular?' Nikki already knew the answer.

'Nothing specific, although we both agreed that the hurt they felt was . . .' he paused, '. . . normal? If you get my meaning. Something terrible happened to wreck their family, but their anger and their suffering at the loss of two family members seemed totally justified.'

'And no one,' added Yvonne, 'exhibited the same kind of manic, bitter fury that William did originally. No one registered as devious or dangerous.'

Nikki heaved a sigh. 'So, we relegate them to the back boiler?'

'I'm not sure we can do that, although I wouldn't consider them too highly on the list of contenders.' Joseph poked around in the bucket for another chicken wing. 'How about your trip, guv? Dave used the word *harrowing*. That sounds ominous.'

Nikki told them what had happened, and didn't forget to praise Dave for his observational skills regarding the trip-wire. 'I was seeing the red mist. Thank God, Dave had his professional head on!'

Joseph and Yvonne had both leaned forward to listen.

'So, we have a real suspect in Morton?' Joseph's eyes flashed. '*And* he's gone AWOL from his country retreat, so he could be somewhere here?'

'Yes, he could be Snipe.' Nikki sighed. 'He's proved he's ruthless by killing his animals.'

'And he has a computer that was valuable enough to take with him when he left.' Dave tried to stifle a yawn, and failed miserably. 'Sorry, ma'am, can I take you up on that offer of calling it a day? I don't think I'm going to be much use until I've had some sleep.'

Nikki smiled. 'Go, and thanks again for what you did today. I owe you one.'

'Forget it, ma'am. We're a team, aren't we? What one misses the other picks up on. That's how it works.'

'Thank heavens!' She looked at the others and saw two tired faces staring back. 'And by the look of you two, I think we should all take a leaf out of Dave's book and get some rest.' She finished her coffee, watched Yvonne and Dave leave the room, then looked back to see Joseph clearing up the remnants of his makeshift meal. 'And Tamsin? Can I assume from your calm exterior that she's made it home?'

He bagged up the rubbish and threw it in the bin. 'She's safe. Well, I hope she is.' He grimaced. 'First thing in the morning, her mother and her new partner Gavin are taking her to stay with a cousin for a few days, and even I don't know the address. I thought it best that way, as long as they phone in regularly to assure me of her safety.'

'And Niall?'

'He grabbed a couple of hours' sleep and he'll be on his way back now. I told him to go straight home and we'd see him tomorrow.' He stretched, then smiled. 'He's a good kid, and he certainly made an impression on Tamsin.'

'I'm not surprised. Niall's a nice-looking young man and he has a lot of good old-style values.'

'She could do a lot worse, I guess, except for one thing . . .'

'He's a copper, and the last man you want your girl involved with is a copper, right?'

'We've lived it, Nikki, haven't we? Your husband? My wife? Very few people really understand what drives us.'

'I know, and even if they do, they can't always cope with it.' She shrugged. 'Still, they'd make a brilliant couple with his looks and her . . . well, I know she's your daughter, Joseph, but she's a stunner.'

Nikki saw the pride in his eyes, and hoped against hope that father and daughter could make things work. 'Come on you, let's go before I fall down on the office floor in a deep sleep. And let's pray that Snipe gives us a night off.'

Joseph pulled on his jacket. 'Amen to that.'

* * *

While her colleagues wearily made their way home, Cat was wide awake and working steadily on her computer. The boss had asked her to use her new search pathways, as well as some of the old ones, to see what she could unearth about Jeremy Bow, both past and present. But although she had discovered a multitude of interesting facts, nothing really made her sit up and take note. Bottom line, it was all pretty sad stuff really. The guy would not, or maybe could not, admit that his son had caused his own death, that of a close friend, and injured another boy. It was far easier to blame someone else, in this case the police, than admit that your talented and precious son was off his head whilst in charge of a lethal weapon.

Cat sighed, blinked a few times to ease her aching eyes, closed the laptop and sat back against her pillows. She didn't know Jeremy Bow, but she recognised a grieving parent and a man who, if the blogs and articles she had found were to be believed, probably pushed his son far too hard into getting good grades and succeeding. And from the messages placed on Facebook by his school friends after his death, there had been no need to pressurise him. Adrian was brilliant. He would have sailed through to university with no trouble at all.

Maybe it was all she had been through in the last few days, but Cat felt tears welling up and spilling over onto her cheeks and into her dressings. She dabbed at them with a tissue. 'Silly cow', she muttered to herself, but the thought of such a bright teenage life being snuffed out so tragically had really got to her. Life suddenly seemed so precarious, every wrong move or bad decision left you vulnerable. Like Danny. If he'd gone out with Dave instead of her, he'd be alive now and his little boy would still have a father. The tears fell faster.

With a snort of disgust at her weakness, Cat grabbed her glass of water and drained it. Hell, she'd just closed up Operation Windmill, which was no mean feat with no PNC and no team to back her up, and here she was blubbering over a crack-head from an old case. This would not do at all. And it wouldn't help her to find Snipe. She reopened the laptop and double-clicked on one of Travis's underground info sites. Work was obviously the antidote to feeling bloody sorry for herself. And with Snipe still terrorising her friends, she was the only one who had plenty of time and every opportunity to do some unorthodox detecting. In fact, it was her duty.

'Okay, who is next?' She narrowed her eyes and typed in "*William French*." 'Right, William, my dead little friend, it's time to tell me your secrets.'

'And do you like communing with the spirits of the dead?'

Cat turned abruptly, and saw the agency night-nurse lounging against the doorframe. 'Pardon?'

'Asking the dead to divulge their secrets? Sounds pretty spooky to me.'

Cat tried to recall the man's name, but ended up squinting at his badge. 'Sorry, Todd, and not that it's any of your business really, but I'm just doing some research on the Internet.' She glowered at him. For some reason she felt uncomfortable when he was around. He asked questions that had nothing to do with her health and, as far as she was concerned, as a nurse that was all he should be interested in.

'Ooh, a tad touchy tonight, aren't we?'

He threw her a wide smile, but it only served to make her feel more irritated.

'Well, if there's nothing I can get you, I'll leave you to your *research*.'

After he'd gone, Cat stared long and hard at the empty doorway. Even though she knew that a police officer was stationed outside and only a few feet away in the corridor, she felt unaccountably nervous. 'Creep,' she muttered, returning her attentions to the computer, 'The sooner I get out of here, the better.'

CHAPTER TWENTY-SIX

The night had been Snipe-free, something that worried Joseph almost as much as facing an immediate threat from him. His silence left Joseph fretting that the killer had taken a day off from Lincolnshire bobby-baiting in order to head north and stalk Tamsin. It wasn't until he'd spoken to her that he felt any kind of relief.

He looked up from his computer and saw that even though it was just after eight thirty in the morning, the team was at full strength and hard at work. To make things easier they had commandeered the whole CID area as a central work hub, and the place was humming. Printers were spewing out documents, phones were ringing and officers swapped information, and then swung back to their computers.

From the relative calm of his tiny office, Joseph noticed the two IT guys, Stuart and Travis. They were sitting facing each other across a shared table, staring avidly at the screens of the extra computers that they had set up the night before. Niall and Yvonne were working together at desks hastily pushed up against Dave's, and somehow, DI Jim Hunter's team had slipped in seamlessly to join them. Joseph had to admit that he had never seen such a well-managed combined effort for a single case. Then again, it was a case that involved colleagues, one dead and two injured, so it was not to be wondered at. Outside her office, Jim Hunter was talking animatedly to Nikki, and although Joseph knew that she had deferred to Jim taking the lead, there was an unspoken agreement that they share the role of officer in charge.

Four whiteboards had been set up, one for each possible candidate for the role of Snipe. Three bore only a name and a centralised photograph, but one had two names and two pictures, those of James and William French. In a relatively short time, when the morning meeting had finished, the boards would be filled with information, data that could make one stand out above the others.

Joseph scanned them carefully, taking in each face as if memorising it.

Windsor Morton. The photograph showed a tall man with hair cropped so short it was impossible to tell the colour. The face was that of a fighter, with a spread nose and sunken eyes, and his stance was aggressive. He wore a thick hiker's anorak with a check shirt beneath. The photo had been taken not long after his sister had been sentenced for murder, and the anger at what he felt was a set-up burned steadily from those deep-set eyes.

Stephen Cox. This was one face that Joseph didn't need a photograph to recognise. He shuddered, deciding not to look at the picture at all. He still saw that face in nightmares, one half devastatingly handsome, and the other half devastated. Burnt, scarred and twisted, like the man's black heart. Joseph's gaze moved quickly to the next board.

Jeremy Bow. Unkempt, even back then, at the time of the enquiry. He had long hair, was unshaven, and wore clothes that looked as if they had been slept in, and indeed that was most likely the case. Intelligent, piercing eyes set in a face ravaged by grief and another emotion that Joseph decided could be guilt. A father who had failed his son, but could never admit to it?

And lastly, James and William French, both deceased.

James was an upright man with a full head of wavy grey hair and an expression that showed both strength and a sense of humour. He looked the epitome of a lovable rogue, and the kind of man any orphan would dream of having for a father. And William did share a family resemblance, but there it ended. A newspaper shot of the young man at James's funeral clearly showed anger, anguish and bitter resentment of what had happened to his father, and there was a desolation too, a terrible, inconsolable grief.

Joseph stared hard at that last board. He had a strange feeling that there should be a third photo up there, someone else, someone living. Someone who mourned either James or William with a hurt that could only be assuaged by taking revenge?

He sat back and wondered who that could be. As Yvonne had noted, the rest of the family showed none of William's fury. And from the little information they had unwillingly given up, there was not a brother, an uncle, a cousin, or a best friend that seemed deep or devious enough to be Snipe. He let out a sigh, then saw that Nikki was closing her office door and approaching the front of the CID room. He stood up and collected his notebook. It was time for the morning briefing.

* * *

Nikki looked around at the assembled officers, at their pensive faces, and opened the meeting by cutting immediately to the chase. 'The person who is targeting us has no scruples and wants us dead. We and those around us are in acute danger until we have a name and someone to go after.' She leaned back against the wall. 'The superintendent, DI Hunter and I have done an extensive analysis of old cases, and we can find nothing other than the four men that we are now investigating. So, Jim and I are asking you to give us all the time that you can afford to make a concerted effort with this search, and every piece of new information that you dig up, bring it to either Jim or me, okay?'

There were murmurs of assent.

'Then we'll take each of these old cases in turn and see what we know. Okay, Yvonne? Perhaps you would be kind enough to add our findings to the boards?' She passed the older woman a marker pen and turned to the first board. 'I'll start here, with Windsor Morton, as this is the man Dave and I were working on. It should be noted that he went missing from his home over a week ago, and that makes him a strong suspect for Snipe.' Nikki took a breath. 'This is a brief overview of the original case.' She paused and indicated the photograph. 'Windsor Morton is the father of Ruth Engle, nee Morton. Ruth and her husband Brandon Engle were convicted six years ago for the murder of their lodger, Charlie Bardell. Morton was convinced that the police falsified evidence and although it was proved beyond doubt that the Engles were guilty, he continued to harass us for several years. Briefly, Brandon and Ruth appeared to be the salt of the earth, entering zealously into charity work and saintly good deeds.' Nikki gave a sour look. 'But it was all a facade. In fact they were predators, and they preyed on the vulnerable. Although Charlie Bardell had learning difficulties, he was completely integrated into society. He was, however, easily influenced and he soon fell under the spell of the charismatic couple. Pretending kindness, they offered him a home, then bled him dry. They drained his quite substantial savings, and when he had nothing left to give, they bludgeoned him to death and blamed a local drug addict, another poor soul that had been taken under their roof in the name of charity.'

'Why was the father so adamant that they were innocent?' asked DI Jim Hunter, 'Sorry, this case was before my time here.'

'Mainly because Ruth was his golden girl and could do no wrong. He totally believed her to be a good Samaritan and that evil spongers had taken advantage of her generosity. However, before she married Brandon Engle, his daughter had had a brief affair with a young police officer. Apparently it ended badly when Engle arrived on the scene. Windsor Morton stated that the police officer had practically stalked Ruth in order to get her back and had threatened both Ruth and Brandon on several occasions. He reckoned it was payback, and that evidence was planted at the scene in order to get her convicted.'

'That would be a bit extreme,' said Yvonne flatly. '*If* it were true, which it isn't.'

'You were here then?'

'I was, and I know for a fact that it was the other way around. The officer in question soon realised that the sparkling young beauty was not what she seemed. He soon saw a dark side to Ruth and immediately ditched her. I forget the full details but I know it was Ruth who threw her teddy in the corner and stirred up trouble, not the police officer.'

'But Windsor Morton took up a crusade?' asked Jim Hunter.

'With passionate enthusiasm. He involved the media, a host of do-gooders, and enough protesters to frighten the horses.' Nikki recalled it vividly. 'Then when he realised it was all going nowhere, it turned nasty. There were personal threats to some of our officers, cars were torched, houses daubed in filthy graffiti, the works.' She pulled a face. 'Then suddenly he gave up, and that was *really* spooky. We were all waiting for the hammer to fall, but it never did.'

'Bit like now,' said Dave grimly, 'waiting for Snipe's next move.'

Nikki nodded. 'Precisely. But we now know that he had moved to the Yorkshire Moors, where he lived as a recluse. And I *mean* a recluse. Dave and I visited his cottage and it was like a prison.' She passed Yvonne a picture of the isolated cottage surrounded by heather-covered moorland and watched as she attached it to the board.

Dave murmured in agreement. 'And the bastard killed his dogs before he did a runner. Yorkshire Police are looking for him, but so far no luck.'

Nikki went on. 'Regarding family, his parents are dead, he has no friends, and his only brother, Matthew Morton, disowned him around the time of the trial and moved to the West Country. Dave rang him and he swears he has not seen him for years.'

'Where are the Engles serving their time?' asked Niall.

'Ruth is in HM Prison Foston Hall in Derbyshire, and Brandon in HMP Lincoln.' Nikki glanced down at a file on the table beside her. 'We have contacted both prisons and according to them, neither prisoner is suspected of any kind of conspiracy. They send out few visiting orders, and they have been vetted carefully. Both seem to be keeping their heads down. Ruth is in some accredited offending behaviour programme, and Brandon is doing an Open University degree in computer studies.'

'Bully for them,' growled Dave, pulling a face. 'How very commendable.'

Nikki turned and looked again at the photograph of Windsor Morton. 'I find it very worrying that we do not know where he is, and I have to stress that at the time of his daughter's incarceration, he truly hated us.' Nikki took a sip of water. 'Now we'll move on to Jeremy Bow.' She placed the beaker back on the desk and looked across to the second whiteboard. 'This man has bugged us for years. Although I have to say that recently he has been more a slight irritation than a major thorn in our side.' She nodded to Travis Taylor. 'Have you spoken to Cat this morning regarding her computer search on Bow?'

Travis stood up. 'Yes, DI Galena, got all the info from her, and earlier we worked on linked computers so I have copies of her findings.'

'Good. And I spoke to Bow yesterday, so I'll fill you in on that, then you can bring us up to speed on what Cat has unearthed.' She pointed to the picture of the scruffy, stick-thin man. 'Bow seemed to me to be psychologically disturbed in a big way. He's still hanging on to his conviction that we hounded his son into crashing his car.' Nikki sighed. 'I did not feel that he was mentally together enough to be Snipe, but PC Matthew Boyd was observing him and believes that some of his unhinged behaviour could be a cover. He also has very good computer skills, confirmed by his old college.' She looked toward Travis. 'Have you or Cat anything to add?'

The young man stared at his notes, then said, 'Cat has dug up a multitude of blog and chatroom entries, but they are all small stuff. Mainly just gripes and grumbles. We have found nothing really sinister in his present activities, although there are a lot of them. Cat said she doesn't believe he is involved in something this big.' He looked directly at Nikki. 'He seems to do most of his socialising online now, unlike his old habit of taking to the streets with a banner. He does occasionally use a local pub called the Snow Goose, but according to a regular who uses Facebook, he's become the grumpy old man that everyone avoids.' He laid the papers down. 'Cat reckons that he's a one-way street and there's little use going down it.'

Nikki privately thought that Cat was right, thanked Travis, and moved on. 'I don't need to tell any of you about Stephen Cox but, for the record, he's the lowest of the low. He has a history of violence and drug dealing. He is a psychopath, totally without compassion, and not one of the officers in this station would piss on him if he was on fire. He's in Greenborough right now, reportedly has a lot of money with him, and he hates us.' She stared at the photo and felt her own hatred for the man begin to reheat. 'We have been told that he has had plastic surgery on his face, but I suggest that the injury was so great that he would still be scarred. Whatever, I'm thinking that every man jack here would still recognise him. He was my number one until I saw Windsor Morton's compound. Now I'm divided.'

She turned to the last whiteboard. 'And here we have something of an anomaly. Two dead men, James and William French.' She turned to Joseph. 'I'm going to hand this one over to you and Yvonne.'

Together the two officers outlined what had happened to James French whilst on the witness protection scheme.

'If any of these men had reasonable cause to want compensation, it would have been William French, James's son.' Joseph looked solemnly at his colleagues. 'It was a disaster, a complete shambles, and according to all our reports we never discovered who leaked the location of the safe house.'

Yvonne nodded. 'And to be honest, it was no surprise that William took to drink and finally died. According to his family, he was devastated by what happened. They said that it was William who convinced his father to give evidence against the drug dealers. He was eaten up with guilt after his father's murder, and no one could console him.'

'Later, that guilt became anger and he found a powerful brief and went after the police with a vengeance.' Joseph glanced at his notes. 'He was awarded a massive figure as compensation, but he didn't want it. It had never been about money.'

'He accepted it, then, thinking it would get up our noses, went out on the streets dishing out wads of money to every street kid, drop-out, vagrant and druggie that he could find.'

'He admitted afterwards that he didn't think it through too well, as most of it filtered its way straight back to the drug dealers that his father was trying to stop.' Joseph shook his head sadly. 'He was well screwed up by that time, and his family, although they loved him dearly, went through hell with him. When he died, their grief was directed once again at us. Considering what a lovely boy he was prior to all that, the reports make tough reading.'

Yvonne pointed to the board. 'And that leads us to the remaining family members. The sarge and I had the pleasure of meeting them yesterday. We spoke to William's wife, Eileen, who still lives in Greenborough, with their two children, a boy, Christopher, and a girl, Madeleine. We also met a sister, Anna, who William was very close to, a cousin and several uncles and aunts.'

'The whole family are very supportive of each other.' Joseph gave a grunt. 'Even though they did agree to speak to us, they were tight, if you understand what I mean, close-knit, and a long, long way from happy. But even so, no one came across as vindictive enough to kill.' He looked back to Nikki. 'That's all we have at present.'

Nikki decided it was enough. 'Thank you all for your input. I'm going to suggest that we prioritise Windsor Morton and Stephen Cox for our investigations, but don't lose sight of Jeremy Bow or the French family.' She turned to DI Jim Hunter. 'Jim? Maybe you'd like to allocate who does what?'

'My pleasure.' He turned to the room. 'Okay. listen up. Here's your duties for this morning, and don't forget, keep either DI Galena or myself updated on everything you find.'

Nikki stretched and walked back to her office, leaving Jim Hunter organising mini-teams and dishing out their relevant tasks. It felt good to finally have some answers about the mysterious death of Magda Hellekamp, and she was more than relieved to be able to hand the closure of Operation Windmill over to their Dutch colleagues, but somehow it made the threat from Snipe all the more real.

She sank down at her desk. The worst thing was, they were still completely at his mercy. For all their work and the increased man-power, they were no closer to knowing who Snipe was or what 'compensation' meant, than they had been on the day that Danny Wilshire died.

* * *

Cat sat stiffly on her bed. Her private investigations on the Internet had been abruptly halted by the arrival of her surgeon, and now it was crunch time. The dressings on her face had been removed and she suddenly felt vulnerable. No, more than that, she felt very small and very frightened. Every time she slept, whether at night or just a few moments drifting away because of the pain-killers, she saw the mirror and the terrible reflection that was burnt and tortured and was the face of Stephen Cox.

'Are you ready, Caitlin?'

No one ever calls me that, she thought absentmindedly.

Angie, her personal nurse, smiled encouragingly at her and held out a pink plastic-backed hand-mirror. 'Hey! Where's that rebel who slunk off to the toilets to sneak a peek?'

Cat wasn't sure, but she certainly wasn't present right now.

Her face felt cold and bare, unprotected and exposed. For a moment she wanted to ask them to put the dressing back on. She would have liked to stick her damaged head in the sand and forget about what had happened to her. Her arm felt heavy, as if unable to take the weight of the mirror, but somehow she found her courage and slowly lifted it up.

Cat closed her eyes, saw again Stephen Cox's mutilated and tethered skin, then snapped them open. Nothing could be as bad as what she was imagining.

She stared for an age, turning her head gently one way and the other. The doctor was speaking but it seemed to come from a very long way away. Words, distorted and garbled, drifted in to her consciousness but meant nothing. And then she was back, and giving the man a watery smile. 'Thank you. Thank you so much.'

There was still dark congealed blood around the black stitches and the skin was drawn and bruised into a myriad of colours, but even at this stage, Cat could see that the surgeon had done a brilliant job. She couldn't take her eyes off the face that looked back at her, because she saw Cat, not Stephen Cox. Just Cat Cullen.

'As I said, we need the initial trauma to heal, then we'll consider a way forward.' His smile was genuine. 'You were very lucky, my friend. The slightest difference in position, depth and angle, and you would have needed the expertise of several of my colleagues, not just me.' He pointed to the side of her face, just a little further back from her laceration. 'This is the route of a major artery and close to it, vital veins and nerves that affect all sorts of functions, like tear formation, facial expression, swallowing, and eye movement.' He moved his finger to a spot beneath her ear and her lower jaw, millimetres from the scar. 'And this is where the parotid gland is located, and the salivary ducts. Again, so close.' He patted her shoulder gently, his smile fading. 'Although I have to tell you that there was some nerve damage. It will take a little time to mend, but hopefully it will be minimal. You will, as I originally told you, have a scar, although I will do my best to make it as invisible as it can be. And apart from that, a slight one-sided weakness maybe, but to be honest, and if I were a betting man, I'd put money on full recovery of all your facial functions.'

Cat had almost stopped listening. She felt totally elated. If she turned the mirror just a little further, all she saw was the face that she had been born with. She let out a sigh of relief. She'd always believed that it was the unknown that caused the problems. The imagination was a powerful tool, but until now she had no idea just how powerful it was. Now, seeing the reality, Cat knew that she would cope.

'And the leg is starting to respond to the antibiotics, so basically, it's good news all round, I'd say.' Angie beamed at her.

Cat opened her mouth to speak but the nurse stopped her. 'I know exactly what you are going to say, and the answer is two days, *probably*, and that's only as long as the leg wound continues to improve.' She held up her hand, as if she were stopping traffic. 'And absolutely no arguments.'

'I can live with that.' She would have preferred one day but, heck, life was looking better by the minute.

Five minutes later she was alone. She had asked Angie to leave the mirror behind, just in case she fell asleep and dreamed again about Stephen Cox.

But right now she was buzzing, and as there was little else to do in the quiet room, she reached across and retrieved the laptop. The first thing she did was to check her emails, and found one from Travis. She smiled as she read it.

Hello, old bag. Can't get in to see you today. Your boss has commandeered Stuart and me into the hunt for Snipe. Looks like we could be chained here for the duration. She says to ditch Jeremy Bow and look at one of the others instead. Use the back alleys that I told you about and see what you can find. T.

I'm ahead of you there, thought Cat. William French and I are already getting well acquainted. With one last glance into the mirror, she sighed with relief and typed French's name into the search engine. 'Let's see what else you can tell me, shall we?'

CHAPTER TWENTY-SEVEN

Joseph exhaled, wiped a hand across his sweaty forehead, and finally decided that the tie had to go. The evening had brought with it a stupefying humid airlessness, and all around him he saw that sleeves were rolled up and shirt collars were now open to try to cope with the failed air-conditioning.

Yvonne's boards were now covered with information and photographs, but Snipe had remained silent. No more calls and no nasty occurrences, and that fact alone made everyone jumpy.

At around nine thirty there was a loud exclamation from Travis Taylor, and all faces looked in his direction. 'Bloody hell!' He beckoned to Joseph. 'Come and look at this, Sergeant Easter.'

Joseph saved the search he was working on and pressed print, then stood up and stretched his aching back. 'What have you got?'

'Something really weird!' Travis tapped a series of keys on his computer. 'I was taking a break from searching archive stuff, and thought I'd check out the day when DI Galena's car had that bloody message scrawled in the boot.' He pointed to the monitor. 'I was just trying to clear my head — all those names and dates were kind of mind-boggling. This is more my line.'

Joseph stared at the screen and saw it was the CCTV footage of the station car park, in particular the L-shaped area where Nikki parked her 4x4.

'If we hadn't spent time working on the security system at Waterside Quay for Operation Windmill, I'd never have thought of this but, hey! It's exactly the same thing! Someone froze the cameras! There's a two-minute gap!'

Joseph asked Travis to rerun the footage, and saw for himself the tiny flicker in the digital display of the time and date. 'Jesus!' he whispered. 'So Snipe was right here in the station grounds.'

'And I know how he got in and out,' said Travis excitedly. 'When we checked the system on the day it happened, we noticed that one of the cameras was not aligned properly. It focussed on the personnel gate close to the main building. But that alone didn't mean much, as the cameras on the inspector's vehicle were working fine and we could all see that no one went near it. But someone did go near it! In the two minutes when the system was frozen.'

Joseph tensed. 'Snipe entered in a blind spot, the system went down, somehow he accessed the vehicle, painted the message, then when the system kicked back in, slipped out through the same dead area that he used to enter.' He took a long intake of breath. 'Am I right?'

'Spot on, Sarge.' Travis looked reverently at the monitor. 'Genius!'

'Evil genius, more like,' muttered Joseph. 'Excellent work, Travis. Now I'd better go find the boss. Tell her that you've solved another seemingly unfathomable mystery.' He clapped a hand on the young man's shoulder. 'Great stuff.'

Travis dropped his head, embarrassed by the praise. 'Thanks, but this guy we are up against is the one with all the great stuff.' He looked up and his face darkened. 'He's one scarily brilliant son of a bitch.'

Joseph silently agreed and turned towards Nikki's office. As he did so, he caught sight of Stuart Broad, Travis's techie sidekick. The look on Stuart's face was anything but pleased.

Everyone else was crowding round Travis's desk, applauding his achievement and clapping him on the back, but not his closest friend.

Joseph paused mid-stride. The look was gone now, but what had it said exactly? He wasn't sure, but there was an element of surprise there, and anger, and something else. Had there been suspicion on his face?

He continued on his way to find Nikki, but that strange look bothered him and he wondered if he had hit upon some deep professional rivalry, or something else, something more personal.

* * *

Nikki listened in silence to what Travis had discovered. Thoughts crowded in on her. She pointed to a chair. 'Sit down, Joseph, but close the door first.'

They sat close to each other, just the corner of her desk between them. She leaned forward and breathed. 'What the hell are the odds on that?'

'What? The same security scam being used on two totally different jobs? Heaven knows!'

Nikki exhaled. As she breathed in again she could smell Cool Water, and realised that she had become very accustomed to the fresh aromatic fragrance that Joseph wore. Sometimes she tried to identify the distinctive blend — mint, lavender, sandalwood and cedar and the other familiar scents that could have been jasmine or maybe orange blossom? Right now, its various notes meant nothing. All it did was make her dangerous world feel a little bit safer.

'Shall I get Travis or Stuart in? Get one of them to give us a ball park guess on the chances?'

'Yes.' Nikki suddenly shook her head. 'Second thoughts, no, don't. Let's run it past Vinnie Silver. He's a security boffin, so he'll know what kind of crook uses that sort of method.' She paused. 'He *is* still around, isn't he?'

'Yes, he rang me half an hour ago. He's organised what he called a "virtual command post" for us to monitor the cameras that he's set up, and once he's shown us that he wondered if we needed him anymore. I told him to come in and see you. He should be here any time now.'

A few minutes later Vinnie was sat next to them. They swiftly filled him in on what had transpired and his face filled with an expression of disbelief.

'Sorry, guys, but I'd say there's little doubt that the same skilled operative did both jobs. It's far from simple, and to do it in exactly the same way is, well, almost impossible.'

'But that means that Magda Hellekamp's death and Snipe are connected.' Nikki drew in a gasp of air. 'But we know that the Operation Windmill killer used a team of crack professionals to support him that must have cost a fortune!'

'I've been thinking about that team, what did you call them? Rent-a-Crook?' Joseph nibbled on the inside of his cheek. 'And something has been bothering me about the attacks on us.'

Nikki looked at him unblinking. She had a sneaky feeling that he was going to say exactly what she was thinking.

Joseph looked from her to Vinnie. 'It started with a fire, set by a very competent arsonist. The fire investigator called him very clever and said that he was no amateur.'

Nikki nodded then added, 'Followed up by a complex, deliberate and lethal hit-and-run carried out by a professional. And someone who dared to take the stolen vehicle that he used to my place and park it in my barn.'

'*After* using steam and special cleansers to render it free from all trace evidence.' Joseph finished off.

Vinnie joined in. 'Your cars, your phones and your homes have been placed under surveillance. Okay, maybe not using the most hi-tech spy-ware, but using very efficient and almost untraceable gear.'

'Then someone calmly walked into the nick, froze the CCTV and tampered with my car.' Nikki felt her eyes narrow. 'And we still don't know how he opened the car without the alarm going off.' Her face tautened, 'Or what has become of our old colleague, Brian Faulkner, whose blood was used.'

'And some evil sod placed a vicious acid in a bouquet of flowers causing indiscriminate harm and suffering.' Joseph's face was full of bitterness when he spoke those words. 'That's terrorism.'

'And Tamsin's phone was stolen very professionally in a cleverly organised ruse to derail her plans and send her to your place,' Vinnie put in.

'And don't forget the dummy bomb in Joseph's shed.'

'And the scam to send Dave's life savings round the world on the trip of a lifetime.'

Nikki let out a long whistle. 'So, we have murder, attempted murder, arson, theft, deception, money laundering, cybercrime, abduction and terrorism. What does that tell you, my friends?'

'That it's not the work of a single criminal,' Vinnie stated. 'Your Snipe has employed a crack team to get at you, all experts in their different fields.'

'Rent-a-Crook. Is that possible?' Joseph's voice was low.

The more Nikki thought about it the more possible it became. As Vinnie said, no one man could be so adept at all those different crimes, unless he was some kind of super villain. No, Snipe had help, professional help. 'But he'd need money. Lots of money,' she murmured, almost to herself.

'Possibly, but not necessarily,' Vinnie said quietly. 'You know what Rent-a-Crook's cybercrime department did with Dave's accounts. As long as Snipe had a moderate sum to put down, he could use them to 'generate' as much as they needed. And another thing, Snipe could be on Rent-a-Crook's payroll. You never know, they might even give staff discount!' He gave a short bark of laughter. 'Mind you, I reckon some of his crooked mates might jump at the chance to take a pop at the police, purely for the love of it.' He leaned back in his chair, tilting the front legs off the floor and the grin faded. 'But that doesn't answer why he's doing it in the first place. All that crap about compensation. What the hell is that about, and excuse my language, but who *is* the fucker anyway?'

Nikki had no answers. But she had the feeling that for the first time in a long while, they were on the right track. She glanced out of the office window and saw Yvonne still working on the whiteboards. Someone wanted compensation, and she was sure that person was within touching distance. 'Okay, you two. We are agreed on this. Although I don't know what the hell the connection between our two cases means, it has to mean *something*. So let's go share it with the troops.'

* * *

Most of the others had been stood down for the night, but Yvonne and Dave still laboured away in the almost empty CID room. Through the DI's office window, Yvonne could see the boss and the sarge still talking to Joseph's friend. A little earlier they had shared their thoughts about Snipe using the international criminal agency that they had nicknamed Rent-a-Crook, as back up. It made perfect sense to her. Trouble was they still didn't have an ID on Snipe.

Yvonne sat back, pulled out her phone and tried Cat's mobile number. After a couple of rings, the girl answered. The line faded a little, but the signal was fair.

'How's life in solitary?'

'Bloody awful!' Cat didn't mince her words. 'Now I feel so much better, I'm going stir-crazy! Even the nurses are starting to look like foreign spies! Still, I should be out either tomorrow or the next day.'

Yvonne smiled. 'That's brilliant news. And heavens, the team certainly misses you! Niall and I are doing our best, but we are foot soldiers, not detectives. I'm far more comfortable outside, people and situation-watching. I like to see faces in front of me, not a computer screen.'

'I'm sure that's true, but you have one hell of a police-man's nose when it comes to gut feelings. The boss is always saying that you're the best there is when it comes to hunches.'

'Well, they haven't served me too well this time.' Yvonne sighed. 'My first intuition was the French family, but I've sat with them and talked to them, and I guess I'm wrong there.'

'No dodgy characters in the family tree?'

'Not one. And although they were all still gutted by what happened to James, and then William, their anger was somehow tempered, sort of diluted down to hurt and sadness.'

'That's what you'd expect as time passes. I've seen it before. The raw pain gives way to a different kind of grief.' Cat paused, then added. 'I've been looking at William French too, only using some of Travis's sites. I have to admit that William came over as a very well-balanced and reliable young man, until his father was murdered. Blogs and postings on the Internet all recognise him as a genuine, all-round good guy.'

Yvonne agreed. 'It was as if someone threw a switch, and the peacemaker, the quiet, honest lad turned into a dark and vengeful warrior.'

'Then lost it totally and hit the bottle.'

'And anything else he could get his hands on.' Yvonne grunted. 'And not being a regular user, the chemicals would have had a much stronger effect on him, poor little devil.'

'Well, I'll keep looking. If you have a feeling about that family, I'm with the guv'nor regarding your hunches so I'll run with it. I trust your instincts even if you don't.' She exhaled. 'And I've nothing else to bloody well do here, have I? God! I want to get back to work!'

Yvonne felt the girl's frustration pulsating down the phone. 'Hang on in there, kid. Just a day or so and you'll be a free woman again. But you haven't told me how you're really doing? I mean physically?'

'Fantastic. The facial dressing came off this morning and hell, Yvonne, I was scared, but it's okay. Honestly, it's going to be one heck of a lot better than I feared. If it wasn't for this wound infection, I'd be home by now. But still, the doc reckons that the antibiotics are getting on top of it.'

They talked for a bit longer and then Yvonne hung up and sat staring into space.

Gut feelings were a strange phenomenon. She knew that it was a mistake to ignore them, but for the love of Pete, she couldn't fathom why she felt so twitchy about William French.

It was like reading a page on a report, and knowing that there was a spelling mistake somewhere but you couldn't identify it. Or knowing that someone had just told a lie, but you couldn't prove it. It was that feeling of unease in the night when you are about to walk into a dark alleyway and the foreboding you feel before you enter a silent, derelict house. Yvonne drew in a deep breath. It was all that, but subtler. Much subtler.

'Sod it!' She stared at her notes on the French family. 'Come on, Yvonne, get a grip. There's something here. There has to be! So *what* am I missing?'

CHAPTER TWENTY-EIGHT

Joseph stared at the dregs of his coffee and decided that his failing brain cells needed another, a stronger one. As he walked to the vending machine, he went over a call he had just taken from Yorkshire. The last sighting of Windsor Morton had been five days ago, in a trucker's cafe outside Hull. So he had been heading in their direction.

'Got the same idea, Bunny? More caffeine?' He had not noticed Vinnie walking up behind him.

Joseph nodded and fished in his trouser pocket for some more change. 'Black, three sugars?

Vinnie nodded. 'Good memory. And your boss would like a top-up too.' He leaned against the side of the machine and looked carefully at Joseph. 'Are you quite sure that you and her are not having a fling?'

'I'd know, wouldn't I?' Joseph shot back, with what he hoped was a flippant air. 'No, Vinnie. We are close, but as friends and colleagues. We've been through some pretty heavy stuff together and . . .' He shrugged. 'I care about her. I care a lot, but that's all.' He looked directly at Vinnie, but could not quite read what his old friend was thinking.

'Then you're a fool, Bunny-boy.' Vinnie heaved in a long breath. 'I've seen her look at you and I'd give my eye-teeth for someone to look at me like that.'

Joseph looked down at the coffee dribbling into the beaker. 'Like what?'

Vinnie raised his eyebrows, then shook his head. 'I give up. There's none so blind, isn't that what they say? But I'd watch out, soldier, cos if you ignore what's right in front of your nose for too long, someone else might not be so lily-livered!' He took the beaker from Joseph and grinned broadly. 'I never thought that Joseph Easter would be a wuss when it came to romance. You were one of the bravest guys I ever had the privilege to fight alongside, but put you in front of a beautiful woman, and a bowl of porridge would have more guts!'

'Don't push it, Vinnie. That woman has gone to hell and back over the last few years and she cremated her only daughter just weeks ago. Even if I did think there was a chance of something between us, and I *don't*, do you think she'd welcome that idea right now? And smack in the middle of a murder enquiry? One that is affecting us all? Get real, man. I'd scare her off in seconds, and maybe ruin a great friendship and working partnership too.'

'Ah-ha! And there you have it in a nutshell. You *are* scared! Scared to lose what you already have, even if it is second best.' Vinnie was in his face. 'I think *you* should get real, Joseph Easter, or prepare to lose something amazing.' He raised his coffee in a salute. 'Think about it. Even if you've never admitted it to yourself before, think about it now. Take time off from crime and think, before it's too late.'

As they walked silently back towards Nikki's office, Joseph's reverie was broken by a shout.

Dave's voice rang across the CID room. 'Sarge! There's been a sighting of Stephen Cox! On the Carborough Estate.'

Joseph dumped the coffee on the nearest desk and ran for Nikki's office.

When he got there she was on her way out, car keys in hand. 'Heard it! With me.' She beckoned to Dave, 'and you, and Yvonne too. Come on.' She paused, then called across to Vinnie. 'Stay here! We need to talk again as soon as we're back.'

'Can I come with you? Another pair of hands and all that?'

'Sorry, Vinnie. This guy is dangerous.'

'And I'm not?'

'You may well be, but you are a dangerous *civilian*. It's more than my job's worth.' Nikki threw him an apologetic smile, and ran towards the lifts. 'Joseph, find out more details from the desk sergeant while I bring the car to the back door, okay?'

Two minutes later, Nikki's father's old car was flying out of the gates. 'By the sound of it he was in the vicinity of Archie Leonard's place.'

'Alone?' Nikki swung the big Countryman onto the main road leading to the Carborough.

'That hasn't been confirmed, but he could have been with two others. He was spotted by a uniformed officer answering a domestic violence call nearby.'

'What's he doing going near the Leonard family? Has he got a death wish?' asked Yvonne. 'If Raymond Leonard sees him he'll be wearing weights and swimming vertically in the Wayland River before midnight.'

'Best place,' muttered Joseph. 'Let's hope Raymond sees him before we do.'

As they approached the estate, Joseph saw two chequered police cars ahead of them, then he heard their radio crackle into life advising the cars of the areas to patrol.

'We're very close, so we'll go directly to Archie,' said Nikki. 'Maybe he already knows that he has something nasty in his neighbourhood, but if he doesn't, then we should warn him.'

'Ma'am! Wait!' Yvonne clutched Nikki's shoulder over the back of the driving seat. 'Pull up! I've just seen a shadow where there shouldn't be one!'

The car slid to a halt, and before anyone could say anything more, Yvonne was out and running.

Joseph threw open the back door, leapt out and raced after her, calling back as he ran. 'Guv! This is probably just some kid scared by the police presence. You go see if Archie is okay. And if this is Cox, he's running *away* from Archie's place! Not towards it!'

The narrow lane led along the rear of the houses in Archie's street. There were tall wooden gates and fences between them and the poky yards and gardens attached to the back of the properties. It wasn't as grim as it used to be, but it was still dark and unwelcoming. Ahead of him, Joseph could see the outline of Yvonne, running flat out and far faster than any woman of her age should have been able to. Joseph was pretty fit, but he was still out of breath when he caught her up.

'Down here!' she gasped. 'I swear it's Cox! He's just gone over that fence immediately ahead of us!'

'Then we need to get him fast, because that alley leads back to the main road.'

One after the other, Yvonne and Joseph heaved themselves over the high fence. 'There!' Yvonne pointed, and Joseph saw a figure slip from the shadow of an old garage and make a dash for the road some 100 yards ahead.

As he ran, Joseph remembered that the man had once been a professional footballer, and he clearly still kept himself in shape. He was running like the wind, but Joseph felt a rush of adrenalin and took off after him like an Olympic sprinter.

'Come back here, you bastard!' called out Joseph. 'You and I have a score to settle!'

Maybe he heard a reply, or it could have been his own rasping breath, but somehow, just like Yvonne, he knew it was Stephen Cox's feet that were slapping rhythmically on the pavement ahead of him. 'Radio for back up!' he yelled to Yvonne, and he saw her lessen her pace and pull out her radio.

'Go, Sarge!' she called back. 'Don't let him get away.'

He knew that he was gaining on his adversary, but the road was very close now, and Joseph had the horrible feeling that a car would be waiting. What the hell had Cox been doing? He felt a chill of concern for Archie Leonard.

Just a few more yards!

They burst from the lane with Joseph's outstretched hand close to the runner's shoulder. Light from the street lamps shed an unreal amber glow into the darkness. Joseph willed his body into one last push, and he grabbed at the man's jacket. As his fingers closed around the smooth material, he was side-swiped by a blow that made him think of his last university rugby match, the one that had broken three ribs and punctured a lung.

Air blasted from his chest and he went to the ground with a bone-jarring thud. As his watering eyes focussed, he looked up and saw someone standing over him. He also saw another man, arm raised and ready to pole-axe the next person to emerge from the alley.

'Yvonne! Look out!' His voice was barely a rasp, but it was enough.

As he took a vicious kick in the ribs from his assailant, he saw her break her headlong run, sidestep and grab at the man's raised arm.

Even as pain burnt through his body like wildfire, he took delight in hearing the satisfying crunch of a dislocating shoulder and the scream of agony that followed it.

'Leave them, you idiots! Get us out of here!'

Joseph's throat went tight and dry as he recognised the voice. He rolled over, gasping as his ribs came in contact with the hard ground, and saw the man who had tackled him hauling his injured mate from Yvonne's grip.

'The bitch has done my fucking shoulder in!'

'Get in the car or I'll do the other one myself!' Cox opened one of the back doors of the 4x4, then ran around to the driver's side. 'Sorry, Joseph, I'd love to stay and go over old times, but don't worry, we'll meet again.'

For a moment their eyes locked, and Joseph was gripped by both pure anger and a terrible flash of remembered pain from the last time they met. If they ever did meet again, Joseph was sure that one of them would die.

Cox threw himself inside the car. 'I promise!' he called out.

Joseph staggered to his feet, clutching his side and saw Yvonne dive at the man who had hurt him. Then he saw the man slip an evil-looking knife from his pocket.

'Leave him, Yvonne! He's got a blade! Let him go!' Fear pulsed through his veins and his own memory of facing a knife threatened to overwhelm him. 'Let him go! Okay? That's an order! He'll kill you.'

As the car's engine roared into life, he saw Yvonne pause and step back. He heaved a painful sigh of relief, and fleetingly saw the driver of the vehicle staring at him as he drove away. Cox had certainly been under the surgeon's knife, but although the skin was less tortured, the evil written on his face had not changed. Not one bit.

* * *

Nikki and Dave hammered on Archie's door. There was no answer. 'This is all wrong.' Nikki tried to see through a window, but there was no light in the front lounge. 'Get that bloody enforcer out again, Dave.'

In a few moments he returned with the heavy metal device that made short work of locked doors in times of emergency.

'Forgive me, Archie. If I'm wrong I promise to pay for the damage.'

The door lock shattered and the front door swung inwards.

Joan Leonard lay on the hall floor, a trickle of blood feeding a growing puddle around her head.

'Jesus! Dave, get an ambulance. And tell them to make it fast!' She knelt down and felt the side of Joan's neck. 'She's alive, but her pulse isn't good.' She called out her name, but apart from a slight tremor in her eyelids, there was no response.

Nikki heard Dave urgently requesting help. She stood up, wondering what else she would find as she moved deeper into the house. She went into the lounge and pulled a throw off the sofa and took it back to cover the unconscious woman.

'They're on their way.' Dave crouched beside her, helping to keep the woman as warm as possible. 'Who is she, guv?'

'Archie's daughter-in-law, Joan. She's been looking after him.'

'Archie's ill?'

Nikki didn't want to admit it, especially to herself. She heard herself whisper, 'Archie's dying.' She was grateful that Dave didn't ask any more. 'You stay here with her, Dave. I'll check out the rest of the house.'

'I think you should wait for back-up, ma'am.' There was real concern in Dave's voice.

'Whoever did this, and I think we know exactly who that was, is now busy being pursued by Greenborough's finest, so I'm perfectly safe, Dave.' She stood up and walked through the house, putting on lights as she went.

'Police! Is there anyone in here? We're here to help.'

Nikki checked the ground floor and found nothing. Then she moved to the stairs. She called out as she went up step by step. 'It's the police! Is anyone there?'

On the top landing she stopped and looked around. She thought she had heard a noise, but wasn't sure where it came from. 'This is DI Nikki Galena! Come out, please.'

Nikki eased open the first door she came to, but as light flooded the big bedroom she saw that it was empty. She moved to the next room and the next and found them the same. The noise had stopped. Had she imagined it?

A corridor stretched ahead of her, one she knew led down to Lisa Jane's old room. She really didn't want to go, but she had no choice.

'Archie? Are you alright? It's Nikki.' Her voice echoed down the silent hallway. And then she heard a moan. A low, animal-like noise that made her blood run cold.

'Archie!'

Nikki pushed open the door, and saw that the room had been all but destroyed. Furniture and ornaments lay shattered and broken. Posters had been torn from the walls, and an oxygen cylinder and its metal trolley lay on the floor. There was a heavy metallic smell of blood mixing with the familiar jasmine room fragrance that Joan liked to use.

'Oh my God!' Nikki ran to the figure that half lay, half leaned against the far wall. His head had taken a vicious blow and thick blood was clotting into his wavy hair. He cried out, clearly in great pain.

'Mickey! Oh no!' She ran back to the door. 'Dave! We need another paramedic team up here! It's Mickey, and he's in a bad way.' She ran back to the boy. 'Oh, sweetheart, I'm here. It's Nikki. I've got you now.' She sat down and held him to her. 'Help is on its way. You're going to be fine, you hear me? Just fine.'

'Inspector Nik?'

His voice was slurred. Nikki didn't like the sound of it. He was just a kid, and he was talking like a stroke-victim. 'Shh, Mickey, you keep still now. We'll talk later when you feel better.'

'At least they didn't get Archie.' The words were laboured and slow, and then his eyes closed.

'Mickey? Stay with me! Come on now, it's not the time to sleep! Wake up, Mickey!' Nikki felt panic welling up and hot tears were burning her eyes and straining to be released. No more dead kids. Please!

The boy gave a little moan and she breathed a sigh of relief. 'Don't you dare do that again, or Sergeant Joe will never forgive you!'

'Sorry,' he murmured. 'So tired.'

Sirens filled the night air, increasing in volume until they finally came to a halt outside. And as the green-clad paramedics filled the doorway of the small room, Nikki finally allowed herself to let the tears fall.

CHAPTER TWENTY-NINE

Joseph eased his aching body up off the pavement and winced. Nursing his bruised ribs he threw a half smile at Yvonne. 'That went well.'

'I've radioed in the vehicle registration, but something tells me they will find that 4x4 either abandoned or burnt out.' Her face twisted into a frown. 'I just wish that I'd—'

'Don't go there,' interrupted Joseph. 'I'd rather see the bastards get away than see you with a knife stuck in you.' He looked at her seriously. 'It's not something I'd recommend.'

'Sorry, Sarge. If anyone should know, it would be you.' She looked up as Nikki's car pulled into view. 'It's the guv'nor.'

Joseph tried to breathe normally as Nikki and Dave stepped out of the vehicle, but knives still stabbed mercilessly in his chest, making him suspect a couple of cracked ribs. ''Fraid, we lost him, ma'am. It was Cox, but he had two goons with him and they . . .' He stopped mid-sentence when he saw bloodstains on Nikki's shirt and Dave's jacket. 'Oh no. Not Archie.'

Nikki was slow to answer, and he began to fear the worst.

'No, not Archie.' Her voice held a faint tremor. 'I'm sorry, Joseph, but both Mickey and Joan were attacked. They are on their way to hospital.'

Joseph tensed. Mickey? He closed his eyes. 'Is it bad?'

'Bad enough. They both have head injuries, but judging by the mess in the house, it looks like young Mickey put up one hell of a fight before he got coshed.'

'Cox actually went after the Leonard family? Is he off his trolley?'

'Well, if he was looking for Archie, he came unstuck. Archie's already in hospital. A neighbour told me that he had a breathing attack early this morning, and the ambulance crew took him into A & E. He's pretty poorly, by all accounts.'

'And Mickey? Have Peter and Fran been notified? Maybe I should go and be with him.' Joseph made no secret of the fact that he was fond of the boy. Years ago, he and Nikki had all but saved the boy's life. He'd never quite fathomed out how he felt about it, or why. You'd think it would be the person who got saved who would be the one with the burden of obligation — forever in your debt, and all that. But strangely, after Mickey recovered from his injuries, Joseph had felt responsible for the boy and what happened to him. And he still did, although now he had backed right off and allowed Mickey's new family to look after him.

'Peter is already on his way, Joseph. Leave it for a while, okay?' Suddenly she noticed his injury. 'You're hurt! Joseph, what happened?'

'Got taken out by a Harlequin's prop, or that's what it felt like.' He tried to straighten up. 'Shit! That's painful.'

'Okay, X-ray. Now.' Nikki shook her head. 'Come on, I'll drive straight to the hospital. Lord, everyone we know seems to be in Greenborough General at the moment!'

Joseph decided not to argue. Little could be done for cracked ribs, but they could give him some pain relief so that he could continue working.

As they drove, they talked about Stephen Cox. None of them could understand why he had gone anywhere near Archie Leonard. And although he had run off alone, the neighbour said that after hearing a terrible commotion, her family saw three men run from the house. Two went in different directions from the back, and one from the front.

'Star-burst,' said Yvonne. It was standard procedure, especially when exiting a stolen car. The villains know that if you're on your own, you can't chase all of them.

'It happened less than five minutes before we arrived,' Dave said. 'I don't think they had expected to find a police presence on the Carborough and they decided to leg it when they realised things were hotting up.'

'Did he speak to you, Joseph?' asked Nikki tentatively.

'Oh, we just passed the time of day, promised to catch up sometime. The usual.'

'Very droll.'

'And I need to keep it that way. I still can't think too deeply about Cox and what he did.'

Nikki glanced across at him. It was a fleeting look, but it was filled with sadness and compassion — and something else Joseph couldn't quite identify. He heard Vinnie saying, "I'd give my eye teeth for someone to look at me like that." Was that what he meant? Because Joseph saw only concern and a shared memory of difficult and painful times. Was Vinnie seeing something different? Something he was missing? His mind stopped spinning and although he knew it was not the right time to be thinking this way, he stared at Nikki. Could Vinnie be right?

'I can't believe that Cox has out-run us, yet again,' Yvonne was grumbling. 'And even if there were ten squad cars on the Carborough tonight, Cox has the luck of the devil. He'd have got away.'

'We need to hope that Mickey rallies quickly, then maybe he can tell us why Cox was there,' Dave pondered.

Joseph dragged his thoughts into the present. 'What if he wasn't after Archie? Mickey knows a lot, and he has a knack of seeing and hearing things that maybe he shouldn't be seeing or hearing. And now he is part of the Leonard family, who is he going to tell his secrets to?'

'Archie.' Nikki nodded. 'Maybe Mickey *was* the intended target. Perhaps he'd found out who was hiding Cox and was about to pass the information on.' She carefully guided the old car into the hospital gates. 'Maybe we should go see Mickey after all.'

'*And* organise a uniformed officer to keep a watch on him,' emphasised Joseph. 'Cox is still out there, so the boy is vulnerable.'

'Deja vu!' Nikki pulled into a space close to the entrance. 'Just like the good old days!'

'Some say,' muttered Joseph. 'I've known better.'

* * *

As Joseph waited to be seen in the A & E department, Nikki waited too, for news of both Mickey and Joan Leonard. She also enquired about Archie, only to be told that he was still in ITU and at present visits were restricted to close family members. She could have flashed her warrant card, but when she heard that Raymond was with him, she decided to leave it.

As she walked towards the area where Mickey was being treated, she saw Peter Leonard approaching. He was an intelligent, fine-boned man in his early forties, with light, sandy hair and dark-rimmed designer glasses. Nothing about him betrayed his family's criminal background. They met at the door and he immediately held out his hand to her, clasping hers warmly.

'Inspector! What happened?' The words gushed out. 'Was it Cox? We heard he was in the area, then I got the call about Mickey and Joan. This is terrible.'

'I'm so sorry, Peter, and all on top of Archie being taken ill. If there's anything we can help with, just say.'

'By the sound of it you've already done plenty. It seems we have you to thank for getting Mickey here so quickly.' He finally let go of her hand.

'Thank God, we did.'

'Mr Leonard? DI Galena?' A nurse practitioner was beckoning to them. 'You can go in for a while.'

'How is he?' Nikki asked.

'He has a nasty head wound, but that kid must have an iron skull! We can't find any internal bleeds. He has concussion, but no fractures, which is really amazing.'

'You'll be keeping him in though?' said Peter.

'Oh yes. We need to monitor him carefully after a crack like that. Plus he has multiple other bruises and abrasions to sort out.' The nurse looked from one to the other enquiringly. 'They say he was attacked?'

'That's right, in his grandfather's house.'

'Mm. Well, whoever did it meant business. He's lucky to be alive. If he'd been left any longer, he could have died.'

Again, thought Nikki grimly. Then she felt Peter's hand on her arm. 'Was it Cox?'

'It appears that way. I'm hoping that Mickey will tell us more. Joseph gave chase to one of three men seen running from the vicinity of Archie's house, and he was certainly Stephen Cox.'

Peter looked across to where his adopted son lay on the trolley, then pulled out his mobile. 'You go in, Inspector. Tell him I'll be right there, but I have a call to make.'

Nikki narrowed her eyes. 'Officially I have to tell you that if your family goes after Cox and anything happens to him, you will be in serious trouble.' She raised one eyebrow. 'And *un*officially, your brother Raymond is upstairs with your father.'

Peter gave her a grim smile. 'Thanks for that. He's just the man I want.' He waved to Mickey, then turned and hurried out.

Nikki walked over to the boy and shook her head in exasperation. 'We've got to stop meeting like this! You in a hospital bed and me with no get well card.'

Mickey gave her a weak grin. 'Inspector Nik! Where's Peter gone? And where's my friend the sergeant?'

Mickey never called Peter his father. To him, the words "father" and "dad" meant neglect, alcohol, and cruelty, so his adoptive parents were always referred to as Peter and

Fran. 'Peter will be back in five, and your Sergeant Joe is getting patched up himself. You weren't the only one to get clobbered tonight, although you are way ahead of him on the injury stakes. He's just being a wimp.' She smiled at the teenager. 'How are you?'

'Head feels like someone's holding a rave in my skull.' He blinked. 'Thanks for helping me. I'm a bit foggy over what happened, but I remember you shouting at me not to sleep.'

'You scared me, kiddo. I had no intention of losing you too.'

He reached out a hand that was stained with dried blood, and took hold of hers. 'I know where you're coming from, and I'm sorry I scared you.'

Nikki squeezed it gently. 'What can you remember, Mickey?'

He closed his eyes for a moment, then said, 'Not much. I heard a cry. I suppose it must have been Joan. I was up in Lisa Jane's room tidying up. The ambulance guys had had to move furniture and stuff to get Archie out on the carrying chair. Then all hell broke loose. They just bust in. Two guys came at me with a cosh of some kind, then Cox arrived and I thought I was a goner, Inspector Nik, really I did.' He shivered. 'Then it's blank, until you were there with me.'

'Did he say anything?'

The boy shrugged, then winced. 'I can't remember. Sorry.'

'Have you any idea what they were after?'

Mickey sighed. 'None whatsoever.'

'If anything comes back, tell the officer who will be looking out for you, okay?'

'I get protection?'

'Sure do.'

'Surely he wouldn't try anything in a hospital?'

'We are talking about Stephen Cox, Mickey, so rather be safe than sorry.'

'And Grandfather?'

'He has family with him. Raymond, to be precise.'

'Then God help Cox if he tried anything in there.' He flexed his neck painfully. 'Joan's badly hurt, isn't she? Have you seen her yet?'

'No. She's still unconscious. They are talking about transferring her to the Royal Hallamshire Hospital in Sheffield. They have a special brain injury unit there.'

'That's so unfair. Joan's a bit of a grump, but she's really good to Archie. She didn't deserve to be hurt like that.'

'Cox doesn't care who he hurts. There's not an ounce of compassion in his whole body.'

'Get him, Nik. Please? Get him, lock him up, and see that he finishes up on the same wing as one of the Leonard family. They would put an end to it once and for all.'

'Oh, I'll get him, Mickey. You can be sure of that, and though some would call it rough justice, your idea is a good one, a very good one.' Nikki looked up as the nurse returned.

'We need to do some obs, Inspector. You can come back later, but this young man needs some rest now.'

Nikki explained that a uniformed officer would be close at hand, waved to the boy and left the unit. As she passed the doors to ITU, she saw a throng of people all still working on Joan Leonard. Mickey was right, she had never been exactly friendly, but she cared about Archie and their family. Nikki prayed that she would either make a proper recovery, or die, because the alternative would be a living hell. Nikki knew all about that. A lump formed in her throat. She didn't want to be here, in the hospital that had been home to her child for so long. 'Oh, Hannah,' she whispered. 'I miss you so much.'

She stopped walking for a moment as the urge to run from the place became almost overwhelming. Then she thought about Joseph and knew there was no time for that sort of emotion. She needed to be firing on all cylinders, and so did he. Time to check out his injuries, find Yvonne and Dave, then get back in the ring. Because there was a fight going on, and she was damn well not going to be the one to hit the canvas.

* * *

275

Cat looked up as the door opened and Yvonne and Dave slipped into her room. 'We've had to slip under the radar,' whispered Dave. 'There's a Rottweiler of a male nurse lurking ready to pounce.'

'That will be Agency Todd.' Cat frowned. 'He's a weird one, and boy is he nosey!'

'We don't have gowns or masks, but we promise not to breathe on you.' Yvonne sneaked a look over her shoulder.

'Forget that! I'm out of here tomorrow, so breathe away.' She screwed her face up in confusion. 'But why are you here so late?'

Dave swiftly gave her the basics. 'But it seems he's only got badly bruised ribs. The sarge'll soon be one hundred per cent again.'

'Phew! That's lucky. What about Mickey and Archie's daughter-in-law?'

'We don't know yet. We haven't tied up with the boss.' Head tilted to one side, Yvonne looked critically at Cat's scarred face, and then she smiled. 'Well, well! I see what you meant about your surgeon being a top guy. That looks fantastic!' Then she glanced down at the laptop lying on the bed. 'Still working? Any luck?'

Cat shook her head. 'There's still a load of stuff here to go through, but it seems that William French was one seriously good bloke. I haven't found one single bad remark about him. He was well-loved by his whole family and his friends, he ran a kid's club from a room at the back of a church hall, he was a scout leader and regularly did sponsored runs to raise money for Save the Children and cancer-related charities.' She puffed out her cheeks. 'And *he* was the one that convinced his father to go to the police about the drug dealers.'

'How did James French know about those dealers?' asked Dave.

'They worked at the same company, a big importing warehouse. He'd been suspicious for months, but was scared he'd lose his job if he went to the police.' Cat gave a little sigh. 'But he finally did the right thing and he lost his life, not his job.'

'I wish I knew who leaked the location of that safe house,' said Yvonne darkly. 'They have an awful lot of blood on their hands.'

Dave looked at his watch, then across to Yvonne. 'We'd better go find the boss. If Mickey's in safe hands and the sarge is okay, she'll probably want to get back to the station.' He blew Cat a kiss. 'See you tomorrow, angel-face.'

'Yes, see you soon.' Yvonne paused at the door. 'Email me anything of interest about French, won't you? Perhaps together we can build up some kind of profile, even if just to eliminate him.'

'Will do. In fact I'll pass on everything. You might pick up on something I've missed.' Cat didn't want them to leave. She felt so safe, so at ease with her friends, but it was late and she knew that they would have been working flat out since dawn. 'I'll ring you the minute they say I can go. Would one of you be able to pick me up? With this leg, I won't be driving for a while.'

'I've got a better idea,' Dave said suddenly. 'Come and stay in my spare room until you are more mobile. And when you feel ready, I can ferry you to and from work until you're up to going solo again, if that's what you'd like?'

Relief flooded through her, as comforting as slipping into a warm bath.

'Really? Are you sure, Dave?'

'Right, that's sorted!' He tipped an imaginary cap. 'Your chauffeur will be here as soon as you request him and we'll go pick up some of your stuff and get you settled in. So sleep well, and I'll see you then.'

After they left, she saw them pause to have a few words with the uniformed officer outside then hurry down the corridor. A feeling of intense emotion flooded through her. They really were her family. Her own mother, bless her heart, and heaven knows it wasn't her fault that she was sick, had never been there for her. In fact, it had always been the other way around. No. As the years had passed by, her work colleagues had become her nearest and dearest, and she knew that she'd do anything for them. Anything at all.

She lay back on her pillow and decided that tomorrow couldn't come soon enough. Meanwhile, she pulled the computer closer. One more run at William French and she'd call it a day.

* * *

It was well after midnight when they got back to the station. On Nikki's desk was a note from Vinnie Silver saying that he'd gone back to his digs and to ring him any time if they needed him.

Nikki sent Yvonne and Dave home, then she and Joseph sat in her office drinking coffee. 'How's the ribs?'

'Somewhat numbed, but at least I can breathe now without thinking that someone is sticking a screwdriver through my chest.'

'Mickey sends his love.'

'I tried to see him while you were hunting down Dave and Yvonne, but Peter said he was asleep. I'll go see him tomorrow.' Joseph yawned, gripping his rib cage as he did so. 'I'm knackered. And seeing Cox again is giving me the heebie-jeebies. I dread trying to sleep for fear of nightmares about him. I can hardly face the drive home.'

She nodded and stretched her aching shoulders. 'I feel the same, but we don't have to go home, do we? There's one futon in here, and either a couple of blankets on the floor, or a night in the cells. Which is it to be?'

'I don't think I'll want to lie down anyway with these aching ribs, so you have the futon and I'll push a couple of chairs together. I'll go grab some blankets, and then if we can't sleep, we can always play I-Spy.'

'Yeah, right. I haven't done that since . . .' Her words tailed off. Since Hannah was a little girl.

'I'm sorry, Nikki. I didn't think.' Joseph looked crest-fallen. 'I'm such an idiot.' He stood up. 'As penance I'll pick up another coffee as well as the blankets.'

As he left, Nikki felt a sadness creep over her. There were going to be so many of those moments. So many people, without intending any malice at all, would accidentally wound her heart. She guessed that in time she'd learn to deal with it. She'd simply have to.

She stood up. These thoughts would have to wait. Right now, she'd check the emails, put the computer to sleep and hope that she could do the same. Although that last idea was somewhat doubtful.

She signed in and waited, her eyes only partly focussed on the screen. God, she was tired. Between Snipe and Stephen Cox, if they weren't one and the same person, she felt both hyped up and totally wrung out at the same time. If Snipe was going for melt-down, there was a very good chance that he would achieve it, and in the not too distant future if they didn't find him soon.

As she waited for the mail to load, she pulled out the futon and unfolded the duvet that they had brought in for the night when Tamsin had stayed. Luckily they had also bought two pillows, so she took one, and placed the other on a chair for Joseph. As she did, she looked across to the monitor screen, and froze.

Seven words filled the screen: YOU ARE PATHETIC! WHAT WILL IT TAKE?

Her blood turned to ice. Nikki ran across the office, threw open the door and shouted for Joseph. There was hint of panic in her voice and she hated herself for allowing her emotions to surface so publicly. But more than that, she hated Snipe for engineering it.

Joseph dropped the blankets and ran towards her. 'Nikki? What is it?' Concern blazed from his wide eyes.

'Quickly! Look!'

Joseph grabbed the monitor and swung it round, and as he did, the words dissolved and slid down the screen into a dark puddle. Then there was nothing.

'Snipe!' he hissed. 'And *that* is a sodding virus.' He turned to her. 'Your computer is blitzed. We need the IT boys in here first thing in the morning.'

'A virus can do that? It was so fast!' Nikki looked at the dead screen.

'In the grand scheme of things, this is peanuts. All because of a virus called Agent.btz, the USA had to form a whole new military department, US Cyber Command. Hell, there are viruses that can bring down the software on massive industrial operating systems, like Stuxnet, the one that damaged Iran's uranium enrichment programme.' He shrugged. 'Although right now, Snipe is far more of a worry to us than superpowers playing war-games.'

If Nikki was exhausted before, she could hardly describe the dreadful sick tiredness that was eating through her now. She flopped down into her chair and stared up at Joseph. 'We have to get him. We need this to end. I'm not sure how much more I can take.'

Joseph reached out his hand and took her arm. He squeezed it gently and smiled down at her. 'It's almost one in the morning. You've been to hell and back in the last few months and you are at a very low ebb. You feel like shit, I know, but I can promise you that Nikki Galena, pit bull, bulldog, terrier and bloodhound all rolled into one, will be back on duty after she's had some sleep.' He pointed to the futon. 'I'll listen out for further developments, don't worry. We've been waiting for him to make contact again, we knew he would, and now he has. But there's nothing you can do about it now, so rest and recharge, okay?'

Nikki knew he was right. She sank back onto the sofa bed and allowed Joseph to drape the duvet carefully over her. She didn't even have the energy to say goodnight. She closed her eyes and sleep rolled over her, like a sea-fret gently drifting off the water. Before the mist claimed her completely she heard him whisper something, and although she had no idea what he said, it made her feel safe. For a moment she was very young and back at home at Cloud Cottage Farm. She had woken in the night, frightened of something, and then she heard her father's deep voice assuring her that it had all been a bad dream.

Nikki sighed and fell asleep with the breath of his kiss on her forehead.

CHAPTER THIRTY

Cat emerged from the loo to see Todd placing a cup and saucer on her locker.

'Brought you this before I go off-duty.' He lifted her laptop from the bed-cover, placed it on the table and began to straighten her pillows. 'Home today? If the leg is okay?'

Faster than greased lightning, sunshine, thought Cat. And I won't miss you one bit. She nodded and lowered herself into the armchair next to the bed.

'Good luck then.' With an odd smile, he left, closing the door quietly after him.

Cat mouthed, 'Bye,' and watched him go through narrowed eyes. She was certain that as she opened the bathroom door, she had seen him looking at her laptop.

'Morning.' Her new "guard," PC Geoff Barry stuck his head around the door. 'I hear you're ready to roll?'

'Hi, Geoff. Oh yes, just as soon as they let me.' She looked at him thoughtfully. 'Would you do me a favour?'

The constable nodded. 'If I can.'

'You've been here on and off for a few days. Are you friendly with any of the nurses on this ward?'

'Fairly good terms. In fact one of the ward aides, Linda, is married to my cousin.' He gave her a quizzical look. 'What's up?'

'Can you find out all you can about the agency night nurse called Todd? He left this room a few moments before you came on duty.'

'I know the one you mean. Sure, I'll make a few discreet enquiries. 'He hasn't been a naughty boy, has he?' His cheerful face clouded over, 'Because if he has I'll happily knock seven bales out of him for you.'

'No, no, nothing like that,' she laughed. 'Although I do appreciate the chivalrous offer, Sir Galahad. I just need to know that he's kosher. It's probably just his manner that's got up my nose. I'm far from my best right now.'

'Linda will be in this morning. I'll certainly talk to her, but I do know he's genuine. I heard one of the other nurses talking about him yesterday. Apparently, although he's good-looking, he's not popular, and they are quite pleased that he's being relocated tomorrow.'

She watched Geoff return to his post outside her door, then sipped her tea. She pulled a face. Lord, it wasn't difficult to make a simple cup of tea, but this hospital stuff had to be on a par with bilge water. She replaced the cup and lifted the laptop from the table. At least Todd wouldn't have seen much if he had been nosing around. The last thing she'd done before going to sleep at around two in the morning was to email some copies of press cuttings about William French to Yvonne. Nothing indiscreet and certainly nothing that would interest a sneaky-peeky night nurse.

Cat checked the time. Almost seven o'clock. The ward round was at ten, and she'd have to wait another three hours to know her fate. So apart from breakfast, there was nothing else to do but keep working. She opened the file that she had set up for William French, and began to go over it again. Nothing but praise and good reports until his father died, poor guy. She stared at the screen, then her thoughts ground to a halt.

Without her aid, the cursor was moving slowly from section to section. Then it clicked on Close, and the folder disappeared. Cat stared, dumbfounded. What on earth had just happened? With no thought for the time, she grabbed her phone and dialled Joseph's number. It stuttered and coughed and the signal went before she'd even connected. She looked closer and saw two green blocks, indicating that there should be fair network coverage. It must have been Joseph's phone that was in a bad place. She bit her lip, then punched in a different number. This time it rang, although he took a while to answer.

'Travis? It's me, Cat.'

'What?' The voice was slurred with sleep. 'Old bag? What's the time?'

'Five past seven.'

'Shit! I was meant to be in early! And now I've overslept. I'm not surprised, though. I had bloody Stuart on the phone at midnight bleating on about that security system at Waterside Quay. Damn, damn, damn!'

Cat didn't know exactly what he was doing but she had a picture of him hopping buck naked around his room searching for last night's clothes. 'Listen, Travis, I think someone is remotely accessing my computer.'

There was an immediate cessation of frantic movement. 'What do you mean?'

'I was working on the French enquiry and something took control of the cursor and closed me down.'

'Have you given anyone passwords to that machine, Cat? Other than me, that is?'

'No one.'

'Are you sure? Right! Okay, well, you hang on and I'll wake up my computer and try to gatecrash.' She heard him swear as he tripped on something, then he was cursing at the lump of junk to speed the fuck up!

A moment later she heard him sigh. 'Okay, I'm in, but . . . what the . . . ? Shit! I'm using a state-of-the-art multitasking web app here. I should be able to get remote access and collaboration, but I've got sweet zilch.' She heard him swear again, then he said, 'I'm blocked out, Cat.' He paused. 'I don't like the look of this. Close your computer right down. Don't use it for anything, especially emails. Just shut it down. I'm going to ring DI Galena and explain what's happened. Meanwhile, is your friendly policeman still on guard at your door?'

Cat looked up, saw Geoff's shadow through the glass, and said he was.

'Then tell him to look after you really carefully. Sit tight, old bag! I'll talk to your boss, then I'm on my way.'

* * *

Once again the team was at work hours before their shifts officially started. The only exception was the two IT boys, and despite their promises, no one had really expected them to wake at dawn.

Yvonne had not slept well, and by five o'clock had given up trying and got ready for work. She had been at her desk for an hour and a half already, going over the articles that Cat had sent overnight.

She smiled to herself when she thought about how things had changed recently, with all the new technology available to people. Computers were now at the heart of everything. Shopping, banking, driving, watching TV — and catching criminals. No old-fashioned policing, out on the streets day and night, asking questions, watching for that unlocked door or the tell-tale signs of lies and subterfuge. It was all digital now. She gave a small sigh for the loss of the old ways. Sure, there was a side to modern policing that she welcomed, like being able to remain in touch in sticky situations, and the speed that you could process information, especially vehicle registration and forensics, but such a lot was also being lost. Young rookie coppers no longer knew how to communicate with people. They were taught aggression, not law, and that was wrong. And at the top of the ladder? With the exception of Superintendent Rick Bainbridge, all the powerful, upper-echelon officers that she once looked up to seemed to have been magicked into administrators, politicians and accountants overnight.

Yvonne stared at the monitor and decided that she was lucky to have seen the best of those times, because they would never return.

But then again, in the past, Cat would never have been able to hitch herself up to Wi-Fi from a hospital bed and keep working. In fact, without technology they would still be groping about in the dark with Operation Windmill, and Cat wouldn't have had a snowflake's chance of solving it.

She sipped at a plastic beaker that held an apology for coffee and mulled over the scientific turn that crime had taken.

'Penny for them.' Joseph paused at her desk.

She shook her head. 'Just wool-gathering over our brave new hi-tech world, Sarge. Everything is about technology. You need to be an expert or have a real interest in the subject just to keep up these days.' She pointed over to the door. 'And talking about experts, your friend has just arrived.' She indicated the big, rugged form of Vinnie Silver.

Joseph lifted a hand in recognition, then turned back to her. 'Funny, but I keep worrying about technology too. Did you hear that Snipe nuked the boss's computer last night?'

Yvonne nodded. 'She told me as soon as I arrived.' She looked around the CID room. 'We could do with Stuart or Travis getting in early. Who knows who Snipe will close down next?'

'They said they'd be here at the crack, but you know what these computer boffins are like.' He made to move off. 'Let me know when one of them gets in? I'm scared to open my computer until I know they've checked it out.'

Yvonne said that she would, and returned to the story of William French. Why, when they had a real bad guy like Stephen Cox, and a dangerous weirdo like Windsor Morton haunting them, was she worrying about a dead young saint?

She rubbed her hands together thoughtfully. Neither she nor Cat had found anything to indicate that any of William's friends or relatives should be suspected of being Snipe, but still there was that awful itch that couldn't be scratched. That uneasiness, that occasional flare of a distress signal in a dark sky, the one that made you squint as you tried to understand where it came from and what it meant.

* * *

'You look pretty pensive,' Nikki observed.

'That or he's wishing he could have another shot at the one that got away,' Vinnie added. 'Shame on you, Joseph. There was a time . . .'

Joseph threw his friend a warning glance. He loved Vinnie to pieces, but he was in no mood for jokes about Stephen Cox. There was nothing remotely funny about that slimeball. 'I'm thinking about something Yvonne just said, and what we all thought ages ago. Snipe is all about technology.'

Vinnie lowered his large frame into a chair. 'But we know that Rent-a-Crook has a vast array of specialists in every field. And they might be criminals but they are running a smart, progressive organisation. They will use technology for absolutely everything. It's just the way things are now.'

'I'm wondering if we should run yet another check on everyone who has advanced computer knowledge and has an immediate connection to us.'

'Jim Hunter's team were thorough, Joseph, but if you think we should, then go ahead. Get Dave and Yvonne to tie up with Jim and initiate a complete background check on all personnel here who might be capable of destroying a computer.'

'I hate to tell you this, but give a high-school kid a couple of Red Bulls and he could do that from the privacy of his bedroom.'

'This is no kid, Vinnie. This is someone who has learnt how to hate over the years. Finally his time has come. And, believe me, he is dedicated to destroying us.' He glanced up as a tall, rangy young man wearing a sweatshirt with a logo on the breast and cargo pants with pockets in every seam walked past Nikki's office. 'Look, see that guy? He has a security pass around his neck and I vaguely recognise him, but I don't know his name *or* what he does.'

Vinnie stuck his head out of the door and called the man over.

With surprise on his face he nervously stepped into the office.

'Sorry, but can you tell us exactly what you do here?' Vinnie asked.

'I'm a sparky, sir.' He pointed to a box that was held under his arm and labelled Halogen. 'Got some lamps out in the conference room.'

'What's your name?' Joseph tried to sound friendly.

'Paul. Paul Saunders. Why? Have I done something wrong?'

Nikki took over. 'No, Paul. We were just talking about the civilian workforce based here, that's all. You've worked here for a while, haven't you?'

'Almost three years, Inspector.'

'Same company?'

'Yes, T J Littlewood, electrical contractors.'

'And do you enjoy working here?' asked Joseph, for want of justifying the conversation.

'Can't say that spurring wall sockets and changing lamps was my dream job, but it *is* a job and I'm grateful for that.'

Nikki thanked him and after he had hurried out, she looked at Joseph. 'I see what you mean. Three years he's been wandering around the police station. Once you begin to recognise a face, they just blend in and you don't question their right to be here.'

'And you didn't even know his name,' Vinnie added. 'How many dozens of others are there — and a lot of them will be tech-minded.' He shrugged. 'And something else you should consider. Don't just look at those immediately involved in IT or security. There are a lot of people who are au fait with computers, even if they don't work with them. Think broad spectrum is all I'm saying.'

Nikki nodded. 'I get what you're saying, but we have to start somewhere, so we'll kick off with the pros. As we know there is a connection with the death of Magda Hellekamp, we'll also run a check on the company that are in charge of the Waterside Quay Apartments. I don't know if Mr Alan Brady and his crew of techies were checked first time around?' She looked at Joseph.

'Not sure. I'll get Dave and Yvonne onto it immediately.'

Joseph hurried out to the CID room and put the wheels in motion, before returning and closing the door. 'Any news on Windsor Morton?'

'Nothing. He seems to have evaporated after that last sighting near Hull.' Nikki shook her head. 'And even though I know that the Leonard clan are out in force hunting down Cox, he too has done a disappearing act.'

Vinnie leaned his big frame against the wall, then looked up and asked, 'Do you still have access to that CCTV footage of your station car park? The part where your IT lad discovered the glitch with the cameras?'

Joseph nodded. 'Of course. Want to cast an eye over it? I got Travis to send that section to my computer.' He looked across to his office and hesitated. 'I've not booted it up yet, for fear of Snipe's virus.'

Vinnie shook his head. 'I wouldn't worry. I'd be dead certain it was another of his "statements" to get your attention. He's not out to bring down the whole system. Go load it up and show me that footage.'

A few minutes later Vinnie let out a long breathy whistle and raised an eyebrow to Joseph. 'Well, well. I think you should get your boss-lady to see this.'

Nikki hurried in. 'What is it?'

'Your IT guy was perfectly right about everything he told you, but he missed something.' He grinned. 'Probably because techies think differently to soldiers and coppers.' He pointed to the area where the CCTV cameras had been out of alignment. 'As he rightly said, it usually focuses on the

289

personnel gate close to the main building, but it should also show this.' He stabbed his finger on a closed door in the side of the building. 'Exhibit One: a fire door.'

Joseph let out a low groan. 'So although Snipe could have slipped undetected *out* of the personnel gate, as Travis surmised, if he'd previously unlocked it, he could just as easily have slipped back *into* the station.'

Vinnie nodded and turned to Nikki. 'I think you should go ahead with that staff record check, don't you?'

* * *

'I need to give this to Jim Hunter. It's going to be one mammoth task.' She threw Joseph an anxious glance but before she could say any more, she heard her desk phone ringing.

They hurried back to her office and she lifted the receiver. 'Sorry, it's a bad line. I can't hear you! Is that you, Travis?'

Joseph watched her frown with concentration as she tried to make out the young man's words. After a while she swore and hung up.

'I think he's driving. The signal is rubbish and he sounds really worked up about something.'

'Ring him back. See if the line is clearer,' Joseph urged.

She did, but there was no connection. 'I caught something about a computer and remote access, whatever that might be, then I'm sure he mentioned Cat.'

'Remote access?' Vinnie sat upright. 'Travis said that he and Cat used that method to collate information. That was how they worked on putting the file together on that other guy, what's his name, Jeremy Bow?' He looked from Nikki to Joseph. 'It's simple. Travis uses software to gain access via passwords to Cat's computer. Most big firms get their IT support and maintenance in the same manner. It saves man-hours and travelling time.' Vinnie grinned. 'Some geeky techie in Cardiff can fix a glitch in your office computer in Greenborough without getting off his bum. My company uses it all the time.'

'So why is Travis telling me that? Why a specific call about something that's old history?'

The three of them sat in silence, trying to understand what the call had meant. Finally Nikki stiffened. 'What if he was trying to tell us that someone *else* is using that method to access Cat's computer?'

'Shit!' Joseph stood up and pushed his chair roughly back. 'What's the betting our Cat has found something about Snipe in one of those underground sites she's been accessing?'

Nikki was also on her feet. 'She could be in danger.'

Vinnie chipped in. 'And so could Travis, if he's trying to be Superman and save the damsel in distress. From what I've seen of him, he's going to be as much use as a wet lettuce!'

'Well, he was certainly driving, so he could have been heading for the hospital. He wouldn't have rung me if he was on his way here. And you're right, Travis has no police training at all.' Nikki's face was gaunt with worry. 'Joseph, ring the hospital. Check on Cat and make sure that the uniformed officer doesn't leave her for one single second! And get hospital security to get up to her room, fast. If Snipe has intercepted something on her computer, he's going to want to silence her.'

Joseph was already listening to the phone ringing on Cat's floor. 'Come on! Come on!'

After what seemed like an eternity a nurse answered. Joseph hurriedly explained and then heard the slap of her soles as she began running down the corridor. A moment or two later she was back on the line, breathing hard. 'I'm sorry, Sergeant, but she's not there! The patient has disappeared, and so has the policeman who was stationed outside her room. They've both gone.'

CHAPTER THIRTY-ONE

The next few minutes were a furore of telephone calls and shouted commands. Nikki informed the superintendent, then she collected a team of uniforms and taking Joseph, Dave and Niall, headed for the hospital. They also took one extra civilian. This time Vinnie Silver had managed to convince her that he could offer serious professional advice in what might be a very difficult situation.

Yvonne was left in the office with the manager, Sheila Robbins. Sheila's task was to coordinate phone calls and pass on messages. Nikki had asked Yvonne to go over every single word of the information that Cat had sent to her via email. She was convinced that Cat had stumbled upon something, even though she probably wasn't aware of it. There was something in those articles and blogs that had scared Snipe into action and it could be something that would give them a clue as to who or what they were dealing with.

Even though she was shaken to the core with concern over Cat, Yvonne pitched in immediately. What she found could be vital. She'd already skimmed the ten pages of stuff about William French's past life, but had not read them all in depth. In her job, she was used to knowing about the bad things that people got up to. Reading a long list of good works and exemplary behaviour did not resonate in the same way that spotting evil doings did. Now she began to read every word, study every date and take note of every other name mentioned. She gritted her teeth. Whatever Snipe had seen as he skulked around inside Cat's computer, it was nothing obvious, or Cat would have homed in on it. Yvonne drew in a long determined breath. Well, for Cat's sake, whatever it was, she'd damn well find it!

* * *

DI Jim Hunter and his team had gone immediately to the hospital's security centre and were already checking through the CCTV. It only took a few minutes to find the footage of Cat's floor and check all the cameras, then he hurried up to Cat's room, where Nikki and her team were talking to the staff.

Nikki looked up as she saw Jim approaching. 'What have you got?'

'CCTV showed a nurse or an assistant of some kind approach PC Geoff Barry. They talk for a few moments, then a male nurse arrives with a drink for him. Then, shortly after that, he hurried away from his post. He's seen on the corridor leading to the nurse's station, then we can't find him again.' Jim looked perplexed. 'I've left my lads searching for him.'

'Geoff is a good copper. He'd never leave his post. What's the betting there was something in that drink he was given. And what about Cat?' Nikki asked urgently.

'Okay.' Jim stared at his notebook. 'One minute after PC Barry left, Travis Taylor arrived and entered her room. Two minutes after that, he left in a furtive manner. The cameras picked up Cat Cullen standing, almost out of sight, in the doorway to her room. She was looking up and down the corridor.'

'She wasn't held or restrained in any way?'

'No. She looked as though she was keeping watch for him.'

'What on earth for?' asked Niall incredulously.

'Taylor returned with a wheelchair. The camera showed him helping her into it, and — I have to make this clear, *helping*, not forcing her. Then, after keeping an eye on the nurse's desk for a while, when the coast was clear, they left the room and he wheeled her down the corridor that leads to the service lifts.'

'They are trying to get away from someone, aren't they?' Joseph stated.

'It certainly looked that way, Sergeant,' said Jim Hunter. 'But we don't know where he took her, because they did exactly what PC Barry did. Disappeared.'

He looked apologetically at Nikki. 'I've got every available man and woman either watching CCTV footage, or on the ground hunting for them. They can't just disappear. This place is bristling with cameras since they adopted the zero tolerance to threatening behaviour policy.'

Joseph shook his head. 'Snipe and his henchmen from Rent-a-Crook could scramble those cameras in a nanosecond without even being here.' He turned to Nikki. 'Liam Feehily told me that the members of Rent-a-Crook's criminal task force are very much like the sleepers that government agencies use. They all have bona fide jobs and respectable home lives. They are ghosts that steal away from their routines, commit or assist in whatever crime is required of them, then slip calmly back under their covers.' He paused. 'Any one of them could be a doctor, a nurse or a hospital professional. After all, it's not just the poor that need money. Men and women much higher up the ladder can be "persuaded" if they have serious cash problems.'

Nikki's eyes narrowed. 'The nurse that spoke to PC Barry?' She looked at Jim Hunter. 'Male or female?'

'The first was a female. The second, the one with the drink, was male.'

'Well, I know who the first one is,' said Dave, 'because I've just spoken to her. Linda Marshall. She's a distant relative of Geoff Barry's. She's admitted talking to him as soon as she arrived on duty, and she told me he asked her about one of the agency nurses.'

'Why, did he fancy her?' Niall asked.

'No, it was a male nurse called Todd. Shall I go get her back to fill in the blanks?'

Nikki nodded, then turned to Jim. 'Can you get a still photo printed off of the person who gave PC Barry that drink?'

Jim pulled out his phone and spoke hurriedly to one of his team. He flicked it shut and said, 'On its way.'

Nikki gave a little shiver. They should have kept a closer watch on Cat. If anything happened to her after all she'd been through, Nikki would never forgive herself. And searching Greenborough General would be a nightmare. It wasn't one of those rambling old Victorian structures like Greenborough's original hospital, the Gordon Peace Memorial, had been. The General had been built around thirty years back, forcing the closure of the Memorial, and it had been renovated, added, to and extended over the years until it was a disjointed rabbit warren of wards, departments, clinics, laboratories, ancillary and administrative buildings. 'Where on earth do we start?' she whispered almost to herself.

'Here, I guess.' Joseph pointed to Dave who was hurrying toward them with a youngish woman with light blonde hair and a plump face. She was wearing flat shoes and a ward aide's uniform.

'This is Linda Marshall, Inspector. She'll tell you who PC Barry was asking about.'

'He said that Cat Cullen felt uncomfortable about one of the male night nurses.'

'In what way uncomfortable?' asked Joseph.

'Oh not like that!' She looked down and added coyly, 'Not sexually, I mean. She just felt he was prying into things that shouldn't have concerned him.'

Nikki's brow knit together. 'Cat's very astute. What is the man's name?'

'Todd Ramsey.'

'Is he here now?'

The aide shook her head. 'His shift ended a while ago.'

Nikki turned to Dave. 'Get his details from HR, then find him. We need to talk to that man.' She swung back to Jim Hunter. 'Would you think that the cameras have been tampered with, Jim?'

'Almost certainly, although they've not been knocked out or vandalised. According to the security guys here, they just don't seem to be covering the directions that they usually do. They reckon they could have been realigned electronically.'

Vinnie nodded thoughtfully. 'That's possible.' He looked at Nikki. 'Then if I might suggest, we really need your IT boys on the case, and as Travis is playing Robin Hood to your Maid Marion, why not pull in the other guy? What's he called — Stuart?'

Joseph pulled out his phone and rang base. 'Sheila, could you put Stuart on the line please?'

Nikki watched as his expression changed.

'Well, has he phoned in?' Joseph asked. There was a pause and he added. 'Yes, please, Sheila. And give him my number and tell him to ring me immediately.' He closed his mobile and stared at it for a moment. 'He's not turned up for work.'

A small shudder passed across Nikki's shoulders, but she said nothing. She was thinking about technology, about those close to them, about people in their trust and about something Joseph had mentioned to her. About an odd look that Stuart had given Travis when his friend blew apart Snipe's secret method of getting to her car. Was Snipe even closer than she ever dared suspect?

Joseph's phone rang and he snatched it open. 'Yes?' This time he pressed the loudspeaker button. 'Sergeant Easter?' It was Sheila. 'I've just rung Stuart's home, and his flatmate told me he went out very early, around five o'clock.'

'Did he say anything else? Did he know why he went out?'

'He said he'd been up half the night working on his computer, then apparently he stormed out without saying a word. He hasn't been heard from since, and his phone is switched off.'

Joseph thanked the woman and closed his phone. 'I think we should circulate Stuart's photo, don't you, ma'am?' His voice was solemn.

'And his vehicle registration.' Nikki felt physically sick. Stuart Broad had been an integral part of their work-force for years. He was bright, intelligent and generally well-liked. Could all that be a facade? Had he been hiding in plain sight? Nurturing his hatred of them behind a show of friendly comradeship? She swallowed. Much as she hated to think it, it *was* possible.

Nikki felt a cold numbness creep through her body. Disappointment and shock were replaced by anger, and with outrage at someone who played games with human lives, those of her friends and colleagues. 'Right, Joseph. Ring Sheila back and tell her to get those fliers of Stuart's face printed off and out here to us as fast as she can. And as I get the feeling that our nurse Todd will have already done a runner, there's nothing more we can do here. It's time we joined the others and helped to tear this hospital apart. We have three colleagues in terrible danger. We have to find them.'

CHAPTER THIRTY-TWO

An agonising forty-five minutes passed before Nikki took the call that they had all been praying for.

'We think they are in a disused block at the back of the hospital, one of the old dental surgeries, ma'am. It was being renovated but work was aborted because they discovered asbestos insulating boards.' The security officer's radio crackled. 'An off-duty nurse saw two patients in wheelchairs being taken along a covered way close to that area.'

'Two?'

'A man and a woman, both wrapped in blankets. They were with a porter and a male nurse. She thought the nurse must be agency from the kind of uniform he was wearing.'

'And Snipe was the porter,' murmured Nikki. 'Are they aware of your presence?'

'No, ma'am. We are well out of the way and awaiting instructions.'

'Then keep it that way until we get there.' Nikki called to a hospital security guard, 'Take us to the old dental surgery, now!'

As they ran through the corridors and down stone stairways, Nikki rang Superintendent Rick Bainbridge and brought him up to speed. 'We need an armed unit, sir, to meet us there. Have you got layout plans of that part of the hospital?'

'I have, and I've secured a heat-seeking camera from the fire service. All entrances and exits will have a firearms officer posted. Just go very carefully, Nikki. Stuart Broad's car has been spotted in the main car park, so there's little doubt that he is Snipe, but we have no idea how he'll react when cornered.'

'I just want Cat and the others safe, sir. She's been through too much already.'

'So do I, but as I said, be careful. Remember his last message: "What will it take?" Don't underestimate him.' After a second he added, 'And he's not alone either. As Todd Ramsey cannot be tracked down, we have to assume that he is the other man seen pushing a wheelchair.'

'Whatever Snipe has planned in his sick little head will be catastrophic, sir. But believe me . . .' Nikki panted as she ran. 'I will not underestimate him. I just have to stop him.'

* * *

'They are in there.' The guard pointed to a deserted building on the other side of a grassy area. It was in the early stages of renovation, the front covered with Keep Out tape and No Access warning stickers. The windows were boarded up and thick, heavy-duty plastic was draped across the front double doors. 'There are two ways in. Through that protective plastic sheeting,' he indicated forward, 'and from the back. There is a service door, a fire escape that opens into a small disused operating theatre that then connects to one of the dental suites.' He frowned. 'I have to tell you it's a labyrinth in there. The place is a death trap, stuff everywhere. Work had started, so walls are half down and there's debris all over. When they discovered the asbestos, health and safety had them down tools and that was that. It hasn't been touched since.'

Nikki did not like the sound of such a large area to hide in. 'Have you any idea where they are?'

'Sorry, ma'am. We followed up the sighting and checked the CCTV that showed them entering the building, but the rest of the place is not covered by cameras. They were all dismantled when the building work started.'

'Perfect. Just perfect.' She turned to Joseph. He and Vinnie stood close behind her. 'We can't have the armed unit storm the place. We'll lose Cat for sure. And I'll bet a pound to a penny that there would be no negotiating with Snipe.'

'He might. After all, he did ask for compensation,' Joseph said dubiously.

'I wouldn't bank on it, not at this stage of the game,' Vinnie said darkly. 'But I do have a suggestion.' He glanced at Joseph. 'That's as long as Bunny here hasn't lost some of his old skills.'

A strange light came into Joseph's eyes, and Nikki decided that if anyone could rescue Cat and the others alive, she was looking at him.

'The old skills never die.' Joseph's gaze locked on Vinnie. 'But, as I recall, the last time I used them I was holding an M-16 assault rifle.'

'So borrow the two best shooters that your armed response unit has to offer. Do you have any names?'

'Andy White and Liz Braden.' Joseph's reply was immediate. 'They've both done the training for Specialist Firearm Command with the Met and, believe me, they can do a lot more than just shoot straight.'

'Ah, experts, that's good. And have they knowledge of distraction devices?'

'And pyrotechnics, plus they can abseil. What are you thinking of?'

'No heroics. You just need good solid back-up from someone who won't pull the trigger if some bugger sneezes. Oh, and you need ground plans.'

Nikki turned to Niall. 'Contact the super to request White and Braden to come here immediately, with ground plans for the old dental block. We could be running out of time. Well, Cat could be.' She turned back to Vinnie. 'You do realise I *cannot* involve you directly. I know you have all the skills, but you are still a civilian and this is a police matter. Just tell us what to do and how to do it, okay?'

Vinnie looked at her as though summing up her capabilities. 'If you agree to my plan, you will be the central character in this little drama.'

Nikki breathed in. At last, some action. 'Just hurry up and tell me what to do.'

'We mustn't rush this,' Vinnie warned. 'Getting it right before you go in will keep you all safe. Nothing will happen to your girl yet. Snipe will have a plan, and it won't be bumping her off and doing a runner. He's waiting for his audience to witness his finest moment.'

'You are the white flag, Nikki.' Joseph looked far from happy, but he obviously knew exactly what Vinnie had in mind. 'We locate them using the heat-seeking camera, ascertain who is in there and their exact positions. Then you tell him that you are coming in alone, and you want to talk. Stuart Broad is a psychopath, so that will be precisely what he wants you to do. Get him to talk, and keep him talking. You know him, Nikki. He'll want to point out all your failings, and boast about how clever he is.' Joseph looked at her earnestly. 'Remember, it doesn't matter what he says, you are just buying us time. Okay?'

Nikki nodded, although she privately wondered if she'd be able to keep her hands off him.

'Another officer and I will split up, each with armed support, and use a pincer movement, one at the back and one at the front. We'll assess the situation and act accordingly.'

Vinnie smiled appreciatively at Joseph's immediate understanding of his thoughts. He nodded silently.

'How can you "act accordingly" if you have no radio contact?' asked Nikki.

Vinnie answered, 'Because I'm going to shadow the other officer. Joseph and I don't need contact. We are trained to evaluate and proceed as a single unit.' He drew in a breath. 'Only one thing bothers me.'

'Booby traps?' asked Joseph.

'Mm. We know he's unbalanced, extremely dangerous and has a sidekick, but have they had the time to set something up?'

Nikki turned to the security guard. 'How often is this area checked?'

'No one is allowed in until the asbestos has been removed, and we have no idea when or if that will happen.' He bit his lip. 'I'd suggest it hasn't been entered for weeks.'

'There's your answer, Vinnie. They've had time.'

Vinnie's face hardened. 'Then perhaps we shouldn't ask you to be the one to go in.'

Nikki gave him a glare that could freeze hell.

'And then again, you could be ideal.'

'Glad you realised your mistake. Now, as soon as the two SCO19 officers get here, we'll go in, okay?' She looked around at Dave and a small band of other uniforms that had just arrived. 'Now I know that Cat is one of our team, but we also have PC Geoff Barry and Travis Taylor to worry about. The witness only saw two people in wheelchairs, and I'm assuming they were Cat and Travis. We can only hope that they took PC Barry in earlier because he was the first to go missing. He hasn't been discovered anywhere else and I would expect Snipe to keep them all together.' Nikki hoped that she sounded confident. 'I want you to cover the two entrances, in case anything goes wrong and he or the nurse Todd Ramsey make a run for it. *If* Snipe runs, don't tackle him. Keep the field commander aware of every step and let the armed officers do what they need to.' She stared directly at Dave. 'I want no more officers injured or killed, understand?'

'Why don't you let *me* go in?' Dave's voice was hoarse. 'I wouldn't let Cat down.'

Nikki felt a surge of warmth for the older detective. 'I know that, Dave. And thank you, but this is not one for me to delegate.'

'Then good luck, ma'am. But can I volunteer to go in with Joseph? '

Dave would not have been her first choice, but he had sense and he would not panic. 'Yes, just follow Vinnie's advice to the letter.'

'I'll do that, never fear. Thank you, ma'am.'

As he spoke she heard footsteps and saw Niall, closely followed by the welcome presence of two black-helmeted figures. The two officers quickly introduced themselves and asked the present status of the incident. Nikki briefed them and decided that they were well up for the job. They wore specialised protective vests, kitted out with an assortment of equipment. They carried Heckler and Koch semi-automatic carbines and had Glock pistols in leg harnesses. Best of all they had a grim determination set firmly on their partially obscured faces.

'Joseph? Here are the floor plans and the camera. You and Vinnie instruct officers White and Braden, then I think we've waited long enough.'

Nikki drew in a long breath and held it. In her head she asked Hannah and her dad to keep watch over her. She repeated this over and over, like a mantra, until everything else was wiped from her mind. Suddenly she felt the nerves calm and the fear dissipate, as if they had been washed over by gentle waves on a sandy beach.

'Ready?' Her voice was steady.

'Ready. We cross the road two hundred yards down, then approach unnoticed, keeping close to the walls of the building.' Joseph touched her arm and held it for a moment. He seemed to have reached a similar place, for although she knew that the men were hyped up for close-quarter battle, his expression was almost serene. She smiled at him and felt his strength flow back to her, heightening her resolve.

'Then let's put an end to this, take our sniper out, and bring Cat and the others home.'

He smiled back. 'Let's do it.'

CHAPTER THIRTY-THREE

Yvonne was on the last sheet of Cat's document, and was beginning to feel sick. Nothing had stood out as being of the slightest interest, certainly nothing to upset Snipe and bring him out into the open. Snipe. Or should she say Stuart Broad?

Since Sheila Robbins had told her the news, she had felt stunned, although the more she thought about it, the more she realised that he had so much access to them. It would have been very easy to target them and their weaknesses. Even so, it went against the grain for a so-called friend and colleague to have brutally killed one officer and maimed another.

She drew the last sheet closer to her and began to read. It was a series of cuttings from old newspapers. Yvonne began to lose heart. She was wasting time here, she should be out looking for her friend. With a great effort she dragged herself back and began to read the headings out loud. 'Teenagers help child with life-threatening illness.' William French and a small group of other young men and women had raised enough money to take a sick little girl to Disneyland in Paris. She read again, 'Local teenager, William French, Nominated for Award.' She looked closer. What had Saint William done this time? She scanned down and realised that as a youth leader on an outward bound course in Cornwall, he had saved a boy from drowning.

Something made her stiffen. She had no idea what it was, but something made her read the whole thing again. The young canoeist had been attempting an Eskimo roll, but he had been too far out in the river and got dragged along upside down. His cagoule had got snagged on a submerged tree branch and it held him fast. William swam out, dived down, released him and dragged him to the bank, where he found the boy had stopped breathing. William managed to revive him and keep him alive until the emergency services took over, and the already popular young man was suddenly a hero.

Yvonne realised that she had stopped breathing herself.

If you were an impressionable youngster, how would you feel about a good-looking teenager who everyone agreed was the perfect role model, saving your life? No, more than that, bringing you back from the *dead*? She gulped in air. Hero-worship? Adoration? Well, it would depend on what kind of child it was, but if the kid was insecure, impressionable or sensitive, it could become exaggerated out of all proportion. Yvonne went back to the article, but there was no name for the boy who drowned.

Exhaling loudly, Yvonne skipped out of the emails and into Google, putting in the date and location of the rescue, and waited for the hits. Pages sprung up. Even after years had passed, William French's bravery was still remembered. She double-clicked on one after the other, but each time it came up as an "unnamed boy."

'Shit!' Yvonne continued to open link after link, but could find nothing. 'There must be something somewhere about that kid!'

Sheila Robbins left her desk, hurried across the office, and hung over her shoulder staring at the stream of words flashing down the screen. 'Would it be worth trying the local police force? Where was it, Cornwall?'

'It was such a long while ago.' Yvonne sighed. 'It would take too long.'

'Let me make a few calls. Where did this rescue happen exactly?'

Yvonne sat up. 'Bude, I think.' She rummaged through the papers. 'Yes, that's right.'

Sheila hurried back to her desk and accessed her computer. In moments she had the numbers she wanted and was talking to the Devon and Cornwall Police.

Yvonne heard the words: *long shot, incident involving a young man named William French, and outward bound.* She held her breath and prayed.

'Really? Would you? Thank you so much.' Sheila rattled off a phone number, replaced the handset and exhaled. 'Sometimes talking to the right person beats technology hands down.'

'And?' Yvonne was almost beside herself.

'*And* someone will be ringing you on your direct line. And it's someone who might recall the boy's name.'

Yvonne stared at her phone, willing it to ring. When it did she grabbed it, almost dropping it in her haste.

Three minutes later she hung up, then logged in to her emails, her heart racing. 'They are sending a copy of a report. The boy's name was never released because he was considered vulnerable. Childhood abuse was mentioned.' She paused, 'and the boy had been so affected by what had happened that he had almost turned stalker. Apparently his idolisation had made French's life a misery for years. The boy had followed him around him like a lovelorn puppy.'

'But who *was* he?' asked Sheila.

And then the email came through and Yvonne saw it, the name of the boy brought back from the dead.

For a moment nothing made sense. Her mind was a maelstrom of jumbled thoughts, then everything crashed into place. 'Oh no!' She rubbed at her temples, then turned to her colleague. 'Sheila! They're going after the wrong man!'

Yvonne grabbed her phone and rang the DI. 'Shit!' Her phone was switched off and Yvonne knew that they must be preparing to take Snipe. 'Oh, dear Lord! Hurry up!' She was now ringing the superintendent at the field command post, and praying that she was in time.

* * *

Heart beating like a jack hammer, Nikki eased her way along the rough red-brick wall of the old dental block. Ahead of her, and moving fast, but with a light-footed, almost delicate precision, were Joseph, Dave, Vinnie and the two marksmen.

Nikki knew that her solo performance was not only hazardous, it was critical to saving Snipe's hostages. Even so, she'd never felt so well protected. If anyone could defuse the situation safely, she believed that it was Joseph.

As she watched, they disappeared beneath the heavy plastic. She saw in her mind's eye the turning of the key that they had obtained from security, and the big doors opening.

Nikki waited as they had instructed her, not taking her eyes from the door. She knew that there was a small army of officers behind her, but to all intents and purposes, Nikki was alone. She went over in her head what she would say to Snipe, if he allowed her to get that close to him, but after a while she decided she was wasting her time preparing. She would simply have to react to the things that he said to her. As Joseph said, she was simply buying them time.

Her eyes snapped up as she detected movement close to the door. Then, to her surprise, she was not beckoned forward, but directed by one of the sharp-shooters to hold back.

A moment or two later Joseph backed out onto the pavement, dragging an inert form with him. Nikki tensed with fear, but it took only a second to realise that it was not one of their officers. It was a male, wearing a navy nursing tunic with epaulettes on the shoulders. Although she'd never met him, she was sure that she was looking at Todd Ramsey.

She took a ragged breath in. This did not bode well. If Snipe could kill his only ally, then his victims' lives would hold no value at all. And neither would hers.

She watched as Joseph felt the side of the man's neck. Then he nodded, did a thumbs-up sign, and gesticulated for two of the officers waiting behind her to approach him. He held his finger to his lips, telling them silently that he wanted the man evacuated as swiftly and silently as possible.

So he wasn't dead. But he *was* out of the game. Nikki felt a rush of excitement. When she finally got to confront Snipe, it would be him and her. Just Snipe and Nikki Galena. She thought about Bob Wilshire's son, Danny, and she saw again the bloody dressings on the floor beneath the trolley that Cat lay on. A steely calm took possession of her.

In that moment she decided that the most dangerous person in the whole scenario was not Snipe, neither was it big Vinnie Silver, Joseph Easter, nor the officers with the rifles. It was her. Hate and contempt for what he had done threatened to consume her, but she couldn't let that happen. She would channel it, use it, make it work for her and for the hostages.

She looked back to the doorway. Vinnie was beckoning to her, and without hesitation she moved towards him.

Inside there was chaos. Broken furniture was heaped into one corner of the big reception area, boxes and packaging in another. Some of the ceiling panels were down, exposing a crawl space above and tangled plaits of plastic-coated wiring for old strip lights.

Joseph stood silently at a junction of two corridors, the heat-seeking camera in one hand. He pointed down the right-hand aisle, a harsh look of concentration on his face.

Nikki moved up close to his shoulder.

Joseph spoke in the softest of whispers. 'Three doors along. Small operating theatre with back and front access. Four thermal images, two lying on the floor, one seated, and one standing.' He looked at her with the oddest expression. 'Are you sure about this, Nikki?'

'Don't piss about, Joseph. I'm absolutely certain,' she hissed.

She glanced back to where Vinnie, Dave and the armed officers were standing. They looked impassive, immobile, and very threatening.

'Then buy us all the time you can, but don't trust or believe a word he says. Don't rise to any bait.' Sincerity flooded from him. 'Remember, whatever happens, I will be there if you need me, okay?'

Nikki brought her hand up and gently touched Joseph's cheek. 'You always are.'

She slowly moved off down the corridor and away from safety.

As she passed the first door she called out, 'This is DI Nikki Galena. I want to talk to you. I am alone and I'll stay that way, as long as you allow me to see my detective constable and the others.'

She waited, and in the silence a touch of the old fear tried to creep back into her heart. Bugger that, she thought. 'I know you have Cat Cullen and two others with you. Can I please see them? I want to know they are safe.'

'You are not alone, DI Galena. Don't lie to me.' The voice sounded a little muffled, but it somehow served to pinpoint what she had to do.

'I had help in finding you, that's true. But I promise I will come in alone.'

'But you'll be wired?'

'I am not.' I don't need to be, she thought.

'I don't care if you are. Come in.'

So this was it. Nikki took a moment to centre herself. What happened from now on in was crucial to saving her colleagues' lives — if there were any lives left to save. She had to get this right.

'I said come in.'

Nikki closed her eyes, offered a quick prayer, took a deep breath and walked coolly towards the door of the disused operating theatre.

The big area was full of shadows. There was still power to this part of the building, but the only lamp left undamaged was a single low wattage bulb in a lamp over a battered metal instrument table.

She tried to be professional, to observe everything impassively and accurately. But it didn't work like that. Nikki saw a tableau displayed in front of her, and it seemed surreal and almost ghostly in the gloomy half-light. But the first thing she needed to ascertain was whether Snipe's three hostages were still alive.

She raised her eyes and looked at Snipe. He was standing casually behind an old low-backed chair, and in front of him, tied tightly to it, was Cat. He had one hand resting gently on her shoulder, and the other held an open plastic bottle. It was just inches from Cat's already injured face.

'Acid. I think you met it before, didn't you?' he asked amiably.

Nikki nodded but said nothing. She couldn't. Her mouth had gone dry and her throat was constricted so tightly that she could barely breathe.

Snipe watched her with amusement. 'Not who you expected, guv?'

Now she recognised the slightly melodic intonation in the voice.

Travis Taylor? For a second or two, nothing computed in her brain. This changes nothing, she told herself. But it did. It changed everything. She had believed Travis to be one of Cat's few real friends, and she knew Cat thought the same. This made it so much worse, and it also made Snipe far more damaged than she had realised. He had maimed Cat, killed a man right in front of her, then visited her in hospital in the guise of a friend. Bile rose in Nikki's throat and threatened to choke her. And now the sick bastard was standing over her with a bottle of acid!

Clarity returned in a flash, and the confused, befuddled woman was once again a skilled and capable police officer.

Her eyes flew around the area, missing nothing.

Cat was alive, although her head was bowed and she appeared sedated.

Two other figures were in a corner, slumped on the floor in a heap. She recognised PC Geoff Barry immediately, then realised that the other man was Stuart Broad. Their wrists and ankles had been secured with duct tape and there was also a strip across their mouths. Neither moved. Nikki looked intently at them, searching for a sign, something to tell her that they were still breathing. Travis hadn't killed Todd, so maybe he would spare these two as well? But why were they so still? Why was their breath so very shallow?

'A strong sedative.' Travis answered her unspoken question. 'Not sure about the dose, though. Todd kindly administered that for me, but I think he was less than attentive to his work by that time. I think I managed to scare him somehow.' Travis looked mildly irritated, then glanced over to another open plastic bottle that was balanced precariously close to the edge of a shelf immediately above the men's heads. 'Let's just hope they stay asleep, shall we?'

Nikki stared at the bottle, then at the two thick plastic protective containers that stood next to it. She took in the bright yellow hazard warning stickers on the side and the fact that their wide screw-tops had been removed. She swallowed hard. Then she turned and looked directly at Travis Taylor, her nostrils tingling at the odd, acidic chemical smell that permeated the room.

Travis moved his thin frame a little closer to Cat. 'We *will* talk, DI Galena, but first, there are things you should be aware of.' He smiled coldly at her, but there was a strange sadness about him. 'I know that I will die here, and that's fine. It's my choice. I know that your friend Joseph, your other buddies and quite probably a couple of impressive armed units are hovering impatiently outside.' His stare intensified. 'But I'd advise caution, Nikki. This,' he indicated the bottle, 'is that most insidious of substances, hydrofluoric acid. If one of your marksmen shot me, I would pitch either forward or backwards. Even a head shot would cause an involuntary spasm, and either of those actions would have a rather devastating effect on our Cat here, don't you think?' He looked thoughtfully at the bottle's wide mouth. 'I would only have to open my hand just a little, and . . .' he wriggled his thin fingers slightly, making the liquid move within the container. Then he gave a little shrug. 'They can come in if you like. Joseph? Dave? Yvonne? Whoever is out there! The whole gang! Why not?'

Buy us time! The words echoed through her head. 'I'd rather it was just you and me, Travis.'

'Okay. You're the one I really want to talk to.' His smile became a look of disdain. 'So, how does it feel?'

Nikki tried not to stare at Cat. She wasn't as sedated as the men, she did not appear quite so out of it. What would happen if she woke? 'How does *what* feel?'

'To be a loser. To have failed. To have failed to even *play* the game, let alone win.' He glared at her. 'You have blood on your hands, Inspector. If you'd been up to the job, you would have stopped me. Everything that's happened has been *your* fault, just like it was before.'

Nikki had no idea what he meant, but considering that Cat's last investigation had been about William French, she guessed that he was the connection. She decided not to tackle that right now. 'You gave us nothing to play with, Travis. The game was stacked in your favour from the start, we were just pawns. So I don't really feel like a loser, I just feel rather cheated.' As she spoke she was aware of the slightest movement in the shadow behind the chair where Travis stood. She tried to ignore it, to keep the man speaking, but then she saw there was more than one dark figure in the background. Now she was really frightened. She must not allow Travis to realise that she was no longer alone, or Cat could die in agony.

'What have you done to Cat, Travis?'

'A mild sedative and Midazolam, I think. Date rape drug. If she survives, she'll have no recall of any of this. That was Todd's area of expertise. He slipped a sedative into her tea and later, after I'd "helped" her escape, he injected her with the relaxant. I didn't want her fighting and getting this all over the place.' He gave the bottle a tiny, frightening shake. 'Todd turned out to be very useful, especially when my all-too-clever partner turned up unannounced.' He threw a scornful look toward Stuart.

'If he was so useful, what happened to him?'

'He was new to the organisation, and it didn't take me long to realise that he wasn't totally committed, so . . .' He shrugged. 'It's *au revoir*, Todd.'

But it's not, thought Nikki. He's still alive, and he could put you away for a very long while.

'Enough of this. You are changing the subject. We were talking about your spectacular failures.' He gave a short bark of laughter. 'Ha, you would *never* have worked out about Magda Hellekamp's locked room! I had to practically draw you pictures!'

Nikki gave a small laugh of her own. 'Hardly surprising, considering it was you who orchestrated the technology for her murder. How long have you been part of Rent-a-Crook?'

'Since college. I was headhunted.' He looked at her disparagingly. 'And by the way, they are not impressed by your ridiculous nickname of *Rent-a-Crook*. It's an organisation that makes your police force look like muppets.'

Nikki watched him intently, praying he would be so caught up by what he was saying that he wouldn't notice the silent figures gathering behind him.

'And you were happy to join up, considering you hated the police so much?'

'You have no idea!' Travis spat out the words.

'I don't know what happened, Travis, and I realise you have a deep loathing of the police, but why hurt Cat? She cares about you, I know she does. She's your friend, for heaven's sake! We were all your friends, but Cat thought you were special.'

Travis looked down at Cat, a bewildered expression replacing the anger. Then he lifted his head and stared at her. Nikki could see that some kind of battle was raging in the young man's head.

'Did she? No, no, she's police,' he said flatly.

'She was friend first, Travis, then a police officer.'

He chewed on the inside of his cheek, then bit on his bottom lip. 'No, no, that's not right. Not right at all. She's police! End of.' The anger was returning. 'And the police and their bungling ineptitude took away . . . Ah!' He almost shook with a sudden burst of fury. 'Your incompetence in dealing with his father destroyed him! Remember the so-called *safe* house? Remember that innocent man in your protection? The one that you and your buddies allowed those thugs to walk right in and execute! Some protection!' He almost spat the words at her. 'And because of that, the most courageous and amazing person ever suffered so badly that he took his own life!' His manic eyes drilled into hers. 'I found him!' Tears welled up, but the madness remained. 'I found him dead and cold on his father's grave.'

Nikki finally understood who he was talking about. She had no idea why he was eaten up with hate because of William French's death, but he was. He was consumed beyond any reasoning with taking revenge. 'William?' she whispered.

'William.' It was one word, but it was brimming with grief and anguish.

For a moment she thought he would collapse, then his eyes widened and he stared at something directly behind Nikki.

'Freeze! Armed police! Keep absolutely still, or we will shoot!' And she knew instantly that officers White and Braden were behind her with their carbines pointed at Travis Taylor.

Fear for Cat's life hit her like a runaway truck. But almost before she could compute what was happening, three figures had moved towards Travis with lightning speed. In the blink of an eye, a strong arm had snaked around the man's upper body and a big hand had fastened itself around Travis's wrist, holding it and the bottle immobile. His other arm was pinning Travis's free hand to his side in a bone-crushing bear-hug.

As Vinnie was executing his vicelike grip, Joseph and Dave had appeared on either side of him. Joseph, his hands enclosed in thick gloves, grasped the bottle and prised it from Travis's claw-like fingers. He then handed it, with incredible steadiness to Dave, who thrust something oval and bulky beneath the open bottle 'Got it, Sarge,' she heard him whisper. Then he whisked the container away and called out, 'Secured!'

Then, as relief washed through her, she heard a low, painful moan and she remembered the others.

Nikki spun around and saw that the drugged men had begun to move. Despite the duct-tape bonds, they were trying to get to their feet. 'No! Geoff! Stuart! Don't move! Keep still!'

Everyone looked towards the corner, at the two half-conscious men and at the innocent looking plastic bottle on the shelf just a few feet above their heads.

'Acid!' screamed Nikki. 'The bottle! It's more acid.'

Stuart Broad sank back down with a groan and tried to pull Geoff with him, but Geoff Barry seemed to be the only one in the room who didn't understand what she was saying. His system was still flowing with the powerful sedative. His eyes rolled and, to everyone's horror, he heaved himself upward.

In the next few moments time moved in slow motion. Nikki saw a hand flash out and, as the open bottle tipped, it fastened around it. She saw droplets of acid fly up and splatter the fingers, but it held fast. And then Joseph was there, and with his own gloved hands, removed the bottle from the clenched fist, placed it directly into one of the protective canisters and screwed on the top.

By this time, Travis had been handcuffed and lay face down on the dusty floor with Dave's knee in his back and two guns trained on his head. It was then that Nikki had a chance to realise who had just taken a handful of agonising burns to save PC Barry.

Superintendent Rick Bainbridge slid down the wall nursing his injured hand. 'Not exactly the kind of swansong I'd have liked, but hell, I'm not having any more of my officers hurt.'

Nikki ran to him, and saw a uniformed police woman already approaching with a large bowl of clean, cold water. 'Sergeant Easter said we might need water in case of another acid attack.' She carefully took hold of the superintendent's arm and guided his hand into the bowl. 'Looks like he was right. In here, sir, as quickly as possible. Irrigation is our best chance to slow it down. Help is on its way.'

Nikki crouched down beside her boss. 'What a way to leave the job.'

'Well, can't go out with a fizzle, can we? We're used to sky-rockets in this division.' He winced. 'My God, this stuff hurts like hell!'

'You saved PC Barry and Stuart Broad from some horrific injuries, sir.' She took his other hand in hers. 'I've known it for years, but maybe I should tell you to your face. You're a very brave man, sir.'

'No braver than the woman who just walked into a psychopath's lair to save her colleagues.'

'Touché, sir, but I had one heck of a back-up team.' She looked up at the others.

'That's not a civilian, is it?' Rick looked towards Vinnie with narrowed eyes.

'My fault,' Joseph pulled off the protective gloves. 'Last minute change of plan. Two of us could not have contained the acid satisfactorily, so I called on Vinnie for help. I take full responsibility, sir.'

'I see, and as a conscientious member of the public, he could hardly refuse the officer's request, could he?' Rick grimaced through the pain. 'Thank you.'

The big man gave a courteous bow, followed by a salute. 'My pleasure. sir.'

'Medics are here!' someone called out.

Two paramedics pushed through the gathered officers and knelt down beside Rick Bainbridge. 'A & E are expecting you, sir. They are ready to start treatment immediately.'

'I'll be over to see you as soon as we get this mess tied up,' Nikki called after him.

'Just get that man locked up, Nikki. Before someone tries to lynch him for what he's done. Not that I'd blame them.'

'Do I stop them if they try?'

'I'll leave that to you.'

Nikki walked over to where a doctor was shining a light into Cat's eyes. 'How is she?'

'Away with the fairies. We'll get her back on the ward and run some tests, but she should sleep this lot off overnight.'

Nikki squeezed the girl's hand and whispered, 'You're finally safe, kiddo.' She looked around her. It was hard to believe it was all over.

The armed team were being stood down and officers were escorting Travis Taylor out to a waiting vehicle. Medical staff and paramedics were helping the two drugged men to get free of their restraints prior to taking them across to A & E for a check-up.

Joseph, Dave and Vinnie came over to her. Each one in turn gave her a hug. 'Nice work, guv.'

'Ditto, lads. You guys were right on time, and I'll give you ten out of ten for team work!' She looked up at Joseph suspiciously. 'Although I'm not sure if I believe all that about a last minute change of plan? It looked very well-orchestrated to me. However, I have to say that your amazing rescue was marred by one thing.' She tried to look sternly at him, then felt a nervous giggle building up inside her throat. 'Was that actually a plastic bed pan that Dave used to protect Cat from the acid bottle?'

Joseph tried to look miffed. 'Don't knock it, lady. That there was an ingenious bit of improvisation.'

'But . . . saved by a bed pan?' All her tension welled up and she exploded into paroxysms of relieved laughter. 'Oh, poor Cat!' she roared. 'She'll *never* live this down.'

THREE MONTHS LATER

Nikki and Joseph watched the gleaming white camper van turn onto the fen lane, hands waving a vigorous goodbye out of lowered windows. Rick Bainbridge's wife had never looked so happy. And Rick was transformed! His hand was badly scarred, but gone were the deep ridges, furrows and worry-lines that made him look so much older than he was. Now he looked healthy, suitably wrinkled for his years, and well-weathered. Even Archer, their pet Springer spaniel, had acted like a puppy, leaping and barking at Joseph to play with him.

'So they are off to the Peak District to get a feel for the open road?'

'And freedom at last.' Nikki watched as the vehicle moved into the lane out of Cloud Fen. 'There were times when I thought he'd never make it this far.'

'Good luck to him.' Joseph stood beside her, a hint of sadness in his voice. 'I really wish him a long and satisfying retirement. He'll be missed, that's for sure. He was one of the good old boys.'

Nikki turned to him, smiling broadly. 'And what about you, Detective *Inspector* Easter? Will you follow his footsteps?'

'As long as I have a breath in my body. I don't want to be a dinosaur, but there are certain values that I will not compromise.' He grinned at her. 'I could ask the same of you. Did you know that Rick had put in a recommendation for your step up to DCI?'

'He intimated as much, though I'm still not sure that I want that next rung on the ladder. I'm comfortable doing what I do, but hey, I'll consider it, if only to keep the team together.' She touched his arm. 'And that reminds me. By way of celebration, I've got a bottle of bubbly chilling in the fridge. Shall we sit outside for a while?'

'Why not? It's still warm and it's going to be a long winter. Let's enjoy Cloud Fen while we can.'

Nikki walked into her kitchen and opened the fridge door. She took out the champagne, found two glasses and tore open a large bag of crisps. As she tipped them into a bowl, she realised that Cloud Cottage Farm felt like home again.

It had taken a long while to rid the dark corners of menace and threat, but now, well, it felt safe once more.

Joseph was seated at an old wooden picnic table that her father had made back when she was a girl, and was staring out across the sunlit marsh.

'I can't believe it's all over, can you? As we were waving the Bainbridges off, it dawned on me that I'd stopped looking over my shoulder.'

Nikki laughed. There was a spark, a flash of understanding between them that told him she felt the same. She sat down opposite him. 'No more Snipe. It's hard to get your head round it, isn't it?'

'And if the word on the streets is to be believed, no more Stephen Cox either.'

'Do you think Raymond Leonard really did find him?'

'Mickey's certain of it, although even he hasn't uncovered any details yet. We do know that Cox was never after us at all, just Archie, and he had a lot of old scores to settle.' Joseph smiled and shook his head. 'The Leonards must have charmed lives. Mickey is back to normal, Joan is making a remarkable recovery and Archie's back home again, although he knows he's on borrowed time.'

'Policing in Greenborough won't be quite the same without Archie Leonard,' said Nikki wistfully. 'He's a one-off.'

'That reminds me. I'm reliably told that Raymond has radically changed his opinion of you, after all you did for Joan and Mickey. He's still a villain and always will be, but he's going to keep his dirty dealings away from our patch. I think you have a new ally.' He grinned at her. 'Maybe Archie's successor will rule the empire like his father did, when the time comes.'

'We can but dream.' Nikki's smile slowly faded, then she said, 'Have you heard any more about Windsor Morton's disappearance?'

'Nothing definite, but North Yorkshire police had a call about a suicide. A jumper went off some chalk cliffs near Flamborough Head. There's no body, hence no identification, but Morton's car was seen that day leaving Bridlington and heading towards that area. They haven't found it yet, but they are pretty sure it's him.'

'One less to worry about I guess, but still very sad. That must be why he killed his dogs.' Nikki stared up into the blue sky. 'Can we talk about Snipe?'

'Sure. Now that the spy cameras have gone and the fen feels good again.' His eyes lost their sparkle. 'I would never have dreamed that Travis was such a disturbed soul.' Joseph shook his head. 'And the fact he was recruited by Rent-a-Crook directly from college meant he spent almost half of his life as a covert 'spook' criminal.'

'And all that hate inside escalated because he'd never coped with his idol, William French, destroying himself.' She pulled a face. 'Or more to the point, he never forgave *us* for letting down the man who saved his life, the man he worshipped.'

'Yeah, hero-worship taken to the level of insanity. And now he is locked up with no access to his precious computers. That will finish him completely.'

Nikki nodded. 'Did Cat tell you that she went to visit him?'

'Yes, she did. She said he was skin and bone, looked like death. I really wish she hadn't gone.'

'She did it without telling anyone. She contacted him and asked him to send her a visiting order. Said there were things she needed to get straight in her head.' Nikki poured the sparkling champagne into their glasses. 'She really liked him, you know. They'd been friends for years, or so she thought.'

'Is that what she wanted to clarify? Whether at some level he cared for her too?'

'I think so. Although she said he was little more than a zombie.' She passed a glass across the table to Joseph. 'I got the feeling that she's happier now. She said it was because when she said goodbye, he called her 'old bag' again. It seemed to tell her something.'

'You know that he tried to top himself yesterday?'

'No.' She sighed. 'That makes the third attempt. He'll succeed in the end. I just wish he'd tell us what happened to Brian Faulkner before he does.'

'He swears he doesn't know. He says that the other cell members carried out the specialist crimes. Travis supplied the names and the addresses of any remaining serving officers who had been on the team that should have been protecting James French, and let the professionals take it from there.'

'At least we know now that poor Danny was a "sins of the father" choice. His dad, Bob Wilshire, was one of the officers on duty when James was murdered. Sergeant Brian Faulkner was another, and thinking back, I would have been too, if little Hannah hadn't been poorly that night.'

Joseph stared into the glass and watched the bubbles rising. 'It was enough for Snipe to target you and your team.'

'I don't think he cared who he hurt as long as he managed to get his *compensation* from Greenborough Police. You can tell how long he'd been planning it from the length of time he'd been working with us. He'd worked alongside Stuart for over five years.'

'Well, I'm glad Stuart has decided to stay on. It must have been one hell of a shock when he realised that Travis was up to something. He told me that when he discovered that his friend was remotely watching Cat's movements on that old laptop, he believed that Travis was doing it because he fancied her.' Joseph shook his head. 'Then when he suspected that it could be something more serious, he did a bit of remote hacking of his own.'

'Then he dashed to the hospital to talk to Cat and warn her off, and walked right into a needle of sedative, courtesy of our new and very verbal grass, Todd Ramsey.'

Nikki sipped her drink, 'And talking of Rent-a-Crook members, how's the crackdown in Ireland going?'

Joseph leaned back and stretched. 'Well, Liam's whistle-blower has come up trumps. With the promise of a new name and a new life with his family in another country, he's been churning out names nonstop. They'll never get them all but hell, there is one massive great spanner in the works at Rent-a-Crook HQ!'

'Good.' Nikki stared at her glass and suddenly saw in her mind the beautiful face of Magda Hellekamp. 'And the Dutch police have nailed Daan for Magda's death, although heaven knows what the courts will do with him. Apart from all his disabilities, he's apparently lost it completely.'

'At least they have him, and we can be happy with the part we played. We didn't let Magda down.' Joseph grinned at her. 'And in a lighter vein, I've had a text from Tamsin. She's coming to stay for a week next month, for a proper visit.'

'That is great news! I'm really pleased for you.'

'I suspect an ulterior motive. She mentioned young Niall Farrow twice in the same text.' He laughed. 'But hey! That's a small price to pay to get my girl to spend some time here.' Joseph leaned back. 'So, what now?'

She frowned and looked at him, her head slightly to one side. 'What do you mean?'

'Now the dust has settled, what do you really want out of life, Nikki Galena?'

Nikki drew in a long breath and thought about it. There were things she could never have, but they were things that were far beyond her control, like holding her lovely daughter again, or getting her old dad back to health. Now she needed to think forwards not backwards.

She looked up at the familiar old stone farmhouse that was her home, and then across to the man who sat opposite her. Suddenly she realised that the raw pain of the past months had subsided, and she allowed herself a long, sighing breath of relief.

She held out her glass to Joseph. 'Right now? If I'm honest? Nothing that I don't already have.'

His glass clinked against hers, then he took her other hand in his. 'Funnily enough, I feel exactly the same.' He raised the glass in a toast. His smile was warm and honest.

'To us.'

THE END

THE JOFFE BOOKS STORY

We began in 2014 when Jasper agreed to publish his mum's much-rejected romance novel and it became a bestseller.

Since then we've grown into the largest independent publisher in the UK. We're extremely proud to publish some of the very best writers in the world, including Joy Ellis, Faith Martin, Caro Ramsay, Helen Forrester, Simon Brett and Robert Goddard. Everyone at Joffe Books loves reading and we never forget that it all begins with the magic of an author telling a story.

We are proud to publish talented first-time authors, as well as established writers whose books we love introducing to a new generation of readers.

We won Trade Publisher of the Year at the Independent Publishing Awards in 2023. We have been shortlisted for Independent Publisher of the Year at the British Book Awards for the last four years, and were shortlisted for the Diversity and Inclusivity Award at the 2022 Independent Publishing Awards. In 2023 we were shortlisted for Publisher of the Year at the RNA Industry Awards.

We built this company with your help, and we love to hear from you, so please email us about absolutely anything bookish at feedback@joffebooks.com

If you want to receive free books every Friday and hear about all our new releases, join our mailing list: www.joffebooks.com/contact

And when you tell your friends about us, just remember: it's pronounced Joffe as in coffee or toffee!

Milton Keynes UK
Ingram Content Group UK Ltd.
UKHW041117061224
452240UK00005B/299